The Winds of Change

Written By Marie Daley

Dedication

3

To My Mom and Dad: Tom and Hilda Daley.
To Barb, Kirsten, and Kyleen, whose love and support I cherish!

And to the Rest of My Wonderful Family!

Love and Chaos Abounds!
Sometimes we just call it Family!

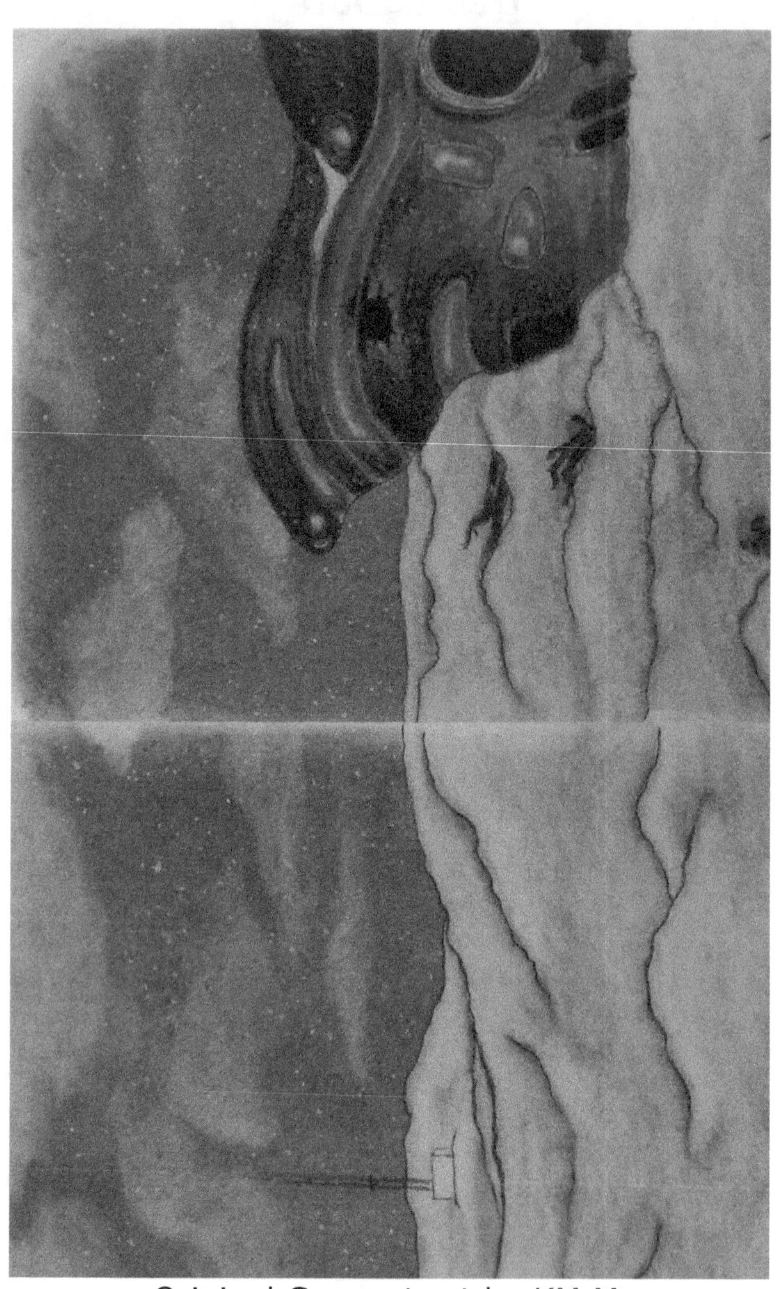

Original Concept art by KM Morgan

The Adventures of Ryes and Garth

Tayna's Dawn

Winterhaven

Winds of Change

Table of Contents

A Hasty Retreat

"All secure with the regular cargo containers. The specimens are packed in; safe and cozy in their suspension tubes, Dr. Cruthers." Bethany MacKenzie walked with accustomed ease through the narrow aisles of tied-down stacks of crates and equipment. It seemed they barely arrived and established their research base on this lush, green world when the military barged in and hustled them off into space once again. Suddenly they'd become a part of the front of a new war zone; forced to leave their new base and most of everything behind because of a faceless, murdering alien people. Most of the research would have to be started over again, hopefully at some point in the near future. She sighed, appearing thoughtful as she approached her mentor and superior.

"Did comp confirm the mass distribution?" Dr. Ethan Cruthers asked, barely glancing up to see his slim assistant nod her head in response. He bobbed his head in return, and turned his attention back to the large, supine figure before him.

"Do you need any help?" she inquired, as she slipped her comp into her thigh shipsuit pocket. She knew better than to intrude when he was busy; if he wanted her help, he'd let her know. His years were catching up with him, but he was determined to hold them off by keeping as active as possible. Even if they'd been out for decades, he felt that too many of the rejuv drugs and treatments were still in the experimental stage, so opted for the old tried-and-true efforts like regular exercise and a good, balanced diet. Bethany did her best to be ready when he was feeling tired, like today, with the hasty evacuation and all the extra work it encompassed for them both.

"If everything else is finished, a little help would be most welcome indeed," Dr. Cruthers replied, as he finished giving his subject an injection and set the hypodermic aside. His hands were beginning to shake with fatigue. He wouldn't tolerate any mistakes made when it came to the care of their charges human, or otherwise. Bethany stepped up as he reached for the sensor pad array and began to help him untangle the slender leads. They both worked as quickly as they could, with skill that comes of much practice.

"There Bethy, finished at last," he said in relief as he straightened back up to his full six foot-four height. He patted his shipsuit and lab coat pockets, absentmindedly searching for his pipe, momentarily forgetting the shipboard ban against smoking. A sad smile dawned upon his jovial, suntanned face as he remembered the restriction and that Bethany had packed them away to keep him out of trouble. Readjusting to ship life was going to be a trying experience after over two years on such a lovely planet. He'd grown quite fond of relaxing after the day's work with a fresh cup of coffee and his pipe while watching the bright colors the orange-red sun painted across the evening sky as it set.

"We're even fifteen minutes ahead of the time the First allowed us," he commented, as he returned to the here and now, noting the clock overhead. Bethany politely didn't comment upon his lapse and search. She knew he'd get through it again. She helped him carefully push the sliding slab into the waiting gray-metal box. He attached the sensor plug into the receptacle inside then pushed the activation button on the readout panel. The box brought up the metal front plate and sealed itself, beginning to cycle the artificial hibernation. These were their strongest and best chambers; even better than their own.

"She was always so much easier to handle than him," she commented as she checked the sensor readings as the final stages of hibernation began. The female she spoke of lay already encased in a similar box above his. Bethany checked her readouts for the hundredth time.

She worried about her pregnancy and having to be put into suspension so suddenly. Would the child survive? It was risky, but they had little choice. Due to company policy, they would've had to euthanize them to prevent possible epidemics in the native population from any microbes they might've been exposed to at their research facility. Not wanting to see such a thing happen with this couple, they chose to take them, along with some others, to be with them on the starship. They had stored as many of the better behaved natives, who were a part of their own studies, that they could, putting them in every extra stasis tube or box they could grab on the ship. Off-hand slaughter had never been a part of their department policy. But this couple had become very special to them both, so were stored here in the main lab compartment, so they could keep a better eye upon them. Bethany remembered the way they tried to take care of each other even in the stress of their captivity. It bespoke of a deep commitment to each other and their relationship had sparked more than a scientific curiosity in both researchers.

"Now, now," he scolded with a twinkle in his eyes, "You wouldn't be too friendly either, if a pack of strange-looking creatures took you captive and began to poke and prod you in places you didn't know could feel pain. The little lady was gentler because you kept Dr. Ortiz and his crew of internists away from her, yourself." She smiled guiltily, nodding her head in agreement.

"All right, he does have cause, and he was better once he could trust us," Bethany replied as she looked down with endless fascination at the distinctly feline features, which carried a hauntingly human cast, on the chamber's vid display. The surprises their DNA strands had revealed were still being debated by the different science teams both on the base and on Earth.

He looked golden-furred, but it was actually a thick body hair and a full head of hair like a human. He was a bipedal humanoid with two arms, legs, ears and round-pupiled eyes, but was not human. His spine and hips were fused – exactly like theirs – instead of a cat's far more flexible spine. He had retractable claws instead of fingernails, and large tufted-round ears which were fixed in place, again like a human. He had a slightly flattened nose and a split upper lip like a cat. He looked like a cross between a human and a lion. His face was human in shape and range of expressions, with exposed skin on his face, hands and feet. His teeth were omnivorous rather than a cat's tearing teeth. He stood man high and was solidly muscled from the hard, primitive life he'd led. But he was highly civilized, too. He wore sturdy, colorful clothing, sandals and had a well-made steel belt knife. He'd also worn a pendant which was delicately hand-tooled in gold and set with small, blue gemstones. Even the spear he used to defend himself with was made with apparent skill and craftsmanship.

"I wish we had more time," Bethany said wistfully. She was thinking again of the brilliant moons dancing over the ruins of a once great city on a special night she spent with a certain young man.

"Give them a few months and this so-called war will have passed this entire sector. Then we can come back and study these people `till our hearts' content," Dr. Cruthers reassured her, as he put his arm around her shoulders and gave her a brief hug to his side. "Don't worry. Those ruins will still be there when we return. They stood as a city for over a thousand years before their destruction; a few months won't change them much. Now, let's get to our own suspension chambers before that Lieutenant Dawe of yours comes looking for us," he teased.

She knew he'd seen how close they'd become in the time they spent together on their off-duty hours. It looked like it did his heart good to know she'd finally found love and with the slow courtship, it seemed to give him some relief. She was aware he wanted her settled and happy before his coming retirement and required return to Earth for discharge. She imagined her parents would be shocked with the thought of their daughter marrying a military man, but felt it was what was best for her and Jim which was more important.

She'd seen Dr. Cruthers had a second fledgling to worry about with the addition of Dorthea Burnes to his staff. He'd never allow her to be abused again, as he found was happening from the recordings she'd made for him at his direction. He still struggled with what he'd seen on the recordings. Dotti was already in her suspension tube, since they could handle the natives by themselves. What was he going to do for Dotti to ensure she found some happiness in life once again, she wondered? Ethan let her go and headed out of the lab compartment, still smiling.

Bethany blushed as she smiled and followed him. As she safely sealed the hatch, she wondered how much he did know about her personal life? He was a good friend of her parents and tended to look after her with a father's zeal, even if he'd never had children of his own. But when a certain young officer began to take an interest in her, Dr. Cruthers at first stayed near, then backed off and would leave them alone to chat. She never knew how to handle such attention, being raised at various installations on a score of worlds. She rarely had people her own age around as she grew up. Still she couldn't deny that she was falling for Jim hard. She rushed to catch up to Dr. Cruthers, when suddenly the lights overhead shifted from a neutral white to an alert red. She froze in a moment of panic, as she looked to her mentor for guidance.

"We weren't quite quick enough," he commented in a low voice, as the alarms started their whine and a prerecorded message instructed everyone to report to their assigned stations. He grabbed her arm and hauled her down the corridor to the hibernation tubes designated for the passengers.

"In you go, young lady. This may be our only chance for survival!" He quickly shoved her within and activated her tube before she could voice any protests. Lt. Dawe rushed around the corner and saw her chamber sealed and cycling. A look of relief flooded his face as he saw Bethany was safely encased. He looked up to Dr. Cruthers with a smile, which was quickly replaced with astonishment as the good doctor pinned his arms to his sides and pushed him into his own chamber. His shout was cut off as the hibernation tube was activated and sealed.

Dr. Cruthers smiled to himself as he again patted his pockets for his pipe, and then turned towards the Star Quest's bridge. He wanted to find out more about this mysterious alien people, who wanted to eradicate all humans wherever they found them. Why? Several thriving colonies had been found decimated with very few to no survivors, per the reports he'd just read earlier today. The stories they told and recordings made were horrific dark tales filled with violence. The Dark Ones, as they were now called, attacked from their ships then landed and either killed every human found, or took them captive and used them for food. No one was intentionally left alive in their wake. There was no mercy in their hearts. It seemed very much like they had a hive mind and were swarming through the habitable worlds.

There was tension running free on the bridge when he arrived and snagged an observer's seat. The First, Dan Hagg, saw him, but was too busy trying to keep the situation in hand to bother. Captain Bill Bice had his eyes glued to the large projected display of the action outside in front of them.

"We're not heading directly home?" Dr. Cruthers questioned after several long minutes, noting their course. Bill turned to look back and saw him, his lips twisting into a grimace.

"We can't risk leading them back to Earth or any of the surviving colonies, Ethan. So, we're taking a long roundabout route to an isolated battle station. There's a signature of something unknown approaching. The Siberian's trying to intercept it, to let us get free and clear," he told him, indicating the display. Ethan stood and approached his chair, getting a good look at the deadly dance, which was moving in slow motion.

"Sir, we have a report of several crewmembers that are unaccounted for," Mr. Hagg reported as a frown crossed his brow. "Their PT's aren't registering at all. It's like they've vanished."

"They're probably in tubes in one of the dead zones," Bill answered, waving him off. "We have more important concerns right now, Mister." He indicated the Siberian Bear, which appeared to be under attack. The enemy ship easily dwarfed the brave cruiser, which stood in its way.

"Can we make it?" Ethan pressed as he inwardly prayed for the brave ship's crew.

"It's going to be tight. The problem is there's too much of the neighboring systems around us, which are unknown. We don't want to jump right into a system full of Dark Ones." Suddenly they saw the cruiser blossoming into a bright ball of fire.

"That was way too fast," the navigator breathed out, breaking the silence on the bridge. "Did anyone survive that?"

"Evasive maneuvers," the Captain crisply ordered, bringing them back to their own dilemma, "get us out of here! See if you can put that planet between us and them." Ethan saw they were fast approaching a colorful world with three moons and a ring of rocky debris. The great enemy ship moved far more quickly than the Star Quest and began its attack before they could even make the shelter of one of the moons.

"It's a Hunter!" Mr. Hagg identified the signature of the ship. "Concentrate shields up axis," he ordered, "and keep a close eye on them."

"Aye, Sir," the defense board officer replied. "Launch the fighters?" he asked.

"To die? They can't buy us enough time," Commander Hagg returned, trying to think of a solution.

"I see it," the Captain replied, calming as he wracked his brain for answers. "I wish I had their drive system," he commented in a low voice. "And Dan, get our guest to his stasis tube!" he demanded, looking to his First. Dan signaled security, knowing the doctor might prove difficult.

"But I may be able to help," Ethan protested, "I've lived a long life and deserved some adventure now." He had the most important parts of the future already safely encased in their hibernation tubes; if there was any safely left aboard this ship.

"Ethan, I don't tell you how to run your labs, so don't worry about the Quest. Stay safe, Old Friend," Bill urged, giving him a brief smile and a nod of his head in farewell.

"Wow! Look at that!" the communications officer shouted out. There were missiles being fired up at the enemy ship from the planet, as they passed close to it. These missiles were getting through the enemy ship's shields and scoring, at least. The Hunter altered course, heading further away.

"Who could it be? We don't have any bases out here!" another crewman voiced, astonished.

"Who cares? They're doing the job!" one of the women declared.

"Angels of Mercy," another answered him, too, as she smiled.

"Maybe this is where our city builders fled?" Ethan breathed out, wondering.

"Let's take advantage of the help. Can you maneuver us so we can bring them back in line with that fire-base? Tease them in closer?" Captain Bice questioned, appearing to appreciate the help, even if it might mean putting themselves at risk from the same missiles, too. They all knew it couldn't be anyone from Earth, or they'd have known about the base well before now. Who could it be, Ethan wondered?

"We'll take a pounding doing it," his First warned, not liking the idea, but seeing it as their only hope to escape. "I want to shake those people's hands, if they have any," he added. The security men gestured for Dr. Cruthers to leave with them. He balked, wanting to see more of this deadly dance, so they each took one of his arms and gently urged him towards the exit. They had their orders to clear him from the bridge.

"Sir, please?" the one pleaded in a low voice.

"Just as it's getting good?" he questioned with a huff of a laugh.

Bill turned his head, giving them a nod to proceed. Their chances were still slim at best. Yet now they could hope. If only they could take advantage of it, without getting hit, themselves.

The men hauled Dr. Cruthers out with little struggling, heading quickly for his assigned chamber. Finding it occupied; they pushed him into the next available one, as the ship was rocking. They were taking fire from the enemy ship.

"Please, I'm old. Let me watch the action, just once?" he pleaded one last time, knowing it was a thin chance.

"Sorry Sir, we have our orders," one of the men told him. Ethan suddenly felt a chill up his back and knew he'd never see these two men alive again. Was it their lives he feared for or his continued own? He wondered. He'd seen and done many things in his time and was about ready to call it quits. Life was a burden, offering him few chances at a promising future. The city's ruins had been his last, great chance.

"Good luck," he wished them, then the door sealed and it began its cycle. His last thought was of his precious wife Shelley, who had already crossed over from this life ahead of him.

Now and Then

"What're you making?" Maren asked, as he trailed Ryes into the kitchen. They had a quick talk, away from the others, and both felt better for it. Raya was already in there, pulling things out to get ready for dinner. She smiled at the two of them. They were more like brother and sister than Maren and Tennan, who actually were siblings.

Raya mused for a moment on the last few months. On their journey away from the ruins of Hailys, she, who originally came from the Moondance plains tribe, followed them for a day and felt they were her only chance for survival. Garth led the small band of adventurers out of Matlowe Village, which lay far to the south and east of Hailys. She finally revealed herself that evening, as the lure of food overcame her fears; not to steal, but to beg. Ryes practically befriended her on sight. During their journey southwest along the pathway they found, she melded in with these former villagers, as if she'd begun the journey with them from the start. Before they found their home, she'd discovered her life's love in Kovin. Moving into Winterhaven, which was an abandoned underground human place, had merely been finding the home she felt she'd always belonged. Even if Ryes and Maren knew little of the plains tribes, they were her true family.

"Lenoon soup, which I made for lunch," Ryes told him. "I hate having to pluck all those tiny feathers from those little birds, so I started it yesterday. I wanted Garth and Sabin to have some to take with them. The computer told me it was going to rain today and I knew it'd make them feel better if they had something hot to drink for lunch. I packed a large thermos full for them."

"Ugh, lenoon soup," he commented, making a face. She made a face back and then offered up a taste for him.

"Oh come on cubling, try it," she cajoled him, smiling. He sighed, knowing it didn't smell anything like what his mother made, then took a sip. He smiled as he closed his eyes, savoring the flavor.

"It's not lenoon soup! It's wonderful," he told her. "Can I get a bowl now?" he begged, looking hopeful. She laughed at him, shaking her head no.

"It's for lunch," she asserted. "You'll just have to wait like everyone else." He sighed in surrender.

"It's my turn for watch, but you'd better make sure I get a big bowl of that soup!" he warned, grinning as he pulled one of her braids. She shooed him out, smiling as she shook her head. He snagged some bubblenuts on his way out, to snack on until then.

"I wish I had a cousin like Maren," Raya sighed with a smile. Ryes shook her head as she chuckled at this.

"I wish I'd gotten to know him better, years ago!" she told her. "Rowan and I lived apart from everyone and I'm only now getting comfortable with the people here," she admitted. Raya looked surprised to hear this; they all seemed to get along so well.

"You're going to tell me all about it, but first, I need to see if we have any fresh eggs available. I'll be right back," she promised as she set down her recipe parchment. She grabbed a basket walking out the door, just as Rein was coming in. She gave her a smile.

"What is that heavenly smell?" Rein asked as she saw Ryes still in the kitchen, mixing some ingredients in a bowl. She smiled at Torr's mother in greeting.

"I made some lenoon soup for lunch," Ryes explained to her. "I packed some for Garth and Sabin to take with them this morning."

"Lenoon soup?" she asked, the smell tugging at her mind. "May I have a taste?" Ryes gave a nod of her head, as she dipped a small amount into a tasting bowl, then went back to work. Rein sipped it, and looked at Ryes in shock.

"It was YOU!" she stated, surprised. Ryes looked up from her mixing to meet Rein's eyes, shock in her own.

"I…" she suddenly stammered, her heart hammering, as the color left her face. She set down the bowl, before she dropped it.

"Sit down," she ordered, pointing to a chair. She hadn't meant to frighten the cub, but wanted some answers. Ryes sat upon one of the stools, as she took another. "How old were you, then?" she demanded.

"Wait," Ardis cautioned in a low voice, hearing Rein and Ryes talking in the kitchen. Their voices sounded strange to her ears. They met Raya in the hall outside, as she was leaving and they were headed into the kitchen to help. Seena held back as did Raya. They listened in, hearing what Ryes was telling her. Then Raya decided to tap in on Ryes, her way, grasping their hands so they could "hear" her too, dropping her basket.

"I was all of twelve years old," she replied, blushing darkly, knowing she had to tell her the whole story, now. It was so long ago! "I was out watching the stars and moons by the Yuri, when I noticed you and Tobin had come out to watch them, too. You both looked so happy. I saw you were pregnant with Rand and was going to go home, when I caught a whiff of Old Korman. He scared me, having tossed me through the air like I was a toy, when I got in his way accidentally, once. So, I froze not knowing what to do. As I sat still, I heard him issue a challenge cry. I couldn't believe it! How could he challenge Tobin, when you were already carrying his child? You were well past your season!" she told her, looking up to meet her eyes, seeing an intensity there she'd never seen before. She truly didn't know the woman, but understood she had to own up to her own actions - no matter how long ago it'd been.

"Go on. I recall it all too clearly," Rein urged; her voice now husky with deep emotions.

"I saw him attack Tobin and kill him, cutting him up with his beltknife, to make sure he was dead. I wanted to run back for Rowan, but was so afraid Korman would kill him, too. And I didn't have anyone, but Rowan, in all the world," she said; her eyes tearing at the memories. "I saw Korman beat and claw you up; like as if he wanted you to lose the cub Tobin fathered. He took you, as if you were in season, and then left you crying and bleeding on the bank of the Yuri. By the time I found the courage to approach, you'd passed out from shock. I carried you home, but no one was there. I didn't know where to even look for Torr, not even knowing his name back then. I had no idea where to turn for help at that time of night. So, I washed out your scratches and bandaged them, then prayed for your tiny one to survive. I cleaned you up and put you into your bed."

"I went back for Tobin's body, but left it in your great room. I'd made some lenoon soup earlier that evening and some sweet muffins, so went and got them for you. I was starting to sew up Tobin's shroud, when you started crying out in pain. I finally decided to risk my Aunt Tanns, so went and got her. She was so mad at me; you would've thought I'd been the one to hurt you. She ordered me to leave and gather the herbs she needed. By the time I returned, half the Village was there, so I left them and ran home. I think I was afraid of being blamed, because I didn't get Rowan to break things up. I just couldn't... I was so afraid of losing him and having no one left to love me. I'm sorry, it was so selfish of me," she whispered the last, looking down as she cried. Rein jumped off her stool and wrapped her arms about Ryes, hugging her tightly.

"There, there, cubling. You probably saved both Rand and I that night," she comforted her, understanding many things now. "It was a lot of responsibility for a twelve year old to take on. It's all right, believe me," she assured her. Ryes wiped at her eyes, and sniffed back her tears, as best she could.

"I didn't know what else to do," she told her, looking up to see the tears and smile upon Rein's face.

"You did just fine," she assured her in a soft voice. "And you make the best lenoon soup I've ever tasted," she teased as she chuckled. She finally got a real smile out of the cub, again.

"My gosh," Ardis breathed softly. Raya had looked inside of Ryes' head, using her Talent and because they were all touching her, they saw it as Ryes recalled that night. She'd been terrified of her Aunt Tanns and what the villagers would do to her for not getting help sooner. And just as terrified of losing Rowan to Korman's claws.

"Why would she be treated so?" Raya whispered, wondering as she dropped the linkage, feeling drained.

"Because she was an outcast for too many years," Seena replied, seeing how wrong they'd been, for far too long. "She didn't have a mother, nor siblings... only Rowan to care for her from the time she was an infant," she told her, sighing as she thought of all the things they'd said, or did to her through the years, heartlessly.

"I'd better go get those eggs," Raya said as she scooped up the basket and headed outside, reviewing it all again, wondering about these people she now felt were her family, too. At least they regretted their previous behaviors.

"Computer, we've heard enough," Maren told the machine, having heard the whole story, as Ryes told it to Rein. He looked over at Torr and Shadd as they sat in shock, too. He had it play them the conversation, as he saw them sit down to talk. Something about Rein's behavior had alerted him and he wanted to be ready, in case Ryes needed his help, or backing.

"Affirmative," it replied as it cut out the audio reception in the control room from the kitchen sensors. It continued to monitor and record everything the natives said, or did, for any of its authorized, human personnel to review, when they returned.

"It's like Garth said before, we all owe her so much. Do you think her Healing Talent might've awakened then?" Torr asked, looking to Maren. It was like reopening a stab wound, as he recalled his father and that horrible night.

"What do you mean?" Maren asked, and then suddenly understood. "When a person prays for an unborn cub, they put their hands upon the mother's stomach, as they offered up their prayers," he said.

"She was at the right age for it and probably too scared to note the change within herself," Shadd added, thinking on it. "She saved Rand and probably Rein, herself."

After a wonderful lunch, Ryes jumped out of her chair in the control room and sat down far back from the console, across the room to the wall. The one time she went Time Walking from the chair when it was before the console, she appeared within the body of one of the computer operators, Neil Jarrett. It was a very strange experience, which left her with chills for days. Since that time, she made sure she was across the room when she traveled back into time. It was very rare anyone would be against this wall.

She closed her eyes, relaxed and began to cast herself back into time, again. She was now making these short trips about three or four times a week. As she learned more, she found there was still so much more to learn. And she gained a better understanding as she followed Neil's lessons for her on the computer. She found herself in the room alone, which was very unusual for this place. She instantly willed herself to be unseen, then stood and waited to see who was on duty. She was learning the temporal differences between the two times from the past to her present, but knew Neil didn't believe her. Still, she wanted to make sure she kept to linear time in his life here for her visits. Monty suddenly appeared and took his seat, and then she understood. He was young and a little reckless, and took short breaks; thinking the computer could handle things while he was gone, instead of getting someone to relieve him.

Chuckling, Ryes went to see if Neil was in his room, so headed down the stairs and the lower main corridor, toward the crew's quarters. He wasn't there and she decided to look elsewhere when his door opened and Brenda looked in. She didn't see anyone, so she slipped in the rest of the way, closed it and began to undress, throwing her clothes over the back of his desk chair. She slipped into his bed, turned the light to a lower setting, and lay waiting. Ryes shook her head at this. Neil told her Brenda was pregnant and "safe" to play with, since it wasn't his baby. She wondered at this. Why would she have another man impregnate her, but spend every chance she got with Neil? It didn't make sense! Suddenly, the door opened and Neil walked in, closing it behind him.

"Ah, my two favorite ladies," he declared merrily, smiling a huge smile. Ryes giggled as she shook her head in denial.

"Oh no! You're not going to start in with that native ghost girl, again!" Brenda demanded, looking disgusted.

"I was just leaving. I'll see you later," Ryes promised. Neil was the only human she allowed to actually see her. They were friends and she considered him her mentor.

"Come on, Ryes. Let Brenda see you. This is impeding my love life," he pleaded. He was smiling, but there was something in his eyes which told her he truly wanted her presence verified. She sighed. Garth had never forbid it… and wasn't here to do so, now.

"Alright," she gave in, then willed Brenda to see her too. She smiled at her as she waved her hand. "Hello, Brenda. My name's Ryes and I want you to know that I'm not a ghost. I'm Time Walking from the future. In other words, you're in my past… sort of…" She never was quite sure how to explain it to a human. They didn't have Talents and it took a lot to convince Neil, alone!

"Oh my God!" Brenda gasped out, clutching the thin sheet to herself as she sat up, surprise written upon her face. "What are you?" she asked, astounded. There was a native girl dressed in one of their loose T-shirts and sweatpants, with sandals upon her feet.

"My physical body is in my own time. I've only cast my spirit back in time, to your time, to get to know you better," she explained as Neil laughed, happy to have finally won. She denied him this for almost two months, now.

"Yes!" he declared, shaking a fist at the ceiling as he laughed.

"Are you a subject in one of our studies?" she asked, frowning. This native spoke English very well, even if she spoke it a little slow, as if considering each word she uttered, first.

"No. In my time, you humans have been gone for years. We needed a place to stay for the winter, so your computer has let us live here. We're very careful about messying?" she questioned, not sure of the word she was using, looking to Neil. He laughed as he sat down in his chair, calming down again.

"Messing," he corrected her. "You're getting better at your English, now." She smiled and gave him a nod.

"We're careful about messing with things, so as not to bother what you don't want touched. Even if the large metal doors are open, we keep the labs and offices locked up. We don't want the cubs to accidently wander into them and either get hurt, or damage something. When I told Garth about the bombs in storage, the only thing he wanted to know was if they could go off by themselves. He's relieved that no one in our time can get to them. We saw the sizes of the craters at Hailys and we don't need such things in our world. I forgot to thank you for showing me how to check the safeguards, to make sure they're still active," she told Neil with a smile.

"What's Hailees?" she questioned, wondering. It was a lot to swallow and her mind was in a whirl. She had a million questions to ask.

"The ruins of the city of our ancestors. Its proper name is Hailys. We know the dust down inside is still deadly, but need to recover our own technology, instead of having to rely upon yours. We've collected all the memory rods we can find, but now need to find a way to extract the information they hold. It's supposed to be done with light, but not regular sunlight," she explained, knowing this was the next project Garth had slated for her and Mitt to tackle. Why they should be stuck with this, was beyond her? She felt she had enough with trying to learn to operate the computer and take care of the Winterhaven villagers.

"Sounds like a laser reader of some sort," he said aloud, thinking about it.

"You're from the future, but need our help from the past," Brenda stated, shaking her head at this. She laughed. "This is just so incredible, Neil!" she told him, smiling.

"I told you, but you never believed me before," he affirmed.

"How is it that I see you now, Rye?" she queried.

"Ryes. Because I willed you to see and hear me," she explained. "It looks like you two wanted to spend some time alone. I'll come back another time," she offered, smiling.

"You look like you're pregnant. Are you pregnant?" she suddenly asked, wanting to know more about her, personally.

"Yes, I am. I should have my cubs by the end of the winter. I'm expecting four, so I'll probably be too busy when they're born to Time Walk. I'm trying to get as much out of the time I have before then. There's so much to still get done here in Winterhaven!"

"Where's this Garth you were talking about? Shouldn't he be helping, too?"

"He's my husband. He and Sabin had to go return a bad man to his own chief, out among the plains tribes, and make sure they understand where we established our own boundaries. We don't need murderers and worse, as Toron is, attacking us at will. Raya's from his tribe and she told us their chief Dyan was a fair man. We'll see," she replied. "So, it leaves me in charge of things, for now. I have the watches established and we're preparing for the winter. We have plenty of food set aside and are having fun learning some of your games."

"Deck of cards and a tower cam; what more do you need?" Neil put in, chuckling. "So you're not from the plains. Where do you come from?" he asked, his eyes looked intense.

"From a village called Matlowe," she told him, smiling. "It's a fair distance to travel overland, but not by helicopter." She was suddenly unwilling to point it out on a map for him. What if he did something, which caused her not to be born? Time was complicated with many puzzling twists.

"Where is it?" he pressed.

"No. Humans were totally unknown to us, so you must not find it. I don't want you to change my past and possibly make it so I'm not born," she explained. This surprised him, as he sat back and thought upon it. Brenda laughed at this, nodding her head in agreement.

"She's got you there," she assured him, "Paradoxes."

"Okay, I'll leave your village alone. So, what do you plan on doing with Winterhaven?" he asked. She smiled at this.

"We want to build Tayna anew. We know it'll take many lifetimes to accomplish, but with the technology we're learning at Winterhaven, it's a start. And if you humans ever return, we'll be there to greet you back with joy. What we really want to find out is what happened to our world of origin, Kahmarr? Why did they abandon Tayna, when it was attacked and Hailys destroyed? Tayna was a small outer world, a game preserve, but they should've sent someone... at some time," Ryes trailed off, not understanding why no one from Kahmarr came to see what happened to Tayna?

"Maybe they were too busy fighting the same enemy who destroyed Hailys?" Neil questioned. The thought that these weren't natives surprised them both. They were merely thought of as a civilization recovering from a devastating planetary war, not that they were attacked from off-world and originating from another one, all together!

"Do you know who attacked Hailys?" Brenda asked, becoming concerned. "There's a battle raging a few sectors away, with an enemy we don't know, nor understand why they're doing what they're doing to us."

"No. They attacked without warning, coming out of the dark of the stars. There was great thunder, fire and terror, and those who would know how to find out, were killed. People fled and through time established new, smaller cities and villages. The plains people fled all technology, believing it'd be the only way to be safe from another attack. We've lost more through the years as the old surviving equipment's broken down long ago and is no longer usable, and we've forgotten how to repair things. No one's tried to recreate our technology, and the old ways of living without it aren't always the best. Simple things like waste chairs... toilets not only make life easier, but are better for our health. The elders have turned their backs; refusing to listen. So, we're trying. We're not many, but we hope. We're learning how to maintain your rovers, helicopters and other pieces of equipment. Someday, we'll learn how to rebuild our own."

"Remake your world and hope the beasts who beat you down the first time, won't find you again," Brenda commented, understanding more than she thought possible. Being able to directly communicate with the natives made a big difference! She'd have to revise her papers and rethink her studies! "It's incredible!"

"We are the Star People and someday we'll regain the stars. If they're still out there, then we'll have to learn to deal with them," Ryes assured her. "It's almost time," she told them, seeing she was fading. "I only have so much energy to work with, now."

"Next time, then," Neil told her, smiling as he waved his hand farewell. She waved back, then pulled herself back to when she belonged.

"Now that was a lot to swallow," Brenda commented as she leaned back against the wall behind Neil's bunk. "How long have you been seeing her?" she asked, trying to recall when he started talking about his little, native ghost girl. He smiled guiltily.

"Almost three months. She spoke very little English when she started coming to me for computer lessons. I knew she said they were the Star People before, but never understood why she referred to themselves in such a way. In her own tongue it's more like `anei manis,'" he told her. "I said it in passing once to the woman native we have captive and I thought she was going to either faint, or swallow her tongue. Bethy gave me such a tongue lashing over it, you wouldn't have believed it!" He chuckled to himself about it, still. "I know she understood me!"

"Why is it she only let you see her, before?" she questioned, puzzled.

"She said it was because I was like Torr. I laugh and smile a lot and she felt comfortable with me as her mentor," He laughed at this. "She asks the craziest things, sometimes." He stood up and started to loosen his shirt, pulling off his tie.

"How often does she come visiting? I want more opportunities to talk with her," she asked.

"About three times a week, sometimes less, sometimes more. Usually, it's in the evening. The first time she appeared, she was in the same spot I was sitting. It was the strangest sensation! Since then, she tries to pick other, more out of the way spots."

"Why the computer?" she asked, worried about this sort of beginning.

"Because it's the task Garth set her to learn. They need to be able to operate the equipment safely and you know the computer controls over eighty percent of it, here. She's accessing the tutorials and is even learning programming. Her English is almost up to our level. She's bright and quick. I'm going to love seeing where she's at, in another couple of years."

"I thought you're due up for transfer in another year?" she pressed, her eyebrows raised in question.

"I might stay right here, after all. It's like helping a kid sister. I just can't desert her," he said. Then quickly undressed and got under the sheets with Brenda. He rubbed her growing stomach, feeling the baby moving, now. "And we have a little one to raise. It'll be better for her if I'm here with the two of you, too." She sighed as she snuggled down with him, thinking. She wasn't due up for transfer for another four years.

"If you're sure you can handle all three of us," she teased, when he suddenly turned and kissed her. As she returned the kiss, his grew more passionate, leaving her practically breathless.

"I love you Brenda, and no matter what, I'm not leaving your side," he assured her. "Will you marry me?" he suddenly asked, feeling it was too important to put off any more. If what Ryes told him earlier about the emergency evacuation and subsequent desertion of the installation was true, then he wanted to make sure they had as much time together as possible. Why hadn't they returned to this this world? Were they caught up in that war? He wanted her for his wife, no matter how much time they may, or may not have left. He couldn't believe their lives would be extinguished so tragically.

"Do I get to think on this?" she teased, then saw the look in his blue eyes. Neil was dead serious. "Yes, I will marry you, Neil," she finally breathed, "After all, why not? It was about time we settled down with our little one due soon." Neil was everything she found she wanted in a lifelong companion.

"Dr. Turner, so kind of you to come on such short notice. This will only be an informal briefing," Dr. Ethan Cruthers said as he gestured for the head internist to sit down. Ted gave him a nod of his head. There was no mistake in his mind as to why he was summoned to the office of the Director of Research; he thought he'd glimpsed Bethy in their lab observation room earlier tonight.

"It's no problem, Doctor," he assured the elderly man as he took the indicated chair. Bethany left, closing the door quietly behind her. In his hand he had printed copies of his last several reports, which Dr. Ortiz had rejected. He said they required further tests, before he'd sign off on them.

"I want you to know that as of now I have officially transferred the male native back to my own department. No more physical explorations will be performed upon his person, without my personal, written consent. Nor are we seeking any new candidates for your team's studies at this time, either."

"Yes, sir," Ted replied, giving him a nod. "Here're the rough drafts of my reports. I thought you might want to review them, since he's been returned to your care. They detail what's been done to date, with the tentative results tabulated, so far." He knew he was damning himself and Ortiz with these papers, but felt he could no longer stand by. Tonight had been the worse. "Dr. Ortiz has yet to review, edit and sign off on this work."

"Dr. Ortiz was placed under house arrest. His access to the laboratories and personnel are now severed. I'm appointing you to act as department head, until Amitell can send out a more suitable replacement," Dr. Cruthers stated, taking the reports and glancing through the top one. This was no rough draft! It was a completed research paper ready for publication! It was as he suspected for quite some months. He looked up to see the surprise in Turner's eyes as he digested what he'd been told. Ethan smiled to himself, glad to see there were no obvious signs of protest immediately voiced.

"May I ask upon what evidence?" he quietly questioned, wondering.

"Several pieces, including computer data, video and audio scans. I've already transmitted my report in, it's been acknowledged and the go ahead given for the actions proposed. I want to inform you that Dotti will also be transferred to my department. She's excellent in computer modelling; a skill Bethany sadly lacks. I hope this shortage will not cause any problems?" he asked. Ted sighed in relief. There was hope and sanity here, after all, he thought.

"No Sir. We'll find a way to manage," he assured him with a slight nod of his head.

"Very well, you're dismissed. We'll hold a more formal review of these drafts of yours, later this week. Please pass down the information I've given you, with all due discretion, to the others in your department only at this time. The circumstances of Dr. Ortiz' removal will not be up for discussion within this facility. If there are any matters which require more immediate attention, please let Bethy know and she'll make sure they are handled as quickly, as possible," he informed him. Dr. Turner gave him a nod of his head in understanding, and then stood up.

"Thank you, sir. We won't let you down," he promised with a smile as Dr. Cruthers stood and took Ted's hand, giving him a warm handshake and smile in return.

"I know you won't," he agreed, then watched as the young medical doctor turned for the door and left quickly. He had yet to do his review of the rest of the department personnel, to determine if further reprimands needed to be issued. He hoped lopping off the head had killed this snake.

Return

They rode, tracking those who'd been part of Toron's raiding party, as they returned home. There were some signs of the riders trying to hide their trail, but as they neared their home territory, there were no further attempts. This was the first time they realized all Ryes had taught them about tracking, so they never lost their tracks. Once they were in Moondance Tribal territory, they removed the blindfold and left their prisoner blinking against the bright sunlight.

"I'm an important man in my tribe!" Toron warned them, shouting. He saw he was tied down to a sled they had tied behind one of their windracers. He strained against the ropes but found these colorful ones made of some strange fiber didn't give at his flexing his arms. They didn't stretch out, either. And they tied down his whole arms and legs, not just his ankles and wrists. It was frustrating.

"So important they're all out looking for him and just happened to miss us, out in the open, heading their way," Sabin commented loudly, as he snickered to Garth. Garth smiled, giving him a nod of his head in agreement.

"After what we saw, I'd almost rather have Korman hanging around, than him," he agreed. "I know I have my days when I'd rather tear and shred the frustrating machines the humans kindly left behind for us, but then, I have Ryes to cajole me into letting go of my frustrations and approaching the problems from another angle. I know I'll never sink to the level of this Toron." He missed her terribly already and they'd only been gone a few days. The lenoon soup she packed for them had been such a blessing with the chill from the rain their first day out, but then, Ryes always looked out for him. He wanted this chore done as quickly, as possible. They had cubs on the way and he vowed to himself to be there for their birth, no matter what Maren said he and Ryes saw. He and Sabin could be out hunting, after all.

"I don't know. Korman can be brutal to the women, if the mood's on him, and has killed several good men," Sabin commented, "I'd rather they both party in hell together, locked up behind the seventh gate away from all decent people." Garth chuckled at this, giving him a nod of his head in agreement, breaking free of his inner contemplations.

"Let's check the map," he suggested later, since they decided to take a lunch break and let their mounts rest in the shade of an old, gnarled tree. They had a copy of one of the human aerial reconnaissance maps of the area they were travelling. They'd overlaid their own markings, so they had a more complete picture of what lay around them. Before they left, they made sure Ryes, Torr and Mitt knew their route, so they'd keep a watch for their return. He made sure his sister didn't try to follow them in the flyer. He didn't want it to be an accepted sight. He'd rather use it as the women had, to help add fright to any who chose to oppose them. The plains tribes were still an unknown element. If they couldn't reach an agreeable understanding, they might need every minute advantage they had within reach of their claws.

"I'm hungry, too!" Toron complained.

"After we eat, then we'll feed you," Sabin reminded him patiently, as he'd done so for the last few days. If he didn't get this small reassurance, he'd keep up the yelling until either they answered him, or stuffed a rag into his mouth. He was tired of the man and hoped to find his encampment soon. Garth studied the map, checking the compass, to make sure they were still headed in the right direction. It should be either later today or maybe by tomorrow morning, by Raya's estimation of where the tribe camped this time of year. They'd be setting up for the great hunt of the large plains animals called the korom, which they used for food, and getting ready for the winter months. Menna, the harvest moon, would soon be in the right setting for their semiannual, Great Gathering, so they had to get there, before they left the area entirely for the event.

After they'd all eaten and the windracers had gotten their fill of fresh water and grass, they filled their waterskins, then stripped down Toron and bathed him, as well as themselves in the cold, swift-moving stream. Toron protested loudly, so Garth shoved him underwater for a few moments, to remind him who was truly in control. He pulled him back up, chuckling to see the panic in his eyes, as he was coughing and choking.

"This is dangerous and unhealthy!" Toron asserted, sputtering and gasping for air. He was indignant with being made to bathe. "It's not spring, yet!"

"The stench coming off your hide's unhealthy," Garth told him. They brought out soap and scrubbed him down thoroughly, then got busy with themselves. They washed their clothes and blankets, then set everything out for the warmth of the afternoon sun to dry. Both Garth and Sabin felt much better, now that they were clean. Toron sat and glared at them, glad there weren't any breezes to give him a chill. At least his lunch was still warm. He noted that while they had brought their hunting weapons, they didn't use them, anymore. Raya, or Gleds, must've warned them about hunting upon Moondance Tribal lands, without the head elder's permission.

"Where did you get that Badge of Passage?" he finally demanded, wanting to know this, at least. "They're not given out often, and this one's from Dara, the Great Chief Elder of all the plains tribes, making it being handed out extremely rare!"

"If you must know, it belongs to my wife," Garth said, as he fingered the very distinctive badge he wore upon his left shoulder. "She's held in some esteem," he told him smiling, seeing it made him nervous to see him wearing it. Ryes gave it to him, telling him it was for free passage through the plains tribes' territory. It was given to her by Darman, in case she should ever decide to leave Matlowe for the wider world. The only one who could deny her leave was the head elder of all the plainsmen, Dara, and he was a close friend of Darman's. He carried letters from both Darman and Ryes. Darman's was to remind Dara and of the value he placed in the person he'd given this token to, and Ryes' letter explained as to why her husband carried the Badge in her stead.

"How could she know Dara?" he challenged. Garth and Sabin merely laughed at this, as they started packing their now, dry clothing and supplies away.

"Ryes knows much of the world. More than any of the three of us," Sabin said, giving Garth a nod of his head at this. Their challenge with her had been more than enough proof for his purposes.

"Get back on the litter," Garth ordered. Toron hesitated, knowing that if he tried to run off, they'd merely ride him down. He stepped over reluctantly, hating this more than anything else. They tied him down again, and then mounted up to continue their journey.

"I only see two of them," Sabin breathed to Garth as they set upon their windracers again.

"That's all I saw. Perhaps they'll come out and give us an escort in soon?" Garth cast his eyes upon the horizon, back from where they'd come. He knew if he called for help, Ryes and Mitt would be out very quickly in the flyer, but he refused to take that step until absolutely necessary. He kept the computer's gift of the emergency transmitter, safely in his coat pocket, only letting it charge in the sun where Toron had no chance to spy it.

"It shouldn't be too much longer, now," Sabin returned. "Let's see how far they intend to let us go." With this, he kicked Spur into motion, mischief in his eyes as he glanced back.

"Not fair!" Garth protested, as he nudged Pacer in the ribs, urging him to catch up. It wasn't fun for Toron, tied to the litter as he was, when the two of them got playful, but Garth suspected Sabin did this to get back at him for being the way he was, too. They galloped for a few minutes, and then slowed to a walk once more. The mare pulling the litter caught up to them, Toron yelling at them for their recklessness. They laughed at this, paying him no attention at all. Their two escorts, at a distance, had become four.

As they topped a gentle rise, they saw a party of swift riders coming toward them at a fast gallop. They stopped their mounts, waiting for them. None had their spears leveled in their direction, which Garth thought was a good sign. About a dozen riders broke into a circuit of their small knoll, riding around them in a circle, as two of their leaders came forward to speak with them, directly. Sabin noted they saw the Badge upon Garth's shoulder and noted their attitude was one of respect. The riders stopped, facing them.

"What do you seek in the territory of the Moondance Tribe Traveler?" the older one asked Garth.

"To speak with the elder known as Dyan," he replied. "We have messages to deliver to him from Gleds and Raya."

He didn't mention Toron's presence. He didn't need to. He saw none of the tribesmen tried to approach to cut him loose, nor even to talk with him. Curiously, Toron was quiet for a change, not even demanding his release. The other riders stopped their mounts, facing them from all sides. They held their spears pointed straight upwards, butts grounded within the carriers made for them, upon their saddles.

"Come, guest Travelers," the spokesman invited, then turned and led them forward, toward the camp. It was as reported. One bearing a Badge of Passage looked to be seeking them out with Toron as a prisoner. "This promises to be an interesting evening."

"Ryes, you'd better get in here," Shadd's voice spoke up over the loudspeaker overhead. Ryes, who was helping to paint a mural they decided to put up in the dining hall, put down her brush with a frown upon her brow.

"On my way," she assured her, standing up, and then looked to Seena with apologies in her eyes. It was her fairly detailed sketch of Hailys they were trying to paint, after all.

"Go on. We'll figure it out. You've given us quite an insight into what our ancestors lived like, with just living here," she told her with a smile. This got chuckles from the others as she smiled with an embarrassed nod, then trotted for the door.

"I think she and Garth mean to build our civilization anew, using both what the humans have left us and what they can recover from our ancestors," Minn commented.

"Yes, to make a stronger city, which would stand up to sudden attacks from the stars," Ardis added, smiling. It was what she and Sabin wanted to see, too. It was a future she wanted for her cubs. To be able to play in a field of flowers with no worries, nor concerns.

"I only hope we're up to the task," Tennan teased with a laugh. She looked lovingly down at her sleeping daughter, Tian, named for Rowan's grandmother, and hoped for her sake. It was a grand vision, after all and Maren had gotten her to share it, too.

"As I understand it, they expect this venture to take several lifetimes. They want to find out what happened to both the humans and Kahmarr, itself. So, if we can leave our cubs the knowledge of what was, and give them the dream of what can be," Sana said, first pointing to the wall they were painting, then to the one which stood ready, whitewashed and full of promise. "All they'll need will be the strength to continue with our work."

"Ahhhh, a hope of a future, instead of an existence only in the here and now," Marla sighed as she sat back upon her heels, to survey their work. It was very colorful and inspiring! "I never realized how depressing Matlowe truly was until Garth brought us here." Garvin chuckled as he stopped to give his wife a loving hug.

"You're absolutely right," he agreed, smiling merrily.

"I can't believe how beautiful this city was," Gleds commented, still enraptured by the metropolis, as it unfolded before him with all its shapes and colors. He wished he could've seen it, as was when it was alive and full of people!

"Neither can I," Raya agreed with him. She saw it, as Ryes had seen it, from her trips Time Walking into the past. It was even more spectacular than their painting suggested. She sighed wistfully, "I wish I could Time Walk, too."

"Show it to me!" Gleds requested, suddenly recalling what Raya could do, now. "Please?" This got surprise out of the others as they realized it, too.

"I could try," she offered, "but I'm afraid I could accidently hurt you. I'm still learning how to use my Mind Voice Talent," she warned, still unsure. Ryes told her it was an ancient Talent and that's what it was so named upon Kahmarr.

"You didn't hurt any of us last week," Seena scolded. "Please show us what Ryes has seen?" she begged, wanting this very much. Raya gave in with a small smile. She got a nod from Kovin, who granted her his support in this venture.

"You won't ever hurt us with your Talent," he assured her. He realized he'd fallen in love with his wife. "And it's good practice."

"Alright, form a circle and join hands. I don't know how well this will work, with so many," she advised, feeling nervous. Then she remembered the time Ryes took them on that adventure within where they explored the lives of the nearby animals and even met Tayna, herself. And Ryes is new to her Talents, too. It lent her courage. She could DO this!

She sat down in the middle and calmed herself, as well as she could. She closed her eyes and centered herself, as Ryes, Maren and Sabin all showed her how to do, then extended her hands to opposite sides of the circle. The excited people also closed their eyes, as Kovin and Ardis reached for Raya's hands. She reached out to their eager minds, taking control when their small eddies of thought tried to distract her, unintentionally. Then, she began to unfold the memories she got from Ryes from her three views of Hailys. The views from her first, accidental trip into the past, then her second one, and finally the one of its destruction, which Tyra gave to her in a horrible nightmare. Each memory they went over again, to explore their ancient city and marvel at it anew; taking it as slow as possible.

"What's the problem?" Ryes asked, as she entered the control room. Shadd indicated the large monitor, which displayed a view from the tower cam. She already had it zoomed in and Ryes immediately recognized it. "It's Kort's van!" she declared happily. "It's a little early for them to be headed back for Matlowe, but then, they're all alone. Caravaners never traveled alone - unless there's a good reason for it!" She watched it for a few more moments, thinking upon the matter.

"It just appeared a few minutes before I called for you. I haven't seen any others and it's just barely within our range," Shadd told her, noting her look of concentration.

"They could be in trouble of some kind. Where's Maren and Mitt?" she asked, looking to meet Shadd's eyes.

"Maren's at one of the workstations in the classroom, taking an English lesson. He's been working so hard, you'd think he was being driven," she commented with a smile. Ryes returned the smile, knowing what did drive him. It was knowing his blonde, human woman actually existed somewhere. "Mitt's out doing maintenance on the flyer. She has Mason with her and I think they're doing a little more than just maintenance," she told her, pointing to one of the smaller screens. Ryes smiled, shaking her head.

"Well, Garth's not going to be happy with her hooking up with Mason. He doesn't trust him for some reason. Do you think you could ask Torr about it? Maybe there's something the men haven't told us about him, yet?" Ryes requested. She still knew so little about the villagers, still in so many ways. Shadd laughed lightly at this, snickering.

"Mason's one of Korman's sons, a half-brother to Maren, and he's very opportunistic with the women. Anyone who'll give him the slightest chance. It may be that Garth's more worried about him trying to go Korman's way, than trying to fit in with the rest of us. The best we can do is reinforce Mitt's decision, if she ever decides she'd rather someone else, later," Shadd explained. "Don't worry; we'll all keep an eye on things, there. Mitt was too young back in Matlowe and Garth kept a watch out for her, so he probably knew better than to go near her, before."

"Some of life's lessons are too hard, at times. I'll have a little talk with Mitt later, too." Ryes sighed out. "Maren and I'll go out in a shuttle and check this out. You keep an eye on things and we'll report back if there's anything to be worried about."

"Won't the shuttle scare them?" she wondered aloud.

"Of course it will!" Ryes agreed, smiling mischievously. "But, Garth would give me such a spanking, if I even thought of using Honey," she related, giving her a wink. "He's afraid my riding a windracer might hurt the cubs." She put her hand on the side of her stomach, feeling the squirming within. "It feels like they're playing a game of field ball!"

"Well, you have half a team in there," Shadd agreed with a laugh. "You make me glad to only be having one," she admitted.

"And the work doesn't truly begin until they're born," she agreed with a laugh. "Now, I wish I were only having one! I'll be back, soon," she assured her, as she turned for the door.

"All right," she replied, then turned back to the console. She was trying to read a very interesting story about a human boy named Tom Sawyer, which had been translated to Dolbith by the computer. She was picking up the language as she compared the Dolbith page with the English one, side-by-side. It was odd that they viewed their own people so different for small things like a different coloring of their skin. It didn't matter among starmen on the color of their skin! She was still puzzling it all out while learning the language; glad Ryes had finally given it some understanding of Dolbith.

"Come on big guy," Dotti urged the native, helping him to stand up. She'd taken him to the back area where the staff showers were, to scrub him down. No one was here this time of night. She usually gave him sponge baths, but since Dr. Cruthers ordered he be returned to his department tonight, she thought she'd better get him cleaned up properly. He was usually pretty weak after a battery of tests, so she knew he'd need her help. She changed quickly into one of her old swimsuits, before trying to remove him from the trolley. She tossed her dye-stained sanitary napkin, relieved the ruse had worked!

"What is this place?" Alda questioned, seeing she was now wearing a skintight, skimpy tunic, which left little to the imagination. Did she need his services, he wondered?

"I promise to take the time to get to know your language better real soon, but for now, let's get you cleaned up for your pretty lady," she suggested. She smiled as she got him propped up against a wall of one of the stalls, then turned on the shower. She made sure it was the proper temperature, then urged him under the falling water. He smiled a genuine smile as he willing let her pull him under it. He spread his arms in thankfulness for this gift. Dotti chuckled merrily as she grabbed a bottle of soap and washcloth. He was truly enjoying this!

"Ah, to be clean once more!" he told her, delighted. He saw she was happy to see his reaction and saw her pour some sweet-smelling liquid upon a cloth. She gently washed his body all over, trying to clean away the stench, the accumulated dead skin and dried blood. She was chuckling as she worked, being careful of his freshly sealed wounds. He felt bad, being so weak and helpless that he actually needed her help with this!

"You sound so happy. I should've done this long before now!" she said, as she worked quickly, making sure she was doing the job thoroughly and well. She knew Bethy was fussy about matters like the cleanliness of her study subjects, and didn't want her best friend upset over the condition the native had been allowed to deteriorate to, while under Ortiz in his labs! She hoped she got the evidence she needed to keep him out of Ortiz's hands for good!

"Let me wash there," he asked, gesturing for the washcloth. Dotti looked up into his eyes, seeing his need to wash his own genitals and probably to check if everything still functioned, after what he'd been put through for the last several weeks. She smiled as she turned the cloth over to him, letting him finish washing his front. She took up another cloth, soaped it up and started on his back. She noted he was sighing in pure pleasure. She didn't know if it was from the shower, itself, or being able to take some care of himself once more.

"Now big guy, I'm going to need to wash your hair," she told him, as he was rinsing himself off. She took his cloth and her own, throwing them onto the trolley. She grabbed her bottle of shampoo and opened it up. Suddenly, he took her into his arms and hugged her tightly against his body. Her heart was hammering as she froze in fright. But, he started talking to her in a low voice as he stroked her wet hair. She realized he was trying to comfort her, in spite of his obvious erection. She suddenly threw an arm around his waist and they stood under the warm, flowing water for several long minutes as she started crying again. His gentle voice soothing her inner wounds. In this moment, she didn't care if he wasn't human. He was a gentle man, who seemed to care. It was far better than she received from any of the men here… ever…

"I'm okay, now," Dotti assured him, as she finally looked up to his face, which seemed so very human to her eyes. She wiped at the tears in her eyes as he suddenly bent to kiss her. Her heart was hammering once more as she found herself returning the kiss. It was almost right.

"No, I can't," she told him, as she finally pulled away. "We have someone who's missed you and needs you far more than I do," she told him. Alda saw her regret, but there looked like some kind of promise in her eyes. So, he released her and let her finish her ministrations.

"Perhaps I'm not your type," he teased her, smiling. She returned the smile as she urged him to help her rinse out his hair. He realized he was starting to feel free and alive once more, as she washed it a second time to be sure. Then rinsed it again.

"I wish you were him," she suddenly sighed out as she turned off the shower and activated the blowers to dry them off. "There's this sweet, golden-brown eyed, native man, who's been with me in my dreams for months, now. He holds me in his arms and talks to me in a warm, rich voice and I think I'm in love with him. You're just not the right one, but I do appreciate the comfort you gave me," she said, looking up into his golden eyes. "Now, let's get you dressed."

She handed him a pair of skivvies, then had to support him as he dressed. This impressed him and there was a definite sense of self about him, again. Next, she helped him into some sweat pants, then a T-shirt. Once he was dressed, she pulled over a wheelchair and urged him to sit down. She changed back into her own clothes, in front of him, then gathered her soaps and swimsuit. She handed her things to him and he held up her swimsuit to examine it, looking puzzled as she blushed and urged him to put it back down onto his lap.

She pushed him out; noting the hallways were empty, in relief. She made a beeline for her own room per her instructions from Dr. Cruthers, feeling great to have had a hand in freeing him from Robert Ortiz! She opened her door and pushed him inside. She helped him up onto her bed, grabbed a box of her things, and placed it onto the seat of the wheelchair in his place. Dotti rolled it back out into the corridor, and rushed back in to assure the puzzled look in his eyes.

"I'll be right back with someone you've missed a whole lot," she assured him, as she brushed his hair with her own brush, trying to make it look neat. She held her hands up in front of him as he tried to grab for her again, ready to kiss her, but she managed to pull away. Dotti laughed, feeling wonderful. This was going to be some surprise! She went back out into the hall, secured her door, put the wheelchair in a nearby closet, picked up her box of things, and rushed to Bethy's quarters. She hit the call button and waited. Her friend opened the door, still dressed and looking wide awake.

"Well?" Dotti asked, "Did Dr. Cruthers get him transferred?"

"Yes, and you're now working in our department, too," she told her, not wanting to discuss such things out in the public hallways. "Come on in," she invited, seeing the box in her hands.

"You're getting a roommate for a few days," she teased, grinning. "I'm transferred too? It's beyond a miracle! But we need to fetch your lady friend. I know a certain gentleman who can't wait to see her." Bethy looked surprised at this, and then nodded her head in agreement.

"The native woman just started her mating cycle this morning. Perfect! Get your stuff in here and come on," she ordered, as Dotti moved to do just that. They hurried down to her lab section and to the small room behind her desk. She keyed it open and saw they awoke the native with their light and noise.

"Come," she urged in her own language. She hoped this was what she was saying. They still had so much ground to cover, yet! The woman looked puzzled, but got up and came to the door and the two waiting women. She suddenly caught Alda's scent from the blonde woman's clothing. She grabbed her white coat collar and breathed it in, in longing.

"Alda," Ptan sighed, missing him so very much!

"Their sense of smell is far beyond ours and I think she knows what our surprise is all about. I believe Alda is his name," Bethany told Dotti, chuckling as she noted the longing and smile upon Pattan's face. "Let's go." They led her out into the corridor and down several others, until they came to Dotti's own. Dotti keyed in her lock code and the door opened. He was sitting upon the bed waiting, looking around the plain room, curiously. His eyes flew to the door as it opened and he saw his beloved mate. As she ran to him, he jumped to his feet and wrapped his arms about her, as if he never intended to let her go, again. Dotti sighed happily, to see them so joyous to be together.

"Now that makes me feel good," she told her friend.

"Are you sure the drugs are cleaned out?" Bethy asked, wanting to make sure any children he fathered would have a good chance of being as healthy as possible, circumstances being the way they were.

"I ran the tests right before that last battery of tests tonight. His blood was clean, sperm count was up and they looked very healthy. So, the only thing affecting them will be whatever they put into him tonight. And when I was showering him, he was making sure everything was working, so I think the chances are good," she assured her as they watched them from the door. Bethy sighed, relieved. If nothing else, she knew Dotti was excellent in patient care.

"Great. You keep an eye on them, while I go make a few quick entries and get the things we'll need," Bethany ordered, giving her a smile in assurance. "Until we get the remote cameras installed and recording, you're just going to have to play Peeping Tom." Dotti chuckled at this, nodding her head.

"The things we do in the name of research," she replied, smiling. "I can manage them," she assured her.

She and Alda had their friendship well established, as she'd been the one to care for him practically since they were captured. She trusted him and hoped he'd intervene if the woman tried anything. But, as a backup, she always carried her stunner ready in her pocket whenever she handled him. Bethy gave her smile as she left. Dotti sighed as she leaned against the doorframe. They were passionately kissing and talking in low voices. Alda turned around and saw her standing in the door, a puzzled look upon his face.

"Sorry Alda, I have to maintain our observations and guard duty," she explained, trying to appear as if she had no choice. He gave her a nod and sat upon her bed, still looking spent, pulling the woman down next to him. Dotti cast her eyes out into the corridor, seeing no one else was out and about at this early morning hour, in relief. When she looked back she saw they were talking to each other as he held her in his arms. They were soon kissing again. She smiled. They looked so sweet, young and in love.

"What's going on here?" A too-familiar voice demanded from behind her. Dotti turned around quickly to see Ortiz approaching her door. She went to hit the touch-plate to seal them inside away from him, but he pounced and brutally grabbed her wrist, pulling her hand away from the lock. "Suddenly, I'm sealed out of my own office," he growled with menace. "And I can well bet you're behind all this! I'll get things straightened out, and then make sure you understand what happens to anyone who tries to get in my way." He shoved her back, and looked into her quarters. She quickly blocked him with her own body, gripping the doorframe, her anger finally rising.

"He's no longer yours! Dr. Cruthers transferred him back to his department to complete his studies," she warned him. "And along with him, he transferred me, as he's familiar with me and I can handle him." She knew Bethany wouldn't lie about something like that to her. She only hoped it was already in the computer!

"So you can pimp him out? He's going back to his holding pen, right now!" Ortiz ordered. But she didn't move, nor tried to comply with his order. He swung back his hand to slap her for her insolence, when his arm was roughly grabbed from behind.

"Enough of that!" Dr. Cruthers ordered. Lt. Dawe held Ortiz by his arm, having pulled him away from Dotti and around to face the Director. "Lt. Dawe, place Dr. Ortiz under arrest. Considering the obvious lack of professionalism displayed, please place him in a suspension tube until he's transferred back to Earth," he ordered.

"You can't do this to me!" Robert shouted, his face now turning a bright red.

"You're endangering my staff and experiments," he told him. "And from the review of the computer files, there will be quite a few charges leveled against you. I've already received authorization from Amitell and the authorities back on Earth. Lieutenant, do your duty," he ordered, knowing Jim Dawe would have matters well in hand. Ortiz shouted his counter threats as the lieutenant took him to the suspension chambers in the main medical section.

"Now, now, my dear," Dr. Cruthers spoke up, stepping closer to examine Dorothy's face. It was turning a dark color from the earlier battering she received at Ortiz's hands. "You were very brave, but next time, go for help," he gently scolded. She lowered her eyes, nodded and blushed. "How are our two native friends doing? Did they miss each other?" he asked, peering in over her shoulder. The male was right behind Dotti, looking as if he intended to intervene, if any further violence happened. He smiled at this and chuckled. "Bethany?" he called.

"Yes, doctor?" she asked, stepping forward. She had a small, wheeled cart loaded with the equipment needed, ready.

"It looks as if he's feeling better and ready to defend his ladies," he commented. "Please help Dorothea set up our observation equipment," he requested, unwilling to step into a room the male looked to consider as his own territory. Bethany gave him a nod of her head, as Dotti shifted and smiled back to Alda, trying to reassure him it was fine, now. He saw the surprise and relief in her face and smiled in return. He extended his hand to this tall human elder, hoping his trust wouldn't be betrayed. Dr. Cruthers chuckled as he lay his hand across the native's palm, guessing what his gesture implied. There was far more warmth in his smile as he gave him a nod of his head and stepped back from the doorway.

"Far more civilized than I suspected. Perhaps they were the builders of that city, after all?" Ethan commented, as he stepped back out of the way, so the women could get the equipment set up. The male returned to sit upon the bed with his woman, relief in his eyes. He held her in his arms as they watched the humans. Once everything was set up, they took them to the bathroom, to let them perform any necessary functions, brought them each a tray of food and water to drink, then closed the door, sealing it to give them a sense of privacy. Lt. Dawe had returned and was talking to Dr. Cruthers in a low voice, by the time the women were finished.

"All ready," Bethany told them, smiling happily at Jim; glad he happened by earlier.

"Very well," Ethan replied as he stepped over and input a special code into the door lock for Dotti's quarters. "Now, only you two ladies and I can open it. Let's let them rest and we'll get some sleep, too. The real work starts tomorrow," he teased, warning them with a smile.

"Yes, Sir. Thank you," Dotti replied, relieved it was truly over! She couldn't believe they were truly free of Ortiz! Now if only she could find her dream man. He had to be SOMEWHERE on this planet!

Travelers

They rode into the camp. It was in a large clearing and was composed of a few simply-built, temporary wood and sod structures, which were surrounded by a small sea of tents and animal pens. This was one of their main campsites, and according to Raya, was sheltered from the worse of the fall winds and rain storms by the high cliffs around them. The only permanent structures they had were at their winter camp, which was further northwest. The rest of the year they followed the herds and lived in tents. There was a plentiful supply of water here, provided by the small river which ran nearby. The river also supplied them with fish, which helped when their other supplies ran low. There were lots of trees around them, which concealed the camp, until you were upon it. The nearby cliffs gave their lookouts an advantage of sight over anyone below. Sabin observed it was a well-thought camp placement.

"My younger brother, Sook, who is son of Dania, will care for your windracers with full honor," Shins, the escort leader told Garth, as they dismounted. A teener stepped forward, taking their reins appearing proud to be given such a responsibility.

"Thank you," he replied, with a nod of his head in respect and gratitude. Then, they went to untie Toron from the litter; still they left the binder on his hands. It was a symbol of his continued rank as their prisoner. They hauled him to his feet and each noted the look of pure hatred he had in his eyes for them, even if he didn't voice his anger anymore. After seeing what this man's mind and heart held, it didn't surprise them at all.

"We're ready, if Dyan's ready to see us," Sabin informed their escort with a smile.

"He's expecting you," Shins replied, then led them to Old Dyan's lodge. He'd seen the hatred Toron had for these travelers; giving him a chill up his back. The rest of the camp was out and gathered around them, watching quietly. Toron was casting some of the plainsmen looks of pure malice, too.

The entrance had a small wall of sod blocking the doorway about two paces inside, to keep out any gusts of wind and rain. A heavy, painted hide covered the actual opening, at an angle to it. Shins held the hide aside to let them in. There was a wide sheltered space within with a vent built for the fire pit in the middle. On one side was a scattered gathering of at least two dozen tribesmen and women. On the other side were ten elders with one seeming more prominent than the others, sitting in the center. Their seating was built up a little higher than everyone else, so they could see the room clearly. A line of younger and older warriors sat before the elders, as if ready at their call. There were mats upon the dirt floor and the elders sat upon well-cured hides. Food was being passed around, as well as mugs of simple mead. None of the elders were women, Garth and Sabin noted. The firepit had a low-level fire that provided light for the building as well as candles around the room to supplement it. Wax dripped down the holders freely, creating frozen waterfalls of wax that were very colorful.

"Welcome Travelers, welcome," an elder greeted them, as they entered the lodge and paused to let their eyes adjust to the lower light. "Please take a seat and warm yourselves by the fire." They did as they were bid, making Toron sit upon the mat-covered floor beside them. He glared hate at them, but didn't speak one word. His glare and their indifference was noted by all in the room.

"We thank you for your welcome," Garth returned, a smile upon his lips. After seeing what these old men let Toron get away with for years, he didn't trust any of them very much. Young women brought them leather mugs of sour mead and a clay plate with a roasted bird upon it. The bird looked burned in places and the mead was a far cry from what they used to make, themselves, when they lived back in Matlowe! Not sure if he was being deliberately insulted, he deiced to opt for better manners in return. Sabin watched for his reaction.

"Good," Garth lied, lifting up the mug in indication. He knew he needed their goodwill and cooperation.

"I'm told you have something for me?" Dyan asked, seeing his visitors looked uncomfortable in his lodge. He truly didn't want them here, but had little choice now.

"Yes, we have messages from Gleds and Raya," Garth told him, as he removed them from his belt pouch and passed them to Sabin who stood up, extending them to their escort. The man gave him a nod of his head in approval of this sign of respect, then took them and passed them to Dyan's hand. Sabin sat back down. The elder nodded and smiled as he unrolled each message and read them carefully by his candlelight. Everyone in the lodge was quiet as he slowly read the messages.

"So, they've each chosen to live with your people. What makes you so better?" he demanded as he passed the parchments to another tribal elder, who sat upon his right. There was anger flashing in his eyes at this, Garth noted. He stood, signaling Sabin to remain sitting.

"We have a vision of what the future can be and they've each chosen to become a part of it and help to build a better world. In Raya's case, we encountered her upon the road on the way to our new home, which we now call Winterhaven. She was starving, so we took her in as a part of our group and she stayed. Later she mated to one of our bachelors and even when she knew where the Moondance Tribe's lands lay and could easily return home, she chose to stay with us," he told him, meeting his eyes calmly. "She felt she was given more choices to live her life as she willed in Winterhaven. As for Gleds..." he paused with a sigh, but the elder signaled for him to continue.

"We were out with a small hunting party, well within our own lands, when eight riders from the Moondance Tribe rode down upon us with their spears leveled against us. We stood our ground, showing them no fear, so they stopped to talk with us, first. Toron became incensed with the idea that Raya would reject his claim of ownership, and charged us with his spear leveled at us. Our women used two of our machines to drive away most of the raiders. Toron was thrown from his windracer, but Gleds had cast his spear at the machine which held my own wife. I shot him with an arrow, bringing him down. Our Healer took care of Gleds, returning him to health. When we took them back to Winterhaven to question them about the attack, Gleds related that he knew they were well outside the Moondance hunting markers, and had only thrown his spear at the machine, not realizing my wife was within it, until too late. She was unharmed and he apologized to her. He later decided he wanted to stay with us. Like Raya, he was free to leave if he wished to return home. Since neither wanted to do so, I asked them to write what was in their hearts to their own people, and that we'd deliver the messages to you."

At the end of his story, voices all over the lodge rose as everyone was discussing it among themselves. Even the elders were conferring with each other, appearing greatly agitated. They finally came to a decision and returned to their own places. One of the elders finally called for order in the rest of the lodge and plainsmen then subsided. Toron just appeared sullen and defiant.

"How do you know where the Moondance markers lie?" one of the other elders demanded, having read the two notes, already.

"Raya showed us and later, Gleds verified them," Garth explained. "We wanted to know, so as to not encroach upon your tribal lands, but we also have come here to make it clear that we won't tolerate encroachment upon our hunting lands, either. If there's extreme need, you may approach us for permission to hunt upon our lands and then we can discuss it. We're not cold-hearted and can well understand with the hunts being so poor these last two years."

"Where do you originally come from?" Dyan asked, thinking upon what this young hunter was asking of him. He stood straight and tall with a strong bearing of command for one so young. It caught at him as he wished his own sons carried themselves this way.

"Matlowe Village," he replied, steadily holding his eyes.

"You're a far way out of Matlowe," he commented. "And what of this one?" he demanded, indicating Toron as if seeing him for the first time in their company.

"He meant to murder us all, if he could. We brought him back to you, to do with as you see fit. If he's ever seen in our territory again, his life will be forfeit. It was clear, if nothing else, that he was freely leading his hunting party well outside of the Moondance Tribal markers to take whatever he could. He has a dark, evil heart."

"I'll take him back. Release him," Dyan said, looking unhappy, but gave Garth a nod of his head, as he accepted responsibility for this burden. Sabin had out the cutter tool and cut the binding cord from his wrists, freeing Toron at last. He cast them a wicked grin as he rubbed his arms to return the circulation.

"Now you'll get to see how we do things here in my tribe," he gloated as he got to his feet. He started to step over to Dyan's side when Shins stepped between them.

"Lawbreaker, you're not fit to sit near the Great Elder," he stated, then signaled for his removal from the lodge. The shock on Toron's face gave Sabin's heart a small lift. Apparently, he expected to be rewarded, not taken away for a punishment, yet to be determined. He struggled wildly and it took six men to take him captive. He yelled his curses down upon them all, until he was knocked unconscious and dragged from the lodge.

"May I know your names?" Dyan asked, as if Toron's outburst never happened.

"I am Garth and this is Sabin," he introduced them.

"You come from the place of the flashing lights?" he pressed, curious. Garth smiled and gave him a nod of his head at this.

"Yes and the computer machine refuses to turn them off. So, we live with the lights, whether or not we wish to," he agreed.

"What is that?" an elder asked appearing puzzled, not knowing the words used.

"A machine which controls other machines," he explained. "They interact with us as well as with each other. It's something like the great machines of old, before the thunder and destruction." This seemed to upset all the tribesmen again and they needed to be called to order, once more.

"How do you defend yourselves, if you don't carry any spears?" one of the other elders cut into the quiet, appearing to wonder about their strange ways. "For you to brave men mounted with spears."

"We used our hunting bows," Sabin told him, smiling. "They work well and are a lot lighter to carry around, but can be just as deadly."

"Show us these hunting bows," Dyan urged, his eyes bright to know all their secrets. He wondered how much he could get out of Toron about them and their winter haven?

"Not in here; outside," Garth suggested, wanting to get out of the stuffy lodge. He could now appreciate the air movement they had back in Winterhaven, much more. Sabin gave him a nod of his head in agreement at this, feeling much the same. He had enough of this closed-in place! And the tribe members in here seemed more hostile than welcoming.

"We'll go outside to see these hunting bows and how well they work," Dyan declared, standing up. His son had his coat ready, as his grandson, Shins, now stood between him and these strangers.

They all went outside and the entire tribe gathered around the area the elders designated for the demonstration. This crowd seemed far happier and looking forward to see something new and exciting for them. Garth explained the basic design of the bows, leaving many small points out. There was a lot of doubt expressed of them even being able to work, among the plains dwellers. There were cheers and jeers as Garth and Sabin loosed their first arrows at the designated target, both hitting it squarely. In this way they also demonstrated the accuracy of their arrows. Garth and Sabin were proud of their skills, but didn't want the plainsmen to learn the new weapons too quickly.

Dyan was delighted with their display of the new weapons, so pressed them to accompany them on a hunt the following morning. He wanted to see them used on the herd animals, to see if they worked well there, too. He assured Garth that once they brought in enough meat for the winter, he'd sit down with them and together they'd work out a peace treaty. The Winterhaveners weren't too happy with the delay, but couldn't protest it at this time.

Then, they were shown to a small empty lodge, for the night. It had sleeping furs and good hides upon the mat-covered floor to sit upon. There was an attached pen and their own windracers were already set up there in apparent comfort with plenty of food and water. Shins had admired the brand they sported on their hindquarters, which seemed to delight to two men, too. But finally they were left with food and drink for the evening to enjoy in peace.

There was no chance for a mix-up with their windracers bearing a "brand" Gleds insisted they burn into the hide of all of their animals, as a mark of ownership. It was a symbol of a bird made of fire rising into the air out of a great fire, which Ryes found in one of the computer files. They decided it was perfect for their use, since such a bird didn't exist upon Tayna and it symbolized a new life out of the ashes of the old. So, the Phoenix became the symbol of the people of Winterhaven.

"I wonder if this might've either been Gleds', or Raya's?" Sabin conjectured as they cozied down for the night, having already brought in their things. It was almost a homey feeling.

"I wouldn't doubt it," Garth agreed. "I think I'll call and let everyone back home know what's happening," he decided, taking out the transmitter.

"That's a good idea," Sabin concurred, "Just as long as I get to speak with Ardis."

"Of course," Garth chuckled, understanding him too well. He longed for Ryes' voice, himself. He activated the non-emergency contact switch.

"Maren?" Ryes asked, as she stepped into the classroom. There were smaller computers in here, mounted to the desks. There were other desks to the one side, which didn't have any computers, so they used these to give the cubs their lessons. She went back in time and saw the humans writing upon the white panels, mounted upon the walls, with pens of light, but had yet to take the time to figure those out. Maybe when the snows hit and she'd have too much time? It wasn't important for the time being.

"Here," he replied in English, raising his hand so she could spot him behind his monitor panel. "What's up?" he asked, grinning.

"There's a lone caravaner's van moving down the road west of us, toward Matlowe. It's too early, so I suspect there may be trouble of some kind. Want to drive me out there to check it out? I figure the shuttle might not frighten them as much as the flyer," she explained, also in English.

"Okay, now say that in Dolbith. I don't think I got any of it," he admitted with a laugh. She now spouted the human tongue, as if she spoke it all her life! She came closer laughing, then did as he requested, repeating herself in their own language.

"What kind of trouble?" he questioned, concerned.

"It could be anything from a family disagreement, to a punishment doled out by Darman, to a death in the family, or even some kind of sickness. It could even be that they did so well with this year's trading that they decided to come in early, because they didn't need to work the last few towns and villages, before the winter. Although, that'd be extremely rare," she assured him. "I just feel better knowing for sure, since neither I, nor Rowan, will be in Matlowe to help if it's real trouble."

"And heaven would only know what mood my mother would be in, if they needed her help with anything," he agreed. He returned his attention to the console and exited his program, shutting it down properly, as was now automatic for him. The human machines had to be handled in such precise ways! "Give me a few minutes to change into something warmer," he suggested, then noted Ryes was only wearing her thin T-shirt, shorts and sandals. "Looks like you need to change, too," he scolded. She smiled and gave him a nod.

"Meet you outside. Let's take good old number seven. We don't use it as often as the other two," she decided. He gave her a nod in agreement as they headed for their separate quarters.

"Mitt?" Ryes queried, stepping into the open, flyer hangar. There was no obvious sign of her, but she wanted to let her know what was happening. Suddenly a window opened in the back of one of the flyers and her head poked out. Her hair was disheveled and she didn't look as if she were wearing a tunic, nor T-shirt.

"Yes?" she asked, and then caught the sly smile Ryes threw her way. "I was just checking a few things out," she explained.

"Maren and I are going out in one of the shuttles. You might want to leave your radio on, in case we need any aerial backup. There's a lone caravan wagon heading toward Matlowe and we want to check it out," she explained. Mitt's eyes widened, as she suddenly became more businesslike about the situation.

"I will," she promised. "And, if there's a chance tonight, could we have a little talk, later?" she requested, her eyes full of conflicting emotions. Ryes stepped closer, the smile melting from her face.

"That's never a problem, Mitt. You should know that by now. We can talk as soon as I get back, if you want. If things aren't totally out of hand," she teased, the smile returning. Mitt gave her a nod of her head.

"Thanks, Sis," she breathed, then ducked back inside her flyer. Ryes smiled to herself as she turned for the shuttle garage entrance, which she saw was just opening. Maren was inside at the controls for the door. He signaled to Ryes and she went over to the passenger door of number seven, opened it and settled herself within, securing her seat straps. Maren jumped in and did his quick check, then buckled in, too. He activated the machine, bringing up the reception of the main screen from the computer control room, so he knew what Shadd was looking at.

"How should we approach them?" he asked, wanting her opinion, since she'd been around the caravaners since she was a cub. She smiled as she considered it.

"Go ahead with full speed, until we're close. It's fairly open land, so there's no chance of hiding ourselves. When we get close, slow to whatever speed their windracers are doing and I'll open the window and try to assure them it's only me."

"Then we'll just cross our fingers that it isn't something we can't handle," he returned, as he pulled up the ramp and away from their tower building. She sighed, giving a nod in response.

"I forgot to ask, why you picked that room you're using?" Ryes questioned, recalling she meant to ask him about it before. It was away from the rest of the ones they used and she was curious. After years of her living as an outcast, it hurt her to see her cousin distancing himself from them.

"Actually, it's HER ROOM," he admitted with a wry smile. "Her scent still lingers very faintly and even if I've never met her before, I'd know it anywhere. I just feel closer to her, when I go to sleep at night," he explained. She smiled warmly at this. He knew her scent only from dreams? It was amazing!

"I think I'm starting to agree with the others. You'll see her someday, and I hope she's worth it all. The humans seem a strange people at times, and I'd rather not see them treat you callously, or hurt you," she admitted her own fears for him.

"I'm old enough and tough enough to handle it," he told her, appearing touched. "Alright, not as tough as you, Sabin and Garth, but tough enough," he teased. She smiled and gave her head a small shake at this.

"I'm not as tough as Garth and Sabin," she admitted with a small laugh.

"From what I heard from them, they think it's the other way around. The three of you never told us what you did to them to get them to drop that challenge - cold. That was a feat in itself!" He looked over to see her blushing at this.

"How about, after Mitt and I have our little talk later today, I'll show you what I did. It's hard to explain, otherwise," she suggested.

"I thought you were planning on Time Walking, today," he returned. "I'd rather go with you into the past, than show me what you did that day. If you don't mind some company?" he requested.

"So you can see your lady fair?" she teased, chuckling. He was smitten, for sure! He blushed at this, and gave her a nod of his head.

"Sure, why not? I miss her terribly. I wonder sometimes, if maybe in another life we were of the same people and true-mates? It's like she a part of me and I won't be whole again, until we're together." He finally voiced aloud what he thought he found in his heart. Ryes felt her heart constrict in panic for him. It wasn't beyond probability of actually happening, but it had to be so extremely rare! Did he actually risk his soul, believing such a thing, she wondered?

"We'll seek her out. I know about something which happened to her, which you should be aware of, anyway," she told him. "It's not that I kept it from you to hurt you, but to keep you from hurting over something where you have no power to intervene." She knew she was making this harder for him by not outright saying what it was...

"What?" he demanded, suddenly worried about everything again.

"It's better if I just show you," she pressed. "I think they see us," she commented, seeing the van's windracers picking up their pace. "It'll be all right, Maren. Remember Alda said they'd be rescued. I think I know how," she assured him, clasping his shoulder. He relaxed somewhat, after he recalled what Alda told them, too.

"Better get your window down and be ready," he advised, "It might be better to catch up to them first, then slow down to match their pace, so they'd know they're outmatched from the start and not run their animals to death." Ryes quickly lowered her window and stuck her head and shoulders out, so she'd be recognized quickly, she hoped.

"KORT!" she shouted as they drew up beside the wagon. "KORT!" she repeated. He finally looked over and saw her wave to him from inside this strange, metal monster. "Slow down. We just want to know what's wrong," she shouted. He began to rein back, slowing their wild dash down the treacherous road, still surprised it was her riding in the thing.

"What in the seven hells are you doing in such a machine?" he returned, worried as he got his team slowed to their normal walk.

"Rowan and I are living in a place the humans built. This is one of the machines they left behind. My cousin, Maren, is driving it for me today, so I could let you know it was only me. What's wrong Kort? You're never in Matlowe this early!"

"Nils is sick with a fever. We fear for his life. We were coming ahead to see your Aunt Tanns, to see if she could do anything for him," he told her, pulling his team to a full stop. Maren braked the vehicle, set it to standby, then jumped out his door.

"Let me see him," he urged, coming to stand next to Ryes, who jumped out her door, too. The van's door popped open and Nahees was there, her stricken, young son in her arms.

"Oh, Ryes," she sighed out, happy to see her out in the middle of nowhere. "If you have some twisted eon root, it might help," she begged.

"Maren's my cousin and a Healer. Let him try first, Nahees," she suggested. She looked doubtful, but was distraught. She just came off her third season and was now carrying Kort's second child. She didn't want to lose his first one is such a way! She saw the truth in Ryes' eyes and knew she never lied. Tara would've never tolerated it! So, she extended her precious cub to this cousin of hers and prayed in her heart. Kort jumped down, putting his arm about her shoulders in comfort.

"Let me see you, young Nils," Maren crooned as he saw the cub distressed to be handed over to his care. It must be hard for them to trust strangers, being surrounded by them wherever they went, he thought. He sat down upon the ground, right where he was and reached within himself to find his center. He then reached outwards to the child, to do what he could for him. He was still a very long time, it seemed. The parents were anxious as they stood nearby, waiting.

"Don't move," Ryes cautioned Nils, seeing his eyes brighten and it looked as if he'd never been sick. "Wait until Maren says it's all right," she stressed, knowing if his eyes were still closed, there was still work which needed to be finished. Maren opened his eyes at last, smiling down at the cub in his arms.

"There you go," he told him, helping him up to his feet. "Now I want to check your parents, to make sure they're all right," he stated, standing up and brushing his jeans off.

"NILS!" Nahees shouted, happy to see her son as healthy as he if he'd never had the fever at all. Kort gave Maren a nod as he stepped closer, extending his hand palm up, claws retracted.

"If ever you need anything," he vowed, meeting his eyes. Maren smiled at this, crossing his palm with his own.

"First, I want to check the two of you, to make sure you're all right, too," he told him. "Then we should clean out your wagon, to make sure you don't carry this fever to others upon your travels," he suggested, feeling this was too important a matter. The more he learned from the humans, the more he understood the way things worked in the world. Diseases could be spread too easily through carelessness and he intended to stop this one from going further.

"Ryes!" Shadd's voice came over the shuttle's radio. "Is everything all right?" she demanded, concerned. They had stopped, but it was hard to see what was happening. Ryes smiled to the caravaners, then ran back for her open door. She reached across and grabbed the mic.

"Maren's services were required. A child had a bad fever. We're checking everyone before returning. Tell Mitt to go ahead and stand down," she reported.

"Okay," she replied. Ryes chuckled, as she hung the mic back up on the dashboard.

"What's so funny?" Maren asked, hearing her chuckle.

"It's just that we've all picked up some of the human words, like `okay.' I wonder what they'd think of that?" she speculated, as she turned back to the others, seeing Nahees' younger sister, Nalin, and older daughter, Aravan, looking out at them from inside. "Is there anything you want me to do while you're busy here?" she asked, wanting to help, too.

"Use your Talents to see if you can see anything inside, or around the van, which might be the cause of this fever, or still hold its root? Your own Healing Talent should find it and be able to kill it," he instructed, hoping she could do it. This time Maren settled upon a nearby rock, then motioned for Nahees to come closer. She was obviously just pregnant and he wanted to check on both her and her cubs.

"If you insist, cousin of Ryes," she told him, as she stepped over to him.

"Maren," he replied with a smile and nod. He then closed his eyes, as she offered up her hands. He lightly grasped them, as he reached out to her from within.

"Tara's little Wild Child has finally grown up," Kort chuckled. "When are your cubs due?" he asked. She blushed darkly at this, lowering her eyes shyly, as the others gathered around them now. They knew her as a part of their larger family and were comfortable being near her.

"We think by the end of the winter. So, several months off still. I just started feeling them move not too long ago and now they keep me up half the night. I'm going to have my hands full when they're born," she admitted.

"Where's the father?" he asked, then suddenly recalled Korman and his menace. She laughed at this and shaking her head, as if guessing his thoughts.

"His name's Garth and he's out trying to make a treaty with the plains tribes. We had one of their hunting parties try to attack one of our own. Luckily, we women keep a good look-out and chased most of them away with our shuttle here and our flyer. We hope to get things settled with them before winter. It'd be nice to be able to plant our spring crops without having to constantly chase them away," she explained.

"You're family," Kort told her. "If your husband can't get them to listen to reason, Darman will enforce the peace." He looked her in the eyes, meaning it. She suddenly understood why few ever attacked the Caravans. If they did, they were shunned until they had made proper reparations to the parties involved. The caravaners wielded their own power, after a fashion. She did not doubt him.

"We'll see where things go," she told him, glad they had other options available. "But, for the moment, I'd better see about doing what I'm supposed to," she assured him, with a warm smile. Kort gave her a nod of his head, as she moved to stand before their van.

He recalled Tara once telling Darman that it was a good thing Ryes was such a giving, gentle child, because once her Talent awoke, she was sure it'd be very powerful. As they stood and watched her stretch out with her Talent, there was a feeling of great power in the air. It tantalized the senses at a level which was hard to describe. In his heart he thanked the gods that even if the villagers had shunned this beautiful child, they always treated her as family. The power, which almost hummed in the air, was frightening and amazing!

Once done, they all returned to Winterhaven. Rowan was there to greet the caravaners, happy to see all were now well. Nahees wrapped her arms about him for a hug, happy to see him looking better than he had in years. He returned it warmly.

"Rowan, seeing you gives my heart joy," she told him, tears streaming down her cheeks. "I thought Nils was going to die, but thanks to your grandson, he lives and is healthy again!" Rowan beamed at this, laughing and nodding his head, as she let him go.

"He's been one of our best blessings, ever," he replied, his pride clearly seen in his face. "I have to talk to you and Kort, when you both get a little time," he added, looking more sober again.

"What's wrong?" Kort asked, as Nahees appeared surprised at the seriousness in his manner.

"There was a great fire in Riverward at the end of winter and people who were burned out of their homes have been turning up in Matlowe Village," he began.

"We heard of the horrors being done to the ones who survived," Kort said, looking unhappy as he seemed to guess where Rowan's concern might be indicating.

"Metta, being Metta has generously allowed the ones allowed to stay to settle out near the river. I showed them the houses they were allowed to use and which ones were clearly Marked with The Seal, but since I'm now here, I can't keep them out of your homes," he related, appearing worried.

"I believe our coming back early is a sign that we were needed here," Nahees stated while Kort appeared thoughtful.

"We taught some of them how to care for the water gathering and waste elimination equipment, and Gann and a few of the hunters are living out there and helping to keep an eye on things, but still I worry," he admitted.

"I want to rest my team a couple of days and give Nils some time to fully recover, first, then we'll head back to our winter home and see that our boundaries are respected," Kort assured them. "Thank you, for telling us right away, Rowan."

"They survived incredible horrors committed by both criminals in the area, as well as being ignored or abused by the city guard and the city elders. I only hope they don't bring those horrors to Matlowe. It's a quiet village and while most people seems set in their ways, they don't deserve it visited upon them, too," he replied.

"Korman is bad enough, all by himself," Maren commented as he and Ryes joined the others after parking the shuttle back inside. This got nods and laughter from the other Winterhaveners who came out to meet them, too.

"Let's get the windracers settled in the pen outside and then everyone all washed up," Ryes suggested after several rounds of introductions and happy greetings exchanged. It was little like an early Winterfest celebration and made her a little homesick for her old home near the river. "We're having a simple dinner tonight, but maybe we'll have something more special for tomorrow?" she suggested. This got a chorus of approvals from the others gathered near.

"I can help," Jons declared, practically dancing on her toes.

"You surely can," Ryes agreed, leaning down to give her a light kiss atop her head. "You're one of my best helpers."

"Me too, me too!" the other young children chorused gathering around Ryes, laughing merrily. She knelt down to be among them as she laughed with them, giving them all individual attention by turn. The adults were surprised by this; but some recalled she did this with the children in the Village at times. Nils joined in the fun, too. Aravan and Nalin held back, but joined the others in their laughter.

"I think we've found the best home possible, here," Rowan told Kort, as they were grinning to see Ryes and the cubs having fun.

"I believe Ryes has made it so," he replied. "No one seems to be mad at anyone else, nor yelling at each other, as happened all the time in Matlowe. Her love has bonded them into a bigger, happier family, I think." Rowan appeared surprised at this, but nodded his agreement.

    "You could be right," Ardis commented, having heard their conversation. "But we're all a part of things here and have made it our home, too." She smiled as she turned back for the inside, planning on where to put their guests for the next few days, or longer.

53

Choices

"Gosh Mitt, I'm the one who knows the least about the rest of the villagers!" Ryes complained, "Remember who was an outcast there all her life?" She held her eyes a few moments, then said, "All right," giving in with a wry smile, seeing the look in her eyes.

"You're still good with people. I know he's Maren's half-brother and far too much like Korman in some ways, but other than when Korman was younger and what he's managed to father on Tanns, he hasn't fathered any cubs in Matlowe in quite a few years. If I mate with Mason next year, I want to be able to bear cubs, not have empty arms for another two to five years!"

"You really like Mason, that much?" she asked, seeing the way this was tearing her up inside.

"He's great when it comes to free-mating. I can't get enough of him there, but he's kinda backwards when it comes to simple, everyday types of things. Minn's much better there and worse in bed. I can't believe they're brothers! But, Minn's five years older than Mason, and six years older than me. I've no idea who his father is, other than it's definitely NOT Korman. I don't know if he'd be insulted if I came out to ask him, either."

"Why not teach Minn how to be better at free-mating, if he fits into your life so well? It could be a lot of fun after all, and what would it hurt? So, he's six years older than you... it just means he might have enough sense to understand you better. And once you're closer, it'll be easier to ask about his family history," Ryes suggested, but seeing she was still wrestling with it, she added, "There's always Gleds and Spann, too," she reminded her.

"I don't like Spann, at all," she admitted, scrunching up her nose at the thought. "And I hadn't thought of Gleds. I don't know. He somehow reminds me too much of Maren and I think I need something more. Don't ever tell Maren I said such a thing!" There was a moment of panic in her eyes, surprising Ryes.

"Never," she vowed, chuckling, breaking the tension. "But, you never know what'll happen. We still have another trip to make to Matlowe and I've decided, Garth's opinion aside, we're taking two of the biggest shuttles to bring out those who're willing to come, and the rest of our things, which were left behind. Maybe someone more suited will appear, to make you happy, Sis?" she offered in hope. Mitt sighed and gave her a nod of her head at this.

"Maybe it's time to cut free of Mason and see if I can figure out if Gleds, or Minn are more entertaining and can stick it out with me?" she asked.

"I vote for that move," Maren spoke up, coming into the room. He'd been outside listening to them for a few minutes before stepping inside.

"I wasn't asking you," she protested, making a face at him; realizing why the shoes he wore were called "sneakers" by the humans. Maren's face went from his usual smile to looking solemn as he stepped closer to her.

"If you need any help convincing Mason to leave you alone, let me know. I mean it," he assured her. She suddenly stood and stepped closer to him, reaching out as if to kiss him. Maren's eyes widened in surprise at this, as Ryes blushed; both unsure of what to do. He stood stock still for several long heartbeats, as Mitt gave him a long, passionate kiss.

"It's true," she breathed, as she quickly stepped back from him, questions in her eyes. "You really must be true-mated to that human woman. It's like no one else can reach you. I'm sorry," she apologized, now blushing, as she thought on what she'd attempted.

"It's all right," Maren assured her, feeling sorry for her. She seemed so lost and alone without Garth to look after her. "I still meant what I said. I know I'm not as tough as Garth, but I'm here if you need me," he offered, seeing the quick stab of pain in her eyes.

"Thanks, Maren," she replied as she stepped over and hugged him, more her usual self. He wrapped his arms about her, returning the hug. How could he ever get her to understand she was more like his own little sister, than a mate, or love interest? Somehow, he hoped through time, she'd see the truth for herself.

"Now wait a minute. What're you doing here in Ryes' room?" she demanded, pulling back. Ryes smiled at this.

"I promised to take him back in time with me today," she told her. "I'm going to show him something about his lady, which Garth, Sabin and I saw when we traveled back before," she explained.

"But, you said you saw Alda being tortured. How's she involved?" Maren questioned, wondering what else she kept from him, for his own good?

"You'll see when we get there," she assured him.

"I'm going too," Mitt declared. "That way, if we get into trouble, it'll be all together," she teased, smiling again. Ryes sighed, but knew there'd be no stopping her, now. She saw Maren didn't look happy, but didn't object, either.

"Okay, Mitt," she agreed, "if Maren thinks it's all right." She turned to him, but he gave her a nod, appearing to see the hopelessness of excluding her. She knew how to tag along anyway. "Sit down and give me a few moments to prepare." They did, as Ryes found her center, she reached out to the other two. Maren had his own Talent charged and ready. He wanted a solid link with Ryes, so he'd understand their English language as well as she did, which was far above his own level.

Ryes shifted them back to when she'd been before. They were in this room alone, so she willed them to not be seen, nor heard, and led them to the lab where she knew to find Maren's woman. They arrived, but remained outside the small room, beneath the window where she knew the dark-haired friend of this other one was making her recording onto a disc for their elder to see. She was afraid of running into herself, unsure if with Time Walking that she could? They had a good view of what was happening in the room and she quickly felt Maren and Mitt's anger over what was being done to Alda.

"Remember this is what was," she cautioned them both. "We cannot change it; just keep thinking of what Alda told us; that they will be rescued." She knew what was coming and kept a tight hold upon Maren, as this cruel elder assaulted her, once they were alone. But Mitt almost broke free of her, wanting to go punch this man, too. They watched as she was crying, as she removed the tubes and other pieces of equipment from Alda, talking to him in a soothing voice, apologizing, as she knew some of these things were very painful to remove from him. As she helped him onto the cart, Ryes saw the dark-haired woman quietly leave, gold disc in hand.

"What's that other woman doing?" Mitt asked, wondering.

"We think gathering evidence of what was happening, to show her elder. We think this was how these two are finally saved from that one who was hitting her," Ryes explained.

"Let's follow," Maren pressed, pulling Ryes and Mitt after him. Mitt giggled as she allowed herself to be pulled along.

"I guess we will," Ryes teased, laughing lightly, too. He was far too serious for his normal self, she noted. He took this far harder than she thought. Maybe it was being helpless to stop it?

She pulled Alda into an area resembling one where they'd seen her take a shower, before. She left him lying upon the cart, stripping down and getting into a very tiny, skintight, colorful undergarment. She discarded her undergarment padding with a chuckle. Had her season been some kind of ruse to get the elder to leave her alone? She helped Alda rise, supporting him as she turned on the water. When he regained enough of his senses to hold her and give her some comfort for all the pain they'd both been through, her tears almost tore Maren's heart out of him. But, it was her admission that she'd been dreaming of Maren, here many years before he'd even be born, which shocked both Ryes and Mitt! She admitted she loved him, as he loved her. Perhaps it was true? They must've been true-mates in another life, which had carried over into this one. It was incredible!

Maren ached to hold her in his arms; they could feel it too clearly through their Talent-charged contact. They continued to follow them, seeing the two women reunite Ptan and Alda and their discussion about his still being able to father healthy cubs. They saw her elder try to get at them again, but was stopped by the dark-haired woman's elder, who held more authority. Once they saw everyone returning to their rooms to sleep, they returned to their own time and place, their curiosity satisfied, at least.

"So, you are true-mates!" Mitt declared. Maren gave her a nod of his head.

"I think I knew that the first time she came into my dreams. We'll never be able to have any cubs, but it won't make any difference to us, truly," he told them. "Won't she be old by the time she returns?" he asked Ryes.

"I'd think so, but would you turn away from her because of it?" she questioned, still worried for him.

"No. No matter what else happens, we belong with one another," he assured her, his eyes steady. "Sort of like when Rowan found Jana; she was older and he younger, but still true-mates." Ryes looked surprised, but nodded her head in agreement.

"I hope they return soon," Mitt stated. "You truly need her." He gave her a nod in response. Now, she understood why Ryes worried about him so.

"I hope Garth returns soon, too," Ryes added, feeling she needed his strength and wisdom. What could she do to help Maren,

now? This was his one and only! The vows did bind one beyond life!
It was that the binding still held in the next life that was utterly
amazing. She wondered about her parents and grandparents. Wait
until she told Rowan about this!

"Me, too," both Maren and Mitt spoke out at the same time.
Their light laughter filled the air, helping Ryes to let go of her inner
pain.

"Ardis, Ryes, come quick," Kovin urged the women, over the
intercom, seeing they were talking together in the classroom, before
going off to bed. It'd been a long, eventful day and they both had
much to share and were catching up.

"On our way," Ryes replied, fear in both her and Ardis' faces.
Mitt was quickly upon her feet, trailing them out the door. It was
almost time for bed and she worried that it was the wives of both
Garth and Sabin who were summoned. Were they all right, she
worried?

"Here, sit down," Kovin urged them a big smile upon his face.
They now looked puzzled, but did as he asked.

"Ryes? Is that you?" she heard Garth's voice, sounding loud
out of a speaker.

"GARTH!" she cried out in joy, her heart suddenly bounding
with happiness. "Are you all right?" she demanded. She heard his
relieved laughter sound from the other side and knew he was fine.

"Yes. We finally reached the Moondance Tribe's camp, but
Dyan won't discuss any treaties until after the fall hunt is finished.
So, it might be a while before we can head home," he warned her. It
wrenched at his soul to be so far away from her warmth and laughter.

"I understand," she replied, biting back on the tears, which
suddenly threatened to close off her throat. "I sure miss you," she
added.

"I love and miss you, too," he returned, wishing he could see
her face.

"I love you so much," she vowed, closing her eyes in her
longing for his touch. "Is Sabin there? There's someone here who
wants to say hello, too," she requested, knowing Ardis was anxious to

speak with him. Mitt disappeared out the door, running down the corridor.

"Yes. Just a minute," he agreed, knowing they both needed a moment to get ahold of themselves, again. He passed the transmitter to his friend, his surging emotions almost overwhelming him for a moment.

"Ardis?" Sabin demanded. "Are you there?"

"Oh, Sabin!" she replied, now understanding why this was so hard on Ryes, feeling her own charged emotions rising up within at hearing his voice, again. "I love you and miss you," she told him. Sabin closed his eyes and pictured her lovely face in his mind's eye.

"I love you, too. We'll be back home before you know it," he tried to assure her. A feeling of knowing better rose up from within to deny him this comfort. It felt like it came from his Talent, but hadn't opened out into a real Vision, yet. He didn't want it!

"Are you all right?" she demanded, needing to hear it from him.

"Yes, except the food's not much, compared to what you can cook up," he laughed, as he reassured her that he was fine. She laughed with him. A crowd started filing into the tiny, computer control room, everyone hearing their shared laughter. "Garth needs to say something," he told her, and then passed it back.

"Other than that, is everything fine there?" he demanded, needing to know.

"Yes, we're all fine!"

"You should see what the harvest was like!"

"We miss you! Come back soon!"

"You're both shirking your chores here! Get back right now!"

"How much longer are you planning on being out there?"

And several other responses were supplied by the others, who now stood behind the two women, overflowing the tiny room. Everyone was trying to be heard and somehow a round of merry laughter ignited among the family and friends. Garth and Sabin laughed in response, hearing them and recognizing their voices.

"We had some sick caravaners to care for, today. Maren healed them and they're staying here, for now," Ryes informed him, when it died down. "We're all set for the coming winter and are merely waiting for the two of you to return."

"I hope this hunt goes fast and well," Garth told her. "We'll be home, as soon as we possibly can. I'll call again, if there's any news," he promised, reluctant to go, but knowing he had to. The human equipment had limits and he didn't want to expend this one's battery charge since he didn't know exactly how long it'd last. It'd be hard to recharge it in the sun, without questions being raised by the curious, suspicious plainsmen.

"You both had better be careful," Ryes scolded. "I love you, Garth!" she said; the tears in her eyes almost blinding her now.

"I love you, Sabin," Ardis added, crowding close to Ryes by the mic.

"I love you, Ardis," he replied, crowding close to the device Garth held. Garth chuckled, nodding his head.

"We will be careful! I love you, too, Ryes," Garth replied then heard the sounds of the others bidding them a good-bye and sending their love, too. After a few moments, he deactivated the device, letting out a long sigh.

"The sooner we get this hunt finished, the sooner we'll get back home," Sabin sighed, settling into his blankets.

"That's the truth," Garth agreed, putting the transmitter safely away. "You know, I can't even picture our old house in Matlowe, any more. All I see is Winterhaven," he admitted.

"I know what you mean," Sabin agreed with a chuckle. "Let's get some sleep." All he wanted was to feel Ardis' touch. It didn't help to know that with a word, they'd have the flyer heading out to bring them back home. But, not now… not here… He sighed as he turned over and got as comfortable as he could.

"Acting Chief Executive Officer Ryes," the computer addressed her, as it was wont to now. She smiled at this as she turned her attention to the main screen. It was her turn at watch and she'd been looking at a book of pictures of the great cities on Earth, the homeworld of the humans. It was from the library and the cities fascinated her with the different ways they each appeared, as if the humans strove to make each of their cities unique from all the others and as grand as possible. It seemed they celebrated their differences. She wondered what the cities on Kahmarr had been like?

"Computer, what is it you require of me?" She addressed it in English, giving it her full attention and carefully pronouncing her words when addressing it, as she put her book aside.

"The computer onboard the Star Quest reports that all possible repairs have been completed. There is declining power available to maintain the suspension chambers and the Amitell crew members and others within them will die, unless the ship is permitted to land here and the remaining crew members revived," it informed her as coolly as if saying it would be raining later this afternoon. She held her breath for a few moments, as if to be sure she heard it correctly.

"Computer, these crew members are humans?" she asked, as her eyes took on new interest. She sat up straighter and looked more intently into the pick-up camera on the board in front of her, as she awaited its response. Her heart was racing with hope as she felt an eternity passed before it responded.

"Yes, the crewmembers are humans. The Star Quest was attacked at another point within this solar system by an enemy ship of unknown origin. It was abandoned and left for dead by both the attackers and the surviving ship's crew, who abandoned the ship as its systems failed. Through time, the ship's computer maneuvered the Star Quest into orbit around this world and initiated what repairs the systems were capable of accomplishing. It is now at the point where it must land, or the lives of the remaining people will be lost." Ryes sat for several long moments, taking this in while her heart was beating wildly. She finally calmed herself a little, so she could speak.

"And the others, of which you spoke. What are the others?" she pressed.

"They are recorded as native people of this world, in the ship's records," it responded. Ryes nodded her head, thinking of Alda and Ptan and prayed for them. She knew what she had to do with unfailing faith, now.

"Computer, please contact the computer onboard the Star Quest and instruct it to begin whatever procedures it requires for it to land the ship here, near Winterhaven. Computer, please make sure all precautions are taken to protect the lives of those of us who are currently living in Winterhaven. Please project all possible landing places?" she requested, remembering the great, dark bulk from one of her Time Walking trips. There were a million flutter-wings loose in her stomach at the thought of a real human ship landing upon Tayna! This was absolutely amazing!

"Affirmative," it replied, then displayed the possible landing sites. She studied it for a few minutes, her brows knit with concern. She didn't want it between them and Hailys, nor in the middle of their fields and gardens. She finally decided upon an open place southwest of Winterhaven. It just felt right and was away from their underground structures and supports.

"Computer, please direct the Star Quest to land in location grid S116-W46," she ordered. Humans! Real humans! She realized she was getting excited! She wanted to jump up and dance.   She hoped her friends Neil and Brenda survived and were still aboard. She didn't want it to list the surviving crewmen because not knowing still gave her hope. And for Maren's sake she prayed his soul-bound lady was still alive, too.

"Acknowledged," it responded, then blanked the screen, replacing it with the usual, sweeping, tower cam view.

"Computer, how long will it take for the Star Quest to land?" she suddenly thought to ask, wondering how much time they had to prepare? Did they have days to get things ready? She had to get the others ready to assist, as this could be quite a large task for all of them.

"The procedure will require approximately seven hours to seven and a half hours, planetary time, to accomplish. There is some degradation in the ship's systems, which do not allow a more accurate estimation at this time."

"Sounds like just about dinner time. We might have dinner early tonight, as we'll be out watching the Star Quest land," she commented to herself, thinking aloud. "Computer, will you please ready the equipment necessary for reviving the humans from this suspension? Maren may not be enough to handle it, all by himself."

"Affirmative. Do you require a printed copy of the revival procedure?" it prompted.

"Computer, yes, that would be a very good idea and in Dolbith, if possible," she agreed. She sat thinking for a few minutes. They had so much to do to prepare, now! "Computer, please display the proper procedures for base personnel to follow in such an instance as this emergency landing."

"Affirmative," it responded, instantly obeying her command.

"Your aim is not directly at the bull, you said you're going to kill," Shins pointed out as Garth prepared to loose his arrow. He ignored him as he double checked his flight path, then released it. It flew up into the air, and came down, hitting the massive creature's head, dead center and burrowing into his hide. He blinked in surprise then started to buck and shake his head, trying to dislodge the shaft. Garth looked disappointed that he missed the eye of the beast.

"The winds are gusting," Sabin reminded him, chuckling. He drew back his bowstring and loosed his arrow upon its flight. It burrowed deep into the animal's eye, dropping it to the ground, immediately. The bull lay upon his side, still kicking, as his death throes started the other animals near him to shift nervously away.

Yesterday morning, the tribe had herded the animals into a dead-end canyon, then closed off the open end with boulders and rocks and brush, which appeared to have been at the ready and might have been used this way for years. It had been heavy labor, but finally they had a sizable number of herd animals trapped and ready for the taking. They had a raucous celebration last night and he was surprised any were able to help on the hunt today. He and Sabin had sat mostly on the side as observers, unwilling to celebrate anything until they were home once again. He had told Dyan he could not party with them with a heavy heart, as he missed his wife and family. They finally left them alone, so today they were more alert and ready.

Garth had his next arrow ready and shot the next animal through his chest, the arrow buried so deeply within, it disappeared from sight. It caused him to start bucking and throwing himself around, crashing into trees and other animals, making the second shot much harder. It came down on the next arrow he loosed, delivering the animal from its suffering from his first shot. He was still learning how best to take them down quickly.

"The flight of the arrows is more difficult to learn because they're lighter and more easily affected by the winds," Garth explained to Shins and his friends, as they clustered next to them to watch. He smiled at their interest. "But, I've found that the increased distance helps in taking down animals, which would panic with our scent upon the wind to warn them." Shins gave a nod at this, seeing he was correct about these weapons and their potential.

"We've designed different shafts for different animals," Sabin added. "And we have two types of hunting bows, although Kovin was working on a totally new one he and Ryes called a `compound bow.' He was still working on it in the shop, when we left."

"I'll give you my sister, if you'd show me how to make and use such weapons," he replied. This startled both men, as they looked to each other in confirmation of such a concept.

"I think our wives would object," Garth commented, chuckling, as Sabin nodded his agreement, smiling. It HAD to be a joke!

"She's still yours, and I'll throw in two of my best mares," he added, hoping. He could go higher, but his sister, Sayer, held future potential of being able to bear him cubs.

"It's a deal," Garth told him, suddenly appearing serious. He gave Sabin a look, bidding him to be quiet, until they could talk quietly together about it. But, he felt, if this man would sell his own sister, then maybe she'd be better off in Winterhaven with them, than remaining here on the plains. Maybe Raya had been Toron's property, if this was the way they did things here? Sabin seemed to see it too, and gave Garth his nod of agreement.

They'd been out five days trailing this herd of massive, shaggy-hided animals they called korom before herding them here. Now it was merely killing off the ones they felt they needed, then letting the rest escape to build up the herd for next year's hunt. It will still take a few more days to do the butchering properly, before heading back to the winter lodges. At least, this provided the perfect setting to demonstrate the power of the bows, and maybe earn them some recognition as a people to be taken seriously. They'd only brought a little over two dozen of the heavier shafts with them, so they only took out six animals by themselves, then used the remainder to help Shins and his friends get a feel for using the hunting bows after accepting their offers of sisters and cousins, as well as windracers.

Finally, the hunters mounted up and descended upon the herd with their spears, as Garth and Sabin watched from their vantage point. It was a bloody battle, as the beasts tried their best to flee, or attack the hunters, giving them back for the pain they inflicted. Too many of the animals went on suffering, too wounded to do much more than wander around directionless, as the hunters concentrated upon the ones still fighting them back. Too many of the hunters were wounded; many seriously so. It was enough to turn both the Matlowe hunters' stomachs. The waste and pain were hard to watch. Sabin restrung his bow and used some of his lighter shafts, to at least end the suffering of some of the wounded animals.

"If this were for anything other than food and the hides," Garth commented in a low voice. Sabin gave him a nod in return.

"And they have no true Healers even up to the level of Tanns' care. We have Maren, at least," he returned, shaking his head at the vivid scene below them. He turned to face his friend, meeting his eyes. "We're taking his sister and those other women? What are we going to do with them?"

"If they sell or trade their women, like they're possessions, I think they'll be far better off in Winterhaven. Gleds and Raya never mentioned it, but then, we never thought to ask," he admitted. "Still, I can't abide such thinking. Using people as coinage? Once we get home, if they choose to return to their tribe, we'll let them go. You don't think I was missing Ryes so much that I'd settle for any woman?" he chided, chuckling.

"No. That's why I thought it was strange, but I agree. She should be given the chance to decide this, herself. I wonder how old Shins' sister is? Are we going to have to play nursemaids for her, all the way home?"

"We'll find out. Look at that," Garth added pointing to where one of Shins' friends was thrown off his windracer, as one of the bulls charged him, goring his stallion. He got up, retrieved his spear and was trying to get at the animal's flank.

"He's too far," Sabin complained, realizing with the distance, he couldn't help.

"Let's head down to see if we can retrieve some of the arrows they misfired. We might still be of some help, yet," he suggested. Sabin grunted his agreement.

"I only worry about the time we're losing with this hunt, when we could be discussing that treaty, and be on our way home," he returned as he mounted Spur.

"Dyan's been meeting with us each night, trying to feel us out. I think he's trying to discover how strong we are and how we think. This treaty may involve more than simply `you stay on your land and we'll stay on ours' to him. He wants advantages and is hungry to discover where our own needs lie. I'm starting to think this'll end up being a real piece of work and I wish with all my heart that Ryes were here. She may have been an outcast all her life, but she has great insights into others, her Talents aside," he explained as he mounted Pacer.

"I think you're right," Sabin agreed. "If we can't get the full treaty worked out before the end of this week, then let's go for an understanding of some kind at least, then come back in the spring to finish the work," he suggested.

"That's what I was thinking," he agreed, then sighed. "It still lies outside of our hands at the moment. Let's go see what we can do to help," he urged, nudging Pacer in the ribs. Sabin was right behind him, knowing his friend was right.

"I think I did something," Ryes admitted, telling Maren as he came in to check up on her. "If I can get this time telling thing they have here to make sense, we should know if it was something good, or bad, by dinner time." Maren sat down, still amazed with the way she could handle this great human machine all by herself!

"What do you think you did?" he asked, hoping it wasn't something too drastic, which might carry a higher price than they were willing to pay.

"I think I called down one of their starships. It's not running right, but I told the computer to take all precautions to protect the people here in the base first, if it could. I think it understood what I was telling it," she said, her voice projecting the doubts which still played within her mind. "There're supposed to be humans left onboard in a deep, cold sleep. If we can't revive them, they'll die." The pain in her emerald eyes went through his heart, as a knife.

"I only hope they're not hostile towards us for taking over their home," he warned her, thinking they should be prepared for anything. "I'll go warn Torr and the others to be ready. We should call a meeting. This is their base and since they'd know it better than us, we should be ready to evacuate, if they want it back," he suggested, as she nodded her head to his wisdom. He smiled as he got out of his chair and headed down the corridor.

"Is there anything you require?" the computer asked into the quiet of the room. Its sensors indicated the native called Ryes, who was serving in the capacity of acting chief executive officer for this facility, still sat before the board.

"Computer," she replied. "Please keep me updated if there're any problems with the landing. We'll stand by to evacuate this new home, if either an emergency exists which calls for it, or if your humans want us to leave," she explained.

"There will be no hostilities offered to the base personnel?" it questioned. She frowned over the new word.

"Computer, please restate. What is hos..? hos tilli?" she asked.

"Your people do not plan upon attacking the base personnel?" it restated its question. Ryes smiled at this, shaking her head.

"Computer, no. That makes no sense. They'd kill us all, very quickly. If they don't want us to stay here, we'll leave and try to find another new home. My children will then have to be born out in the forest, somewhere."

"Acknowledged," it stated, consulting its subroutines for this situation. The native population peacefully occupying the base was a situation not covered in its original programming and it now had to draw from information stored in its peripheral systems. The fact that the lead native was pregnant with children meant it was supposed to protect the offspring for study, but it also had a duty to protect the human base personnel. It would wait for further instructions from the regular, base personnel, as soon as they would be available for consultation. Sensors aboard the derelict, Star Quest, indicated there were only fifty-one stasis chambers still active and functioning. There was no record of exactly who survived, but there was a chance that one of the department heads, or ranking military support officers, still lived.

Landing

"We have a human starship landing here this evening," Ryes told the gathering of all the Winterhaven inhabitants, as they sat waiting to hear why they'd been summoned so unexpectedly to their new village square. It was in the center of the most comfortable pit any of them had ever seen. The chairs were plush with a thick carpet on the floors, and the cubs were running up and down the stairs having fun. The adults were far more serious.

"There are several humans and some of our own people in their frozen sleep state aboard. We'll have to revive them ourselves, and then see what they're like and if they're willing to let us stay," she explained, her voice carrying easily in this room. She was glad of Maren's idea of using it. Kort and Nahees were wonderfully impressed with the room and she could see ideas dancing in their heads as they looked around.

"Why's it coming here?" Spann demanded into the sudden quiet of the room. He dug his fingers into the cushioned arm rests, looking like he wanted to claw something up.

"The computer said the last of the people will die very soon, as the equipment's failing. The starship was damaged in some kind of attack, long ago. The ship's computer has repaired the damage as much as it possibly could, and now is the best time for it to attempt the landing. It insisted the ship be brought down from orbit and its humans revived."

"Why were they there?" Mitt asked, not knowing they had them overhead, all this time, as she looked up to the ceiling high above.

"The ship was left for dead by their enemy. After several years, its computer managed to make enough repairs, to enable it to return to circle about Tayna in what's called an orbit. I would think to have the humans closer to their own base, in case any other humans came to Tayna to see why they didn't return home. The computer down here was shut down and unable to help. Now that our computer's active, it's been talking with the starship's computer and it's come to understand that there's not enough power to maintain their frozen sleep much longer. It's imperative that it land. So, I authorized it to land near Winterhaven."

"Will they let us stay, if we help them?" Torr asked, wondering what these humans would be like? He knew what Sabin and Garth told him of their Time Walking venture and was uncomfortable with such callous cruelty. They didn't need it here!

"I've no idea. We can only hope. After all, this was the place they built originally. It's not like we truly have a choice here and I'll not see them die, when we can help," she stated. Now that she knew of their existence, she had no intention of letting them die in the darkness of the stars, so cold and alone. "And Alda and Ptan deserve life, too!"

"I would love to meet them," Raya spoke up into the quiet. "They are legend in my old tribe." Kovin gave her a hug at this, nodding. Gleds heard her and agreed.

"How can we revive them?" Marla questioned, as they digested not only what Ryes said, but how. She was loyal to these humans! Was this something which happened through her interaction with the computer, or from her Time Walking? She wished Garth were here to voice his opinion about this situation.

"Maren and I will try with our Talents. We'll see how many we can handle. If there's not enough time, we'll have to resort to using the human methods; using their machinery. I have the computer printing a copy of the procedure in English and Dolbith, and bringing up the necessary equipment to readiness, in case of need," she answered. There was anxiety in their eyes as the magnitude of what this rescue might mean to them was hitting home.

"Where will we go?" Rein asked, "I'm not willing to leave this new home of ours, now." Ryes smiled gently in understanding, giving her a nod.

"Well, if they want us to leave, we'll just have to borrow some of their outdoor shelters and largest shuttles for transports, until we can get reestablished. I think closer to the Yuri, near their main water gathering machinery. That way, we'll still be fairly sheltered from most of the winter storms by the great trees there, and will have access to good water and the humans, too. They don't know Tayna as well as we and might have a use for our knowledge and skills, as much as we do for theirs. It could still work to both our benefits," Ryes voiced her hopes. "We can then build our new Winterhaven on that site and truly make it our own. We've all learned so much since coming here!"

"What do you want us to do?" Garvin and Rowan both asked, as Garvin gave her a nod of agreement. Rowan smiled as he nodded to Garvin.

"Pack your things and have them ready, just in case. There still exists a danger in the starship's landing, as it's badly damaged and not working correctly. If we must evacuate because it's going to crash, I want to make sure we leave nothing behind that we can't replace. If the starship makes a safe landing, we revive the humans. If they tell us to leave, then we must be ready to surrender this place to them. Don't load anything onto the shuttles, but I want the two largest ones pulled out of the garage and ready to move. We can go ahead and pack the outdoor shelters within them for our use, for now," she ordered. This wasn't easy for her, as she considered this place her home. She recalled that flash of Vision she and Maren once shared. If it were true, her cubs would be born in her room, right here. She could only hope.

"Right," Maren agreed, supporting his cousin's plan, standing up and facing the rest. "Let's get to it! We've got a lot of work to finish, before dinner time and the starship's landing. And let's have an early dinner, so at least we'll get one really good meal before giving up such a fine kitchen," he urged, getting a round of laughter, breaking the somber mood.

"You're always ready to eat, Maren!" Mitt teased, laughing.

"Acting Chief Executive Officer Ryes," the computer intoned over the portable link device she had brought with her outside as they watched the fiery jets as the starship was coming in for a landing far overhead.

"Computer, yes?" she replied to it.

"There are some stability issues with the ship's systems. It might crash," it warned them. She nodded, having thought that might happen. She thought on it for a moment, and then gave another nod.

"Let me try helping it with my Talent," she stated. She closed her eyes and centered herself. Mitt noted it and had been curious about what the machine was telling her. She suddenly felt Ryes' Talents called up and power unleashed. She quickly stepped over to her side to support her body while she was concentrating. But in doing so, she was also drawn into a meld.

Ryes recalled how she had fought Tayna's pull herself, when the cart ran over Mitt before and sought to unleash that same ability to help this failing machine to land safely, if she could. Mitt, now in full contact with her, felt it too and urged Ryes to do her best. Ryes reached out with an old Talent named Manipulator, which name she learned from stolen memories, and used it to help stave off the grasp of gravity to help it land safely. She reached for the great machine. Its flight path straightened out as she guided it to the spot she'd chosen earlier. It wasn't using physical muscles, but shaping the raw power which flowed through her being. Slowly, carefully she guided down to land safely exactly where she felt it rightfully belonged. She realized that another Talent awoke in her and assisted. She was reshaping the machine itself to be better. And Mitt was helping! That surprised them both! Their Talents seemed to have an instinct built-in to guile their efforts.

Maren noted Ryes' concentration and stepped closer, in case she needed his help. Mitt was helping to support her, but had her eyes open and watched the landing from both within and without, also giving Ryes both views, too. She smiled and gave Maren a nod of assurance, so like one of Ryes'. He smiled and shook his head in wonder.

"By the gods, look at that thing!" Torr commented in awe, hugging Shadd close to his side, his mind staggered by its immense size, as his eyes were cast skyward. "How can we ever hope to match such building skills?" he asked. They all came outside to watch the landing of the human craft. It was a huge, blackened thing and it was plain to see the damage done to its hide. It landed a ways away from the underground base. The starmen were reluctant to approach it, now that they saw its immense size. The cubs were charged and running about the adults in excitement.

"Were our starships like this one?" Rowan speculated as he watched it all.

"Computer, is it safe for us to board the Star Quest?" Ryes asked the computer, once the ship set down and the engines cut off. She had immediately let go of her Talents so she and Mitt could be free to act, once again. It gave her chills of excitement. A real starship! "Garth should be here to see this!" she breathed out. Mitt nodded agreement.

"Sensors indicate that as long as you do not approach the aft area of the ship, it should be safe to board," it responded.

"Computer, display the aft area," she directed, wanting this to be very clear. The computer projected a three dimensional image of the ship in the air above the minicomp, then highlighted the back area with a red color, to clarify the prohibited area. It was positioned away from the base and personnel.

"The indicated area is the one to avoid," it advised. She showed the display to the others.

"We're not going near this part of the starship. It's still dangerous," she warned.

"Who said anything about you going near that thing at all?" Maren demanded, looking her in the eye. "Garth will be very upset if I let you near it!"

"I have to be there. I'm the only one here who can speak enough English to be able to talk with them," she returned, smiling in triumph as she saw the understanding in his eyes.

"She's got a point," Teris agreed, reluctantly. "None of us have learned it that well, yet."

"Let's only have a few for this first time meeting," Ryes suggested, thinking it'd be better that way. They didn't want to scare the humans, after all. "Maren, Teris, Gleds and Minn, come with me. The rest of you will stay here, wait and watch for our signal - either way," she ordered. There were protests raised, but she just stared them down.

"I have my reasons," she stated, once they were quiet again. "Torr, please try to keep order for me? Come on, guys, let's go."

"Me, too," insisted Mitt, appearing unhappy.

"No, I need you to stay here and help Torr," Ryes replied, putting a hand upon her shoulder. "You felt the wrongness in that ship, too, didn't you? It's not dangerous to us, but still, I don't want any of us inside of it without true reason." Mitt nodded her head and looked down, blushing.

"What WAS that?" she asked in a lower voice, wondering as a thousand questions danced in her eyes.

"I think it's a very rare Talent called Inner Sight, but I'm not sure," she replied. "Stay safe! We'll both look into it later. You have a Talent." With that she turned for their waiting shuttle.

They climbed aboard shuttle number seven and drove toward the great bulk, with the sun starting to get low to the horizon. She made sure no one was carrying any weapons, but they each had their beltknives and some hand lanterns, in case they needed them to see inside of it. Everyone was wearing heavy coats since the weather had turned colder at night here, now.

It was immense and as they approached, they could see more of the damage in the fading daylight. They wondered at what could cause such burning, pits and gashes? Pieces of metal on the side were strangely twisted inward from the structure, as if something huge punched it and torn up the outer walls. It must've been an incredible horror! It was a miracle any of the humans survived the ordeal! They finally reached its side and saw the ramp extended and a door open at the top.

"Here's our invitation," Gleds commented, not liking the look of the thing. Ryes smiled back at him, giving him a nod of her head.

"I think our help must be much needed," she replied as the smile melted from her lips. "Stay alert," she advised. He gave her a nod.

She jumped out of the shuttle, waited for the rest, and then led them up the ramp. As she reached the door, she saw the interior was very dark. She switched on her lantern and shone it about inside. There was a small room with a second door, which was also open and beyond that a larger room. She stepped inside, feeling as if she walked in the company of ghosts and cast her bright light about the room, as she paused by the lip of the second doorway. It was a room with bulky suits hung upon the wall and other equipment stowed in cages, ready for use. It was strange, but seemed to make good sense. You wouldn't want to hunt for the things you needed when an emergency happened, and you needed to run outside of the starship. According to old stories there was no air to breathe in the dark of the stars.

"Look, more lanterns," Mitt noted. Ryes turned, seeing her with their small group.

"What're you doing here?" she demanded.

"Keeping my sister safe, just as Garth told me to," she returned, grinning impishly. Ryes sighed.

"Just stick close and don't wander off," she warned her.

"It's ice cold in here," Maren commented, as they stepped into the room and were looking around them. Ice crystals were evident on everything around them and the breaths they exhaled were like little puff of steam! Teris opened one of the equipment lockers and switched on one of the other lanterns. It operated as well as their own. He handed it to Mitt, who smiled her thanks. Minn cast him a jealous look at this, which they failed to note. As they were doing this, Ryes checked two of the doors built into the sides of the walls of the room. Just more storage... Maren was curiously examining the bulky, hanging suits.

"Look, here's the corridor," Ryes informed them in a low voice, having opened a heavy door on the far side. It moved inwards, then slid inside the wall, operating differently than the others doors they knew. She shone her light down both directions, but they looked much the same to her. So, she closed her eyes and concentrated from within. Maren held the others back, letting her alone to work. "That way," she told them, opening her eyes, once more. Maren smiled as she saw him restraining Minn, who was looking impatient.

"Let's go find them," Minn urged, waving her to lead them onward. It was frustrating with her using Talent for something he wanted to do the natural way - hunt them out. This thing was huge and looked like it'd be a lot of fun to explore, now that he was seeing the inside!

They traveled down a corridor for several long minutes, every echo sounding too loud in their ears. There were some odd creaks and groans from the metal of the ship, as if it was getting used to being on the ground once again. Finally, they came to a large cross corridor and inset into one of the walls, down away from their own passage, were some of the tall tubes Ryes had the computer display for them, earlier. She approached them, her hand held out before her, using Empath.

"This one's dead, this one's empty, but the other two still hold life," she told them, opening her eyes. Maren pointed to the tiny green lights above the ones she said were working, with mischief in his eyes.

"I had that figured out, already," he teased. "They love green lights." She laughed at this, then put a hand over her mouth as it echoed loudly in the empty, metal corridors. This got the rest of them laughing, making a raucous, merry sound, making her smile. Down on the other side, across their original passage, were four more tubes. All of them displayed tiny, green lights at the top.

"Maybe we should practice opening them with the empty one, first?" Maren suggested.

"That's a good idea," Gleds agreed with his friend. He hefted one of the human opening tools, which Ryes named a prybar, and looked for a place to put it. Minn pointed out a good spot, so he put it within the indentation and braced it. He pulled, but it resisted. Minn added his strength to the effort and it suddenly whooshed open. An icy blast of stale air assaulted their senses at their victory. "Whew!" Gleds declared, waving a hand before his face. "That stinks even without one of them in it!" This brought out more laughter, as the rest agreed with him.

"Let's go for real," Ryes suggested, bracing herself within, trying to calm her inner excitement and panic. Ryes reached for the prying tool Maren had in his hand. He extended his arm, keeping it out of her grasp, shaking his head.

"You stand back. This's for we men to handle," he warned. She sighed her resignation; giving in. He wasn't going to let her do anything with her cubs due in a few months. It was now almost the end of the fall! She stepped back to let them work, holding her light up so they could see better, anxious to see her first real human. Mitt took up a position partly in front of her, as if to defend her. Ryes smiled to herself at this, wondering what she'd do without her? She was like a younger sister. She saw their closeness as something to last the rest of their lives - whether or not she and Garth had taken true-mate vows.

Teris and Maren put their backs into this one, as it was more stubborn about opening, than the empty one. Finally, the seal broke and the door whooshed open. Ryes shone her light within and saw a petite form standing with her eyes closed. Maren quickly pulled her out and held her in his arms. Her body was stiff and unmoving. He sat down upon the icy floor, as he opened his Healing abilities up fully, extending himself to this human woman. Ryes was practically holding her breath, waiting.

Suddenly the woman gasped and the strange stiffness left her body. Maren's eyes were still closed, as he held her close to him, not quite finished, yet. Her eyes opened and she blinked against the light, as she blindly reached out for anchorage, gripping Maren's arm. She seemed to realize she was being held, for the first time and calmed at this small reassurance.

"Are you all right?" Ryes asked in English. She nodded her head, and then rested it against Maren's chest, closing her eyes once more. "Maren, are you all right?" she added in Dolbith as his face looked so strange. His shoulders finally relaxed and he opened his eyes.

"That was different," he told her, looking at the prize he held in his arms. Here was his Dream Goddess, lying in his arms and he had no idea what to say to her, as she was cuddled up against his chest! "Are you feeling better?" he finally asked her, knowing she wouldn't understand Dolbith.

She opened her beautiful blue eyes and looked up into his face. She frowned as she realized he wasn't human, but one of the natives. Then realized it was Him! He was the man from her dreams! She was shocked! She had no idea what his name was, but felt so safe and warm in his arms, that she didn't want to leave them, ever.

"What's your name?" she asked him, in return.

"His name's Maren," a native woman answered her, looking concerned as she crouched down next to them. "Are you feeling all right?" she asked. Ryes realized she knew this human! She was the one Maren was so adamantly attached to, as if they were true-mates from another life.

"Oh, yes. I feel so very nice and warm, finally. Please tell Maren thank you for me?" she requested, in return. Ryes smiled at this and relayed the message. This got grins out of the others, gathered here in this cold, dark corridor. Maren wanted to hug her to him, but was unsure if she'd accept such a gesture from him. She smiled up at him and hugged him, herself, causing him to blush, as his heart hammered in reaction. He carefully stood, keeping her cuddled up to his chest.

"I don't think you're supposed to keep them like pets," Teris teased, seeing the possessive way he held this small woman.

"It's her! She's real!" Mitt gasped, looking to Ryes, seeing she knew it, too.

"Ryes, could you ask her name for me?" he requested, now needing to know, while ignoring Teris and Mitt.

"Maren wants to know what your name is?" she asked, smiling merrily at seeing him so happy.

"My name's Dorothea, but my friends call me Dotti. Tell him to call me Dotti, too," she told her. She just realized there were only natives here. The fact that one spoke English, slow but well, must mean they had some contact with humans, but if so, where were they?

"She says her name's Dorothea, but to just call her Dotti," Ryes relayed for him. "Why don't you put her down, so we can thaw out her companions, now?" she suggested. He seemed very protective of her. Ryes knew what she meant to him.

"Do you think you can stand, Dotti?" she asked, wondering if she felt strong enough.

"I don't know," she replied, truthfully. She still wasn't ready to let go of Maren. He really was the one she'd dreamed about for so long! He was real and his arms were as warm and supporting as they'd been in her dreams! "I'll try," she offered, seeing this woman was anxious about something. "What's your name?" she asked in return, wondering why she looked worried?

"It's Ryes," she said. "Maren go ahead and put her on her feet, she's willing to try." He didn't think she acted too willing to him, but set her carefully down upon her feet. She suddenly leaned her full weight upon him, clutching for his support, unsteady as a newborn windracer. He laughed as he caught her up in his arms, once more.

"How about if we find some chairs for now?" he suggested, noting Ryes' budding distress. Could it stem from anxiety over reviving the remaining humans, or seeing he and Dotti together? He'd have to talk with her about this, later.

"I'll go look. There should be some in one of the rooms we passed," Minn volunteered. He disappeared, as Dotti was laughing with Maren, looking up into his golden-brown eyes.

Ryes was sure that once the rest of the humans were revived, she'd focus upon them more and give Maren some breathing room. It looked like she was studying his face, as he was doing the same with hers.

"Looks like love at first sight," Mitt whispered to Ryes, smiling as they waited.

"Yeah, but could a human and starman free-mate?" Teris teased Maren, nudging him. He looked up to meet his eyes, curiosity playing in their depths.

"There'd be only one way to find out," Ryes broke in, before Maren could speak. "And I'm sure once the rest of the humans are awake, her own free-mate will be among them," she warned her cousin. "Dotti's very pretty and must've had a man of her own, before being stuck in cold storage, after all." He seemed to deflate some, as he caught her meaning. She was right. It was a possibility.

"What's wrong?" Dotti asked, seeing Maren's expression. What had she told him, to upset him so?

"I advised him that you might have a man of your own here and that he couldn't keep you for himself," she answered, truthfully. Dotti blushed as she realized what she meant.

"He wants to keep me as his wife?" she questioned, wanting to make sure they understood each other clearly.

"He acts like it and I know my cousin well enough. Yes, he wants you as his wife," she agreed, glad the others didn't understand English well enough to follow them.

"But, we could never have any children," she protested, surprised.

"I'm sure he's got that figured out," she returned, wondering what she was getting at? Did she truly understand these humans, as well as she thought?

"I never dated anyone here. Tell him I'll allow him to court me for now," Dotti offered. She hadn't been interested in anyone in neither the research group, nor the military support, who were there to protect them. Her last love interest had been on Earth long ago. Why not? She could reward him for her rescue by letting him court her, if he really wanted to. It might be fun, she thought... She recalled Alda's embrace, but Maren was the man from her dreams. This would give her the chance to discover if she truly loved him, or if it was pure fantasy. He existed, and that was a small miracle in itself!

Ryes was shocked at this, doubt playing in her mind. What kind of game was this human up to? She didn't want to see Maren hurt, but she couldn't hold the truth back from him, either. This was too important.

"She says that she could never bear you any cubs, but she'll let you court her for now," Ryes told Maren, not looking happy about it, at all. He laughed as he hugged her to him, once more. This got her to laughing, too. She reached up and stroked his ear, sending shivers up and down his spine. He didn't know if she was doing it on purpose, or just in some kind of fascination with the differences between them? If it was by design...

"Found some!" Minn declared, returning with five of the folding, metal chairs. He loved these things. When he first arrived in Winterhaven, he spent hours playing with them, appreciating their simplicity and function. The humans were quite clever in their design! He set them against a wall, as he opened one up for their first human to use. "Here, now you can set her down," he told Maren.

"She just said she'd allow him to court her. We'll be lucky if he ever lets her go again," Gleds informed him, laughing. "I don't know, she looks too small," he advised Maren, hoping he'd get his meaning. He wouldn't want to hurt her.

"Dotti will be fine," he assured him with a wink. "I'm a Healer, after all." This got shocked surprise out of his friend! He bent to set his precious burden upon the chair, then draped her with his coat. He nuzzled her ear in reassurance, as she looked uncertain about being left by herself. She then watched the proceedings, curious about their operation. Gleds and Teris were ready to crack open the last tube on this side.

"Ready," Maren told them, moving back into position, taking in a deep breath, focusing himself, again. Excitement still coursed within him, having not only found Dotti, but having her permission to get to know her more intimately. He couldn't wait!

They strained as Ryes and Mitt held their lights steady for them. It opened to reveal a man within. Maren caught him, sitting down upon the floor to work on him. After several agonizing moments, he stirred. After a small space of time, he opened his eyes and looked up at Maren's face, wondering where he was and why a native man held him? What were they doing back on Beda IV?

"Scott, how're you feeling?" Dotti questioned, having come off her chair to kneel next to Maren's side. She just didn't want to leave him, now that she was sure he was real!

"Dot? Is that you?" he questioned, trying to see with the bright lights shining down into his eyes. She laughed at this. Yes, it sounded like her voice all right, reassuring him.

"Yes. A party of the natives are trying to revive us. Just lie still a few moments more," she advised. "Everything will be all right. Ryes, here, knows English and is playing interpreter for us."

"Why's this guy holding me?" he asked, wondering.

"He's healing your body," Ryes answered him. "You were frozen in that cold tube and Maren's using his Healing Talent to bring your body back up to what it should be," she explained, seeing the shocked, disbelieving look in his eyes.

"Yup. You were like an icicle, just a few minutes ago," Dotti agreed. Maren opened his eyes with a sigh. He smiled as he saw his second human was looking alert and healthy. "Let's get you up into a chair," Dotti advised, as she gestured to Maren with this in mind. He saw she was sitting on the floor beside him and smiled at her with a shake of his head.

"Another woman who won't stay put!" Maren groaned in mock exasperation. This got chuckles out of his friends in agreement.

"Thank you," Scott said as Maren and Gleds helped him up and into the chair Dotti quit. He gave him a nod of his head, figuring what he meant, as he stepped back. Dotti now clung to him again, smiling mischievously.

"And I think she understood me," he added, grinning as he looked into her eyes, again.

"Seems like a good match to me," Teris said, chuckling. "Let's get to the next one. The others outside have got to be wondering, by now!"

"That's right! Mitt, could I ask you to go tell them we're fine and will be reviving a few more, before we'll be out?" Ryes asked, feeling she was best suited for this errand. Mitt pouted but gave her a nod of her head.

"Sure Sis, anything for you," she replied as she threw her arms around her and gave her a hug. Then she went back up the corridor they entered through, heading for the door outside. Ryes chuckled at her display, thinking the night air was far better for her anyway.

"Next," she ordered, stepping across to the four tubes waiting for them. "Which do you think, cousin?" she asked. Minn now folded out the other chairs, having them ready for occupation. Maren closed his eyes a moment, then opened them and looked at her.

"The two on that end will require more strength than I've got, alone, for each of them. How about the other two first, then we'll see if the two of us can tackle the last two?" he requested, pointing to the tubes as he talked about them. She gave him a nod of her head as she understood and agreed. Her Healing Talent may be nowhere near as strong as his, but it did exist and she had a greater pool of power to draw upon, than he. Yes, they made a good team, if she could shunt her power for his use, even with helping to support the ship earlier, she still had plenty to spare. She brought back up her own body temperature, realizing why she felt truly cold, now. It must've been from her efforts to prevent the crash!

"All right," she agreed, as Teris and Gleds took up the prybars, ready. Maren moved into position, as Ryes and Minn held the lanterns up to give them directed light. Scott watched from his chair, still feeling a little out of place. Dotti stood beside Ryes, half leaning against her, waiting. They pulled and the seal gave quickly, spilling out the woman inside into Maren's arms, surprising him as he caught her. He quickly sat down on the floor. Ryes and Dotti were immediately at his side, as he went straight to work. After a few moments, she started moving, and then shortly opened her eyes. She looked bewildered, as she realized she lay in one of the native's arms.

"It's all right, Bethy," Dotti assured her. "Maren's trying to bring you back up out of that cold suspension." Bethany realized she could make out her friend's face over his shoulder.

"Who?" she asked. Dotti laughed at this.

"His name's Maren and he's a healer of some sort," she explained, hoping he wouldn't get attached to her, too. She had Jim already, after all. Maren finally opened his eyes, starting to feel the first touch of his limits. He smiled as he saw this woman looking up at him, puzzled.

"Here you go," he offered as he stood up and placed her onto a chair, having recognized her, too. "How're you doing?" he asked as he put a supporting arm about his blue-eyed goddess, once more. She giggled as Ryes translated for them.

"Fine," she returned, looking surprised to see Scott sitting on the chair next to hers. "It's cold in here," she commented, realizing at least she had her lab coat on, even if it was thin. Ryes stepped over and took off the light coat she wore, draping it about her shoulders.

"This should help," she told her, with a smile. Bethany looked into this native's eyes and liked what she saw. Here was warmth and caring for others, even when she didn't need to.

"Thank you and please thank Maren for me, too," she told her, smiling in return. This brought out a bigger smile, as she gave her a nod of her head.

"Maren, she said to offer you her thanks," she told him as they were getting ready for the next tube. Dotti was standing holding the lantern in her stead, looking a little more steady upon her feet, already. Bethany realized that this English-speaking native looked very pregnant, even in this light. She shouldn't be here, putting herself at risk, she thought.

"How does he do it?" Scott asked, as he saw the tube open and Maren pull out Justin, immediately sitting upon the floor with his eyes closed.

"What do you mean?" Bethany asked, wondering.

"Watch," he offered, indicating what was happening, nearby. She did as he bid her. After a very few minutes, Justin was beginning to move, then a short time later, he opened his eyes. Dotti and Ryes were there to reassure him, until Maren was finished and opened his eyes, once more.

"You know it takes hours to bring someone back, using a controlled bath. It only takes him a few minutes. How does he do it?" he asked, again. She shook her head in wonder.

"It's through his own, natural Healing abilities," Ryes explained. She then set down her light, as she stepped next to Maren, to help with the next one. They might as well do all they could now, then see what they'd be up for tomorrow. "I'm ready," she told him, then cracked a grin, realizing she'd spoken in English. She repeated herself in Dolbith, as the others laughed, teasing her.

"Why do you need to help here?" Dotti asked, wondering, as the men were straining to open the next tube.

"Because Maren's getting tired and he says these two will need more than just he alone can handle. This isn't without risk and my Healing abilities aren't as strong as his, but I do have power that he doesn't and between the two can help boost his remaining strength."

She turned as the tube whooshed open and Jim was dumped into their arms. She helped to lower him to the floor as Bethany stumbled out of her chair to be at their side. Both Ryes and Maren had their eyes closed as they concentrated upon restoring the man they held in their arms. It took longer than the others, but he started breathing and then moving. After a while his eyes opened and he smiled as he saw Bethany's face over Ryes' shoulder.

"Don't touch them," Dotti warned her suddenly, seeing Bethy wanted to reach over Ryes to touch Jim's face. She spared her a surprised glance, but agreed that it was best if they could concentrate, undisturbed. A few minutes later they opened their eyes in relief, smiles upon their lips.

"I don't know Maren. You're really tapped out," Ryes warned him, but there awoke a stubborn look in his eyes, which she knew too well... It ran in the family. "All right," she finally gave in, smiling for him.

"You've got power and then some, to spare. It's too bad your Healing Talent isn't as strong as your other Talents," he playfully scolded her with a wink. She agreed within her heart.

"You just have to keep rubbing it in," she teased in return.

"Need a hand?" Torr asked, as he and Kovin arrived, following Mitt. They brought extra coats with them, too. Teris and Bethany were helping their latest man to his feet.

"Almost done, Torr Strong-arm," Ryes teased him, as Maren helped her to her feet. "One more and we'll call it a night," she said. He gave her a nod, as they watched the operation, handing the human men each coats to wear. As this last tube opened, they found a human elder. Bethany, who was fussing over their last human, gasped as she recognized who they now held in their arms. It was a very long time, indeed, before Dr. Cruthers opened his eyes to look upon the world about him. And even longer yet, before the two natives finally opened their eyes, having finished their work.

"Now, I feel drained," Ryes complained, as Torr helped her up to her feet.

"Since you helped the starship to land and then in other ways since, it's no wonder you're drained," Maren teased. She swatted at him, grinning. Maren and both women helped their elder to his feet.

"We need to get our humans back to their base and see if they mind if we stay here through the winter with them, at least," she said with a sigh. She suddenly recalled her portable unit, pulled it out of her back pocket and activated it. "Computer? Will the remaining tubes with living humans be safe to leave until the morning? We're limited on our restorative abilities," she asked it in English.

"There remains sufficient power levels to maintain the suspension tubes for four planetary days," it responded in English. She smiled relief at this, as the humans gave her astonished looks.

"It responds to you, Ryes?" Dotti questioned, shocked. She smiled and gave her a nod of her head.

"Yes, it does. Isn't it supposed to?" she asked, wondering.

"We never took into account a native who could learn English well enough to issue commands to our computer. I don't see it as beyond the scope of its operations," Dr. Cruthers stated as the friendly-looking natives were offering their strength to help them out of the derelict this ship had become. "What's your name, son?" he questioned a tall, strong, young man who was helping support him, with his own legs still unsteady. He wondered how long they'd been in the tubes?

"Sir, Torr doesn't speak much English. We've been fairly busy trying to establish our settlement here and I've been the only one with enough time to learn it well enough," Ryes offered with a smile, as she walked between him and the dark-haired woman. She wasn't sure if Dotti was supporting Maren, or he was supporting her, or they were supporting each other, but it was strange to see them together as they walked down the corridor, before them. Neither one of them seemed to want to let go of the other.

"A settlement?" he questioned, his eyes merry. "Why out here?" he pressed, wanting to understand these people better.

"Because it has land to cultivate and plant, with a plentiful supply of water. With your underground facil... facil-littie, we'll be out of the coming winter storms. And finally, it's close enough to Hailys, the destroyed city of our ancestors, so we can uncover some of our own techna.. ogy," she explained. "We have plenty of memory rods, but it's getting the readers to work, that's going to be the challenge."

"My, my… You have been busy," he commented, smiling at her merrily. She smiled in return, realizing she liked this elder, as

they reached the ship's personnel boarding and staging room. He was
the one who stopped the mean one from hurting Dotti and Alda any
further.

"We want to ask permission to stay for the winter at least,
Elder Sir?" she pressed, knowing it needed to be settled, as soon as
possible. "I have the others ready to leave, if you don't want us here
with you, but if so, we'll need to borrow some of your outdoor shelters
to get us through the winter," she informed him, hoping. This seemed
to take all the humans by surprise.

"You don't have any laws concerning salvage rights?" Scott
questioned, puzzled.

"What's sallvij rites?" she queried in return.

"That since we left this place behind us, it was yours for the
taking," Jim explained.

"That doesn't make it ours," she assured them with a chuckle.
"You left it against your return, so it still belongs to you. I could see
when it concerns Hailys, with it being attacked by an unknown enemy,
hundreds of years ago and those left alive, left it for good. But,
you've only been gone from Tayna seventy-two years and left your
computer to keep a watch for your return. So, we feel we still need
your permission," she explained.

"Seventy-two years!" Justin exclaimed, startled by this news.
"Are you sure?" he questioned her. She smiled and nodded her head
to this.

"It's based upon Tayna's yearly cycle. I hadn't thought to ask
the computer what it'd be in Earth years," she apologized.

"That'd make it about eighty years, give or take," Bethany
said, tallying it up in her head. It was an amazing concept!

"Yes, you and your people may stay with us here in our
facility," Dr. Cruthers assured her, as they approached the main
airlock doors. "You've saved our lives and it's time we all learned to
live with you natives, as neighbors." Ryes laughed at this as they
started down the boarding ramp.

"We're not native to Tayna. We're the Star People and our
ancestors originally came from a great world called Kahmarr," she
explained. "I had trouble trying to get your computer to understand
this concept. Tayna was a game keep? Preserve? Zoo? And Hailys
was the largest city allowed on the planet. Visitors would come to
study the animals, or hunt here for fun, until the attack and we were
cut off from our stars." There was sudden silence, as they took in

what she was saying, stopping at the foot of the ramp, next to the two rovers.

"Do you know what happened to your other worlds?" Bethany questioned, wondering.

"No. No one who could ask was left alive. I don't know if by having your ship land we might bring back the murderers, but we couldn't leave you up in orbit to die, as your equipment was failing. Also, we need your help. We've lost so much of what our ancestors took for granted. Your machines are different, but not too different," she told them. "We want to have a better future for our children and to build Tayna anew."

"Oh my God!" Dotti exclaimed as she turned and got a look at the hulking wreck of a ship they'd just been rescued from. The rest of the humans turned, shocked as the condition of the Star Quest registered in their eyes, too. Ethan Cruthers gave a nod of his head as he turned back to the lead native woman.

"Uh Ryes, do we get to stay, or not?" Torr asked, seeing she was telling these people a lot of things, which surprised and amazed them. He saw the pain in their eyes at viewing the starship. He felt sorry for them, but was glad it was night with only Shaysa's light to see by, now. He was sure in the daylight it'll look far worse. Ryes smiled at him, giving him a nod of her head.

"Yes, we do," she affirmed. Mitt shouted out in joy, ran ahead and jumped into the smaller shuttle she brought out earlier, to go tell the others waiting.

"She's sure excited about something," Justin commented, smiling, still shocked they'd survived.

"I just told her we get to stay in Winterhaven," Ryes informed him. "She's going ahead to tell the rest."

"Winterhaven," Dr. Cruthers murmured. It was what Brenda Reed said a native called it, in one of her latest reports. Before the emergency evacuation...

Awakenings

The small storm of activity finally settled, with only a handful of the natives remaining with the humans in the dining room. The two prepared shuttles had to be put back into storage and unloaded once more. The former villagers then returned their things to their own rooms, their eyes filled with joy and relief. They shared a late dinner with their newly acquired humans, since they had been too busy beforehand to eat. Most of the people were driving Ryes to distraction with questions for the humans for her to translate and vice versa. Finally, most of the Winterhaven residents went off to bed, as it was late and there promised to be far more work ahead for all of them tomorrow. This left the humans and a handful of starmen.

Maren sat next to Dotti at the "mess hall," as the humans called it, almost nodding off over his mug of hot tea. There was a smile of deep contentment upon his face, which the mean looks Justin cast his way could never touch.

"Dr. Cruthers," Ryes began, a little nervously, "Why is it Neil's always been so friendly to me and yet your Justin isn't so toward Maren? Maren's far more friendly than I've ever been and the gentlest person alive. What has he done to deserve such animalosity?" she asked in a low voice.

Dr. Ethan Cruthers looked at her in surprise as he tore his eyes away from their fantastic murals. Was this what the ruins looked like when they were a living city? And the other one, on the wall next to it, just starting out. What did it portray? Another city here on this world, or one they might have come from back on their own world? But the phoenix rising over it teased his curiosity. Did they have such mythology here about the fiery bird of reincarnation? The burning destruction between was easy to guess. It had to be the fall of their great city. Did it symbolize their quest to reach their original world, again? He sighed as he saw how serious she was and chuckled; she was young and so direct and a delightful surprise.

"Animosity," he corrected her with a smile. "How is it you know Neil? He isn't with us tonight," he probed, wondering. He had assumed she learned her English only from the computer.

"I met Neil and Brenda when I was Time Walking," she explained, with a shy smile as if that said it all. "I never saw them treat me in such a way and am concerned."

"Maybe Justin's jealous of what Maren has, which he doesn't?" he asked in return, far more loudly than they had been speaking. Ryes frowned at this, not having wanted it projected, so Justin might take insult from what she still needed to understand. But it seemed their elder wanted it brought out into the open.

"You mean Dotti?" she questioned loudly, too. "We women here in Winterhaven have decided that it's our choice whom we mate with, and the men just have to get used to it. We're not allowing any challenges, so if that's what Justin plans, please make it clear that the choice of whom Dotti wants to court her is her own, not his."

"Women's Lib has hit the planet," Jim declared with a laugh, as he sipped his tea. "This is delicious stuff," he added, holding up his mug with a delighted smile.

"It's a blend of my herbs and Raya's favorite ones. I like it best, too," Ryes agreed, partly happy with the small distraction.

"She's absolutely correct, Justin. You never dated Dotti before, why the pent up anger, now?" Dr. Cruthers asked directly, wanting to quash any prejudices immediately.

"He's not even human!" he complained, feeling uncomfortable with being put in the spotlight this way.

"Ryes is right. It's not only none of your business; it's not your choice! So, stick your nose out," Dotti scolded him, hotly. "I think he's far more 'human' than someone like Ortiz will ever be!" This got a sudden look of shocked understanding from him. He recalled what Ted told him about Ortiz and his appetites, before. And Dotti had worked in his department until his sudden removal and arrest. From her tone of voice, he could guess she had a personal grudge there, too.

"That's the truth," Bethany agreed with a sigh, looking to her friend and meeting her eyes with sympathy and understanding.

"We will need to get our quarters straightened out," Dr. Cruthers suggested, standing, feeling the subject had run its course and was done. He wondered if Robert Ortiz still survived in storage somewhere on the Star Quest?

"Oh, yes, I forgot. Some of us may already be using rooms you had previously claimed for yourselves," Ryes agreed, standing.

"Let's go down the hall and see if we can get this resolved?" Ethan put a hand upon her shoulder, shaking his head no.

"We'll take new ones. Your people can stay where they are," he assured her with a warm smile, then turned to the survivors. "Tomorrow we'll begin unloading everything salvageable from the ship and start planning to expand the public quarters here to accommodate the increased population. I also expect all my personnel to learn the Star People's language, Dolbith, since we're essentially cut off from our home worlds and stranded upon this one. You can all consider that an order." He met their eyes, seeing surprise and understanding. He looked back to Ryes and smiled as he gestured for her to lead them from the mess hall, heading for their sleeping quarters. The group following looked far more subdued.

"How many do you think you and Maren can revive in a day? Only six?" he asked her, speaking more privately between them as they walked. "You're faster and far more efficient than our own equipment. And you seem to go beyond simple restoration from the effects of cryogenic sleep. I haven't moved this freely, nor felt this good, in years!" he told her. She grinned with pride, giving him a nod of her head.

"It may be more than six," she offered him. "We'll get some sleep tonight and see how tomorrow goes. Maren's our greatest asset, when it comes to Healing. My Healing Talent's so weak compared to the others I have," she admitted, blushing. "And I'm happy you're feeling better, too."

"What other talents do you have, my dear," he asked, smiling, changing the subject again on purpose. She was a font of curious information, but after personally experiencing Maren's Healing Talent, he was ready to believe them.

"I can Time Walk, or journey as a spirit into the past. I used that to go back to learn your language and how to operate the machines here," she told him. "I can go into another's mind to see the truth that lies there, including memories, but Raya's Mind Voice Talent is far more gentle than mine when it comes to determining the truth within. I can use my Catalyst Talent to activate a latent Talent in another person. And I can stop something from moving, if stopping it is very important to me," she told him, smiling with a merry light in her eyes. "I stopped a runaway cart from killing Mitt and it surprised me more than anyone else. Tonight I used it to slow down the crashing starship. And I made sure it landed where I wanted it to go. There may be others which I haven't discovered yet. My mother was said to be very Talented, herself. She was born on Kahmarr, itself."

Ethan wondered at this accounting. Did she mean telekinetic abilities? And what of this time walking she spoke about? She did mention both Neil and Brenda by name! She could have found out about them from the computer, but it felt more as if she'd known them personally. Then there's the matter of Brenda's last report which Wynne gave him, acting as if it had been some kind of jest. He'd have to see if a copy of it was still here on file. And she kept the Star Quest from crashing? That was amazing! They might owe her their lives all over again, if true.

"But your mother never took you home with her to visit?" Bethany asked, curious about Ryes, herself.

"She slept several hundred years in a cold sleep much like yours. She awoke and escaped from Doran's valley of death, then found my grandmother, Jana, wandering in the forest nearby. She went home with Jana and later married her son, Ronn. They were both killed by Korman, who wanted my mother for himself. I was the lone survivor of that attack and was a tiny infant at the time," she explained, telling a very short rendition of the full tale. "I never got to know her, myself." She sighed at this, wishing again that things had gone otherwise. The rest were quiet as they digested what she told them.

They went through the heavy doors next to the stairs and turned towards the crew's quarters' passage and stopped before the first, largest room. It was the one they'd left alone, thinking it suited a high elder.   Rowan had taken the one next to it, which was almost as large. His loom sat in a conference room in a nearby corridor, along with Garvin's cloth weaving machine.

"Ah, my old room," Dr. Cruthers stated, smiling. The door was closed and he wondered if it was occupied? The door to the quarters next to his had a bright, colorful drape over the doorway, with the door itself left open. Ryes smiled, her eyes lighting up.

"Then it's still yours. None of us felt we deserved so much space. It looked like it was for an elder to use," she explained. "Torr? Could I please ask you, Shadd and Mitt to fetch these people some bedcovers and pillows?" she requested, smoothly switching to Dolbith. She'd been doing it all evening long!

"We will," Torr assured her. They quickly left to get them from the storage closet in the next corridor.

"What was that?" Dotti asked, still wanting to know the language.

"I asked them if they could bring out some bedcovers for your use. All the rooms looked so sterile and cold when we arrived. So we left the ones we weren't using alone and empty," she answered, as she opened the door before them. They all looked in, seeming to agree with her statement. Rowan, who had been at the back of the group, came around and disappeared inside his room. He returned shortly with his arms loaded down with blankets he'd made.

"Granddaughter, please tell your humans that I am making a welcoming gift of these, to keep them warm and brighten their rooms," he ordered her, smiling as he said it. She nodded.

"My grandfather, Rowan, says he wants you to each have one of these blankets he's made as a gift, to keep you warm and add some color to your rooms," she informed them as they looked puzzled by Rowan and his loaded arms.

"Oh my, they're beautiful!" Bethany declared, having stepped over to closely examine the one on top. The weave, colors and patterns were a feast for the eyes! Ryes smiled proudly at this, giving a nod of her head in agreement. She reached out and touched the top one, running her fingers across its surface as she smiled, enjoying it.

"They're made of a very tough, but soft when processed, plant fiber, similar to your cotton," she told her, tugging on the fabric of the black T-shirt she wore.

"We couldn't. They're too beautiful to use just to keep warm. They look like they belong in a museum," Bethany told her with regret, as she withdrew her hand, as if afraid to touch them now.

"Please accept them, otherwise he won't understand and it would break his heart to be so rejected," she urged them. Dr. Cruthers smiled as he stepped over and took the top one.

"Please offer him our heartfelt thanks," he replied, gesturing the others to take one, too. "On a second thought, could you please tell me how to say, `thank you' in Dolbith?" Ryes looked surprised for a second, then smiled with true warmth in her eyes.

"Thank you," she said in her own language slowly and clearly enunciating the phrase as possible. Dr. Cruthers and the rest each repeated the phrase, with her correcting them just a little bit. They seemed to get a feel for it, then spoke it to Rowan in earnest. Mitt, Torr and Shadd returned with their arms loaded down with sheets, blankets and pillows, while this was going on. Rowan was smiling jovially at all their thank yous. They were trying to fit in with them and it amazed him greatly.

"So now we get to teach the humans something?" Torr asked with a smile and a laugh. Ryes nodded her head, chuckling at the display.

"Here all these months we've striven to understand the humans and their speech and now we're going to have to teach them our language. It's so strange," Shadd stated, grinning.

"Here you go," Mitt said, offering up the load of bedding in her arms to Justin and Scott, who were the closest to her.

"Thank you," they both told her, smiling at the game. She smiled in return as they lightened her load, passing things out to the others.

"It was no trouble," she assured them. She looked at each of them speculatively, her imagination kicking in now, wondering.

"No. You're not going to try to bed the human men," Ryes whispered, seeing where her interest lay. "Don't you already have enough troubles with Mason and Minn?"

"But Maren's getting to court Dotti," she protested in a low voice, pouting now.

"You know what lies between them is far different! Anyway, I thought you wanted cubs of your own someday? A human man wouldn't be able to do that for you," she reminded her. "I don't even know if one could possibly be able to meet a woman's demands when she's in season," she added, smiling. Mitt sighed as she nodded her head, knowing Ryes did have a valid point.

"What did you just tell her?" Bethany asked, stepping closer, seeing the quiet discussion Ryes was having with this other young woman. Ryes blushed at this, not sure how to express it correctly. Well, direct was usually best.

"Mitt was looking at Justin and Scott as if she was considering them as possible bedmates. I reminded her that she's the one who wants cubs of her own someday, and neither of them would be able to do that for her. She's not due for her first season until maybe next year, so it's not a pressing issue. But she's been trying out several other men here, thinking it will help her make a better decision later," she explained in a low voice, as the rest were busy passing out the bedding. There was a look of surprise and shock in Bethany's eyes as she realized it was the kind of look Mitt had in her eyes a moment ago.

"They're big boys and will have to take their own lumps. I'll make sure to remind them not to take advantage of any of your women, without talking with you about it, first," she promised. She thought it served Justin right with the attitude he'd displayed toward Maren.

"That'd be great," she agreed. "They should have an understanding of what they'd be getting into, first."

"An understanding of what?" Dotti asked, seeing the women discussing things in low voices and moved in closer to hear what was being said.

"Courting and what it entails for the people here," Bethany explained. "That reminds me, what exactly has Dotti allowed Maren by letting him court her?" she asked. "I want to make sure there are no misunderstandings."

"That he can spend time with her, talking and getting to know her better, while he tries to prove his devotion and caring for her. If she wishes, they can free-mate, or physically join. Neil and Brenda were fond of free-mating, but later Neil asked her to marry him, she told me. They both were so happy. If Dotti were to come into season, he wouldn't be allowed to actually mate with her, unless she felt comfortable with him as her husband. Normally, if there were any other suitors around, it's a time of challenges being issued and the woman would be stuck with whoever won the challenge. But, we don't allow that here. We women stick together and determine whom we wish to have as our husbands, or don't want around," she iterated, appearing merry with having to explain it all for them.

"Who's your husband?" Dotti asked, hoping it wasn't Maren. They seemed very close... But she called him her cousin.

"His name's Garth and he's away trying to settle a peace treaty with the plainsmen. We don't need them attacking our hunting parties, anymore. I miss him so much and pray he and Sabin are safe. I hope they'll be back before our cubs are born. I'm expecting four of them and will need all the help I can get. But for now, he's left me in charge of things and the computer keeps calling me the acting chief executive officer, but I've no idea what it means by that title."

"Acting chief exec?" Dotti laughed, speaking loudly now in delighted surprise, then nodded her head as it appeared to make sense to her.

"What does it mean?" Ryes pressed, curious.

"That you're officially the second in command of this facility and that Lt. Dawe here should be saluting you," Dr. Cruthers explained to her, chuckling merrily. "Whom did it name as the acting base commander?" he asked, wondering.

"My husband, Garth. But, he's away trying to establish a peace treaty with the plainsmen," she replied, puzzling this out. "He has a transmitter with him, but has only called once. He said they had reached the Moondance Tribe's camp, but have to accompany them on some kind of hunt. It'll probably be at least another couple of weeks before they'll be able to head back home. I hoped they would've let us come and get them with one of the bigger shuttles... I mean land rovers, by now," she explained in frustration.

"I'm surprised they didn't use one for this journey of theirs," Dotti commented, looking amazed.

"He decided we should save both the land rovers and flyers... helicopters, as defensive devices, to help scare them off if they decide to attack us, again. It's what we did when we saw them being attacked the first time. Mitt flew the helicopter and did scare off most of the mounted riders as they charged with their spears, and I stopped the rover between the remaining two and our men, blocking their attack," she reported.

"Computer?" Ethan spoke up loudly, looking towards the ceiling, sure it'd be monitoring them.

"Yes, Dr. Cruthers?" it replied instantly.

"Have you recorded the incident Chief Executive Officer Ryes has described to me?" he asked.

"Affirmative," it responded, confirming his suspicions and logging his official recognition of Ryes' office.

"Good, then tomorrow we're review your stored data files. Stand down," he ordered it, to let it know there was no expectation of any hostile actions, in case it had previously taken precautions.

"Affirmative," it stated in return.

"You realize, Sir, that you just affirmed its pro-tem promotion of Ryes to an officially recorded position?" Scott pressed, his eyes full of concern.

"Have I now?" he questioned, smiling to see his discomfort. "I think she's already handled the position well, so can continue to fulfill her duties as such. Everyone find new rooms to call your own and let's all call it a night. We have a lot of work to get started tomorrow," he ordered, then turned for his own room, going inside and closing the door behind him.

"I don't believe it," Jim whispered to Bethany. She giggled and gave her head a nod at this.

"Let's get everyone settled," she said aloud. "Ma'am," she added, saluting Ryes with a mischievous gleam in her eyes, "by your leave." Ryes laughed lightly in response, shaking her head in response. Then the rest of the humans joined her, holding their hands to their foreheads in salute, too. Some looked unhappy about it. Her friends and cousin merely looked puzzled with their odd behavior.

"Yes, let's get everyone to their own rooms and to bed. There will be plenty of work for all of us tomorrow," she agreed, returning their salutes properly, as she'd seen in her forays into the past. She led them down the corridors, letting them choose one room, or another. Torr, Shadd and Mitt went off to their own rooms, too. It looked like the ones they claimed as their own, were still available, until they came to Dotti's quarters.

"Maren's already using your room," Ryes advised as they stopped before his door and the colorful drape across the doorway.

"Oh?" she replied, looking puzzled. "Why this particular room over any other? It's away from the rest of yours." Ryes sighed, seeing the look in her eyes, knowing she had to explain this for her.

"He told me many months ago, when we first left our original village forever, that he dreamed about you. He was so deeply infatuated with you that it worried me. He's my cousin and I was just getting to know him for the first time in my entire life and I felt responsible for him. As time passed and we found this place, he rejected even being given the chance to mate with other women and have cubs of his own. He kept saying he'd find you, someday. I took him Time Walking with me once and he knew you on sight when he saw you. Mitt tried to tell him that you might be an old woman by the time you returned to Tayna, but he didn't care. In his mind and heart, he belongs with you, no matter what else happens," she explained, but held up her hands to forestall both their questions.

"He chose this room when we first came here, because he said it held your scent, very faintly and it made him feel better when he slept. On our journey back in time, we found you being battered by an elder. It almost tore him to pieces to be so powerless to help. Then, we saw you crying afterwards as you were helping Alda in the shower. You said you dreamed of someone who sounded so like Maren, as you rejected Alda's offer of free-mating. He took hope from this, thinking you meant him. It was a shock to find you today and even if he's said he loves you to me before, I believe it'd be better for the both of you, if you take this courtship slowly. I'm sure he'd move his things out for you right now, if you want your room back."

"He's dreamed about me and says he loves me?" she questioned with a small catch in her voice. She didn't understand it, for it tore at her to part company with him, even now. Ryes nodded her head in affirmation. "Please tell Maren I'll take the room next to his for now. I'd rather he be right next door to me in case I needed anything," she agreed. She wasn't sure if she was ready to sleep in the same bed with him yet! Still, her heart was flying as she realized what she said all those years ago was still true. She did love him too! But was this all for real, she wondered? It amazed her!

"Maren, Dotti says she'll take the room right next door to yours for now, in case she needs anything. So you'll be close to help her," she relayed to him, smiling, relieved for both their sakes.

"You're sure that's what she wants?" he pressed. "I can move my things out very quickly. It's her room, after all." Dotti's reaction to his being in this room was clear that he'd been right – from the beginning. He smiled, wondering what Ryes had been telling her. It seemed like a long tale.

"Yes," Ryes chided him, still smiling. "Now get ready for bed and get some rest," she ordered.

"All right," he gave in, knowing his protests were useless. He turned to his precious Dotti. "Goodnight, Dotti. I'll be right here for you," he offered. Ryes translated, but Dotti felt she already knew what he said. She smiled, then stepped up, threw her arms about him and stretched up to kiss him, surprising Ryes. He wrapped his arms about her, returned the kiss in kind, her bedding falling to the floor, forgotten.

"Goodnight, Maren," she whispered, trying to imitate the word she thought meant "goodnight." He smiled grandly, not wanting to let her go, but doing so because he realized this was something he couldn't rush now. It had to be her choice, especially after her abuse at that elder's hands! He helped pick up her bedcovers before he went to his door, lifted open the drape, and looking back at her, again. Dotti went to the door of the one next to his and opened it. She gave him a bright smile before disappearing inside and closing it.

"Goodnight, Ryes," Maren sighed, "Thanks," he added, meaning it. She gave him a nod and smile at this.

"Goodnight," she replied. He dropped his door drape and she sighed in relief, turning for her own rooms, glad she'd finally gotten Winterhaven settled down for the night, once more.

"Computer, system status report," Dr. Cruthers ordered, as he sat down in one of the chairs of the computer room. One of the natives was on duty, keeping an eye to the views the various cameras about the facility displayed. She'd acted nervous to be sitting here on watch when he walked into the room, but calmed as she realized he didn't mind her presence and looked to accept her duties in this place.

As the computer gave him the rundown and he made several minor corrections, he thought about this woman. She was trying to puzzle out the words from one of their classic tales which was on display on one of the computer screens. Half of the screen was in an artistic, flowing script which might be their native language and the other half was in English. She looked to struggle with some of the words and phrases and would ask the computer for clarification. It was amazing, he thought.

They seemed so primitive a people and if it weren't for the presence of the ruins of a city Ryes names Hailys, he would've never expected them to not only figure out how to work their machinery in this abandoned base, but to take command of the main computer system, itself. To think they were from a civilization forced into decline... They knew from their earlier surveys that there were few natural minerals available for mining on this world. They conjectured the natives had merely exhausted what little resources the planet had and some kind of war broke out over what was left, which ended with the global destruction of all the major cities. But, with this world turning out to be a planned vacation resort and hunting retreat did finally explain why there were animals and vegetation which looked to have been impossible to develop naturally with foreign protein bases, almost side by side. Their researches, when they could be resumed, would have to be reviewed, corrected and redirected now. He did not doubt Ryes. It fit all too well, now that he could see it.

As he finished the review of the computer systems, he started a quick review of how the indigenous population came to possess the facility. He saw how a small group arrived and quickly learned all that they could grasp. Then there was an influx of the others they brought back from their original village. Through it all, there were two men and Ryes leading and directing the others in their efforts. He could well understand why the computer gave them the designations of acting command personnel, in the absence of the proper humans to guide it.

"Sir?" Scott questioned, coming into the control room. "May I have a few words with you?" he requested, appearing uneasy. Ethan gave him a smile and nod of his head as he indicated the empty, remaining chair. Scott Randall looked relieved as he took it. He saw the native woman was merely keeping an eye to things outside and sat down, hoping she didn't understand too much English, yet.

"How may I help you?" Dr. Cruthers asked, giving him his attention and permission to speak.

"It's about several things," he started, looking a little uncomfortable again. "Who really is in charge of this base? And is there any way for us to contact Earth, to find out what's happening? It looked like the Star Quest and the Beda system was abandoned all together. We were hot property with all the universities and governments back home." He saw one of the screens displaying the ship and was shocked all over again at how torn up it appeared. How had they survived that?

"Who's in charge?" he returned, then smiled seeing where his focus lay as his face seemed to go white. It was a wrenching sight, indeed! "Since we abandoned Winterhaven about eighty years ago, it now belongs to the indigenous population of Tayna which came and settled here to build a new life for themselves. I would say that Garth is now the Base Commander, his wife Ryes is the Chief Executive Officer, and another man named Sabin is the Executive Officer. Maren is the Chief Medical Officer, for good reason I believe, and I'm still the Director of Research. We'll see how many other department heads still survive in the next few days. As for the rest, we'll discuss this after breakfast," he told him. "Anything else?"

"No, Sir," he replied. "This is enough for now." Ethan gave him a nod of his head, dismissing him. Scott got up from his chair and almost bumped into Ryes and another indigenous man, as they were coming into the room.

"Good morning, Scott," she greeted him with a smile lighting up her eyes. He suddenly smiled in return. It was hard not to with the warmth and happiness she projected.

"Good morning, Ma'am," he returned, saluting her. She laughed lightly at this, returning the salute, blushing about it. This got him to chuckling as he stepped around them and escaped the room.

"Dr. Cruthers, do they have to salute me?" she asked, feeling it was an unnecessary gesture. He chuckled and gave her a nod of his head.

"It's a manner of acknowledging your rank," he explained. "Good morning, Ryes," he greeted her. She smiled merrily at his greeting.

"Good morning, Dr. Cruthers," she returned. "With us, we know who's in charge and give respect by paying attention and doing as directed. It seems so useless to stop everything to merely salute each other," she gently protested. She sat down on the chair Scott vacated.

"You have a point, my dear," he agreed. "We'll lay down the law after breakfast," he suggested, smiling as he still enjoyed her directness. He saw the man stepping over to the other woman's side and was talking quietly with her for a few moments. Then she got up, after storing her reading program, and he took her seat. Changing of the watch. Ryes noted his interest.

"We felt that since the computer was displaying what the cameras were recording anyway, this made a perfect place to post our observers. And not only do we have access to a greater range of view, but it's far more comfortable and safer than patrolling outside," she explained.

"It's what this room was designed for, originally," he acknowledged, with a nod of his head. The other woman left after giving Ryes a quick hug. "As far as I can determine, we've lost all contact with the Earth. I plan on ordering a drone launched after we revive all the survivors, to deliver messages from the people here to their families back on Earth and the colony worlds, and to give them an update of our situation. I think this will be safer than deliberately linking up with them using our normal communications methods. After all, we have no assurances if the Dark Ones are still lurking nearby."

"Once, when I was first learning my Talents, I recreated a borrowed memory for Sabin and Garth to experience, but Sabin did something within that recreation which went beyond the original memory. He brushed another mind, which was so very cold, deadly and alien that it scared me. I wondered if he hadn't actually reached out with his and my Talents and touched one of Tayna's enemies of old, by accident. If so, I think it came from about here," she said, quickly keying in the starmap coordinates, as best she could match them up to the computer's perceptions, pointing out the location for him. He studied it for several long moments, thinking.

"Could you show me the memory of this contact?" he boldly requested, meeting her eyes. She mentioned being able to touch other minds last night.

"I'd be afraid of hurting you," she replied, suddenly nervous. Bethany stood in the doorway, hearing their exchange, suddenly uncomfortable with this experiment, too.

"Sir, would it be safe?" Bethy asked, feeling she couldn't stand by quietly in this instance. He looked up to meet her eyes and gave her a nod of his head.

"I have full faith in Ryes and her abilities," he replied, giving them both his opinion. "What do you need me to do?" he requested, giving Ryes his permission and full attention now.

"Close your eyes and relax," she suggested. "I'll try to be as gentle as possible." This could be the best way to truly learn this man's mind and heart in the process, even if she didn't believe he was anything like the other elder.

Truths

Bethy stood, uncertain about what to do in this situation. There was no one else she could go to for help here. The other starman in the room was politely ignoring them with keeping his chair well away from them while watching the screen displays and only occasionally glancing over his shoulder at them. Then Maren appeared at her side. He asked something of Ryes. She replied, giving him a smile, then closed her eyes, relaxing herself. Maren came in and knelt down next to her, closing his own eyes and clutching her arm, as she reached out to Dr. Cruthers' hand with her other one. Bethan wasn't sure if this was a good idea, or not, and was afraid of interfering. Then she realized she wasn't going to be left out, so she came and knelt next to Maren and put her hand over his, closing her eyes.

There was a wash of colors, emotions and images which settled into order once her mind focused in. They were in the command center of a starship, but it was being run by the cat-like people, just like Ryes and Maren. It was focused upon two men and their uncertainty with the requests put upon them by one of the ship's officers. They saw Sabin sit in a chair, assuming the duty of the communications officer. He put the headset on, then just as suddenly and shockingly as he'd felt it the first time, their minds were cast out into the vastness of space. First there was the brief communication with the military vessel, and then as he groped about for anchorage, there was that cold, utterly alien presence noting him, but not from the original memories this scene was drawn from. As the memory wound down, they were back in the command center once more, safe and sound. Dr. Cruthers urged her to finish the rest of this story, with Garth going onward to the bridge to observe operations there. Then it slowly melted and they were once more, only themselves, back in their own bodies.

"Utterly amazing," Dr. Cruthers breathed. He realized he felt like a kid just getting off his first roller coaster ride and wanting to climb immediately back on. He never imagined such a thing was possible! The depth of the venture was like living through it!

"It wasn't just pictures, but the actual experience!" Bethany declared, shocked. "Ryes, how do you do it?" she asked, her mind rushing as it sought to understand it all.

"How do you breathe?" she returned, chuckling merrily. "I've no idea, but since my power awakened, I've found all kinds of new things are possible."

"Someday you're going to show me the whole thing," Maren told her, standing up and helping Bethany to her feet, and eliminating her budding headache, knowing it was from being in contact with Ryes' very strong Talents. "I take it they were amazed by what they saw?"

"Yes," she replied, "Did you need something, Maren?" He sighed, shaking his head.

"I'll talk to you later. I'm going to grab a shower. That thing Sabin touched gives me the chills!" he stated, giving a smile and nod to the others in the room.

He touched Dr. Cruthers' shoulder briefly with his Healing for his headache, then left. After he was out the door, Ethan realized what Maren had done with his light touch and was grateful. Apparently it was something he knew and expected, and took care of immediately. He smiled, as he gave Ryes his full attention, once more.

"So, you're correct with these coordinates, as far as we can determine," Dr. Cruthers said, looking at the starmap and wondering. "I'm glad you're so observant."

"When I first found out about you humans, I wondered if you weren't the ones who originally destroyed Tayna, but then I had the memory of the presence Sabin touched in the challenge. When I went Time Walking, I started to get a feel for what your people were like, and with this in mind I came to understand there was no way it could've been humans. It's not that I think you're perfect, especially after finding the remains of those people in the specimen freezers, but that I know you far better now," she explained. "That presence is from a people I fully believe destroyed both the cities of Tayna and your starship. Is that system too close to this one?" she asked, wondering, tacking back to the original subject.

"Yes, far too close. It's where we first started fighting a faceless enemy of our own," he related to her, grimly. "It may be where they live and hold their own domain. I only hope Earth, herself, hasn't been destroyed. Do you know where your homeworld lies?" She gave him a nod and shifted the starmap and indicated where her copies of the maps in Berrals said it lay.

"Since no one has returned to see what happened here, I can only hope that Kahmarr still survives, too. But it's been far too many years with no word. Could they intercept your drone and find us through it?"

"They might, but they'll be unable to trace it back to where it originated. I'll program in different courses and won't let it run straight to Earth. And I'll only use our base designation, Beda IV, Amitell Research Station number ten thirty-three, not our coordinates. These are uncertain times and we only have each other," he stated, meeting her eyes. "I apologize for taking those lives. It wasn't something I personally wanted to happen, but I was powerless to stop it. I saved those I could by putting them into every spare stasis tube on the ship," he admitted. She gave him a nod of her head, understanding; her eyes were steady and clear. It was enough for her.

"If we stay quiet and keep things out of sight, we might be able to slip by their notice for a long time. Time enough to develop some kind of weapons to defend ourselves from such aggressive people."

"When your people failed before and Earth may have failed, too?" Bethany questioned, worried. She fought with her inner emotions, remembering the day they executed the test subjects for the evacuation. Ryes knew... yet was still willing to befriend them. It amazed her anew.

"They were each alone. We have each other," Ryes assured her. "We have to try." Dr. Cruthers laughed merrily at this, giving her shoulder a warm clasp in comfort.

"Yes, you're absolutely right. We have each other and we'll see what we can accomplish together," he agreed. "Let's get ready for breakfast," he suggested, standing up. He was smiling jovially as they all left the control room. Yes, there were a lot of things he needed to think about before he gave his remaining crew his briefing. This promised to be a busy morning, at least, and a start of a new dawn for this world.

"Maren?" he heard her call out as he was under the fall of water, rinsing his hair out.

"I'm in here, Dotti," he replied, turning so his back was toward the curtain, which blocked the opening. She pulled it aside, saw him and sighed in relief.

"I was looking all over for you," she gently scolded, smiling, knowing he couldn't understand what she was saying.

"I'll be finished in just a moment," he promised her, glancing over his shoulder to note her smile. She came in and shut the curtain again, dropping her clean clothes onto the bench in the small changing area, next to his. She started stripping down, feeling nervous, scared and excited all at the same time! She saw his eyes grow bigger as he saw her approaching and he appeared suddenly afraid to move. Good. He wasn't taking this too casually, either. She placed her soap and shampoo in the holder next to his, and stepped under the water with him.

"I didn't get much sleep," she explained as she reached out and touched his back, running her fingers through the thick body hair covering it. It wasn't fur, it was hair, really noting it for the first time! "Want me to wash your back?" she offered, talking in a low voice, practically in his ear. She felt the shivers travelling up his spine at this and smiled mischievously.

But this was more than a teasing game. She had to get to know him and since they lacked a common tongue, she was resorting to old-fashioned body language. She grabbed her washcloth and soaped it up, then started to gently wash his back, humming softly under her breath. After several long moments, he began to relax under her ministrations. She urged him to turn around and noticed he was aroused by her presence. She continued with her gently massage, washing his body all over, teasing him as she did so. She smiled then handed him her washcloth, gesturing for him to wash her body, now.

Maren got the idea very quickly and noted her arousal and sensuous reactions to his very gentle scrubbing. He noted the differences between her and his sister, seeing they were practically nonexistent as a people. Still, she had two nipples as opposed to the normal four and they were well rounded, as if she were ready to feed a cub right now. He hadn't bathed with his sister since they were young, but recalled the details very well. When he was finished and she rinsed off, she grabbed her shampoo and began to wash her hair, arching her body towards him. He didn't know what she truly wanted and was afraid of touching her out of turn. He didn't know anything about human courting rituals and didn't know what was and wasn't allowed! When she finished and rinsed off, she hugged her body against him, almost causing him to lose his tenuous hold upon his good sense. He finally gripped her arms gently and pushed himself back from her, looking her in the eyes.

"I don't know what you want of me and I think this is not the place an far too soon, for both of us," he told her, wishing he could recall even a few of the English words he thought he knew, but his mind was a blank. He had an idea about this and wanted to discuss it with Ryes, when they could be alone for a few minutes. Dotti saw the look in his eyes and gave him a solemn smile.

"I'm sorry. You're right. This isn't the place for our first time together," she agreed. Then disengaged one arm to shut off the shower and start the drying cycle. This relieved him and she smiled as she leaned up to give him a kiss. This he gladly returned gladly, with passion, feeling more centered once more, even though his panic.

"Wait until tonight. We're going to get to know each other, very well," she whispered in promise. She had come to realize she did want more of him, now. Maren excited her deeply; the first she'd ever felt toward any man! He heard the promise in her voice and thought he could guess what she wanted.

"Whatever you need of me, my dear Dotti," he replied, leaning in the kiss her again.

The computer gave them the exact locations of the remaining suspension tubes which were still functioning, as well as finally locating the boxes Alda and Ptan were stored within. Between Maren and Ryes they revived another eight humans before lunch. Then had to rest as the both of them were drained. By late afternoon, and after a long nap for each, they tackled the next group of cylinders.

"Maren, this one's next," Ryes ordered as he approached, trailing the rest inside. The corridors were now illuminated with a reduced number of light panels as the humans shunted some power from the base to the Star Quest. It provided them power to keep the tubes working a little longer. The humans and starmen were busy off-loading the equipment and supplies they wanted to use or keep for later need. Bethany was here with Ryes, as well as Justin, Gleds and Mason. They found the mechanisms on the tubes were no longer functioning and still needed brute force to open them.

"Why?" he asked, seeing an excited look in her eyes.

"I think it's Brenda, a friend of mine," she told him. "Please?" she begged, feeling this one will need more effort from him. He stood before the tube for a few moments.

"This one's going to be a lot of work," he commented. "She's pregnant?" he asked, unsure.

"Yes. She's expecting a daughter, soon," she affirmed.

"All right," he agreed, then signaled he was ready. Mason and Justin put some effort into it and the tube suddenly popped open, spilling her into their waiting arms. Immediately, they were sitting upon the floor, extending their Healing Talents to help repair and rejuv this woman's body and the small one she carried within. After a few minutes she begun to move, then opened her eyes soon afterwards. Brenda looked up and thought she saw Ryes holding her.

"Ryes?" she questioned, surprised. "What're you doing here?"

"She and her cousin, Maren, are healing your body. Just lie still for a few more moments, Brenda," Bethy assured her, seeing her puzzlement. "How do you already know Ryes?" she asked, wondering. She wasn't mistaken when Ryes spoke about her last night!

"She was Neil's little native ghost girl. I've spoken with her several time when she was `Time Walking,' as she called it, into the past," she explained, smiling. "She doesn't look like a ghost, now!" Ryes and Maren opened their eyes and she smiled down at her friend.

"Of all the people here on this ship, I was so glad to see you survived," Ryes told her, meaning it. "Do you know where Neil might be?" she asked as they helped her up and into a waiting chair. Ryes gave her a quick hug, then draped a blanket over her shoulders. It was still so cold inside the ship! Brenda saw the others and the look of the ship around her, but suddenly felt her baby kicking, just like normal. She closed her eyes for a moment of thankfulness, then opened them to see the concern in Ryes' eyes.

"I think in that one," she said, pointing to the cylinder next to hers. It still had little green winking lights too. "What happened?" she asked.

"We've been in these tubes for almost eighty years," Justin told her, relieved to note she was all right. She carried his daughter, after all, from their very brief affair.

"But they were never designed to be used for that long!" she exclaimed, shocked. Bethany nodded her head, smiling.

"Nothing like being a living legend," she teased, then watched as they moved over to the next tube, which should contain Neil. It was opened and Maren reached in and pulled him out. He and Ryes were immediately on the floor with him, their eyes closed as they worked. "I've watched them revive eleven people so far and it still fascinates me," she admitted as she stepped closer. Neil opened his eyes, puzzled about where he was.

"Ryes? Bethany?" he questioned, looking as if he wasn't sure if he was seeing things, or not.

"Hold on, Neil, they should be finished with you, soon," Bethy assured hm.

"Where's Brenda?" he demanded, not seeing her immediately.

"Right here, Honey," she spoke up, relieved he was all right. She tried to stand, but almost fell. Gleds caught her and returned her to the chair.

"Too soon for that yet," he chided, smiling gently. She returned the smile, guessing what he might be saying and wondering how anyone could have considered them savages.

"Oh Neil, I'm so glad you made it, too!" Ryes told him as she opened her eyes, smiling down at him. Maren helped him up as Gleds lent Ryes a hand. She grabbed a blanket and wrapped it around Neil. Then he surprised her by giving her a hug and laughing.

"You're real!" he told her, as she laughed with him. He let her go and stumbled over to Brenda, before Ryes could move to help him walk. He sat down hard on the chair next to her and wrapped his arms about her, too. "And you're still real too!" he declared, looking so very happy as he gave her a kiss. This got the others to chuckling.

"How do you feel, Maren?" Ryes asked him, knowing Brenda had taken a lot out of him. It was her pregnancy which had taken a deeper draw from his Talent.

"I think I should be able to handle these next two, if you're still willing to lend me your strength," he told her with a sigh. She grinned and gestured grandly for him to lead her onwards.

"At your service, O' Great Healer," she teased. He grinned at this, giving her a nod of his head. They moved to the next tube and readied themselves.

"How do they do this?" Brenda asked, now, as they revived Axel and then Kerry. By the time they were done, they both looked utterly exhausted.

"This is amazing," Bethany told her, "but this morning Ryes showed Dr. Cruthers and I a memory she had of one of their other `Talents,' as she calls them, touching the mind of what we firmly believe is one of the aliens who attacked the Star Quest and maybe destroyed the cities of this world hundreds of years ago. I'm still astounded by the whole thing!" she admitted. "It wasn't just images, but the entire experience! Of course, we both ended up with horrible headaches afterwards, which Maren quickly cured. These people are just astounding!"

"You're as bad as Mitt!" Ryes scolded her, smiling as she stepped closer. "Always jumping in with no warning and with about as much sense," she teased her new friend. "Maren and I are tapped out," she admitted with a sigh. "I think twelve's about our limit."

"How many are left?" Neil asked, standing on unsteady legs, but determined to help.

"Thirty-three more to go," Justin told him, looking grim. "As far as we can figure, most of the ship's crew abandoned her, thinking she was going to blow. We were left to drift in space, while the ship's computer repaired as many systems as possible; bringing her back to orbit Beda IV, or Tayna as the nati... indigenous people call it. When Ryes and Garth got the computer here online, it started talking with the Star Quest's computer and they finally decided it was getting too close to losing everyone, so the computers requested a landing. Ryes agreed and she and her cousin, Maren, have been reviving us, one-by-one. Dr. Cruthers will be briefing everyone shortly. It's almost dinner time, after all," he said, filling them in on what he could.

"And since Raya gets upset when she has to hold dinner, we'd best get moving in that direction," Ryes added, giving Justin a nod of appreciation and a smile which lit up her eyes with humor. They'd learn the rest soon enough.

"I'm actually starving!" Axel commented as he put an arm around Kerry's waist. She giggled at this, then gave the cat people a skeptical look with questions in her eyes. Still, she smiled and shivered, glad of the blanket placed around her shoulders. She was still unsteady on her feet as they supported each other, moving down the corridor. It wasn't only cold in here, but somehow spooky, as if the ghosts of those who didn't survive were all around them.

"Wait, Ryes," Brenda requested, still barely able to walk as she needed both Neil and the plainsman's help to go. "Please thank Maren for me, and I want to thank you, too."

"You're very welcome," she replied, smiling warmly, then translated it for Maren. He gave Brenda a nod of his head and a smile, keeping it simple by now.

"You're going to have to teach me more of their language," he commented as he draped an arm over her shoulders, needing the support as they walked out.

"When we get the time," she promised with a light laugh.

"Ryes, you're going to have to start teaching me your language in earnest," Neil told her, thinking it'd be a good idea with being stuck on this world with no way off. From what Justin said and the condition of the ship, it'd been a miracle they survived at all.

"Maren was just making a similar request, so I'll give you the same answer, when we get the time," she promised, smiling up at his bright, happy face, as he held Brenda close to his side. She was so very thankful that these two humans survived.

Dr. Cruthers gave a very brief set of rules of conduct, informed the newcomers of the real ranking order of command in Winterhaven, and promised more details once the remaining survivors were revived. When dinner was served, everyone was delighted as foods from both cultures were set out. Chuck Swithin, who originally headed the kitchen staff, had been one of the first one's revived this morning, and after they settled their differences, both he and Raya prepared the evening meal together. The starmen were impressed, sampling the human fare prepared correctly.

"It seems your idea of doing things together has already taken root," Ethan chuckled as he sat down next to Ryes. "This looks and smells delightful." Ryes grinned, giving him a tired nod of her head in response.

"Raya and Chuck have inspired each other," she agreed.

"Ryes, it's about time you start teaching the rest of us how to speak and understand the human tongue better," Rowan chided her, hating being left out of things at a time like this. Dinner time was a time of discussing the events of the day and enjoying each other's company for him and now he felt left out.

"I promise, I will," she assured him, looking him in the eyes and seeing his pain. "We need to revive the rest of the people, as well as Alda and Ptan, first. Then we'll begin language lessons for everyone."

"Is your grandfather worried about something?" Ethan asked, noting his look of concern. She appeared too tired to deal with very much right now.

"Only with his inability to understand English," she explained. "I've promised more people than I can recall that I'll start language classes as soon as possible, after we finish reviving the rest of the people from the Star Quest." He chuckled, hearing the note of strained patience in her voice, giving her a nod of sympathy. He'd had similar requests volleyed his way all day.

"I believe you do have your priorities straight," he concurred. "First we finish the revivals, then handle the matter of the language barrier. Although, it seems to me that it shouldn't be too great a task with such delightful concoctions as this," he commented, lifting his fork in emphasis. She and Bethany laughed in full agreement.

The next four days Ryes and Maren spent every moment pushing themselves to the limit, to finish the task of saving what little of the humans still existed. There were hundreds of bodies pulled out of the ship and recorded before putting them in an area they set aside for cremation. This was a sad task for the humans as well as the assisting starmen. Every life saved was cherished because of it, making Ryes and Maren's roles all that more important.

Among the humans, they found four other starmen who'd been pushed into the tubes during the evacuation. Two were caravaners and the other two were from a farm outside a village further to the west. All were welcomed to join Winterhaven until they were ready to return to their homes, if ever. Kort and Nahees welcomed Ottin and Seega back to the caravan and while they tried to bring them up to date, they found out tidbits from their own history they never knew. And they all delighted using the Village Circle in Winterhaven for performance practices!

Finally, Alda and Ptan were found and pulled out of their cold storage. When Alda saw Maren and Ryes holding him, he smiled, knowing he was finally safe and back where he belonged. He felt he'd finally come home. It amazed him that the humans were here too, but he soon saw it was as if they were a large community which was melding together. Ptan was amazed that Dotti and Maren had become inseparable. And Gleds and Raya greeted them both in joy, welcoming them to their new home. This embarrassed them, as they felt they hadn't done anything special to deserve such honor. Still, they found this former place of captivity and torture had evolved into something so much more.

"Come on," she urged, as Dotti pulled the suddenly reluctant Maren into the lab she used to work in, when she was under Dr. Ortiz's department. "I need this to face up to what happened here, so

I can find some healing within," she explained, knowing he didn't understand what she was saying. "I know you saw the one instance of what occurred. Ryes said that it hurt you as much to watch as it as it hurt me to receive the bruises. I'm not doing this to hurt you, Maren. I need to purge this place from my soul. Please?"

He finally gave in, allowing her to lead him inside. She latched onto his hand and walked about the deserted room; pain-filled memories crowded her mind. Maren saw her intense distress and pulled her into his arms to comfort her. She clutched him tightly to her as she cried out her inner agony, knowing she was safe now and free of it all, once and for all time. Dr. Ortiz had not been among the survivors. She'd waited half in fear that he'd be back to try to fill her life with misery once more. The Fates could sometimes be kind. Dotti started to relax her grip a little and started to talk about it, and even if Maren didn't know the words, he understood what it meant to her and supported her with his patient listening; wishing he could do more.

"Dotti?" a voice sounded surprised to find her in the empty lab. They turned to see Dr. Turner and three of the other men who used to work in here with him. "What're you doing here?" he asked. She sniffed back her tears, wiped at her eyes, then smiled uncertainly.

"Purging some old ghosts in the company of someone who cares," she explained with a small smile, holding tightly to Maren. He was her anchor in more ways she cared to admit, now.

"How do you know he cares about you, really?" Justin demanded coldly.

"I know," she countered, the smile melted from her lips. "And that's all that matters!" She gently shoved Maren back behind one of the lab tables, keeping herself close as she put it between them and her former coworkers. She knew she HAD to get him out of here and away from them!

"Why don't we put him through a few tests to see what makes him so different? He can heal, but they can't. Aren't you curious about why?" Wyatt questioned.

"You're not touching him!" she suddenly shouted. It echoed through the lab. Maren could guess from their actions and presence in this room what might be being discussed, so he decided it was time to call in reinforcements of his own.

"Computer," he called out. "Please ask Ryes to come to this room right away? I need her to help to resolve a problem," he requested in Dolbith, knowing it would understand him.

"Affirmative," it replied. This got shocked looks from everyone else in the room. They hadn't known the computer had enough of the starman's language cataloged to understand him. The fact that it responded to Maren as if he truly held rank astounded them. The men stood wondering what he'd requested of the computer. In a few moments, they found out.

"What seems to be the problem, here?" Ryes demanded as she stepped into the room. She noted Dotti looked to be defending Maren from the other men. They saw her and started shifting, uncertain of what to expect now.

"They want to start a series of experiments upon Maren, as they did on Alda, to see the differences. They want to know how he can heal others, as if it could be dissected out of him," Dotti quickly explained with disgust, before any of the men could speak up. Ryes' eyes took on a grim look at this, giving her a nod of her head. It's what she thought it looked like was happening.

"Computer, would you please summon Alda to this room for me? I need his assistance," she said in Dolbith.

"Affirmative," it replied in Dolbith.

"If you want to conduct an experiment, I have a great one in mind," she assured the men in English, her voice suddenly icy.

"Oh gods, they made her mad," Maren commented under his breath. Dotti heard his nervousness. Was it the men he feared now, or Ryes? They soon saw Alda enter the room, appearing uncomfortable to be here, now. Ptan was with him, following slowly and cautiously as she looked about her.

"What do you mean?" Ted asked, appearing curious to see what she wanted to do. Was she going to offer herself up for their investigations, he wondered? What was their last subject doing here? For comparison?

"I want the four of you to gather all the chairs we need and bring them here to form a circle," she instructed in English. After they had the chairs in place, she gave them a nod of her head. "Please sit down and tightly clasp each other's hands," she urged them. She saw the building protests in their eyes. "That's an Order!" she added. Then she turned to Alda.

"I'd like to ask if you could help me show them what they truly did to you, while they were running their tests," she requested. He gave her a nod of his head, knowing she was a Talent, after all.

"What do you need, Lady Ryes?" he asked. Ptan stepped over to stand next to Maren and Dotti.

"Please take a chair and relax. Close your eyes and we'll see where this goes," she advised, smiling in encouragement.

"What now?" Dr. Turned asked now that they were all seated. They weren't ready to play mutiny. They had nowhere else to go on the planet. And he could well imagine what Dr. Cruthers would do to them afterwards, if they tried it.

"Close your eyes and relax," she told him, as she took a stool next to him. Alda sat on the other side of her and did as she'd bade him, appearing hopeful.

"I'm not being left out of this," Maren told Ryes as he came across the room and pulled up a seat next to her. He closed his eyes, centered himself and reached out to put his hand over hers as she clasped Alda's hand. She knew he wouldn't let her leave him out of it. She reached out to Alda, then the humans, but just as they settled down within, Dotti and Ptan joined them in the link. Ryes felt she barely had energy to deal with the rest, but she knew she couldn't exclude them.

She reached for the memories of what Alda experienced in this very room, at their hands. She weighed filtering it for the others, but thought they needed to know what the full experience had been like, to be an unwilling participant in such an environment. The intense pain, the uncaring explorations of his body, the lack of understanding and inability to communicate with them. The hatred, the hopelessness, the helplessness were all there, causing the men to feel what it was like from a very personal point of view, as if they each were set upon the table and used so callously. Through it all, the men now fully comprehended what they, in their driving quest for understanding, did to others who were helpless and suffered for their thirst for knowledge. In this extremely intense intimacy, Alda came to understand his former captors far better and accepted their very heartfelt apologies for all the grief they caused him.

Then Dotti added in her own memories of being hopelessly abandoned, alone in this lab, as the rest of them left once their work was finished. It was as if she were casually given over to the clutches of Dr. Ortiz. The abuse had been physical as well as mental and even now she was still healing within from the bruises no one else could ever see. Then she showed them the gentleness and caring she found in Maren, even if he didn't understand what she was saying. Now they understood a little of why she was so close to him, in spite of their being so different in so many other ways. Ryes released them all gently, opening her eyes, once more.

"I never knew," Dr. Turner murmured, his face ashen. His body was still reacting to just the echo of Alda's memories with his stomach twisting and his hands shaking. Now he knew what it was like to be a test subject with no choice in the matter. It was nothing he could have ever imagined!

"I suggest you either rethink your lines of research, or find more humane ways to conduct the experiments you feel you absolutely must; making sure your test subjects fully understand what you're asking of them, beforehand," Ryes advised, seeing they now understood her fully. Maybe this rank thing wasn't too bad, after all?

"That's why you never get Ryes upset with you," Maren explained to the plains people, with a grin. "The truth can be far more brutal than you're ever willing to face." Ryes laughed out loud in surprise at this, shaking her head in denial.

"Thank you, Ryes, for the insights you've given me," Alda said, offering her his hand, palm up. She blushed, but crossed it with her own and did so with Ptan, as she shifted closer to offer her hand, too. "It's time for bed, my wife," he teased her, as they stood and left. He pulled her closer to his side, putting an arm around her shoulders as she put one around his waist. They looked much happier now.

"Ryes, there's one more thing I'd like to ask of you. I know you're tired, but it's important," Maren requested, putting a hand to Dotti's arm as she had stood and come closer. She sat back down in Ptan's chair, as he shifted and took Alda's. "Could you give me an understanding of English, as you see it?" he begged. She met his eyes and realized he had the right idea.

"Yes! And let me give our small gathering of humans an understanding of Dolbith, too," she agreed. "Wait, Dr. Turner, gentlemen. Maren just had a great idea. Why don't I try to give you an understanding of Dolbith, so we can all get along better?" she asked, as they were getting out of their chairs. This got surprise and concurrence from them, as they quickly sat down, once again.

Ryes smiled, closed her eyes, as did all the others, and centered herself. They joined hands, once more. She reached out to the humans first, giving them the concepts she knew as her native language, both spoken and written. Then to Maren she gave the concepts she understood as English, with the humans filling in more and correcting some of her misconceptions. They opened their eyes together, smiles all around at their accomplishments.

"I'll have to pass this on to Raya. It'll be easier for her to handle it for the rest," Ryes said, grinning as she looked to her cousin. "Thanks for such a wonderful idea, Maren!"

"It was insightful," Ted agreed, "Thank you Maren," he voiced, also speaking in Dolbith.

"You're welcome," he replied in English, laughing. Ted, Wyatt, Justin and Cliff got up and goodnights were bid all around. They left the room, talking quietly among themselves.

"One more thing, cousin," Maren urged. She held up her hands as she laughed.

"Enough," she pleaded, smiling merrily, then sighed as she saw the look in his eyes. "What is it now?"

"Just give Dotti and I a few moments to truly know each other's minds from within," he requested. Dotti looked surprised, then nodded her head in agreement, blushing.

"Yes, if you could," she coaxed, hoping.

Ryes gave in with a smile of understanding, then joined them once again within. This was a deeper contact, one where she felt the intruder, even if it were her own Talent forming the bond. Maren had tried to do this himself, the last few days, but was unsuccessful. He'd been reluctant to approach Raya about it, because he felt this was far too personal. Ryes knew and loved him and would never betray him in such an intimate inner joining. She saw the truth. Maren and Dotti were true-mates and were finally reunited, the way they were meant to be... their hearts and minds were now joined as one and complete within themselves and together.

Ryes found she had trouble going to sleep that night, because of what she now knew of Maren and Dotti's inner connection. They were each other's other half of their souls. Ryes missed Garth all the more because she knew he was the other half of her soul, too.

Duties

"I know I should've consulted you first, but you'd already gone to bed. They were so eager to run experiments on anyone they could, that I felt they needed the experience themselves, so they'd get the full effect from the stresses Alda was undergoing, while under their almost nonexistent mercies," Ryes apologized and explained to Dr. Cruthers first thing in the morning, finding him in his office after breakfast. The remains of his breakfast tray were sitting on the credenza. She felt it was his due to know what she'd done to discipline his staff. "I couldn't let them go on hurting others, without truly knowing what they were doing."

"Your command of English has improved, immensely," he commented, smiling, "and you're not pausing as you pick your wording, plus your pronunciation is remarkable." He saw this weighed upon her very soul, to be put in the position of having to mete out punishment to humans. The fact that she hadn't backed down from doing it impressed him more than anything else. And she used a method of punishment that didn't involve any direct violence was very intelligent. She blushed and nodded her head.

"Maren's idea was for me to directly teach Dotti, and the men involved yesterday, Dolbith as I perceive it, and to teach him English. In the process they added to my perceptions of your language and corrected some of my misunderstandings," she admitted. "I'm going to give Raya what I've learned, so she can pass it onto the rest of Winterhaven, since I know she's far more skilled and gentle than I am at direct mind-to-mind contacts." Dr. Cruthers looked surprised and delighted, not having thought of such a quick, obvious solution.

"Could you please give me an understanding of your language, too?" he requested. "And I'll see if your English might need any further refinements." Headaches or no, he relished such a contact! Ryes smiled, guessing he'd want this, so gave him a nod of her head.

"Yes, I can. Please relax and close your eyes," she instructed with a sigh. She closed her own eyes and centered herself, then reached out for his hand; which he grasped eagerly. She projected her perception of her language, and then learned even more about his, than she thought possible.

Now, he pressed for an explanation of the murals in the dining room, since they were in close contact. She opened up her memories of her two Time Walking experiences in Hailys, showing him the city as it was, when it was filled with thriving, busy beings. He wanted to know more, so she projected her recollection of her encounters with her great Aunt and her protector, Hadu. He was fascinated with them both and everything she knew about them. She then sent some of what she saw, when she went back to learn what she could of them, here in Winterhaven. This seemed to delight him, as well. He then wanted to know what the village she grew up in was like. She gave him both the view of what most of the villagers knew, then one of her and Rowan living very peacefully beside the bank of the Yuri. She showed him her favorite time of year, when the caravaners came to winter with them near the river.

He started showing her of his home back on Earth, itself. He showed her the great cities of his homeworld falling into decay, with the masses of people feeling they had nowhere else to go, as the colony worlds seemed so far away and it was expensive to leave Earth. There were his views of the colony worlds, some fantastic and beautiful, some very simple and barely starting out. He projected his favorite thing to do in the evenings, to sit and enjoy his cup of coffee, watching the sunset while he smoked his pipe. She opened her eyes feeling awed by all she learned, not having the words to describe it to anyone else. He opened his eyes, chuckling in delight.

"So you chose the phoenix," he commented, at last. "Very well thought out, my dear," he said, agreeing with her choice. "Don't worry about Dr. Turner and his assistants, they'll be fine and you may have granted them a perspective they needed. I'll log that I'm in full agreement with your actions. Is there anything else which might be important?" he asked, sighing as he now knew what Hailys was truly like. So much more civilized than the great cities on Earth were today. And with her showing her trips into the past to learn this facility, verified her Hailys sights for him. The roller coaster rides only got better!

"Monty had a terrible attack of gas last night. Maren took care of him very quickly, but I was wondering if we could use some of your staff and labs to analyze our foods; to see if there might be any problems for your people in trying to digest them. And tests run on your foods and their effects upon us. I know there're areas upon Tayna where the plants and animals would be extremely toxic for any of us to consume, and I wouldn't want to see any humans, nor starmen, suffering due to a food intolerance, or allergy," she suggested.

"A very good idea," he concurred, smiling to see she did possess foresight and had the health and welfare of everyone at heart. "I'll have Dr. Turner and his staff see to it today. That will keep their hands busy and out of trouble for a while."

"That's all I truly wanted to cover," Ryes told him. "Is there anything you might need me to look after?" she asked.

"Yes, to take the day off. You and Maren deserve it," he replied. It was the least they were due for saving their lives!

"But..." Ryes started, then saw a shift, as he felt she was challenging his will on this matter. She smiled, giving him a nod of her head. "It'd be a nice day for a drive out," she agreed, then stood up.

"Yes, it would. Pack a picnic lunch and have a good time, my dear. Enjoy yourself," he ordered her with a chuckle, standing up to see her out the door.

"Thank you," Ryes said, as she paused before opening it up, smiling with a happy gleam in her eyes. "I've wanted to see what Earth was truly like, since we first found this place."

"You're more than welcome. Now git," he urged. She opened the door with a light laugh and quickly disappeared outside. He closed it thoughtfully behind her.

"Mitt?" Ryes called, as she approached the flyer hangar. She saw her head bent, trying to discuss a piece of equipment with one of the humans. They were pointing at things but she wasn't sure if either truly understood, but it didn't seem to be in contest, which was a relief. Mitt's head snapped up as she saw her, then a grin blossomed upon her face.

"Sis! I've got to ask you a favor," she declared, stepping over in front of her. "Could you do that language thing for me? I need it to truly understand all this machinery," she requested, looking as if it were the most important thing to her, in all the world. Ryes laughed lightly at this.

"I gave my understanding of English to Raya. She's far gentler than I am," she reminded her.

"But it doesn't cover enough of what I need to know! Please?" she begged. Ryes sighed, giving in.

"We never did get the chance to explore that Inner Sight Talent we unlocked in both of us when the ship landed. We haven't had the time," she confessed, questions were dancing in her eyes, but Mitt gave her a nod.

"We'll tackle that when the winter snows lock us in and we need some distractions," she offered, smiling. "This is different and I need it now."

"Does he understand what you're asking?" she volleyed in return, wanting to be very sure before attempting this venture.

"Axel? I think he understands, but he doesn't believe," she admitted.

"Axel?" Ryes called out. He put down the device he had in his hand and stepped over to the ladies. "Mitt wants to learn all about the flyers... helicopters. Is it all right with you, if she learns it directly from your mind? I'm not as gentle as Raya, but she's been pretty busy this morning and may not have time for something more specialized like this, for several days," she explained. He huffed a laugh and gave her a nod of his head in consent.

"Sure, no problem with me," he told her. "What am I supposed to do?" he asked. His disbelieve was plain in his eyes. Ryes smiled, seeing his opinion in his expression.

"Just close your eyes and relax," she instructed. He did, so she did too, centering herself. She reached out and gripped his hand, then took Mitt's, knowing she knew the procedure by now. First she made sure he understood Dolbith and she English, then she gently delved into his store of knowledge concerning these machines and passed his experience onto Mitt. In a very short time, they were finished, so she released them both and opened her eyes. There was surprised shock in his expression. "Are you all right?" she asked, worried about him. Axel cracked a smile, giving her a nod.

"Just kinda took me by surprise is all," he assured her. "You really can touch another mind!"

"Yes, I can. If you have any problems, Torr's in charge today," she told them with a smile. "I have orders to take the day off from Dr. Cruthers."

"Have fun!" Mitt told her, giving her a quick hug and kiss. She smiled in return, giving her a kiss and hug back.

"I think I might," she agreed. Then she noted Jim Dawe and Bethany Mackenzie were coming across the outside courtyard toward them. At least Jim was in regular clothes today!

"I don't know. Maybe I'm not quick enough, anymore?" Mitt saw them and laughed merrily.

"It's all those cubs you're carrying," she teased. "You would've been long gone by now, if we were back in Matlowe." Ryes looked at her and realized she was right. When had she gone from the shy outcast, to one of the leaders of this motley mix of humans and starmen?

"You're not supposed to be out without an armed escort, Ma'am," Jim informed her, saluting. She smiled and returned the salute, seeing he wouldn't drop his arm, otherwise.

"I thought we eliminated these salutes," she teased; his grin widened with mischief in his eyes. "And I seem to remember hearing something about an escort, somewhere," she agreed, as she saw the garage door opening nearby. Dotti was already strapped into number five, as Maren was operating the door. "Just make sure to strap in. I'm driving today." Mitt laughed at this, as Bethany looked at her in surprise. Ryes was already walking toward Maren to let him know, too. She had her fall gathering of spices and medicines in mind and there were a few places she wanted to investigate, first. She hoped they'd have enough time.

"Garth, Sabin, Dyan said he wants you to come to his tent," Shins said, poking his head into their tent. Garth had been going back over their copy of the treaty they penned in Winterhaven and looking at the sheets Dyan wrote in response. His demands made no sense, no matter how many times he read them. He looked up and gave Shins a nod of his head.

"We've been waiting long enough," Sabin started, then caught the look in Garth's eyes and subsided. He sighed and nodded, too.

"We only want to be heading home, soon to our wives," Garth voiced for them both. Shins gave them a nod of his head. He kept hoping to catch them using the women they'd acquired here as he thought a man should, but they seemed very devoted to their wives. It was hard for him to fathom.

"I'll tell him you're coming," he replied, smiling at last, then turned to leave.

     "After due consideration, Traveler Garth, we feel you need to
present your case directly to Dara, High Chief of all the Plains Tribes,
himself," Old Dyan informed him. They arrived at the winter
encampment, having dressed, dried or salted the meat they gathered,
as well as processed the rest of the korom parts for other uses, too.
Still, it took far longer than either Garth, or Sabin thought it should;
and now this?

     "Would it be better if we returned in the spring? We both
have cubs due to be born very soon, back home," Garth pressed, only
wanting to be free of this place. He truly wanted Ryes by his side for
these negotiations and thought their cubs might be old enough to
leave home for a few of days by then. Of course the next time, he
promised himself, he'd use one of the shuttles and make it a much
faster trip! They'd had such a time teaching them how to make their
simple bows; he knew they'd never comprehend what lay behind their
machines! And Ryes once told him they could be set to only respond
to certain people, so as to make their theft much harder.

     "No. We're leaving in the morning for the Great Gathering of
Tribes. As a bearer of a Badge of Passage, you're required to present
yourself before Dara. It's spelled out clearly by our tribal customs,"
he insisted, seeing their reluctance with the delay. "It'll only be a
week or so, travelling to our gather field. Once Dara approves the
treaty, then you two will be free to return to your own home." Garth
saw the stony look in his eyes and knew there'd be no appealing his
decision. He gave him a shallow bow in acknowledgment.

     "Then if it's required, we shall gladly attend," he replied,
trying to sound as reasonable as he could. His inner ire burned. "If
you'll excuse us, we must ready ourselves for this journey, too."
Dyan gave him a nod of his head, dismissing them. They didn't put
up a fight. It was almost a disappointment. He half believed the
Badge was merely something they'd found; now he began to truly
worry. Garth and Sabin quickly left the stuffy lodge, heading for their
own.

     "I don't know about this, but it's exactly as you predicted,"
Sabin said in a low voice. "I guess this means we have to bring along
our women and all these windracers we've come to own," he
chuckled. "Which is going to make the final trip home far too slow."
Garth smiled and nodded his head at this.

     Shins' payment of his younger sister, Sayer, and the two
mares was only for them to teach him, his cousins and brother how to
make and use the bows and arrows. He insisted that if anyone else
wanted to learn, they had to either pay them, or him for the lessons.
Since he was charging far more than they were, they now had Raby,
Katas, and Dodi, plus another dozen windracers. Shins commented
yesterday that they were quickly becoming very wealthy men. Of the

women they now owned, Dodi was the only full adult and was their age. The rest ranged in age from twelve, up to fifteen years old. They finally managed to convince the women that the only things they wanted out of them were for them to cook, clean and take care of the windracers. And to stay out of their personal things!

"We'll make it," he assured his friend with a heartfelt sigh. "Let's wait until after dinner, and then give our wives a call. They should know what's happening. I'm sure they're worried about us," he said. He worried about Ryes. He was afraid she'd push herself too far with that Time Walking, unless he or Sabin were there to make her behave. Maren was more inclined to go along with her wild ideas, than police her, even if he promised otherwise before they left.

"I wonder what they're having for dinner tonight?" Sabin voiced aloud. "I'm sure it's not this endless, tasteless, stewed meat." Garth chuckled at hearing this.

"Whatever it is, they'd better save us some, whenever we do manage to make it home," he agreed.

"What're we going to do about the girls, when we make our call home?" he asked, suddenly concerned, stopping just outside their lodge. He didn't want to needlessly worry their wives!

"We'll ask them to keep quiet, but since I made sure to give the transmitter a full charge, yesterday. We'll have plenty of time to explain things to Ryes and Ardis, if we need to. They're not going to believe THIS," he assured his friend with a laugh. Sabin nodded his head in agreement, laughing too. He missed Ardis all the more with having the others fussing over him. He'd rather do things himself, than be constantly catered to. Then he noted a woman approaching them, appearing determined. He gave a nod in her direction and Garth turned around. She was the image of Raya, only older. He smiled as he turned to greet her.

"Where's Raya? Why didn't she come home?" she questioned outright, before either of them could speak.

"I'm Garth, leader of Winterhaven," he introduced himself, first. She gave him a nod, then seemed to recall herself.

"I am Rana of the Moondance Tribe. I'm only a tanner," she replied. "But I want news of my daughter. She left so suddenly and never said any goodbyes." Her inner agony was plain in her eyes. Garth gave her a nod at this and invited her inside their dwelling.

"I'll tell you her tale, so to put your heart at ease. She's safe and happy and now has a good husband with two cubs on the way," he told her. She saw his truth in his eyes, so accepted his invitation and went inside.

"How much are you going to tell her?" Sabin asked in a low voice before going inside, himself.

"The whole thing. She deserves to know," he replied, smiling.

"She does," he finally replied, realizing it himself. "I wonder if she can teach these girls of ours how to cook?" he wondered aloud, getting Garth to chuckle. Smiling, he went inside and settled down for the long tale.

"Isn't that plant extremely poisonous?" Bethany asked, seeing how carefully Ryes was collecting this particular one. She used her boot to step on it, flattening it to the ground, then her beltknife to cut it loose from the main stem, not letting the sap spray outwards. Now, she used a pair of tongs she'd brought along and was placing it within an empty collection box, all by itself.

"Yes, it sure is," Ryes agreed, smiling as she sealed the box, wiped off her beltknife and tongs on the thick grasses, then rinsed them off, for good measure. She wiped the bottom of her boot, making sure no bits of the plant were clinging to it, then rinsed it, to be sure. "But, once it's dried and cured properly, it's an excellent ingredient for both a tea and an ointment, which helps Rowan's joints in the winter. Now that we have Maren, I don't know if he'll need it, but it's always best to be prepared," she informed her. "I always gathered this one very carefully and keep it stored away from all others. I wouldn't want someone to mistake it for a spice plant, or anything they could handle casually." She was teaching them the plants in the area the way she knew them, for her new friends to understand this world better.

"So, you were the village alchemist?" Dotti asked, smiling. Ryes had a vast store of knowledge about the local plants and animals, telling them far more than they could possibly remember, for just this one outing! Wait until Wynne Baights heard this! She'd be in seventh heaven! Dotti was recording everything for her; the drone catching everything.

"An herbalist, maybe. I usually gave most of what I collected to my Aunt Tanns, who prepared the concoctions the villagers used for their medicines," she explained. "She's probably upset with us moving out, because she has to do her own gathering and I'm sure has no idea where to begin, anymore."

"It's about time my mother did something for herself." Maren laughed at the thought of his mother out in the forest gathering plants. "She treated you poorly for all the work you did for her."

"She is the way she is," Ryes chided him, then sighed. "She was always so busy with the cubs to look out for."

"Now, you're going to be too busy when yours are born, so it wouldn't do her any good to have us back there," he returned.

"We still have to make a trip back - to gather the things we left behind - and the others who might've changed their minds about joining us," she reminded him. "What do you think about later this week, after we finish the burial of those who didn't survive the Star Quest's cold sleep?"

"Wait a minute," Jim objected. "You're not going out wandering about the countryside, leaving Winterhaven," he cautioned. Not only was she pregnant, but was the Chief Executive Officer for the site and far too valuable to endanger in such a venture.

"I know," she replied, mischief dancing in her emerald green eyes as she smiled. "Garth's already forbid me to go anywhere near Matlowe. He's afraid Old Korman might go off in a fit and try to kill me, even if he's already won a challenge against him. All I want are the remotes up, to be able to see what's happening." She saw relief in his eyes at this and chuckled.

"The only one who can make her properly behave is Garth. Too bad he and Sabin are still out on that winter hunt. I hope they get back soon!" Maren exclaimed, missing his friends all the more for recalling their absence. Ryes' eyes took on a pensive look.

"Just a few more, then we'll call it a day," she suggested, finally recalling why they were out here today. Bethany noted the way she seemed to suddenly go quiet; her mind upon something else. Who was this Garth, she wondered? She knew Dr. Cruthers had reviewed the computer's recorded files from when the starmen first come to Winterhaven. Maybe he had some insights into what he was like? She felt he had to be someone very special for Ryes to be so deeply loyal to him.

"Calling Winterhaven," Garth said into the transmitter. There was a few moments' pause, then a voice came through.

"This is Winterhaven, who am I speaking with?" came the puzzled reply. This had him frowning, not recognizing the voice.

"This is Garth. Is Ryes, Maren, Ardis or Torr available?" he questioned, not quite ready to be worried about this stranger. Maybe they'd taken in some more strays?

"Base Commander Garth? Sir, I'll get Ryes, immediately," was the quick, fumbling response.

"Base commander?" Sabin questioned with a chuckle. "What kind of games are they playing now? Too fond of that darned computer, for sure!" Garth shrugged, trying not to laugh, himself. The stranger had sounded so serious about the matter.

"Maybe the population's grown, again?" he returned, smiling.

"GARTH?" he suddenly heard Ryes' voice. She sounded excited. "Are you all right?" she asked, breathlessly.

"We're both fine," he assured her, finally chuckling, tears springing to his eyes. "How're you doing?"

"Well, your cubs are now so squirmy that it's hard to sleep at night," she scolded him with a laugh. "I love you so much!" she told him.

"I love you, too. I wish I were home, right now!"

"I could send out a large shuttle for you two, one to accommodate the windracers," she suggested, wanting him back as soon as possible!

"They now say we're required to go before Dara, the great chief of all the tribes, at their gathering. We've been looking at the maps and think we already have a quick overland route back planned, but it'd be better if you, Torr, or Ardis were here to make sure we're doing this right," he informed her, knowing it was best to break the bad news, first. There was laughter coming over the transmitter which didn't belong to Ryes.

"I tried to teach you how to read the maps too quickly," she stated. "If worse comes to worse, find the Caravaner's Road and stick to it. It may be slower, but it'll get you back here. It should be well marked on the maps." Her heart was heavy with the thought of it still being longer before they'd be home. Torr, Maren and the others, crowding in behind her, were adding in their comments, too.

"But that way looks far too long," Sabin protested, crowding in next to Garth. "Is Ardis there?" he suddenly asked, as Garth surrendered the transmitter to him.

"I'm HERE!" she shouted, sitting down next to Ryes, tears in her eyes too. "Are you keeping out of trouble?" she demanded, smiling. She was so excited to hear his voice.

"No more than usual," he teased her. "I love you and sure miss you, woman! Are you all right?"

"Yes, I'm fine. We've been busy trying to get things done, but we're managing. I love you, too. Are you sure you can't just go see this Dara in the spring?" she asked, hoping.

"No they can't," Ryes told her. "They carry the Badge of Passage and must go before Dara to explain how they came upon his lands, and that badge."

"That's what they told us. Oh, yes. We forgot to tell you, we've got some new members for our little community, whom we'll be bringing back with us," Sabin told them. "There were a few things Gleds and Raya never told us about their people."

"We've acquired a few new people, too," Ardis said, smiling mischievously. "And are you two going to be surprised when you get home!" She winked at Ryes, as the others behind them were laughing merrily at her secret. She felt it served them right, with being gone so long!

"We guessed that much by the way we were greeted when we called in," Garth commented, wondering who they were?

"Oh, that was Monty. He's still very excitable about things," Ryes assured him, laughing. Dr. Cruthers, sitting on her other side, was chuckling. It was a good description of the former ensign.

"Is Raya there?" Garth asked, remembering.

"I'm here!" she called from by the doorway. The crowd shifted to let her get near the console and Marla came in, in her wake. "Yes, Garth, what do you need to know?"

"Your mother was here today and wanted us to let you know she loves and misses you," he related, wishing he could've let her speak with her directly. They heard a loud gasp from the other side and a pause.

"If you see her again, please let her know I love her so very much," she finally was able to voice around the tightness in her throat. Tears were now flowing down her cheeks as she was smiling happily.

"I will," he promised, understanding what she must be feeling.

"And I love and miss you so much, son," Marla said, getting as close to the desk as she could, standing behind Ryes. She shifted and tried to surrender her seat to her, but she shook her head, refusing the chair. "Your father and Jons do too!"

"I love and miss you so much, mother; all of you!" he replied, truly wanting to be home all the more now! "How's Myran doing?"

"Growing up fast," she laughed out, smiling, "you'd better get back before she starts crawling!" He laughed at this, nodding his head.

"Sabin! Sabin!" Lixi called, trying to squirm closer. Sana picked her up and moved through the crowd. Garth passed the transmitter back to his friend, taking a moment to wipe away his tears.

"Hurry back, brother," Sana insisted, then smiled. "I love you!"

"I love you, too!" Lixi voiced, giggling.

"I love you both! I'll be home as soon as I can," he promised. "Help take care of Ardis," he asked.

"We take care of each other," Ardis told him, laughing. She and Sana now held each other's hands.

"That's what you should do," he declared, laughing now, himself. He passed the box back to Garth.

"Is everything truly all right?" Garth finally asked.

"We ARE taking care of each other," Ryes assured him, "and everything is great here. We finally got a device made to read our crystals from Hailys and Aunt Adina was right... most of it is frivolous stories and news items. You'd be laughing at what they thought was so important they had to preserve it for centuries. Are you both truly all right?"

"We are. We may have to call you, to help in dealing with Dara," Garth told her. "I wish you were here with me, my wife," he said, his throat tightening up, again.

"I do, too," she assured him, "I'll be here waiting, but next time, you're staying here and I'll go out to settle the treaties. This is far too hard to sit and wait!" she scolded.

"Next time we're using a shuttle," he assured her with a laugh. "And you're faster at driving that thing than I am! We'll call you from the gather site. Be good and don't give Maren and Torr too many headaches," he warned. He heard her laughter, blended in with the others, as they added their own comments and goodwill wishes for them.

"I'll try not to," she replied in promise.

"Don't believe her!" he heard Maren shout with a laugh.

"Bye," he called, reluctantly.

"Bye," Sabin added. "I'll see you soon, Ardis!" They heard a chorus of voices wishing them well and to hurry back home, then after several long minutes Garth reluctantly turned off the box and sighed heavily.

"I wanted so much to have them come out in that shuttle right now," Garth said, as he put the transmitter away.

"Those were the voices of your wives and friends?" Dodi questioned, getting up and coming closer. She sat down near them and saw the burden they bore in their hearts, with being far away from their home. The other three girls were amazed with the whole experience, appearing curious about this magical box they'd used.

"Yes," Sabin affirmed. "Both our wives are expecting cubs very soon and we want to get back home to them."

"I didn't catch last year, so have to wait for my first one, still. How many cubs do you two already have?" she asked, wanting to know more about these quiet, gentle men. They didn't want them for free-mating, saying they had their wives waiting for them at home. There'd been a promise of other men, who still wanted pretty wives, back in this Winterhaven, but she hadn't believed it until now. They could actually talk with those so far away, from way out here? It was amazing! It wasn't something that could be made up!

"These will be our first," Garth told her, "Maren says Ardis is carrying two, but he and Ryes have kept it a secret from me about how many she's going to be having. She keeps saying cubs and I know of one son for sure, but otherwise..." he shrugged with a smile. "I'll find out when they're born."

"Who's this Maren?" she returned, wondering.

    "He's Ryes' cousin and our Healer. You'll get to meet everyone there soon enough. Let's all get to bed and get some sleep. We have a long day ahead of us, tomorrow," he urged her and the other girls. Dodi returned to her furs and settled in for the night. The love they had for their wives had been plain in their faces and voices as they spoke with them. It was what she wanted, more than anything else... to be loved so much, that even when far apart, no one else mattered. She wanted so much to find a man whom she could love and live with in such a way, too. There was now real hope.

Trust

Aylita and Chel opened the back door to Rowan's former home and stopped in shock. The very clean and organized kitchen appeared as if everything had been pulled off the shelves, or out of the cabinets, and left lying wherever they came to rest; tossed aside casually, as if the different cups or containers didn't matter. The door to the cold keeper was open and the contents inside appeared as if wild animals had gone through what foods were still stored within. The honey bowl was lying on the floor in front of it smashed and sticky with the remaining honey.

"Who did this?" Aylita practically growled. Her eyes lit up with smoldering anger.

"Someone who's stupid," Chel replied, her eyes were alight with fire, too. "It was a trust for all of us to keep safe."

"I'm going to see if the farga's still here! He or she has some serious cleaning to do!" Aylita declared. She righted the baby pen and straightened the thick pad and small blanket within so Chel could set down Amarr, who was still sleeping in her arms. Chel set him carefully down and then gave Aylita a nod. Aylita picked up a fallen metal ladle and swung it experimentally, satisfied and appearing ready. Both women started checking the different rooms. The bath tub looked untouched but the waste closet was a mess. They went out into the great room and saw it was mostly undisturbed. There were a few cushions tossed about and chairs knocked over, but nothing else that was obvious. Then they looked into the room the loom had sat before and saw the sideboard doors hanging open and some colorful yarns had been pulled out and left on the floor. They were now a tangled mess!

Going back into the bedrooms' hall, they found the caravaners' room was also violated with their possessions scattered. It appeared some things might be missing but with the tumble, it was hard to tell. Ryes' room had also been ransacked, but there had only been a few boxes left and the clothes and other small things had been dumped all over the floor. And finally in Rowan's own room they found a pair of men they'd known from Riverward. They too had been burned out of their homes, but from everything they seemed to have hanging out of their over-stuffed backpacks near the door, it appeared they'd turned into thieving maggots.

They walked in and Aylita brought the heavy ladle down upon the sleeping head of the farthest man while Chel wrapped her claws around the front of the throat of the nearest one. Both awoke with a start and realized they'd been fully caught.

"Jain, I never knew you were so stupid!" Aylita stated with anger dripping with each word. She had her arm ready for her next, harder swing. He put up an arm in self-defense, which she dodged and scored on the top of his head with a hard thud. The months living out here had returned the strength to her body and had filled out her frame. She was now even stronger than she'd been in Riverward.

"Aylita, let me explain," he started, as tears of pain sprang to his eyes as he realized he was far more frail than she was now.

"There's no explaining being a common, dirty thief and a desecrator of a Caravaner's Seal. You know they'd simply have put you to death and still might, seeing the way you wrecked their home! How stupid are you? Truly?" she demanded. The astonishment on his face said it all.

"We'll put it back – all of it," Joce, his brother, tried to say with his throat being constricted by Chel. He'd put a hand on her wrist, but then she'd put her other hand, claws all out, digging into the flesh of his arm. He appeared afraid to move. Chel was a strong woman now and he couldn't match her grip. Jain mutely nodded his agreement, but was afraid to move, too.

"You're not alone," Chel suddenly said, turning to look over her shoulder. Siah and Nali stood there, having heard the commotion and come down from the loft. There was shock written on their faces too. Siah shoved her brother Nali hard and slapped him.

"You dragged me into this?" she screamed at him.

"All four of you are going to clean the whole house up and put everything back the way it was before. Everything you took will be put back exactly where you found it. It does not belong to us and when the owners return soon, they'll want a full accounting of your actions," Aylita ordered. Chel pulled back in her claws, even if her anger wanted to strain against it. She'd rather shred Joce for his stupidity.

"We left Riverward to find a better home and people who we can trust and live with peacefully. And here you brought the worst of what we thought we escaped to this new home! Were you behind the theft of our tools back in Riverward, too?" Chel demanded, the anger still smoldering in her dark eyes. Jain held up his hands before him and shook his head no.

"I swear we had nothing to do with that. We heard that you were living near the Yuri and thought we could take any home we wanted," he admitted. "We didn't mean anything bad!"

"Let's get cleaning up," Siah then voiced, her brows pulled into a frown as she realized the wreck they'd made of this one room. The men mutely nodded agreement and scrambled to obey. "Are there homes out here we could live in?" she asked the women as they stepped back to let the others get busy.

"Yes," Aylita and Chel both responded, then grinned at each other.

"It's a real community out here. There're a number of homes the caravaners have set aside as their winter homes, but it still leaves quite a few others for the rest of us to own as our new homes. We all contribute to keeping things neat and clean as well as repairing the homes that need it. Taroom is building a bigger house for us actually in Matlowe itself because he says he has lots of work to do there," Aylita told them. They started to put the room back into order while Chel dumped out their backpacks and looked at disgust with all the things they had stolen.

"Come on, there's a lot of work to do! You made a horrible mess of Rowan's home!"

"You know the owners?" Nali asked astonished, as he knelt down and helped Chel sort out the stuff from the backpacks.

"Rowan is one of the best Elders I've ever known in my life," Chel told him with a nod. "He's kind and a great storyteller and if you truly needed something, he would give it to you. But since he's not here to ask, you're going to put everything here back," she stated in a no-nonsense tone of voice.

"Right away," Siah replied, wondering about an elder like that.

"I'm taking Joce with me to get started on the waste chair room. Gann and the others will be back soon from the morning's hunt and will be very unhappy when they see the kitchen," Aylita stated, grabbing the young man's arm and pulling him out of the room with her. "Good thing they we're the ones to find you here with the house this way," she added, as look of disgust still on her face.

"I'll help you there," Siah volunteered. Aylita gave her a nod as the trio left the room. Jain and Nali finally got the big chest put back upright and now were gathering and throwing back in the things that had spilled out the drawers.

"No you don't!" Chel ordered. "You will put everything back in folded and neat, as it was originally." The protests were in their eyes until she stood up. Then they quickly pulled out everything they had stuffed within and started folding the clothes and linens as neatly as they could manage. She saw it wasn't perfect, but it would have to do. She tossed them things she knew belonged in the drawers from the backpacks and they winced, but got to work in earnest.

"What happened here?" Gann asked as he and Kaytas arrived in the kitchen. It was a mess! A strange woman was mopping the floor as Aylita looked to have just finished washing the dishes. There was a large pot simmering with some fresh tea in it though, and another pot with grains cooking. The woman mopping blushed darkly.

"Stupidity," Aylita replied, "We've some stragglers from Riverward who thought they could help themselves to anything they wanted in Rowan's home," she explained. The other woman nodded mutely and looked down. Kaytas scoffed in disgust, but gave Aylita a nod.

"Looks like you have it well in hand," she replied, then noted Amarr watching them from the baby pen and added, "and Chel I guess is handling the rest?" The other six hunters came in through the door and looked around in disbelief.

"Is this all right," Joce asked as he stepped out of the waste chair room. He stopped as he saw all these strong and very unhappy looking people now in the room. "I think I got it right this time," he amended, appearing afraid.

"Let me see," Leand offered as he stepped up to the shorter man and gestured for him to show him his work. Joce opened the door and blushed as Leand looked inside. "Not done yet. Don't you know how to simply clean? There's the brush for cleaning the bowl and you pull the cord to flush it out," he instructed and stood with his arms crossed as Joce moved to comply.

"I don't think their mothers ever taught them how to clean anything proper," Chel stated as she herded the other two young men into the room. "And they'd come out of their graves and beat them if they knew what they'd done here."

"What have they done besides make a mess of the kitchen?" Tavis asked, setting her hunting spear into the holder by the door.

"They got into everything and were going to steal all they could carry," Aylita told them, still looking disgusted. Mellas came into the kitchen to wash up and then helped her dish out the cooked grains.

"Where's the honey bowl?" Kaytas asked as she looked into the cold keeper. Not much food appeared to be left inside.

"Destroyed," Aylita answered. She pulled out the large jar Rowan used to store the honey in and looked around for something to use in the old pot's place. Siah put away the mop and moved to help Mellas with the bowls of grains. She motioned for her to wash first.

"I'm sorry," she said with tears in her eyes, as she complied. "It was an accident last night."

"I can't believe you all did such a thing in a caravaner's home," Couyle stated in disgust. "You were never that way in Riverward! Or were you behind some of the small thefts in my bakeshop there?"

"Never," Siah vowed. "None of us have ever stolen anything before." She was blushing in embarrassment now, drying her hands.

"We can do better," Jain replied, meeting his eyes. Joce and Leand came out of the waste chair room, finally done.

"Wash up," Leand stated, indicating the sink. "Breakfast smells like it's almost ready."

"I have these eggs to cook up to add to our breakfast," Riss offered, bringing them out of his gather pouch; they filled both his hands. A smile lit up Aylita's face as she took them and put them into an empty bowl. She tousled his hair playfully and smiled her gratitude.

"I'll get them cooked right away," she assured him. "Thank you, Riss." He gave her a nod as he stepped around her to wash up his hands, too. He didn't want to miss out on breakfast when they'd been out before dawn.

"We have a few things to get straight," Gann told them as the newcomers finished washing their hands. He gestured them to sit at the table, while he took Rowan's seat.

"I'll go get Taroom," Chel volunteered in a low voice to Aylita. She nodded her agreement in return. Chel then gave Amarr, who had woken up with the arrival of the hunters, a piece of warm biscuit before she slipped out the back door.

"Why do you think I should be in the role of an elder here?" Taroom asked as both Aylita and Chel confronted him with what had been done in Rowan's house. The thieves were finishing the last of their clean up and placing things where they belonged, under the watchful eyes of the hunters. Chel had found him finishing up a new bed for Couyle and his new wife for their new home and brought him over to Rowan's. His children were now playing hide and seek in the yard area around them. They were sturdy now and laughing happily, as if the fires had never touched them.

"Of all of those who have come from Riverward, you're the most respected and have a wonderful sense of justice. The rest of us look up to you," Chel insisted.

"I'm not old enough," he protested, grinning and shaking his head.

"Garth's younger than you and look at the way he held command, even better than any of the elders in Riverward. We didn't get much time to actually know him, but I felt he was a fair man. I see that in you, too, my husband," Aylita countered. Gann stepped over and put a hand upon his shoulder for a moment, giving it a light squeeze.

"If not you, then who?" he asked, "You have sense, Taroom, and an idea for a new future. That's what's important," he advised. Taroom sighed and nodded his head as he thought on it for a few moments. He nodded to Gann and the women, feeling they were right in what they asked of him. There was no one else among the survivors who seemed smart enough, nor with enough sense to take the leadership of the others.

"We all need direction. I'll do it, but don't expect me to sit around all day doing nothing," he replied. Gann chuckled at this, nodding his head.

"No one here's fast enough to ever nail your feet to the floor," he teased. This got the rest to laughing merrily and Siah, having finished her part of the chores, stepped out and wondered what had happened to cause such wonderful mirth.

"That's the truth," Aylita agreed. Couyle stepped forward and offered his hand to Taroom in friendship. Surprised, Taroom crossed his palm with his own.

"Thank you. We need a leader like you, Taroom," he assured him with a nod. Taroom smiled at this, amazed at the instant support. Other Riverward survivors streamed over to join in things at the firepit site, having heard his acceptance of the position, many of the adults offering him their hands immediately, too. The children, which came over with them, joined in the fun of the game already started.

"Do you see what we and our children are like now?" Aylita told Siah as she stepped closer. "There's nothing to fear here except what we bring with us. And we're all stronger and healthier once again."

"I noticed," Joce agreed, as he came out and stepped closer too. He slung his very empty backpack over his shoulder and grinned. There were smiles now and their faces weren't thin with that haunted look in their eyes anymore. "What happened?"

"We grow our own food and the village hunters give us a share of their catches. We all share with each other and with the main villagers, so we all have a better life. We work for our food and to upkeep our homes, but none of us ever wants to go back to Riverward, ever," Taroom explained. "If you want to keep doing what you did, you're more than welcome to the east road, go north and take the west road."

"Never," Nali vowed, "we've learned our lesson." None of them looked comfortable at this gathering. So, Taroom stepped forward.

"I believe you," he replied, extending his hand in offer to the newcomers. It was a trust he hoped he'd not regret. Nali crossed his palm and smiled in relief. Siah did too. Joce stepped up looking embarrassed and likewise crossed his palm. And Jain, who was just emerging from the home appeared surprised at the crowd now outside.

"Where do we go now?" Siah asked, not sure what they were going to do.

"You can have your pick of any of the available houses to have as your new home on that side," Gann informed them. He then indicated the ones closer to the river side, "and those ones with the Caravaner's seal over their doors are never to be touched. They'll be back to live in their winter homes, soon enough."

"We can pick out a house and it's ours?" Jain asked in disbelief, stepping closer.

"Come," Taroom invited. "Let's see if one suits you. I'm finishing a new bed for Couyle and will be able to start on ones for you next."

"A new bed?" Siah questioned, smiling at the thought. "But first I want to see this new house."

"Will it have a waist chair room?" Joce asked.

"They all do," Leand assured him with a wicked grin. Joce groaned but smiled. It was still worth it.

That evening, before sunset but just after dinner time, six windracers rode into the riverside part of Matlowe. Gann and Kaytas came out of their home with spears in hand to see who arrived. Minn was quickly down from his mount and strode toward his old friends, giving Kaytas a happy hug.

"What're you doing here, Minn?" Gann demanded; glad it was someone they knew. Still his hugging Kaytas seemed to disturb him now that they were trying free-mating. He let her go to give him a hearty hug, too. It got him to chuckling; letting his tension go.

"I came out to exchange some news and to get a few things that Kort and his family need from their home," he explained as Kort joined them, giving the villagers a nod of his head. "And Ryes sent some medicine supplies for Tanns, and finally Rowan wanted some of the extra yarns he left in his loom room."

"It should only take us a couple of days then we'll be headed back to Winterhaven," Kort told them. "Looks like we have more homes out here with new occupants. Did the villagers finally decide it's better to live here, after all?"

"We have more news for you, too," Gann told them. "Come on, let's get your mounts settled for the night, then we'll talk," he advised. Kort saw a long tale ahead and gave him a nod of agreement, then turned back to his mount to get his saddlebags, first.

Taroom finished telling Kort and Minn his whole story about the disaster, the dangers they'd faced in Riverward and why they'd come all the way out to Matlowe Village to start a new home. The fact that they'd found more than they could ever dream of before in this place, as well as new homes of their own, had been beyond belief. Their new extended family was a priceless treasure he'd never give up now.

Kort listened to it all, nodding grimly in parts, as he'd heard rumors of the fire in his travels. It was the talk across the land. But the details of what followed was far more damning and damaging for the people of Riverward. It'd have to be discussed and actions taken, as soon as was possible. There were over a dozen of the survivors seated around them now. Most appeared well and hardy once again, but some still clearly bore the scars of the trials they'd been forced to withstand.

"We're here to apologize for breaking into Elder Rowan's home and eating some food and breaking some dishes there," Siah said, speaking up into the quiet that followed the story. They had each contributed a part of the telling, making it as complete as possible. "We were ignorant of it being a caravaner home and will do whatever is needed for atonement," she offered, standing and bowing at the waist to Kort, waiting for his judgement. Kort looked at her sharply.

"They did clean up the mess they made and put back everything that had been misplaced," Gann put in, seeing the anger in Kort's eyes. "Rowan had allowed that the hunters could have use of his kitchen until the winter return of your people. That's how we all knew about it right away," he explained. Kort gave him a nod of understanding, knowing the way Rowan liked to do things. It meant that someone could dust and clean the house regularly until they returned. He sighed.

"I don't know what Darman and Rinna will say, as it will be their judgement you'll face. It may be no more than care of the windracers, or time helping with some of the winter shops we set up in Matlowe proper, or just watching the children, but just know that normally trespass is taken very seriously by all caravaners and can lead up to death." He saw four of the people pale and others look uncomfortable. Now he understood why these four were tense all evening long! He grinned then, his eyes mirthful. "Since you did confess to it yourselves, put things back and made sure to clean up the mess you made, that will count in your favor, so I don't believe the death penalty will be involved."

"Thank you, kind sir," she replied, finally relaxing in his company. He gestured her to sit again, which she did, quickly.

"And your news, Minn?" Gann pressed, grinning and glad they all insisted every corner had been cleaned and everything back in its rightful place.

"Winterhaven prospers," he reported first off, trying to be positive. This got smiles and nods of happiness from the other villagers and polite happiness from the others. "The human machines have become a part of our daily lives and make living there very comfortable. We might be further north and will get the snows this winter, but we'll be living through them in unbelievable comfort. Still there's so much to do, now, too. But one of our hunting parties was attacked by a group of plainsmen on windracers, with spears." This got gasps of shock out of his audience.

"Were you on their lands?" Mellas asked, appearing unhappy with this news.

"No, we weren't. We were clearly on our own lands. But we have resourceful women who used the machines stored in Winterhaven to scare off all but two of the raiders. One threw his spear at the machine Ryes rode in and Garth shot him with his bow. The other was thrown by his mount, which ran off and we captured him. Maren healed the one that was dying, bringing him back to full health." This got more murmurs of astonishment from his listeners.

"Since when can Maren heal?" Allis asked, looking indignant over the idea.

"Maren told us he can heal when they stopped here to pick up Rowan," Gann chided him. "Healing runs in his family and he said Ryes used her Catalyst Talent to find his and open it up." The villagers settled down again and Minn gave Gann a nod of thanks.

"So to keep them from constantly attacking us while out doing things on our own lands, Garth and Sabin went out to get a peace treaty established with the Moondance Tribe, or at least an understanding with them to stay away. They've been gone for a couple of months, but we've been in contact with them using a box like this." He held up a communications transmitter for them to see.

"How does that work?" Aylita asked, curious. He gave her a grin in response.

"I'll demonstrate it tomorrow," he assured them with a nod. "And the latest is that Ryes, being Ryes, called down a human starship to land near Winterhaven. We've rescued all the living humans and starmen aboard it and had a huge funeral pyre for the hundreds who didn't make it. It was hard for all of us who live in Winterhaven." The sadness of this part of his story was plainly written upon his eyes and heart.

"It was so very heartbreaking for all our remaining humans, as they lost many good souls," Kort added. "But we're learning a lot of amazing things from those we have left living among us. They've said that since Garth and Ryes and the others found the base, as they call it, it belongs to them, or us, or something like that."

"But Dr. Cruthers still remains in charge for his part of things, which I think is a good thing," Minn added with a smile. "So we've learned human speak which they call English and they've learned Dolbith and we've come together as a new community. And Winterhaven is continuing to thrive and grow. We're expanding the community rooms and Kovin and Phil, along with the computer, are planning on building new above-ground homes for us in the spring."

"You're living underground?" Leand asked, surprised.

"Yes and it's so very comfortable. The air is fresh, we have hot showers and waste chairs and things to learn from the computer and interesting new stories and cultures from the humans, while they're also learning a lot of new things from us."

"It's not a cave," Kort added with a laugh, seeing the looks of puzzlement on the people around them. "It's more like Hailys, the ruined city far to the north. Built on purpose underground, so not to disturb the lands above."

"It sounds scary and wonderful at the same time," Tavis put in, grinning.

"So what're your plans for now?" Kaytas asked, directly, wondering.

"To pick up some things from my home to take back with me. Ryes is planning upon another official visit to Matlowe before the winter storms hit and makes travel harder. I want to make sure that our shops are still in good shape for the rest of my people to set up when they arrive in a few weeks. And just to take advantage of the quiet before things truly start to get busy with Winterfest preparations coming way too soon," Kort related.

"It's late. Let's get to bed and see what tomorrow brings," Minn advised.

"Where are you going to sleep?" Tavis asked frowning as she was trying to think where they could fit them in.

"In my own home," Kort told her with a laugh. "And Minn will be my guest for tonight. So, I wish you all a good night," he said, standing up and giving Minn a nod of his head as he also got to his feet. Goodnights were exchanged then and they were escorted by a merry bunch to Kort's front door.

"This is far more than the toy it appears," Minn assured the other hunters as he readied his bow to demonstrate it. He'd set up a target on a tree a goodly distance away and knew without a doubt he could hit with his arrows, but was too far for his old spear. Gann scoffed, seeing the distance. Minn just grinned, closed his eyes for a moment to listen to and focus upon the breezes rustling the tree-tops around them, then opened his eyes and focused on his target. He loosed his arrow and it flew true and thunked into his target, hitting it squarely on one of the inner rings.

"You didn't aim straight at the target," Gann commented as he eyed the target for a moment, and then tossed his spear with all his might. It fell far short of where he wanted it to go.

"That was a great shot, Minn!" Riss declared, clapping his hands. "Can I try it?" Minn chuckled as he nudged a long packet that lay on the ground near his right foot.

"I brought a few out for the hunters," he told them. This was met with happy laughter and cheers. Kaytas knelt down next to the bundle, looking up to him as if to get permission to open it, as if it was filled with their Winterfest gifts. He gave her a nod of his head. "Be careful, they're not as sturdy as spears." She gave him a nod and carefully opened up the pouch, figuring out the closure quickly. She marveled at the zipper, opening and closing it a few times, then pulled it fully open to expose the bows within. Minn smiled, as she pulled a pair of them out of the bag; holding them up for the others to see. He groaned softly.

"What?" she asked, catching his odd smile.

"I just lost a bet with Shadd," he complained, then sighed. "She bet if a woman were to get the bows out that it would only take a few moments to figure out the zipper's operation." He laughed ruefully and shook his head.

Gann chuckled as he took one of the bow staves, as Kaytas started handing them out to everyone. They just had enough to go around. Minn then opened up the case that had the quivers, as Kovin called them, and the arrows carefully placed within. There were also boxes of extra arrowheads, which he set aside for now for another class, later. They all quickly figured out how to don them, seeing his own. The hunters figured out the cords, too. Soon they were all ready to learn this new tool. He spent the rest of the morning teaching the bows to the hunters. By the afternoon they were almost as good as he was with them; making him very proud.

"I want to talk with you about Mitt," Minn asked after lunch, when he finally got a moment alone with her brother. He gave him a nod, curious about what he wanted. He noted the others were elsewhere and they were alone right now.

"What's she up to now?" he asked, knowing if Garth was gone out on the plains, she was free to make as much trouble in Winterhaven as she could dream up. He realized he might have to go visit the place to see if he could rein her in.

"She's been experimenting with free-mating with the different men in Winterhaven. I don't think she's gone so far as to tempt one of the humans to her bed, yet," he stated, coming right out as he needed her brother's advice. The deep shock in Gann's eyes said it all.

"I forgot… she's old enough for that now," he started, the color drained from his face for a moment.

"She started it before Garth left and I don't think he actually knew what she was up to, but I believe that Ryes has spoken with her about it a few times. She's finally decided that my brother, Mason, is not the one she wants, after all. It kind of crushed him," he told him. "I know she tried Teris once and maybe a few others."

"And?" he pressed, sensing something more.

"She finally has seemed to settle upon me," he admitted, blushing.

"But, you're older than Garth and I and more like Karr's age," he stated, astounded. "Why did she think you're her ideal?"

"Ah," Kort said, stepping closer, having heard it all. "I have the answer to that one," he offered. This appeared to puzzle both men for a moment, and then Minn looked to suddenly understand and gave him a nod and smile. "I heard her first was Ponti, but he did try to keep it secret. He's older than you, Minn, and saw in Mitt the potential for a strong caravaner woman. But Mella came into season and wanted him as her husband, which he accepted, but left Mitt with the idea that she deserved more and she had a whole world in front of her to explore," he explained. "Nahees heard it all from Mella, later."

"Mitt told me as much, too," Minn admitted, "So, now she's trying to teach me how to be better at free-mating. It's amazing what she knows, or wants to try out," he added, shaking his head in wonder, still. This got Kort to laughing while Gann appeared unsure what to feel.

"Gann, at least Minn is known and a good man," Kort stated, sobering a little. "She could do far worse."

Gann finally gave him a nod of his head and sighed, realizing that yes, his sister had the right to decide whom she wanted to bed, or not. And within a year or so, she'd be really for picking her real first. He looked up to meet Minn's eyes, seeing the pain in them with having to be the one to tell him about it all. But he realized he was glad he had. He gripped his shoulder and gave Minn a nod.

"Kort's right, better you than someone who'd only use her uncaringly," he finally said, still feeling a knot in his stomach. Still, it was a choice he could live with, too. Minn appeared relieved.

"I'll take good care of her, for as long as she wants me around," he vowed. Gann gave him a nod, then offered his hand to him. Minn understood the gravity of this moment and crossed his palm, realizing Gann was welcoming him into his family. He gave him a hearty hug afterwards and finally it was all smiles for both of them and Kort.

"And I'm sure she'll take care of you, too," Gann assured him, chuckling. "I trust you, Minn, and I'm sure she does too, or she wouldn't be so close to you." He nodded.

"Winterhaven calling Minn and Kort," they heard a voice sounding from Minn's pocket. He laughed as he pulled out his communicator.

"We're both here, Mitt," he said, holding down the button. "What's the problem?"

"With Garth still gone, I am not losing track of anyone else," she replied. Minn gave Gann a nod and held the box near him so he could speak, too.

"So, you drove Garth so far up a tree that he had to run off to the plains?" Gann teased with a laugh.

"Gann?" they heard her cry out. "How're doing? How's everyone else? And don't you dare tell me about Karr, first!" Gann was unable to do more than laugh for a few minutes. Which got everyone else around him laughing too, as the other hunters heard and gathered near, too. A few of the new villagers out of Riverward approached with curiosity written in their eyes.

Chance

"Rand! Lixi! Aravan! Alden! Jons! What're you cubs doing running in the hallways?" Ryes demanded, as she was just about to enter the Botany Sciences lab where her gathered plants were stored. She needed to get them sorted and processed. She'd sneaked out for a short gathering trip for a few more plants, fruits and nuts late yesterday afternoon after Kort and Minn returned with news from Matlowe. If by sneaking out she meant it was with four armed men and women. But, it was the first time she realized she was homesick deep down inside. Her new home here was quickly filling the space within, but there were times when she did miss the house by the Yuri River.

"Ryes!" Jons shouted, turning and running back to her, smiling. Ryes smiled as she shook her head, dropping down to her knees. The cubs all crowded around her, laughing and telling her about all the wonderful new things they found here, while giving her hugs and kisses. She laughed with them, giving them each the attention she used to dole out. "And grandmother says if it weren't for you and Garth, we'd never know how miserable we were in that ol' village," Jons told her, then hugged her once more.

"I'm glad your father let you come here with us. Let's hope he and your mother will move here, too," she said, then saw Damian Hacker rushing down the hall toward them.

"Ah, there you munchkins are," he scolded, relieved. "Are they bothering you, Ma'am? They ran off as I was closing the classroom," he told her, visibly fighting the urge to salute her. It was hard having to learn to behave so informally, but he found he didn't miss having to wear the uniforms! Ryes laughed lightly at this, giving him a shake of her head.

"No. These precious cubs are the only villagers I used to spend my time with before. Where're you going?" she asked them.

"We're going out to ride Honey," Lixi told her, a merry look in her eyes.

"Oh, great! Honey probably feels like we're all neglecting her, now that I have so many other things to take care of. I'm counting on you cubs to take good care of her, for me," she told them, smiling.

"We will!" Alden assured her as the rest chimed in their agreement. She gave them each a hug and kiss, then stood back up.

"Now, I'm also counting on you to mind Damian and do what he says," she added. There was a chorus of agreement from the cubs, then they joined hands at his urging, taking his hands, too.

They continued down the corridor, singing and laughing as they went. Ryes sighed as she turned for the door she was standing outside of. More things to get finished, still... She wished she could've been allowed to go to Matlowe with the others, but knew of Garth's injunction and would never go against his direct order - even if he wasn't here. They left yesterday and should be arriving today; sometime after lunch. She went into the Botany Lab itself.

"Hello, can I help you?" Dr. Wynne Baights asked as the native woman entered her lab. Ryes smiled, giving her a nod of her head.

"I've got to finish sorting the plants I collected, yesterday. Bethy said this is where she put them. If I'm in your way, I'll just take them elsewhere," she offered, then extended her hand. "My name's Ryes," she introduced herself.

"Yes, I recall you and that other young man were the ones to revive us," she replied with a smile, shaking her offered hand, in the human manner. "Thank you for that! So these plants are yours? I was told to keep my hands off, until you had the chance to take care of things, yourself."

"Yes, I need to get them sorted, some set to drying and others delivered to the kitchen. Maybe next time I go out, if you want come along, we can gather plants together?" she suggested, smiling, appreciating her very human solidness. "Sorry, I didn't realize how they piled up from my two trips out," she commented seeing the bins on the tables near the door.

"Oh, you've GOT to go with me!" Dr. Baights demanded, excited over the prospect of learning directly from one of the natives. The plants she had here were impressive and she wanted to know all about them. "We'll just take a quick afternoon jaunt out. No one will miss us, I assure you," she promised. Ryes smiled, knowing if anyone in this place would be "missed," it'd be her.

"The main team should be arriving in Matlowe, shortly, and I must see what kind of reception they'll receive. Perhaps tomorrow? That way we can take our time and I can show you more than we could cover in one short afternoon," she counter suggested. The chief botanist looked disappointed, but realized she was probably right. A whole day was far better than one afternoon.

"Alright, but I'm holding you to that one," she vowed, smiling. "Now, tell me about what you've gathered and why. I need to record all this and get samples and sketches." Ryes laughed, giving her a nod of her head. "Let me get Brenda in here to help," she decided, reaching for her call box.

"Computer?" Ryes called out, looking up towards the camera in the ceiling, nearest them. "Please ask Brenda Reed to join us in this laboratory," she ordered it.

"Affirmative," it responded, then relayed the request.

"My, it does seem to like you," Dr. Baights commented, frowning in surprise as she considered the unappreciated command this native had over the facility. Ryes laughed merrily.

"Neil taught me well and ever since Dr. Cruthers told the computer that I'm the Chief Executive Officer of Winterhaven, it's response time has improved even more so. I think as long as either Dr. Cruthers, or myself remain in the facility, it's fine. So, tomorrow might have to do for our little outing, since Dr. Cruthers is on his way to Matlowe Village," she said. Brenda appeared in the doorway, just as she was telling Wynne this, and smiled.

"We're going out with you tomorrow?" she asked. "Great! I can't wait!" She stepped over to the women, all smiles. "So, do you get as much sleep as you'd like to, anymore?" she teased.

"Nowhere near as much," Ryes agreed as Brenda laughed in understanding. Her own baby was due soon. "We need your help in recording information as I go over these plants I collected, yesterday." Wynne chuckled, not used to having someone else order a member of her staff, in her own lab. "Oh, I forgot to ask how Teris and Shadd are doing?" Ryes asked, turning back to the older woman. "Have they been much help?"

"They've been wonderful, but both have told me if I really want to know more, I have to talk to you. But, I didn't know who you were until you walked in and introduced yourself," she admitted, as she took out her digital scanner, set up her dissection scope and brought up its monitor. Brenda brought out fresh log books and the plant presses they'd need for the samples.

"I would guess because it's taken me all my life to learn what little I have," Ryes admitted, laughing lightly. "I don't consider myself an expert, though. My Aunt Tanns is fairly knowledgeable, as is Rinna, who's Tara's mother, a caravaner and wife to Darman. They're still on the road and won't be back until the winter starts to hit. Either we can go visit them when they get to Matlowe, or perhaps we can talk Darman into spending the winter with us. At any rate, I can show you what little I know, at least," she offered.

"And modest," Wynne added, in comment, causing Brenda to break out in laughter as she sat down at the work table. "Let's get started," she suggested, now ready to begin.

"Ryes?" Shadd said as she entered the Botany lab. She saw them studying a plant under the dissection scope, and she was telling them something about it as they viewed it up close. Ryes turned her head and smiled her greeting.

"Hi Shadd, how can I help you?" she asked, as she looked relieved to find her.

"I forgot, before Bethany left she gave me some recordings from your time in the field last week gathering plants and she also was asking Teris and I about what could be done with that field we had to use for the pyres," she said, extending a box to her.

"Oh, the recordings Dotti made," she confirmed, smiling as she took it and handed it over to Wynne. "This might be more for you than me," she admitted. "It was from our outing last week when Dr.

Cruthers ordered me to take a day off." Wynne took it as if it were made of fragile glass, which got Ryes to chuckling. "I don't know how useful it might be," she added, "but if you could send me a copy, I'd appreciate it."

"It's a start, and a promise for tomorrow," she replied, smiling. "I'll look at it after lunch and send your copy over," she said, setting it over on her desk.

"About that field," Shadd started, then frowned. "Can you do something for it, like you and Maren did for healing the humans?" she blurted out. Ryes eyes took on a look of speculation, and then mischief danced in their emerald depths.

"I can try," she replied. "It's a great idea!" Shadd was grinning while the human women were puzzled.

"What do you mean?" Brenda asked, stepping closer. Ryes turned to grin at her merrily.

"I can try and we'll see," she said. "Let's go see," she offered, having had enough time in the lab today. She wondered how they managed it? "Let's get Teris to join us," she added, "He has good plant sense." It took a few moments to get the two humans convinced to come along, then they all headed outside and over to the broad, open field near the Star Quest where the charred ashes still remained and scarred what had been lush and green before.

"It does look sad," Brenda commented as Ryes spread out a blanket she snagged on the way out of the building. Teris ran up to join them, all smiles.

"Sit down, and let's join hands to see what I can do with your help here," Ryes offered, indicating the blanket. Her long red hair was blowing into her face, so by the time she pulled it back behind her ear, she saw the others had taken her up on her offer and were taking places on the blanket.

"What do we do?" Wynne asked, noting Shadd and Teris had closed their eyes and looking to be trying to relax while still appearing very excited about something.

"Very simple," Ryes advised, noting Monty was now standing nearby with a pistol strapped on his waist. She gave him a nod of understanding. "Simply close your eyes, relax and join hands." She got nods from the women as she sat down between Wynne and Shadd. She did as she told the women and prepared herself. Then she reached out to the others, grasping their hands and from within, too. Once she got them calmed down about being able to share their thoughts with each other, she unleashed both her Empath and Healing Talents.

"I don't recall all the details of what was here before," she admitted, puzzled as she reached out to the field to feel the way the life had been as deeply snuffed out in it as the people sadly burned upon it. There was a pit filled with ashes that was clear to her senses.

"Why not ask Mother Tayna herself?" Shadd suggested, seeing it all herself through Ryes clearly. Teris clearly supported this idea.

"Is she like Gaia? The spirit of the Earth?" Brenda asked, amazed.

"I think so," Ryes replied. She deepened her Empath Talent and delved deeper into her world to find Tayna, herself. She welcomed them into her heart and gave Ryes a deeper understanding of how to feel the rightness of the land, itself. Then they were released.

Wynne was starting to believe it was all a shared dream until this moment. She had her heart touched, understood and welcomed by the spirit of this world. It was beyond anything she could've ever imagined! Amazed, she hung on, now seeing Ryes had more direction and purpose.

Using her combination of other Talents, she delved deep into the earth and broke down the charred remains of those who hadn't made it back to Tayna. She used the rich carbon and refined it further using her Manipulator and then using her Healing Talent, she found the seeds Tayna had sensed all around them in the ground and encouraged them to sprout and grow using the nutrients she'd released. Now Wynne started to add her own direction to what Ryes was doing, making it a more complete task. Teris pulled up his own Talent, which was a specialized Empath Talent just for plants. All of them scattered and directed the plants in the field, encouraging their healing and growth, taping Ryes' and Teris' Talents. Finally they opened their eyes and it took several moments to realize what they had sitting before them.

"I think we need to cut back the jungle now," Monty commented, grinning; having watched the whole thing happen. They were all laughing as they stood up. Wynne grabbed her and wrapped her arms about Ryes in a warm hug.

"I don't know how to ever let you go, young lady," she commented. "You're a blessing from above!" Ryes laughed, blushing, as Wynne did release her.

"Well, we've solved the problem with this field," Teris commented, smiling happily.

"Oh, I forgot," she groaned out, shaking her head. "I never took you to see a tree!" Teris laughed, nodding his head.

"Maybe we could do that one tomorrow?" Brenda suggested, smiling. "I'd like to see what a tree spirit's like, too."

"So would I," the other two women chimed in, laughing.

"Let's go to lunch," Ryes suggested, shaking her head as she grinned. "I could use something after all that work." They turned to survey the field again, pride in all their eyes.

"I forgot to record it," Wynne suddenly groaned out, amazed with herself.

"I got it," Monty assured her, smiling as he held up his minicomp and she then noted the small drone flying over his head. She sighed in relief. They finally gathered up the blanket and headed in for lunch, as he sent the file to her minicomp, as well as Ryes.'

"The scanners indicate this should be the opening below. There are stairs leading down to a big door," Jim Dawe told Dr. Cruthers and Bethany in English, as they stood in the middle of the Village Circle. Maren frowned as he thought on this. Ryes jumped out of her chair, getting closer to the pickup, surprising Neil.

"Tell them to leave it alone and to keep speaking in English only," Ryes ordered Jim. He looked puzzled, not understanding why.

"Ryes says to leave it alone and for us to speak only in English," he relayed, tapping his earpiece. This brought surprise to the faces of the others gathered near him, who understood.

"Please ask her why?" Dr. Cruthers inquired, needing to understand her reasoning. She seemed to display sound thinking, most times. Was this something she considered sacred, he wondered?

"Tell Dr. Cruthers that we'll leave it for the spring. Once Garth is back, we can all go together. I don't want it revealed because the remaining villagers might try to open it and tamper with whatever lies below. For all we know, the place could be trapped, if it was sealed when the attack fell upon Hailys. This is the hardest thing in the world for me, but don't let its location be revealed, if at all possible," she explained. Jim repeated what she said, word for word, as she said it. Maren gave his nod of agreement.

"She's right. They could make their own try at excavation and either ruin what might be down there, or get killed if it's important enough to those who buried and forgot it," he advised, staying to the English. This was becoming pretty handy, as they could speak freely without the villagers understanding a word. Their arrival by rovers had almost given the elders spastic attacks and panicked the rest. Maren smiled to himself. The memory of his father staggering in shock as he casually stepped out from behind the wheel of one of these great machines, was one he'd cherish for years to come.

"A point well taken," Ethan agreed, smiling. "This is only supposed to be a day's jaunt out to the Village, not an encampment and full excavation. We don't have the proper equipment with us, after all."

"Metta? Where's the Book of Truth?" Maren asked, suddenly recalling something, which might actually be of some help. The elder looked surprised to be so addressed, but then, these young cubs were behaving rudely toward everyone today. Their pet hoomans seemed more mannered, at least.

"You're no longer of Matlowe. You don't have the right," he decided, denying him a chance to look at it.

"It's not a real book, but only a reader," Maren explained. "Let Dr. Cruthers and his assistant get a look at it, at least," he requested, knowing he was being short with the old man. But, he was responsible for things out here today and was tired of the delays they'd had with these slow people!

"Your hooman elder?" he asked, as Ethan gave him a nod of his head in affirmation.

"Yes, I'm Dr. Cruthers," he said, in perfect Dolbith. "Could I get a look at this book of yours? I would be most grateful." Metta looked mollified by his courtesy, so gave him a nod of his head and went to retrieve the precious artifact.

"I don't know if it's still operational, but you never know," Maren explained, grinning. Rowan joined them, all smiles. "I wish I'd brought a crystal rod with me."

"We've finished loading our things from the houses by the Yuri," he confirmed. "I've invited two of the other families there to make free use of the one the ladies had picked as their own. I don't think we'll ever be coming back here to live, but I can't answer for Darman and Rinna."

"No, I don't think so, either," Minn agreed, joining the group, smiling. "I just finished getting Marla and Garvin's things they wanted and had to practically fight Karr to get it done. If she were my older sister, I'd rather be out on the plains, too," he commented, smiling.

"There're times when I do feel sorry for Glyn," Maren agreed with a chuckle. "I wonder how long it'll be before she realizes that Mitt's slipped the leash for good? She only listens to Garth and Ryes, and that's about it."

"She minds Axel pretty well," Bethany reminded them with a smile. "But that's only because if she doesn't, he won't let her go out flying. He was saying she's a natural, for the amount of time she's been behind the stick and is pretty good at it. From him, that's high praise," she assured them.

"I can't believe she's picked me," Minn said with a smile.

"She wants cubs of her own, but someone with some intelligence, caring and a heart," Maren explained, with a knowing smile.

"Right!" Minn gave him a nod. "That's why she dumped Mason the way she did. Your father," he said. "My father, Rusan, died trying to save my younger brother, Roos, when one of those old houses he was playing in collapsed. Our mother, Minna, died of a broken heart, shortly thereafter. He used to treat Mason as if he were his own son, too. It was hard for me to watch after him, after all that and this thing with Mitt really has him confused. I'll have a talk with him when we get back. Thanks, Maren," he said, giving him a nod of his head. Maren smiled, glad to have helped straighten this out now, before it became a real problem. Mitt was serious about Minn as her choice.

"So, you and Mason have the same father?" Bethany asked, wondering if she understood them correctly.

"Yes. Our father was a terror upon the women of Matlowe, for too many years. Hopefully, things have quieted down a little, since Garth defeated him."

"Here's our great book," Metta said, rejoining them. He was carrying a very ornate, gaudily painted version of the simple "readers" they found in the old buildings of Hailys. Dr. Cruthers looked delighted as he turned to examine this treasure. Jim had his scanner out, taking his readings.

"I take it, you're not too fond of him, yourself?" Bethy whispered in English. Maren huffed a laugh at this, giving her a nod of his head.

"I had the misfortune to be raised in the one house he considered his own. Let's say I know him too well and know the way I could NEVER be. I don't know if I'll ever forgive my mother for taking him in and defending him, after all the lives he's taken and people who've suffered because of him," he whispered, likewise in English; his eyes dark as he recalled witnessing too much of his father's cruelty. This surprised Bethy, as she realized she needed to ask Ryes what this father of Maren's had done, to rate such hatred from such an otherwise, gentle man.

Minn saw the look in his eyes and understood more of both his half-brother's mind and Maren's. Mason never had to LIVE with what Korman had done, as Maren had. Mason didn't consider Korman to be the cruel danger Maren knew him to be. Perhaps Maren could be the key to saving Mason from trying to repeat Korman's brutality? He had to talk with both him and Raya. He didn't want to see Mason start down Korman's path, if he could help it! Not that the women in Winterhaven would ever let him, he thought, amused.

It took almost six days to reach the plains tribes' Great Gathering grounds. Since the supplies and equipment they brought were only designed to shelter the two of them, they ended up having to bargain with one of the plainsmen to obtain a proper tent and equipment, so they could house their women, too. All-in-all, they considered the cost of one windracer well worth it. They still had plenty of mounts for the women and to carry their things.

"You're in great luck," Shins reported as they just finished pitching their tent and were placing their things inside. "The caravaners are still here, including their great chief, Darman."

"Darman's here?" Garth asked, surprised and delighted. He recalled the old man from the many times he came to the Village Circle to demonstrate his great, magical abilities for the cubs on Winterfest Day. He was the one man Ryes loved almost as much as Rowan; considering him like a grandfather, too. "Please take me to him," he urged, checking to make sure he still had his transmitter in his pocket. He'd made sure the charge was fresh as they rode, earlier today. Shins looked surprised at this request, and then gave him a bow of respect. Now that they were among the great elders, he and the others were showing Garth and Sabin far more respect than they had before. It amused them both.

151

        "Immediately," he replied as Garth caught Sabin's eye, giving him a nod of his head to come along and told Dodi they'd be back soon. They followed him through the maze of tents and campfires, with cubs running and playing happily among them. There were knots of people gathered round to hear stories, or to discuss matters. There were circles where warriors wrestled, or fought each other with clubs, or old swords, in contest. There were people sitting on colorful blankets, selling things in a small market area. It looked to be a huge gathering, with a feeling akin to Winterfest Day. Finally, they reached the great vans, lined up in several rows with the fires and socializing going on between them.

        "What do you need?" a man stood and challenged them, as they came up to the largest campfire. Others nearby noted their presence, too.

        "A few minutes to speak with Darman," Garth replied, starting to feel a little nervous. He hadn't spoken directly to Darman in years, and then that had been to request a piece of sweets he was passing out to everyone. "We're here, originally from Matlowe," he explained. The look in the man's eyes was one of pure shock.

        "Just a moment. I'll go announce you. May I have your names?" he asked. Garth smiled at this.

        "Garth, and tell him Ryes is now my wife. And this is Sabin, my blood-brother," he introduced them. There arose a cheer and laughter, as others quickly stood to come to them, surprising Shins, greatly. Garth was grabbed and hugged and kissed and fussed over as the caravaners asked him a thousand questions about how Ryes was faring and how did they escape Korman?

        "Actually, at their second challenge, Garth defeated Korman. The first one Rowan called a draw, or he would've beaten him then, too," Sabin bragged as Garth laughed his agreement.

        "You defeated Korman and freed Ryes?" a voice asked, sounding astonished, coming up behind them. They turned to see the old wizard, now standing with them, beaming at them merrily.

        "Yes, and we have cubs due at the end of the winter. We're living in a new place which Ryes named Winterhaven," he affirmed with a smile. Darman opened up his arms and wrapped them about Garth, laughing in joy.

        "It's about time!" he declared. "Come my son, tell us more," he urged, gesturing them to sit near the fire. It was getting chilly tonight, so they readily agreed, making themselves more comfortable. They related the whole tale, taking turns to add in details as needed, astonishing those gathered `round to hear it. There was a plainsman elder sitting among them, too. He was delighted and very interested in everything they had to say. Shins listened closely, having never heard this tale before. Everyone in the camp had sat near to hear it, too.

        "And so Ryes lent you her Badge of Passage?" Darman asked. Garth nodded his head to this, then pulled out both the parchment he wrote out himself, years ago and the letter Ryes wrote to go with it. He handed them over to Darman with a smile.

"She knew it might come down to my having to present myself to Dara, so gave these to me to show him," he explained. Darman handed back his own note, knowing it well already. He opened the other and nodded his head; smiling as he read it.

"It's her handwriting and she surely sounds happy to be able to excuse herself because she's carrying your cubs," he agreed. He handed it over to the plainsman elder who read it, then gave it to Rinna, who read it next and smiled as tears sprang to her eyes. She gave it back to the plainsman.

"She does sound happy about it," he stated, smiling; his eyes merry as he handed it back to Garth.

"She was complaining about them squirming too much now, for her to get enough sleep, last week," Sabin added in comment. This got the others to wondering. If she was back in Winterhaven, how could they know of her complaints? Garth saw their doubt and surprise and took out his transmitter.

"We talk with our wives when we have news to pass onto them," he explained. "It's one of the human's transmitters and is very handy, indeed." He activated it. "Hello Winterhaven," he spoke.

"This is Winterhaven. Is that you, Garth?" Gleds asked, sure it had to be him.

"Yes, it is, Gleds. Is Ryes about? I have someone who wants to speak with her," he said.

"I'll call her in, right away! Computer, please call Ryes into the control room, immediately. Tell her Garth is calling for her."

"Affirmative," it responded, as they sat there, everyone around them suddenly going silent, as they listened, too. Garth had the volume up all the way, so they could.

"It looks like she's on the way," Gleds told him, chuckling. "She yells at the cubs for running in the hallways, and now she's doing it, herself," he explained, amused. Garth and Sabin chuckled with him at this, understanding.

"Garth? Is that you?" she asked, out of breath and laughing happily. "Are you on your way back home, yet?"

"Not quite. Hold on a moment," he said as he held it closer for Darman to speak to her.

"Ryes? How're you doing, child?" he asked, seeing the joy in her husband's face. Yes, he was attached to her, deeply.

"Darman? What're you doing out there? Shouldn't you be heading in toward Matlowe, by now?" she demanded, laughing. "I'm fine and Rowan's here with us in Winterhaven." Darman laughed with her, nodding his head. It was her, most definitely.

"We'll be headed that way very soon. How's Rowan doing? Is everything in Matlowe all right?" he asked. It was so strange to think of Matlowe without Rowan living there.

"There's been some kind of trouble back east and a lot of new people have moved into Matlowe. Most are living in the houses near

the river bank. Rowan made sure they left your homes alone, but
gave up Tara's house and the empty ones for them to use. He's
pretty happy here in Winterhaven though, except for complaining of
no river's voice to help him go to sleep at night," she informed him,
knowing this was something he'd need to know. "We also intercepted
Kort's van and Maren, my cousin, healed Nils and the others. We built
a shelter outside to house his van, and they've decided to stay here
with us through the winter." There were voices raised in relief at this
news.

"So, this Winterhaven of yours is near our road?" Darman
asked, wondering where they were living now?

"Kort went out and marked it for you, and we made a good
trail in, using the shuttles," she explained. "So, if you want to drop by
and visit, or stay the winter, you're all more than welcome," she
invited, smiling to herself. "You can't miss it, it's the tower with the
bright, flashing lights on top of it," she added, mischievously.

"Ryes, is there anything special you want us to bring for
you?" Rinna asked, trying to get closer to the magic box.

"Grandmother Rinna! No, I'm fine, but maybe some clothes
for some new infants would be nice," she asked, grinning happily. "I'll
need them for the end of the winter." Rinna laughed and nodded.

"I'll make them myself," she promised. "We need to talk, my
cubling."

"Thank you, so much," she told her, meaning it from the
heart. "We will talk! I promise," she assured her, "we'll have the
whole winter to spend together!" Rinna laughed as she nodded her
head. Darman edged in closer to the box, once again.

"Then we'll look for your tower and visit you, at least," he
promised. "See you soon, cub. Be good," he told her. He heard her
laughing at this.

"I have to be good now, or Garth will get upset with me," she
teased. "He already knows all my tickle spots and loves to drive me
crazy!" Garth blushed, laughed and nodded his head at this. Sabin
clasped him on the shoulder, laughing too. Darman chuckled as he
gestured for Garth to talk with her, himself.

"So, everything there's fine?" he asked her, again.

"Well, Karr was a headache to get settled in," she admitted.
"We didn't expect her to join us. The rest of the villagers who were
coming and a few of the new families from out of the east, just moved
in today, so the place is in a little pandemonium. Other than that, not
much going on," she informed him. Ardis sat down next to her,
smiling.

"You should've seen Karr's face when Mitt turned on her heel
and walked off when she was trying to order her around," Ardis told
him, as Ryes chuckled.

"Garth? Do I have to do what Karr tells me to do?" Mitt
demanded, stepping up closer behind the two women.

"No you don't, Mitt," he assured her. "You're old enough to do as you see fit, even if it isn't always the wisest thing as the rest of us see it," he scolded, smiling.

"I love you and miss you. When are you going to come back home?" she demanded, frowning.

"I love you and miss you too, sis. We'll be on our way home, as soon as we get this peace treaty approved," he promised. "Ryes? I love you," he added.

"I love you and surely miss you; especially at night!"

"Sabin, are you there?" Ardis asked.

"Of course I am, wife of mine," he assured her, grinning. "What took you so long to get to the control room?"

"We've been painting a mural in the dining room and I was working on it when I heard you two were calling," she said. "I love you and miss you so terribly much!"

"A mural?" he asked, wondering. "I love you! You'd better be taking care of yourself," he scolded.

"You too," she quipped back, grinning with mischief in her eyes. "Do you think you'll be home by Winterfest Day?" she asked. "It's seemed like what was only supposed to be a few days, has now stretched into months. You're supposed to be here for these cubs, you know," she scolded.

"It may be around Winterfest Day, with all the stuff we have to pack and carry, now," Garth commented. "We've got to go. I'll show Darman our planned route on the maps and see what he thinks of it," he told Ryes.

"Great! He taught me to read the maps, long ago. I know he'll love those aerial views! You two be very careful. We're waiting here for you."

"Good-bye. I love you, Ryes," he told her, then the caravaners raised their voices in wishing her their good-byes, too.

"Good-bye, Ardis," Sabin shouted, too. "I love you!"

"Good-bye. We miss you two," the others now gathered in the control room shouted, as well as adding in other wishes. After a few moments, Garth turned off the transmitter with a heavy sigh.

"Amazing box," Darman commented. "Can it only talk with the people at Winterhaven?" he asked, thinking it'd make a fine addition to any caravan, out on the roads. Instant communication with others - just as was said from ancient times!

"They're the only ones who can receive the signal this one puts out, as far as I know," he admitted, as he put it away in his pocket. "Give us time to get to know the human machines better. We may have more available soon for others to use, given time," he hedged, thinking it wouldn't be beyond their capabilities. This small comment got the people in the encampment very excited, indeed. Even Shins looked thoughtful, as he considered the implications such a device held.

"What's this peace treaty you need to settle with the plainsmen?" the plains elder asked them, his eyes bright and sharp.

Shins realized who he was, recognizing his voice, and was suddenly afraid to be noticed.

"All we wanted was an understanding with the Moondance Tribe to mind their own hunting markers and to let us hunt in peace upon the lands we claim as our own. If their need were ever great enough, we were leaving them the option to come speak with us about the matter and see if we could make some kind of arrangements with them. We're not cruel, nor a heartless people, but after Toron and his party attacked us upon our own land, unprovoked, we felt we'd better get things settled right away. Dyan and his council have been adding all kinds of stipulations and it's grown into a nightmare. He wants Dara to approve it now, before he'll let us go home. We thought to try to get a delay until the spring, since our wives are due to have their cubs soon, but knew we had to come out here to ask for permission to use the badge Ryes lent me, anyway," he explained, as he tapped it upon his shoulder.

"Do you have copies of this treaty with you?" the elder questioned.

"Back in our tent," Sabin supplied. "We have copies of what we originally proposed and what Dyan wants."

"Please, go fetch them. I want to see this nightmare," he urged. Garth shrugged his shoulders, looking to Sabin. He smiled and gave him a nod of his head. Perhaps this elder could give it a look and advise them of a good approach to use, when presenting it to Dara, himself?

"You stay here, Garth. I'll go get them," he offered.

"I'll go with you," one of the caravaner men stated, standing up. Shins looked surprised, but bowed his head in acknowledgment. His duty was now as guardian and escort to these two strangers, since Garth bore the Badge of Passage.

"Thank you," Garth told the both of them as they turned to leave.

"So, are these your first cubs?" Darman questioned, recalling seeing Garth many times in the Village. He always seemed so quiet, before. He didn't look like a man who could best someone like Korman, but with the added furs, it was hard to truly tell.

"Yes, they are. I've wanted Ryes as my own since we were cubs, but never thought she'd ever want me. She forgave me for all the mean things I did to her, when I should've known better in my youth. There's never been anyone else. We're true-mates, now," he told him, unsure how this man would take such news. He looked startled, as surprised laughter broke out from those gathered around them.

"Then, you're a part of our family, too!" he declared and gestured for the leather mugs to be filled and passed out. By the time Sabin and the caravaner returned, the celebration was well underway. There was dancing, food and ale being passed out to everyone in their camp, and laughter filled the air. Sabin was amazed and managed to get back to the main fire through the press of the reveling caravaners and presented the copies to Garth.

Garth took the copies and bowed as he presented them to the elder he now knew was Dara, himself. It was explained to him that he was a cousin and blood-brother to Darman and had wintered in Matlowe once with the caravaners, when Ryes was about four years old. He remembered her well, which was one reason he gave the badge to Darman for her use, when she got older.

He took several long minutes to look over Dyan's version, then ripped it apart, casting it into the fire. He looked at Garth's, made a few corrections, and showed it to him. He nodded his head in agreement, then signed it and placed the new seal they'd made for this occasion, of the Great Phoenix, upon it. Dara studied his seal for several long moments, nodding his head in approval. He signed it and added his seal, too. He had Shins sign for his grandfather and place his seal upon the treaty, then had Darman add his signature and seal, as the witness. Dara ordered Shins to get his scribe to record the parchment, handing it back to Garth for safekeeping, in the meantime. Garth laughed, relieved to have this chore finished, at last! Now they could start on their way home!

Being Human and Starman

"Where did you say we could put our things?" Kaspin asked a man passing them, but he never heard her, as she realized she'd spoken barely above a whisper. She paused looking around. In truth she actually had little to call her own, but still wanted to find a small corner to call her own, once again. This place was huge! Her younger sister, Keffa was glued to her side, fear in her eyes with the strangeness around them.

"Ladies, come this way please," Ptan requested with a big smile. They returned her smile in relief. She led the women down a corridor, then down the stairs, as they were lightly burdened, to the living quarter's area. The main doorways to the lab areas on this level were closed and locked for now, as was the one that lead to the conference rooms, offices and control room on the main level. The stairs below had their doors sealed too. They wanted their new arrivals to get settled before they started trusting them fully.

"This place is so big for being underground," Keffa commented as she stopped and turned to face them again. Ptan nodded, her brown eyes alit with humor.

"It took me a while to get comfortable here, since I'm from the plains, but I've found it feels like home and I know I'm very safe in this place," she admitted, placing a protective hand on her growing belly. "Oh and my name is Ptan."

"My name is Kaspin and this is my sister, Keffa," she introduced them. She gave them a nod of her head in response, still smiling. People were passing them in the corridors, some bearing boxes, some just looking lost. She raised a hand and indicated a smaller side corridor.

"Here's where we can get you some fresh bedding." They followed her over to a huge closet which was filled with blankets, pillows and bed clothes. Both women stood astounded.

"And we can pick what we like?" Keffa asked, unsure if she understood her.

"Of course. And once a week you can get fresh bed clothes and blankets if you like. You put your soiled ones in this chute, and they go down to the laundry room. Pillows too, if needed," she explained, showing them the chute. They looked down into the darkness, amazed. Ptan helped them pick out some items, so now their arms were full, but they had happy grins plastered across their faces. Keffa kept hugging her pillow, appearing joyful.

"This seems so much," Kaspin commented in a low voice. Ptan shook her head in denial. "I've never had a pillow in my whole life!"

"It's a small thing. And once you get your chore assignments, you can help contribute to the community here and earn it fairly." This got a nod out of both women as they'd been told this before. Another group arrived at the bedding supply closet and she ushered out her charges as Bethy waited, appearing not to want to get their groups mixed up. She and Ptan exchanged a brief hug, then Ptan urged her pair back out toward the main hall.

"Those different people seem so friendly," Keffa commented, finally relaxing a little. Their guide nodded agreement, smiling.

"Where're you from?" she asked as they walked further away from the stairs.

"We come from back east," Kaspin replied, unhappy with the reminder. "It was nice in Matlowe Village, but we heard of Korman and thought this might be a safer place to live. We're only two women, after all," she explained.

"The women here in Winterhaven do not allow challenges. You are both free to pick the men you want to mate with, if they agree to the mating, too," she explained. This had both women stunned, as they stopped in the middle of the hall to absorb this idea.

"You're making fun?" Kaspin questioned. Ptan stopped and looked back, then stepped up to them, smiling again.

"My husband and I ran away from our plains tribe so we could be together in peace and now we're having our first cub. For all of us here it's a very serious matter. If anyone tries to force himself on you, please let any woman bearing this symbol know," she displayed the firebird on her shirt's shoulder, "and we'll make it stop. It's not allowed. Ever. This is the first home in my whole life where I've felt truly free," she admitted. They saw she wore a very colorful tunic, but the firebird was there to be clearly seen. They saw it on the shirts and tunics of several others – both men and women - in the hallway and nodded. A big smile blossomed on Kaspin' face at hearing this news.

"But what can a woman do against a strong man?" Keffa asked, still worried. Ptan chuckled merrily.

"We have many strong Talents here and don't truly need a man to back us," she advised. There was surprise at this but they both nodded.

"Thank you," both replied, smiling with this news.

"Oh, I pity the man that even tries anything whether or not Ryes is home to do something about it," Ted commented, having heard their discussion as he was headed back to get another party of newcomers. "I don't get it Ptan, where I come from it's called rape and the guy would be jailed for some years."

"I think Ryes was saying it was a custom started on Kahmarr thousands of years ago. But I agree, no man should ever think he can abuse a woman whenever he feels he wants to," she replied, shaking her head. "In my tribe the men sometimes own the women, as if they're property, unless her family's strong and protects her." He shook his head grimly at hearing her.

"Slavery should be outlawed, no matter which sex is involved," he stated. She sighed and nodded.

"I agree," Kaspin added in comment. He gave her a grin and nodded.

"Which is why we don't allow it here in Winterhaven," he assured her. "If you can't reach a woman, stop any man who wears the Firebird, or Phoenix as we call it, on their shirts. Or run to Medical. You'll have more help than you'd expect, immediately," he assured both women, smiling for them.

"Ladies, my I introduce Ted of House Turner who is one of our wonderful medical doctors, who will take care of you at need if you get sick or injured," Ptan introduced him, smiling grandly. They both laughed and she gave him a quick hug, then he gave the newcomers a small bow.

"Today I'm tour guide. I've got to go help," he told them and headed back for anyone else who might be waiting.

"Now, do you want separate rooms, or do you want to be together in one?" Ptan asked, curious. "If you want rooms next to each other, that's easy. We also have some with connecting doors inside, but we usually save those for parents who have small children," she explained. She saw the surprise on their faces, once more.

"Together," Kaspin said with surety in her voice.

"Next to each other," Keffa stated, then grinned as she glanced over at her sister, as she blushed. "I don't need to be coddled any more, Kaspin; I'm better now." Kaspin appeared to be about to protest, but then sighed in surrender.

"Next to each other," she finally agreed. Ptan nodded, glad they both decided. She led them over to show them where the main bathroom was and their rooms.

Ardis finally rounded up the last of the newcomers. She'd made sure everyone took a shower and put on fresh, clean clothes. Then got them to the dining hall, as half her thoughts were on the radio call Sabin and Garth had made earlier this evening. She couldn't believe how much she missed Sabin! The sound of his voice and laughter lightened her heart while it made her yearn to be in his arms again. She felt like she was dancing on the clouds, as she hoped he'd be on his way home, soon!

"Everyone please grab a tray and pick out the foods you'd like to try," she invited, smiling. The newcomers filed in and she soon heard sounds of delight as they started to truly see the selections they had for dinner tonight. Ardis shook her head and she went in to get her own dinner. Sana was helping on the other end right now. Finally a few started filing out of the exit.

"Karr, not there, you're over at that table," Sana pointed out to her as she saw she was headed toward Ryes and Mitt, as they just set down with their trays.

"Then I'm dragging Mitt over there with me," she growled out, making Glyn pause, as he'd been following her through all this strangeness.

"Mitt's not yours to order around, she's grown up now," he tried to tell her, to dissuade her from her course.

"What's the problem?" Torr asked, seeing something starting up with the look on Karr's face. Neil stopped on his way in to get his own tray, recognizing budding trouble, too.

"None of your business," she flatly stated with hate in her eyes. "Mitt's going to help me with the cubs!"

"She has plenty of other responsibilities to take care of," Neil stated, standing in her way. "She's our best pilot and doesn't take care of any cubs."

"This is a family matter. Get out of my way!" she practically screamed, "Whatever you are!" Ryes was across the room on the instant; a stern look on her face.

"Karr, you're welcome to join our community here, but we expect you to behave in a civil manner. Lower your voice, and stop insulting one of my best friends," Ryes stated. "What's the problem?" Glyn stood looking unhappy, as he balanced both their trays. Kala was now clinging to his leg crying.

"Mitt's going to help me with the cubs, right now!" she declared, her hands now on her hips. Ryes sighed, shaking her head.

"She's not yours to command any more. She's part of our staff and has duties that sometimes take her into danger. She can't take cubs with her there. You're going to have to find someone else to help you out," she told her in an even voice. Mitt was now standing beside her, blushing darkly as they were now the focus of the entire room.

"Grow up, Karr. Take care of your cubs yourself. Garth said I don't have to do what you say," she stated, unhappy with her older sister's attitude. She tried to throw herself at Mitt with her claws fully extended; fire burning in her eyes. Mitt had stepped back as Neil and Torr moved quickly and had Karr restrained, holding her away from Mitt and Ryes, each grasped one of her arms. Karr struggled; acting wildly out of control. Maren stepped over and put her into a deep sleep with a gentle touch.

"I'll look at her after dinner to see if she has something physical behind her behavior," he said as Garvin stepped over.

"Where do you want her?" he offered, taking her body from Neil, who'd scooped her up into his arms.

"We have some beds in Medical for observation. Let's put her there for now and let her rest," Maren decided, leading him off.

"What do I do?" Glyn asked, appearing relieved and unhappy at the same time. Brenda stepped forward and scooped up Kala, giving him a nod.

"Let's get the two of you settled in near Marla and Myran, so you can both be more comfortable. Jons is there, already," she suggested with a smile. Kala stopped crying and was looking from her father to this strange woman. Glyn sighed, smiled and gave her a

nod. Ryes stepped up and took the second tray from him to help out.
Mitt followed them over to Marla's table, blushing a dark gold.

"Thank you Brenda and Ryes for helping them reach me,
finally," Marla said, now smiling at the sight they seemed today. Glyn
appeared relieved as he sat his tray down at an empty spot. Kala
reached for Glyn and he laughingly took her now.

"She looks tired," Brenda commented, smiling. He gave her a
nod.

"With the move here she hasn't had time for a good nap, yet,"
he agreed. "I thought a good dinner and then I'll put her to bed early.
She should be ready to meet new people tomorrow."

"Da," Jons said as she pulled on his jean's leg. "I missed you,
but not mother," she scolded him. "Why didn't you leave her at our
old home?"

"Because you're a family, Sweetling," Ryes told her, kneeling
down. "You need to teach your mother to become a better mother,
and you need your father and sister to help you," she teased, smiling.
Jons threw her arms around Ryes giving her a hug and kiss, then did
the same for Brenda as she knelt down too.

"I'll do it," she told them, then climbed into her chair, crossed
her arms and looked very serious. Mitt smiled giving her a nod of her
head.

"And I'll help when I can," she told her, then looked up.
"Sorry mother, I didn't help things tonight," she apologized, looking
up to meet her eyes. Marla waved her off.

"It wasn't you, Mitt. It was all her. I don't think Karr's going
to be here long, truth be told," she replied. Glyn nodded in
agreement.

"So Glyn, the question is, when she's ready to go stomping
back off to Matlowe, are you going to stay, or go? And if you stay, are
you going to keep your daughters here with you? In Winterhaven
you'll have the choice," Mitt advised, wanting to actually give him an
honorable way out. He appeared surprised at this news.

"I'll see when the time comes," he finally spoke aloud. Karr
was elsewhere and not fussing at him. He had Kala in his arms and
Jons sitting beside him and felt at peace for the first time in a long
time. "Thank you," he told Brenda. She gave him a nod of her head
and a smile.

"It's my pleasure," she assured him. "Now, I need to get back to picking out my dinner. I'm starved," she said, excusing herself. She grabbed Neil's arm and returned to the line to get their own trays. He'd waited for her.

"It'll be fine," Ryes assured them all as she gave them a nod of her head, then turned for her meal, too. Mitt gave Glyn and Marla hugs.

"I'll stop by before bed," she offered, with Marla giving her a nod. Then she turned and followed Ryes back.

"These strange people seem very helpful," Glyn commented as he turned back to Marla. She laughed and nodded her head.

"The humans have been a blessing and we've all made this new home together the best place for all of us to live," she replied. "You'll see soon enough. You haven't met Myran yet, Kala? She's your new aunt." The toddler looked at Marla, recognizing her, and smiled. Glyn laughed, feeling comfortable for the first time in a long time. He thought it was a shame Karr couldn't let go and just enjoy the small things in life like she used to do.

Early the next morning, Justin sat next to Maren, when Ted came into the room, and pulled a chair over next to him too. They were both ready to see if they could help Karr, in case there was a true physical basis for her constant anger with everyone else around her. Raya was at the doorway, then saw the others gathered and smiled as she came in to join them. She took a chair that was next to Justin, everyone sharing a smile before they got ready. This wasn't a common circumstance, but they felt with the skills all four had, there was a chance to help her and everyone else in Winterhaven.

"Ready whenever you are," Maren said. She gave him a nod of her head, then settled more comfortably into the chair. They grasped each other's hands.

Raya closed her eyes as did the others, established the meld, then mentally sat back as Maren had up his Healing Talent and the three of them started to examine Karr. There were some minor infections which were quickly eliminated by Maren, as the two humans were excited and approving. They could "see" and "feel" the wrongness within Karr with him and could understand more of how his Talent worked. Then they delved deep into her endocrine system, which Ted thought could be a contributing factor.

They fixed some imbalances, which they felt that while these might've been contributing factors, but they were not the answers. They went through her brain chemistry to see what else might help. After over an hour of repairs and rebalancing, they finally let go from within to open their eyes to see Karr now awake and contemplating this gathering around her.

"How did I end up in this little room?" she asked, after a few moments.

"You were a little out of control last evening," Maren informed her. "We felt you might need some rest away from the cubs and everyone else's demands upon you." He tried to be as diplomatic as possible. Ted nodded. The four of them got to their feet, hoping it'd done her some good.

"Moving can be very stressful," Ted agreed. She frowned, as if trying to remember.

"What are you?" she suddenly asked him, sitting up. Ted chuckled as he helped to steady her.

"I'm a human," he explained. "We live here with the starmen. Are you feeling better, now?"

"Truly, yes," she replied, amazed. She then smiled as she swung her legs out of the bed, from under the blanket. "Are you a Healer?"

"Actually Maren is our Healer," Raya explained, as he gave her a nod.

"I'll get back to reception," Justin said in a low voice, as he left the room. He was still amazed with Maren's power.

"And I need to get back to help with breakfast," Raya stated. "I'll see the rest of you soon," she promised with a smile as she left, too.

"I am hungry," Karr stated, realizing it as Ted and Maren helped her stand up. Maren pulled her sandals out from the storage under the bed for her and helped put them back on her feet, noting their worn condition.

"Let's get you some new shoes, first, and then go for breakfast," he suggested. "Everyone should be in the dining hall soon, anyway." She looked surprised as she nodded her head, appearing unsure of herself again.

Feeling like a princess from the old stories, Karr entered the dining hall practically dancing in her new, comfortable shoes; the first new pair ever in her life. She'd picked a pair with glittering stones upon them. Ted and Maren were chuckling as they followed her, hoping their work had cured and freed her from the irrational anger. Once there, Marla met them inside, having been alerted by Raya. She greeted her oldest daughter with a warm smile.

"Good Morning, Karr," Garvin said, walking up to join Marla.

"Morning Father, Morning Mother," she replied, a smile of relief at seeing their familiar faces in this strange place. They looked far better and happier than she'd seen them in a long time.

"Let's get breakfast and sit down and talk for a while, Sweetling," Marla invited, showing her off into the serving kitchen. Karr readily came with them appearing far more calm.

"Sweetling?" Maren huffed out a small laugh, as he spoke in a low voice. "I can think of many other words to call Karr, but not that one." Ted nodded in agreement, having heard of the evening before.

"Maybe her parents will be a key to helping her heal the rest of the way?" he suggested. They waited a few moments to give them time, then went to get their own trays. Maren picked up a tray for Justin, too, then set his beside Dotti and went to deliver breakfast to Justin. He needed a few moments to clear his mind before he'd be ready for their normal morning banter at Ryes' table.

"Maren, I never knew before and am still trying to wrap my mind around it," Justin told him after a big thank you for the surprise breakfast.

"What?" he asked, not sure what he meant.

"The way you can see into the body and effect repairs by what just seems will alone. It's just amazing!" he replied, grinning.

"From our stories of old, the royals of Kahmarr bred the genetic traits we call Talents for over tens of thousands of years into our people. They refined them and we are the result. If your people had bred specifically for your psi abilities for that long, I imagine they'd be much the same," he explained. Justin nodded, seeming to understand. "I'm still learning a lot of how our bodies work, so I can use my Talent more effectively. With you and Ted teaching me, I'm a better Healer."

"We're here for you, Maren. Just ask," he said, looking surprised, but nodding in understanding.

"Thank you," he replied, smiling. "Now I have to go get back to my breakfast. See you soon." Justin gave him a nod, then turned to explore what he'd been brought as Maren left Medical. He grinned as he saw all his favorites, so dug in with relish. The differences between the starmen and humans really wasn't so much, after all. And Maren was a good boss, even if he was younger than himself!

It was late in the evening, and Ryes was getting ready for bed, when there was a scratching on her doorframe. She wondered who, but even if she was tired, she realized she couldn't leave another in need.

"Come in," she called out, putting her book aside.

Mitt came in with Bethy, Jim, Dotti and Maren, all with happy smiles upon their faces. Bethy set down a basket brimming with fresh strawberries from their hydroponics garden, on the small table in her open sitting area. Ryes laughed as she jumped to her feet and gave her friends each a hug, as she was happy to see them. Maren had a small covered pot which he set down next to the fruit, then gave her a hug too, in his turn.

"I was just thinking I needed a quick snack before bed," she told them.

"We wanted to say goodnight, but ask a favor, too," Mitt requested, the hope in her eyes.

"We want to view the world, Ryes-style," Bethy came out and told her, laughing at the knowing look in her eyes. She nodded her head, finally, feeling ready for adventure; having been reading stories of adventure lately from the human culture point of view.

"Alright," she finally gave in to their pleading looks, "let's sit down, get comfortable and give it a try," she invited. They happily did as they were bid and joined hands as they closed their eyes to begin. As Ryes reached out to the others, she felt Raya and Dr. Cruthers join them, too. Raya took over the group meld, easily blending her Talent with Ryes, as they were now well practiced working together.

"Where to first?" she asked the group.

"We both know it was both our Inner Sight and your Manipulator which brought down the Star Quest safely to Tayna," Mitt started. This fully surprised the rest, as no one else had been aware. Ryes seemed embarrassed, so Mitt opened up her recollection of that landing and they could see it clearly. They'd reached out to the crashing ship and did quick repairs, which their Talents told them were needed and just supported it until it was safely down.

"It was… what was needed," Ryes explained to the others. "And we were only lucky to be there and able to do it."

"Or our story would've had a different ending," Dotti supplied, seeing how close they'd all been to dying that night. Jim heartily agreed, shocked.

Mitt pulled them over to the hulk of the ship, now, through Ryes' Talents. She easily pointed out what they'd done to help and they could actually see the ship clearly, as Maren could look into a living body. Ethan directed their Talents now and they delved into figuring out what was still salvageable and what could easily become spare parts or metals to be reshaped to other needs later. Mitt was trying to remember it all to be able to tell Axel about it tomorrow, when Ethan quietly asked Raya to call him over to join them, now. She did so gladly.

"What is this?" he asked as he joined the circle after a few minutes. The request had come at an odd time of the night, but he and Kerry both came since it originated with Dr. Cruthers. Kerry joined in, too and was marveling over everything, now.

"What's left of the Star Quest," Mitt explained, her relief was abundantly clear to everyone else, which sparked amusement all around.

"We're assessing what can still be used and what can be considered salvage," Ryes explained with Ethan's approval for her taking command again. He seemed to consider this for a few moments, then figured out how to view the ship with new eyes, through Mitt and Ryes.

"There're more useful things here than I ever suspected," he finally determined, showing them all what should be kept and what should be recycled. "We've been busy with simple maintenance that I forgot we should've been more actively stripping down the Quest."

"Two shuttles we can rebuild," Mitt breathed out, her joy singing through the linkage.

"Whoa, Hot Shot, you need to learn to fly better before I'll let you pilot those," Axel returned with humor.

"Axel, you know she can do it," Kerry teased. "This Talent thing gives her an edge we never had."

"It sure does," he admitted, finally.

"Are we done with the ship, yet?" Ardis pressed, having joined the meld after Kerry. She'd looked in and saw the gathering, so joined in. "I want to see if we can find Garth and Sabin."

"I don't know if I still have the reach," Ryes warned, "but let's try." She added in her Booster and reached out, feeling for them both across the land.

"There," Maren pointed out, feeling it, suddenly. She focused in and there was joy in her heart as she and Ardis reached out and touched both their husbands gently, as there were deep in sleep.

"They're truly safe," Ardis breathed out, leaving Sabin a knowing that she loved him deeply, as he dreamt. Ryes did the same for Garth, as did Mitt, Maren and Raya for them both. The humans just left the joy of getting to meet them at last.

"They're going to wake up wondering if this was all just a dream," Ryes playfully teased, then reached out to Rinna and Darman, as they slept, too. She gave them her love in their dreams then left them alone, too. She pulled upward and they felt the life of the inhabitants of Tayna as bright sparks beneath them, as Ryes pulled them all back slowly to Winterhaven. She made sure they were each settled back in themselves, then Raya slowly dissolved the link.

"All that and strawberries too!" Kerry commented, smiling as they all opened their eyes. "What an adventure! Thank you, Ryes and Raya," she said.

"And dipping chocolate," Maren added, pulling off the lid. There was laughter around the room.

"That was amazing," Axel said, taking a strawberry from the basket and taking a bite. "So, Mitt, if you think the choppers are something to maintain, wait until you get your hands on those shuttles," he challenged. She grinned broadly at this, giving him a nod of her head; unafraid of the challenge.

"I'm ready whenever you are," she volleyed in return, as she and the rest started to reach for the strawberries, too. Laughter filled the room as they all fell to chatting about the evening's adventure.

After having finally returned to his room for the night, Ethan went over to his computer station and called up the video footage of the night of their landing upon Tayna. He split the screen and pulled up both the view of the ship's landing and the one of Ryes as she stood watching it in horror for a few moments, then suddenly closing her eyes. He saw Mitt noticed and stepped over to help brace her and appeared to have been swept up in the effort, too. Maren stepped closer too, but stayed farther back.

He then saw the ship's wild plunge suddenly slow and level out. Then the main thrusters activated and aided the descent, slowing it even more. With the ship finally settling down to the ground a little harder than it might've done if landing properly. Only then did Ryes and Mitt open their eyes. While the inhabitants of Winterhaven were cheering, they appeared as if chatting about something after Ryes turned to the portable computer to get more information.

He recalled Ryes telling him that she had helped the Star Quest to land, but he thought it was something like navigational assistance using the computer. This was far different. She used her Talents to bring them down safely for both the humans and the starman living here. It was an unprecedented accomplishment, which he'd never heard happening before in all history! And he knew if he'd pointed it out to her, she'd merely shrug it off as unimportant. The lives saved were what mattered to her, personally.

He sat in quiet contemplation for a few moments, then ran it through again, to see it once more. He noted it ran a little slower and saw Dotti, Bethany and Axel were accessing the same files. He chuckled to himself, but watched it all the way through once again. Yes, it would've been a very unhappy ending for all of them if their landing had not been assisted by Ryes and Mitt and their incredible Talents. And with the others viewing it, too; he knew news of it would quickly spread among the survivors. A little humility might be good for some.

Captured

"Are you sure they're EVER going to let us go home?" Sabin asked exasperated, as they readied for another demonstration of the bow and arrows for the plainsmen. They'd both had a very vivid dream last week, where their wives and several others had imparted their love to them and urging them both to get back home soon. When they awoke in the morning they realized it couldn't have been a dream, but Ryes using her Talent to reach them. It made them both long for home even more!

Darman and his caravan had already left, taking with them their women, extra windracers, and Gleds and Raya's things, to deliver to Winterhaven for them. Darman had been quite amused with their predicament, but offered to help, once he saw they were sincere. He delayed his departure for a week, having their aerial maps copied and helping the two men sharpen their map reading skills, so they wouldn't get too lost.

"Dara promised today was the last," Garth assured him. "How about we start home, as soon as we wrap up this class? That way it won't give them enough time to talk us into giving another one," he suggested, smiling. Sabin smiled at this too, having noticed the packs were already full, as were Garth's saddlebags. His own were now packed, too.

"We'll still have to say our good-byes to Dara," he reminded his friend. "Do you think he'll like that bow you made him as a parting gift?"

"I hope so. I put more work into it, than my own. And those small green gemstones we got from Rinna look perfect in it. Let's go get this over with," Garth suggested, clasping Sabin's shoulder warmly.

"The only thing I regret is having to pass by that rock they have Toron strung up on. Do you think he's dead, yet?"

"I hope so. It's not the kind of thing I truly thought these people would do as punishment," he agreed. He would've gladly shot him with an arrow and outright killed him, rather than see him hung up upon a rock, which stuck out before a sheltering cliff face. He'd lasted three days so far, dying slowly and full of misery. It was hard for them to see him this way. Yesterday he'd been screaming, yelling and crying; completely out of his mind now. No one was allowed to talk with him as he died, but all were invited to cast stones at him, as they passed. Garth and Sabin had to abide by the custom, but hadn't put as much energy into their efforts, as the others; only casting one stone each time they passed him. Garth tried to make his casts count, in hopes of ending his misery sooner.

"They live by a harsh code and he was a murderer, as we both knew," Sabin commented. Dara has one of his Talents confirm what they already knew, before he'd strung him up. Garth nodded his head at this. They gathered their things and headed for what they hoped was their last demonstration.

You tire of us so easily?" Dara teased, smiling merrily. He suddenly got up off his chair and crossed the tent, standing before Garth. He threw his arms about him, hugging him as if he were a son.

"It's only that I don't want to keep Ryes waiting any longer," he replied in a low voice, hugging the older man in return. He and Darman had made him feel as welcome, as if they were uncles of his own blood. "I promise we'll be back for The Great Spring Gather with Ryes, Ardis and all our cubs."

"That's a promise I'll hold you to," he returned, as he pulled back from this quiet young man, holding him at arm's length. After spending the last three weeks with him, he could well understand why Ryes loved him enough to exchange true-mate vows with him. He was patient, wise for his lack of years, and willing to listen before acting. He was learning how to draw a line, when he felt it was required, yet was caring and respectful. He knew Darman heartily approved of him, too.

"It'll be an easy one to keep," he returned, smiling. "If you don't mind the noise of our shuttles," he added.

"Bring them out. I'm looking forward to riding in one, myself," he assured him with a laugh. He let Garth go to take Sabin into his arms, too. Garth noted some of the others in his tent were unhappy with this open display of affection, but none dared say a word about it. The politics of the Windsong Tribe did not involve them directly, for which he was endlessly grateful. He'd found enough headaches when the Moondance Tribe tried to draw them into their political structure and was not going to repeat that here.

"You take good care of each other," Dara told him. "I'm looking forward to meeting your wife and cubs, too." Sabin chuckled at this, giving him a nod of his head as he hugged him warmly.

"She said she can't wait to meet you, either," he replied, smiling. "We can't thank you enough for all you've done for us." Dara released him, giving him a nod at this. Garth picked up the well-polished and artfully-carved and stained bow with matching quiver he had sitting on the matted floor, behind their chairs; out of sight.

"We want you to have these, Dara," he offered, extending them, "For all the kindness you've shown us." Dara looked impressed as he took the gifts, examining them, seeing the care they'd given in creating these presents. Each green gem had been well mounted, too.

"You've even painted my own seal on it," he commented, "and the gems appear to be well placed." Then signed to one of his own sons to step forward. "And these are for the two of you." His son, Dace, pulled back the covering skin to reveal two beltknives lying in his hands. The bone handles of each bore their names and the firebird symbol of Winterhaven. Both men were shocked and delighted with the presents, accepting them with reverence.

"Thank you," they replied in unison and smiled.

"You do us great honor," Garth added with a formal bow. Sabin bowed as well, words failing him, now.

"Then we'll look forward to seeing you at the Great Spring Gather," Dara declared, and dismissed them. They had two very anxious wives to return to, after all.

"Chief Executive Officer Ryes, your presence is required in the control room," the computer informed her, as she was in one of the workshops inspecting some new supports Kovin and Phil designed for the apartments they hoped to build in the spring. The foundations were already poured and sealed, but they decided to put off any serious construction upon them until the spring thaw came. They'd had a light dusting of snow once, which melted, but knew their time was running out on getting their outdoor projects finished. The only one in the works now was the hangar for the shuttles off the Star Quest.

"I'm on my way," she replied with a sigh. "I need my own portable hook up to the control room, so I'm not constantly running back and forth through the hallways," she complained, heading for the doorway.

"Why don't you check out a headset and minicomp, so you can ask them what the situation is, first?" Phil suggested. "But the exercise may be good for you, anyway," he teased, smiling. She laughed at this, shaking her head.

"Philippe, you're now a comic? And, I need this?" she volleyed in return, smiling. "Thanks for the idea!" she told him, then waved as she left.

"I'm a man of many talents," he called out, before the door closed, laughing to himself. Kovin was laughing with him.

"What's up, Sadie?" Ryes asked, as she stepped into the control room, a few minutes later. She saw she had something up on the big screen. "The caravaners are here?" she questioned, coming closer to see for herself.

"That's what it looks like. They're taking our turnoff and should arrive in about another hour, or so. That's quite a few wagons," Sadie Saliman told her, smiling.

"Then let's `roll out the red carpet,' as you would say," she urged, quickly disappearing back out into the corridor. She trotted toward the kitchen. They had a quick feast to prepare for tonight! After she first stopped by the equipment room.

It took them nearly another two hours to get the vans parked under the special, protective awning Ryes had constructed, in case the caravaners did decide to spend the winter with them. It was maneuvering them, so they all fit beneath it, which caused the headaches. She thought she'd it built with plenty of room to spare, but found it was barely adequate. Then, they helped unload the vans, bringing the caravaner's prized possessions inside and getting them settled into their new quarters. Finally, with everyone very tired, but in great spirits, they gathered in the multi-purpose room with the tiered, plush seats. Everyone was happy and comfortable. Even as they filled in the seats closest to the center stage, there was still plenty of room to add in more people.

The caravaners were all impressed with the whole room's construction. They immediately recognized it as a center place for entertainments to be performed for a great crowd. They admired the acoustics and types of lighting, as Phil set it up for the presentation. They were very excited, but eventually settled down in the seats, as Ryes gestured for Darman and Rinna to take the stage. Rinna declined, but Darman took her up on the invitation, examining the mic for a few moments before starting to speak into it, as he'd been directed to by Phil, who immediately left the stage.

"I thought that when you were ready to leave Matlowe behind, you'd wait to travel with us, Ryes," Darman scolded her with a laugh; he smiled as he heard how powerful his voice sounded within this large room. Ryes blushed as she nodded her head. "In the morning I'll lead everyone on a blessing of this new home of yours," he announced. There arose a cheer from those who knew the elder caravaner well. Ryes chuckled and nodded her head in full agreement; laughing.

The humans didn't look unpleased, just accepting. Ryes realized there were gaps in the knowledge she passed onto them. This was one and she'd have to explain things to them, as well as the villagers. A blessing ceremony many times ended in a drunken orgy.

"As many of you already know, we're here at Garth's invitation and Ryes has promised the use of the large shuttles to go to Matlowe to fetch our things, which we left stored for our return. We'll also have to harvest the meadow grasses for our windracers to eat. We'll set up our Trader's Market there, but will rotate the shopkeepers we leave in Matlowe, to be fair to everybody.

I want to thank everyone here for your help today in getting us settled, and for those who'll help the day after tomorrow, especially when you start feeling your backs' aching," he teased amid chuckles from the audience. "We look forward to being a part in this great adventure." He gestured toward the crowd, sweeping them all in, in this moment, as if they were truly one community. "And I believe this'll be the most interesting winter we'll ever know," he offered, gesturing toward Dr. Cruthers, the humans seated around him and

the small mix of starmen with them. There were cheers as Darman
smiled, then stepped off the stage. Dr. Cruthers stood, stepped
forward and offered his hand, starman style, surprising him. He
courteously crossed it with his own, then wrapped his arms about him
in a merry hug, amid cheers from the audience. The laughing men let
go of one another, as Ethan stepped up to take the stage, himself.

    "On behalf of the citizens of Winterhaven, I'd like to welcome
Darman and the caravaners as new members of our humble home. I
still look forward to Garth and Sabin's return, even if they have yet to
know anything about us," he said with a light chuckle. His audience
was laughing, "Everyone here knows Ardis' joke. In a little over five
weeks we'll get to celebrate our first Winterfest; a celebration which
sounds very much like our own Christmas, back on Earth. I sent out a
simple drone to see if Earth still exists. In the meantime, we'll offer
our prayers for our travelers' safe return and for what we hope to
build Winterhaven - not only what we plan to add on this coming
spring - but what we plan on building for the next several years. I
think we have a splendid beginning in what I see before me; a
community which is learning to come together in unity of a vision. No
small miracle within itself and from what I know is due largely to our
own Chief Executive Officer, Ryes." He gestured toward her as she
blushed and shook her head at this. There was cheering from the
gathering, as they urged her to stand and take a bow. She finally
took a very brief one.

    "As unbelievable as it appears, I was told she would've run for
the woods, long before now. Living on the edge of the plains seems
to have an advantage; the forest is a bit far for a fast sprint," Ethan
teased, the others broke out in renewed laughter, howls and cheers.
Ryes was almost doubled over in laughter, as Maren and Mitt were
making comments in full support. "We owe Ryes and Maren a great
deal, which can never truly be repaid. Without them, and the rest, we
humans wouldn't be here - alive - today," he continued as the group
quieted down. "The adventure is only beginning and I hope to be able
to see it well upon its way." With this he gave a bow to the assembly
and gestured for Ryes to take the platform. She smiled and stood
amid clapping and cheers, suddenly feeling as if her stomach was
filled with flutter-wings as she walked up the stairs. She stood before
the mic for a moment, as if gathering her thoughts amid the cheers.
Finally they seemed to calm down a bit.

    "The forest IS just a little too far for a quick escape, so I
guess I'm stuck here with the rest of you," she replied, blushing.
There was more laughter and comments yelled out. "We still have
plenty of adjustments and obstacles before us," Ryes reminded them
with a smile, after some order was restored. "But, together we're
more than capable of handling any challenges, as they come. I'm still
learning all kinds of things about the people I grew up near and never
got to know, until now. I'm looking forward to what the next few
years brings us. But, for now, let's go have dinner - I'm starving -
and get to know each other that much better as our new additions

settle into life here with us!" There were shouts of agreement and laughter, as she turned off the mic and stepped down to gather her family and friends and headed out for the dining hall together. The crowd was noisy and filled with laughter as they followed her to the meal they were all looking forward to eating together.

"No, you don't understand, these women BELONG to Garth and Sabin," Darman explained to Ardis, as Ryes sat down with her plate.

"How?" Ardis demanded, utterly shocked, "Can a person OWN another?" Ryes sighed, knowing the tales she'd heard from the caravaners through the years, of slavery and where it was usually practiced.

"There're some places on Tayna where unless you're born into the right family, you're considered the property of others," she explained. "We're descendants of Foresters, so it was never an issue. We were all free. I wonder if such a concept actually came from off-world, where they might have servants for the wealthier families, which when we were cut off translated into slavery?" she questioned, looking to Dr. Cruthers for his opinion. He smiled, noting she hadn't looked to Darman and the expression upon his face at noting this lack.

"It's a possibility," he replied. "What do you think, Darman?" he asked.

"Ryes and I have discussed this before and she may be correct in her view overall, but in the case of the plainsmen, it's only the women who're so treated, not the men. Essentially, since Ryes and Ardis are married to Garth and Sabin, they own these women too, by tribal custom. I have letters for each of you from your husbands, I think explaining the situation," he replied, smiling. He suddenly had both women's eager attention. Rinna laughed, understanding their eagerness.

"Please, may we have them?" Ryes requested, knowing he deliberately waited until the subject was brought up, to tell them about the letters he carried. With a laugh, Darman produced them, handing them out to each of them. "Thank you," she said, as did Ardis. They eagerly broke the seals and opened them. Tears sprang to Ryes' eyes as she recognized Garth's handwriting. Mitt read it over her shoulder. Both she and Ryes suddenly laughed when Garth expressed his distress to have strange women offered to him in exchange for the bow and arrow classes. When Ryes finished the letter, she rolled it back up, closed her eyes and held it close to her heart, feeling closer to Garth, once more.

"Let me see," Maren demanded, wanting to know what it contained. Ryes opened her eyes and looked at him, her heart still very far away.

"Later. Let's eat first," she suggested, tucking it away in her breast pocket. The platters and bowls were being passed around with their special treats tonight, and she wanted to read it again, before she let the rest see it. She and Ardis looked to each other; the understanding and agreement in their eyes.

"Later," Ardis agreed, smiling. Sabin's scent clung to the parchment and she wanted to cherish it for a while, before letting the others handle it!

"Dodi, you and the others are now free. We don't own slaves in Winterhaven and the women can pick and choose their mates, as they will, if the man agrees to it, too. We don't allow challenges and the men are slowly getting used to the idea. If any of the men give you any problems, let me know immediately. We'll all talk later in my office, so you can ask me questions and I can explain how things work here, in a quieter setting," she informed the young women, who were now her latest responsibility, with a smile. Sayer looked uncertain, but gave her a nod of her head in agreement.

"Who'll provide for us and our cubs?" Dodi questioned with a frown, then had a bowl of sweet tubers placed in her hands, surprising her. She looked uncertain, then as Ardis gestured for her that it was all right, she scooped a large spoonful out onto her plate, passing the bowl onto Raby with a smile.

"We're a community. We have artisans, craftsmen, gardeners and hunters. We all look out for each other and no one ever goes hungry," Rowan told her, smiling. Rinna laughed at this, smiling too.

"You've modeled your Winterhaven after the Caravaner's Way," she commented, as she took a basket of fresh, fruit-filled biscuits and put two upon her plate. She passed the basket onto Darman.

"Actually, it wasn't consciously decided, just there are things in which we each are better at, so it sort of fell into place that way," Ryes explained. "The humans are far more specialized than we are and I'm not sure of the wisdom of such a thing. To know one little skill to the point where the person's useless once out of his, or her, field is too dangerous. It makes it too easy to collapse the society, or build discontent because they can't imagine being able to do anything else." Ethan chuckled, giving her a nod of his head.

"It may not be the correct path," he agreed. "We'll see as we go along. But for now, with all the cross-training we're doing, it shouldn't be an issue for many years to come."

"Personally, I want to get in one more hunting trip before the heavy snows come," Maren piped in; many of the others from the Village giving nods of agreement. "I know we have plenty for the winter, but I want to be sure." This got laughter from the humans, trying to imagine this gentle man out on a hunt.

"I'm worried that we've already over hunted this area," Ryes scolded him, smiling. "Why not try up near Hailys? The game that way isn't as wary of us and unused to being hunted," she suggested.

"We also have to finish unloading the supplies and equipment we need from off the Star Quest," Ethan added with a sigh. "So much to finish, before the heavy snows fall."

"But, tomorrow we're holding our blessing ceremony, then the day after we'll borrow some volunteers to bring our things out of Matlowe," Darman reminded them with a merry smile.

"Why does this blessing ceremony take a whole day?" Maren questioned, as Ryes laughed lightly.

"Everyone has to drink to acknowledge each blessing and sometimes things do warm up between couples," Darman explained, knowing Ryes knew what it entailed.

"The last one I saw was for two new vans being added to the Caravan. It ended up in a drunken orgy. I was too young, so watched the little ones while the adults celebrated," Ryes explained. "Since Garth isn't here, I'll watch the cubs again," she offered smiling as she blushed.

"We understand," Rinna told her. "We know…" She smiled, her eyes twinkling.

"What?" Rowan asked, puzzled.

"That Garth and I are true-mates," Ryes explained, recalling she hadn't had the chance to tell him, before. He looked shocked at this news, then thoughtful. He considered how little of the world she truly knew, that she'd want such a bonding from the first man to take an interest in her. He hoped she wouldn't regret it, later!

"When Garth tells me it's true, then I'll believe it," he told her. Now it was her turn to look shocked, as Maren laughed.

"I heard it from the both of them on the same day, as they tried to explain it to the rest of us," Maren assured their grandfather.

"Even so, I need to hear this from him," he stubbornly declared. Ryes sighed, then smiled and gave her grandfather a small bow in agreement.

"Then, when he returns and verifies it for you," she offered. "It better be soon. There's a lot of work to get done around here!"

"How many cubs are you having?" Darman asked, recalling she kept it a secret from her husband.

"Four," she informed him, smiling. "I figure if he knew that, he'd PLAN on being gone as long as he could possibly get away with it!" There was laughter of agreement from the others gathered near her, at the table.

"Oh my, I'll need to make more baby clothes," Rinna declared, surprised and delighted at once. "Just like your mother." Ryes gave her a nod, her eyes merry now.

"Just through that pass, then it's downhill from there," Sabin told Garth as they decided to stop for the night, not wanting to tackle the high pass as the sun was starting to set. He folded the map up, then stowed it and the compass in his saddle bag.

"Do you think we should call them?" Garth asked, feeling uncomfortable and exposed on the rocky trail this way. There'd been a feeling of being watched most the afternoon as they wound their way around a well-traveled game trail, skirting the high peaks of the mountains. Sabin smiled, as Garth put away the human lighter in his pocket, having started their campfire. It was such a useful tool.

"Now that's an idea," he agreed. "We're making good time and I bet we'll be home well before Winterfest."

"Winterfest," Garth sighed. "Our first one together," he added, thinking of Ryes and her smiling face. He wanted to take her into his arms and dance with her around the festive, decorated tree, whether or not there'd be any music.

"I've danced with Ardis before, but this one will be very special," Sabin commented, missing her bright, happy eyes. "I was thinking," he started, unsure of now finishing what he wanted to talk with his blood-brother about. He sat down next to Garth, throwing another stick into their small fire. He saw he had his full attention and a smile of encouragement. "Do you think Ardis might accept true-mate vows, if I offered them to her?" he asked. Garth sighed, feeling the weight of his question.

"I know for years she was after me, but I was never so happy as when she turned willingly to you. Are you sure she's not using you as a way to still be closer to me?" he questioned, wanting him to be sure, before making such a deep commitment. He knew if Sabin did offer her his soul in such a vow and she turned him down, it'd tear him up inside for a very long time.

"I thought that myself, but after mating with her, I don't think you're in her heart anymore. She knows you and Ryes belong together; that your true-mate vows are real. But I don't know if she feels as deeply about me, as I do about her. I know now that I'd be half a man inside, if I had to continue living after she's passed on. Maybe that's why Rowan's the way he is? He never tried for another woman after he lost Jana and he was still young enough for mating, even if he had Ryes to look after," he conjectured. "In fact, with a young cub to care for, it would've been a good move to make."

"Maybe, once you've found the other half of your soul, no one else will ever fill the void?" Garth asked. "I know I wouldn't want to mate anyone else. Ryes is willful and far from perfect, but I don't want anyone else to carry my cubs." He met Sabin's eyes, his heart revealed within his own. "If you feel that strongly about Ardis and you think she feels that way about you, then offer her your vow and see what she does. I don't think she's the type of person to laugh at you, but it might, at the worse, make her feel uncomfortable for a while."

"I've had a Vision of us having four cubs, playing out in a field of flowers under the bubblenut trees Shadd's growing next to the stream, back at Winterhaven. And she's expecting more! I can only believe this one will be true, someday. I feel in my heart, that I have to offer her the vow, no matter what may happen."

"You've never been wrong, yet," Garth assured him, smiling as he clasped his shoulder, warmly. "Go with what's in your heart and we'll hope it'll work out for the best," he advised, thinking this sounded right to his own ears.

"I think I will. Just as soon as we get home," he agreed, feeling much better. If nothing else, he had Garth's support, if it didn't work as planned. "Let's get our windracers fed and unloaded, then some rest. We have a climb ahead of us in the morning," he suggested, smiling.

"Right," Garth agreed, and stood up, looking at the approaching men with spears leveled in their hands, as they stepped into their small camp. "What do you want?" he demanded, frowning. Sabin stood at his side, ready.

"We have to bring you lowlanders before Senah, for you to beg her leave to travel in our lands," the leader told them.

"One of the mountain tribes," Sabin whispered.

"There's too many of them and we don't know the land, as well as they," Garth returned in a low voice, wishing they both knew the human tongue better. That way they could speak freely, without them understanding.

"Think we should've made that call home a little more quickly," Sabin returned, wishing they could summon Mitt and the flyer, now!

"Enough!" the leader shouted, kicking out the campfire they'd just started, extinguishing it. "Come now!"

"We're coming," Garth affirmed. He stepped over to take Pacer's reins, when another of the mountain men blocked him.

"Your animals will be cared for." He was told, then he gestured for them to follow another, who was leading the way.

They trailed after the lead hunter, with spear carrying escorts at their sides and their windracers being lead behind them. The remaining men followed; at least a dozen in their party. After almost two hours, they were finally led to a great lodge, built into the side of a towering cliff. Garth looked up to note several holes were dug into the overhang, one was to vent the smoke from the fires within the structure. They were lead inside, while their mounts were taken around the end of the building, to the pens he could see there. There were other windracers being kept, so hoped theirs would be well-treated.

They entered through a huge double door, which appeared at one time to have some decorative carvings. Once inside, they descended a wide staircase down to the floor of the great hall, which looked to be situated in the middle of the building. There was a huge firepit in the middle, with a chair upon a raised platform at the far end, against the wall. Most of the party hung back on the side closer to the stairs. There were tables and chairs here with food and drink set out. People were laughing and pointing as they passed. They skirted the fire pit and came to a dark circle set into the lighter, stone slabs, which comprised the floor. They were shoved inside this circle and now faced the raised, ornate chair on the far side. On the chair sat a middle-aged woman, who looked as if she rarely bathed and overindulged herself at the table too frequently. The sight of her repulsed them, but after spending a lot of time around the plainsmen, they knew to hold their reactions and opinions to themselves.

"You wear the Badge of the plainsmen, but it doesn't guarantee you free passage through MY lands," she stated, sitting up so she could get a better look at these two, fine, young men. There was no fear displayed, but they were holding themselves too still… too controlled…"What are you doing here?" she demanded.

"We're only passing through. Darman thought the higher road might be our quickest way home," Garth answered. "We didn't know we were treading upon your lands. We saw no markers to warn us away."

"We don't need markers," she declared with a huff. "Where're you from? You have a strange way of speaking."

"We originally came from Matlowe Village, but have moved out to found a new home this last spring. We now live in a place we call Winterhaven, just outside of the Moondance Tribe's lands," he informed her. She jumped out of her chair, coming down the platform to step inside the circle with them. Her stench up close was appalling, Garth realized, trying his best not to react. Urine, sweat, strong body musk and stale sweet oils smells clung to her as a cloud. It was like she rarely bathed, or didn't care for it at all. Her hair was mussed as if she'd just left her bed.

"Matlowe Village is a far place. I've never met anyone from there. Why did you leave it?"

"We wanted a place of our own, for our wives and cubs," Sabin told her.

"The hunts have been poor these last two years," Garth added, giving Sabin a nod of his head.

"They have, indeed," she agreed, her eyes now hard as she surveyed them both, as if sensing their revulsion. "In a few weeks I'll be ready for getting cubs again. You're going to do me the honor of fathering my cubs, then I'll let you go, home… if I'm ready to," she decided, telling them and the others around them. A few of the men had gathered near. There was rough laughter raised, as well as cheers and comments in support of their leader's decision.

"Our own cubs are due very soon," Sabin protested. "We need to get home to our wives." Garth held his hand up against his friend's chest, stalling him.

"I can't help you in fathering cubs. I've already spoken true-mate vows with my wife and my blood-brother plans on doing the same, as soon as we arrive home. Neither one of us would be of any use to you this way," he stated, being truthful about the matter.

"True-mate vows?" she questioned, shocked. It was almost unheard of! They had to be lying! "We'll see. Throw them into our `guest room' until I'm ready for them," she ordered, stepping out of the circle, heading back for her chair. Garth was astounded by the vehemence in her voice. Didn't she believe him?

"It won't matter even if you were in season tomorrow. We can't help you," he emphasized. "You're only bringing a curse down upon yourself," he reminded her. She screeched something they didn't quite get, but they were again surrounded by the same hunting party and urged at spear point toward a door on the east side of the room.

Reluctantly, they let themselves be led away; seeing it was hopeless. The stairs beyond the door lead downwards, deep into the building. They were shown through several doors and stairs down, until reaching a room with a very, heavy door. They were pushed inside and it was closed tightly behind them; the lock making a "clanking" sound as it was shoved into place. There was a small barred window in the upper part of the door and a larger slot in the bottom; neither big enough to allow them a way to get at the locking mechanism, nor squeeze through. Their only light came from a lamp well outside, across from the door. The room was dark and gloomy and smelled moldy.

"Now what do we do?" Sabin questioned, seeing their guards were gone, as they heard them talking and stomping back up the stairs. Garth sighed as he sat down upon the lone bed in the middle of the room. He drew out a small lantern and switched it on. He saw the bed was large enough for both of them, but covered with stale, moldy grasses.

"Try calling home, once they've checked to make sure we've settled for the night. Maybe the ladies can use the flyers to rescue us?" Sabin gave him a nod of his head in agreement.

"They'd sure love the chance at it," he agreed, sitting down. "This place reeks," he added in comment. Garth huffed his agreement, hating it and hated feeling helpless.

"Let's shove this stuff somewhere else. I don't trust trying to sleep on top of it," Sabin suggested. He dug into his backpack and found his small hand lantern, too. Garth stood up as he realized something was crawling on his leg.

"Let's get it as far from us as we can," he insisted, as he crushed the insect he shook off his pants onto the floor, under his boot. "Let's keep our lights with minimal use, so they won't find them and take them from us." Sabin gave him a nod understanding. They started tidying up their new sparse quarters.

Burdens to Bear

"Calling Winterhaven," Garth called into the transmitter. There was a crackle of static for a several long moments, then a very faint voice answering him.

"Th... Winte...ven. Is... you, Gar...?" He thought it sounded like Kovin's voice on the other end.

"Yes. Is that you, Kovin?" he returned, smiling, relieved they reached someone. "Is Ryes around?" he added. There was a wash of static.

"...getti... her... Nei.... try... bett... fix," they heard, then it cleared up.

"How's it sound, now?" another voice asked. Most of the static was gone, but he sounded so faint and far away.

"Much better," Garth assured him, as he turned the volume up to its limit, even if it meant the others in the hold might hear them. "Is Ryes there?" he asked, needing to hear her voice, so very much.

"She's on the way," he assured him. "It's a good thing I was checking on the computer, before I went to bed," he added. "My name's Neil, by the way."

"Pleased to hear you, Neil," Garth returned, smiling at Sabin. "How many new people are there now? And I'm glad you've learned something about the computer! Ryes could probably use help with it." Neil laughed at this.

"There's quite a few newcomers now," he said. "And I'm happy to help Ryes whenever she needs it. And here she is!"

"Garth?" he heard Ryes suddenly. "Darman's here," she told him. "Where are you two? He said you should be here by now."

"We were almost to the pass, when a hunting party caught us. We've been imprisoned by one of the mountain tribes. Some woman named Senah. Ask Darman what we should do to get out of here," he requested, hoping. "It's either that, or you're going to have to come out to fetch us."

"Kovin's getting Darman right now, since he's outside. Are you all right? Have they hurt you?" she demanded. They could hear Ardis' voice as she was asking someone else in the room what was happening.

"So far, they've only tossed us into a locked room in what the humans would call the basement of the building," he explained. "It's cold, but not too bad other than the stench Band bugs. At least we're out of the wind outside."

"Just a minute, Darman's arrived," she told him. Ardis plopped down into her chair as Ryes got out of it.

"Sabin, are you all right?" she demanded, while Ryes quickly explained the situation to the caravan leader.

"I'm fine," he assured her, leaning closer to the transmitter. "I want you to know that I love you with all my heart and I miss you more than anything."

"I love you and miss you, more than I could ever find the words," she returned, now fearful for him. "Just remember, your Visions have yet to be wrong!" she reminded him, hoping it gave him some comfort and hope.

"Garth? Did you say Senah?" Darman demanded, coming closer to the mic's pickup. "Of all the people to be out in the passes hunting!"

"Neil, can we get a fix on their location?" Ryes asked in English, as Darman sat down. Neil gave her a nod of his head, already having the computer working on it.

"Yes, I believe that's her name," he replied, not liking the sound of his voice.

"Of all the luck! She's the only tribe leader who's a woman, and the only one who's recognized by her own people as insane. Be very careful of her. You'd be far safer sleeping with a viper, than as her guest. See if you can bribe someone to get word to Kyma of your imprisonment. He'll recognize your Badge of Passage and get you out of there," he advised, as best he could. Ryes leaned over him, getting closer to the mic.

"We can't get a good fix on your location. It may be because you're deep in the mountains and in the basement, but we can't find your location. We'll get the choppers out in the morning to see if we get a good triangulation," she told him, the frustration clear in her voice.

"A what?" Garth questioned, not knowing the word she used.

"Triangulation," she repeated with a light laugh. "It means to get a fix from three different points, to figure out your real location. We only have it from one right now. And there's a big storm headed towards you, according to the computer. It may hamper us. Set your transmitter to standby in the morning and we'll see if we can find you, before the storm messes things up," she suggested. "I love you and need you here at home!" she added, feeling a touch of desperation.

"We'll be there soon!" he promised, vowing it under his breath. "I love you and definitely want to be home with you, right now."

"Get some sleep and we'll see what the morning brings," she suggested, tears misting her eyes.

"We will," he promised, then turned off the transmitter, as the computer explained it to him, what seemed like so long ago. He checked the device to make sure he knew where the standby setting was before putting it back into his coat pocket. He knew it'd allow any incoming signals to be received. He hoped there was enough of a charge for it to keep it up, until they could find them.

"Now they're worried," Garth commented, smiling as he met Sabin's eyes.

"They're worried? I'm worried!" he replied. "Let's also try Darman's way and see if we can find someone we can trust enough to bribe, to get a message through to this Kyma."

"If we're not rescued by tomorrow, I heartily agree. Wouldn't you know our luck would keep running this way?" he asked, disgusted.

"That's the truth," Sabin agreed, feeling much the same. "Still, Ardis is right. My Visions haven't been wrong yet. They don't always work out like I think, but they've always been right."

"That's true. We have yet to pilot that big flyer you saw," Garth chuckled, smiling. Sabin smiled as he recalled it, too.

"Exactly! And I don't think they have any of those stored around here." Garth chuckled in agreement, as Sabin stretched out on the hard wood platform of the bed. They shoved off the straw and bugs and were using their own blankets, with their backpacks as pillows; glad the mountain men let them keep the things they had on them, at least. "Good night," he said, feeling a little better about things. The women will succeed, he felt.

"Good night," Garth replied as he lay down thinking. He hoped the storm would hold off just a little longer. He wondered if the computer was ever wrong?

"I want the both of you to be very careful," Ryes ordered. It was just the break of dawn and she hated risking them, but was compelled to find her husband. Both he and Sabin were sorely needed here in Winterhaven.

"We will," Axel answered for the both of them, smiling at Mitt as he did. She returned the smile, then turned, giving Ryes a nod of her head in agreement.

"We'll find them," she assured her, then gave her a hug. They quickly left for their aircraft, which were sitting out; ready and waiting.

There was a new, outside shelter going up. A hangar was being constructed to hold two of the space-faring shuttles from off the Star Quest, which were deemed repairable. The remaining two were deemed "spare parts." The starship's crew had left in the ones which were operational. They hoped to get these two fixed and a satellite into orbit to monitor things like communications, and weather conditions here on Tayna. They had yet to discover what happened to the previous satellites the humans had in orbit around Tayna long ago.

And they were planning to link the orbital satellite to another placed further out from the planet, to possibly to give them some kind of advance warning of any other starships coming into this sector of space. It wasn't much, but far better than nothing. Dr. Cruthers was also debating about sending out a second drone with another message for his people back on Earth, but thought it wasn't a pressing issue, yet. If there was an unknown enemy about, he didn't want to attract attention with sending a second one to Earth. Maybe one of the other colony worlds? Maybe by the end of next summer?

Ryes went back in, heading for her office. She had her breakfast early, not being able to sleep very well; imagining Garth and Sabin locked up in a cold, damp, dark hole. She felt so helpless with the distance. They had to find them! There was a polite tapping at the doorframe, as she sat and tried to focus in on her day's schedule, on the computer screen before her. Somehow she still couldn't read the screen even after several minutes of looking at it. Her mind couldn't focus today!

"Come in," she invited, standing up. It was Tennan. This was a surprise. Her cousin had never wanted to talk with her alone, before. "What can I do for you?" she asked with a smile, gesturing for her to sit down. She did, looking uncomfortable, but determined.

"I need to talk with you, cousin," she started. Ryes sat, moving her chair closer, granting her full attention.

"That's what I'm here for," she assured her, "What's the matter?" Tennan looked her in the eyes, then sighed.

"I want my brother back," she finally stated. "He used to spend time with ME, helping, but all he does now is wait upon you and that blonde human he sleeps with!" She was very upset and Ryes wasn't sure if she was about to cry, or throw a screaming fit. She really knew so little about her, other than what Maren told her out on the trail.

"I never meant to keep Maren from you," she said. "He's busy helping to manage things. I'm sure he didn't mean to neglect you. The computer appointed him the Chief Medical Officer and he has duties with managing a staff of humans, who're working for him. And as for Dotti, have you even tried to talk with him about her?" she asked, seeing her words gave her no comfort.

"What could he possibly say about her, that would make me see it any differently?" she demanded, her anger now building. Ryes sat back in her chair a few moments, contemplating her. She was so like her mother, with her opinions so set in her mind; that she'd never listen to any arguments put before her.

"Just a minute," she finally said. Then quickly typed a message into the computer, to relay for her to Raya. She turned back to Tennan and sighed. "There's something I have to show you, but I'm afraid there's so much emotion tied up in it, I'd hurt you. So, I asked Raya to join us for a few minutes. This is too important to Maren, Dotti and myself, to let you be mad at him for something which lies beyond his control."

"What do you mean? They're not having cubs, are they?" she demanded. This got a light laugh out of Ryes, as she shook her head in denial.

"No, they're not," she assured her. "Neither does Dotti control him. Maren does what he wills and beds whom he wishes, even if she's a human and some of her own people object to their union." She realized she wasn't surprised at finding this prejudiced view from her own people, too. Raya appeared in the doorway. Ryes smiled up at her, giving her a nod of her head.

"I know you're busy," she apologized, as she gestured toward the remaining chair, "but, I need your help with this problem," she explained, as Raya grinned merrily. It wasn't very often Ryes needed her help. Except for Maren and Mitt, she found those whom Ryes had direct contact with, much preferred her own, softer touch.

"It's not a problem. We have so many now who want to help in the kitchen, Chuck's had to set up a schedule to rotate the volunteers," she informed them, sitting and seeing the anger in Tennan's eyes. She wondered what the problem was?

"I need your help in explaining something to my cousin, please?" Ryes requested, "I believe with this situation, the deeper the understanding, the better." Raya gave her a nod of her head, then extended a hand to Tennan.

"If you're ready," she offered.

"I don't know why I have to go through this!" she protested, not trusting either of them very much. But, seeing the look in her cousin's eyes, she sighed her resignation and took Raya's hand. She closed her eyes, as ready as she could be, inwardly trembling.

Ryes closed her eyes and centered herself, extending her hand to Raya. Once they managed to calm and reassure Tennan, she projected, as gently as possible, Maren's talks with her about his dream lady, while they were out on the trail. Next it was what she heard and saw of Dotti, when they went Time Walking into the past. Finally, she revealed to them the harmony Maren and Dotti shared. They were now firm in the belief that they were in fact true-mates from another lifetime, come together in this one, once more. Their paths had originated far apart, but now that they were together, wouldn't be parted.

"It's not that any of us meant to take up so much of Maren's time, that he's forgotten you," Ryes sent mentally through Raya, "but that we're all still undergoing a time of adjustment. He hasn't abandoned you, Tennan. I've seen. He keeps an eye to you and Tian, whenever he gets the chance. I think he feels that since we're all here, you're far safer than when we lived in Matlowe," she explained, hoping she'd gotten through. And hoping she hadn't given Raya another headache! She let go of Raya and opened her eyes. Raya and Tennan remained in contact for several more, long moments, then they too opened their eyes.

"I never realized," Tennan said in a low voice. There were tears in her eyes as she finally smiled. "I guess I was jealous of you and Dotti."

"Ryes, I think you ought to check Tennan, yourself. I felt something within her - a glow of power," Raya prompted, feeling it needed attention; recalling the way the madness hit her when her own Talent unfolded, unexpectedly. It felt like it could happen to Tennan the same way.

"What?" Tennan demanded, as Ryes looked surprised. Then she smiled, catching on.

"Your Talent," she told her. "May I please see?" she asked, extending her hand once more. Tennan looked shocked and uncertain, all over again.

"I don't have a Talent!" she protested, then recalled Maren hadn't had one either, until Ryes helped him find it. Finally, reluctantly, she extended her hand and closed her eyes.

Ryes opened herself up to Tennan. She was so very different from Maren; here were the qualities she subconsciously equated with her Aunt Tanns! She felt her resistance, but pushed past and gently delved deeper, searching for the point where this presence of power within emanated. She found it, but first turned her attention to Tennan, before going any further.

"I've found it. It'll be wild when released, but YOU must set your will to control it, yourself. I'll still be here to help, but this is a contest only you can win. I have faith in you, Tennan. You're as strong and stubborn as Maren, and then some," she teased. She felt her uncertainty more clearly, but suddenly there awoke an eagerness, too. She actually had a Talent, herself!

"Ready," she finally returned, feeling this was what her cousin was waiting for. Ryes reached out and touched the sphere, then quickly back off, letting Tennan fight her battle. Raya joined her as well as Maren, which surprised her, but she kept herself calm as she encouraged Tennan to fight. It was over very quickly. She had will and then some, it seemed. The others withdrew from the contact and opened their eyes. Smiles were on all the faces around her, as Tennan opened hers.

"We have another Healer!" Raya declared, happy with the outcome.

"How do you feel?" Maren and Ryes asked, then both grinned merrily.

"Like the world's suddenly in shades of new colors, I never knew existed!" she replied with a laugh, throwing her arms about her brother, with tears in her eyes. He laughed with her, happy with this unexpected turn of events. He only stopped by Ryes' office to see how long it'd be before they had word back from Axel and Mitt.

"What I don't understand is why you're Ryes' younger cousin, yet already have your first cub?" Raya asked, wondering.

"I think," Maren began, pulling back from his sister, his face taking on a more serious look. "Our mother has Healing Talent, but nowhere as strong as mine. She may have subconsciously made Tennan come into season so early because she used to complain about having to help with our younger siblings all the time. I don't know if in her own mind it was a punishment, or to let Tennan see what it's like with cubs of her own to care for... It was probably the same way Ryes and I used to correct and help Rhin catch up with his siblings, so they'd all be born at the same time," he explained.

"Why would you need to catch him up to the others?" Tennan questioned, shocked, not having heard this tale before.

"He's a sport, created when our father challenged Garth a second time. He lost, but Garth couldn't help it with the blood fever," he replied, as Ryes blushed darkly, still remembering that day, all too well.

"He tried," Ryes agreed, "but, I never realized how intensely it affected him. And with him and Sabin being so close, he fell under its influence, too. Now, that was a headache to get resolved!" She sighed, then smiled. "It seemed so long ago, yet it hadn't been long, at all. And it'd been the best use I've found yet, for those memories I gained from Doran!"

"Who truly is this Doran?" Raya suddenly asked, catching a bare glimpse at something of it in Ryes' mind.

"A vile creature," she stated flatly, but felt Raya reaching out to her, needing to know more. She was undecided if she should just block her out cold, or not… She put up an inner barrier, but not without feeling some regret. She felt Raya's utter shock.

"When you and Garth disappeared, while waiting for the creek to drop back down, right?" Maren pressed. "You TOLD us the story, but there had to be more," he stated, urging her to open up and let him know it from her own viewpoint. She met his eyes and sighed, reluctant.

"She's pure evil! Remember your own nightmares?" she pleaded. He took on that stubborn look.

"I'm sure I only saw a very small part of her. How'll we know how to deal with her in the future, if we don't truly know her?" he returned sharply. She sighed again.

"I'll try to filter it," she finally relented, her green eyes shadowed.

"NO! I want the full experience. I need to know this, Ryes!" he demanded, his own anger coming up out of nowhere. He wasn't going to be coddled, as if a child! He knew she liked to curb some of the harsher elements from her, or other's experiences, as she relayed them through, but he'd been in contact with her for a long time now and knew he could handle it. She looked at him stubbornly in return, but saw it was a fairly even match. She finally gave in.

"All right," she told him. She closed her eyes, centering herself very carefully for this inner foray. She extended her hands to Maren and Raya, feeling their contact immediately. Then, she felt the hesitant contact of both Tennan and Bethany. This surprised her, but she had no way to exclude them, now.

She had opened up the full thread of what she saw, thought and felt from the moment Garth led her into the valley, unknowing of the dangers within, until they were finally free of the place. Then she added in her first experience with Time Walking. It felt like an eternity had passed; having relived the whole experience. Shortly thereafter the others dropped out of the link. She suddenly had an idea and reached out to check on Doran from afar... to see if she could. She brushed her consciousness briefly, letting her know who it was and reminding her she was still watching, then broke away and opened her eyes again.

"What did you just do?" Maren questioned, having felt her surge of pure power, but not having enough time to re-link to see.

"Checking up on that witch; making sure she was still safely secure. There's a sense of restlessness and I wonder if her followers are giving her some headaches now, or maybe she's using their Talents to still do as she wills?" she conjectured, trying to analyze the impressions she got from that brief contact.

"It scares me to think such a person was calling me to her service. Hers was the voice which drew me out of the plains," Raya spoke in horror, now shivering in the cold understanding of what she narrowly escaped. Servitude to THAT? She'd been far saner left in Toron's clutches! "No wonder one of the first questions you asked was whether or not I was still hearing her call." Ryes nodded her head, smiling sagely.

"What a nightmare!" Tennan commented, her eyes wide in shock.

"Maybe in the spring, or early summer, when we get all the other chores we have planned settled, we can take a helicopter over to survey the valley? There must be a way to seal it, or take away that power stone of hers," Bethany suggested, shivering herself, over what Ryes experienced. She'd heard Maren's voice raised in anger and only came in to see what could get him so upset, so very early in the morning. And when she saw the commune, she jumped right in.

"I'm glad we're well away from it, here," Tennan commented. "You have courage," she added, meeting her cousin's eyes. Ryes smiled and gave her a nod.

"It wasn't like I truly had a choice in things. At least there was no doubt of where my mother came from after that, and I didn't have to run all over Tayna to find her family!"

"Like Dotti and I, you're deeply connected to Garth, long before you spoke your true-mate vows," Maren observed. "I'm going to check to see where Mitt and Axel are now. They've got to be close," he teased with a smile, as he stood back up. He'd gotten far more than he bargained for! He'd have to talk to Dotti, Ardis, Shadd and Torr about this Doran, before taking the matter before Dr. Cruthers. She was far more dangerous than any of them had believed before. He realized his legs were like pins and needles for a few seconds, until he extended his Talent to take care of it.

"Thanks," she replied, now needing some time to think about things. She felt the limits on her Talents starting to shrink. By the time the cubs come, would she be able to do anything? Would others still be able to tap her Talents to use them at need? She'd have to ask Seena if there were any stories in her family about this problem. Would her Talents return, afterwards? "See you, later," Ryes told him, with a nod of her head. He noted she was worried about something. Had she noted something about Doran which needed investigation, he wondered? He'd ask later.

"Maren, wait," Tennan said, suddenly standing up. "I'll go with you. Talk with you later, Ryes," she told her, smiling back at her cousin. Ryes waved them off, smiling.

"You may be right, Bethy. We should see if we can take away the power stone and possibly those shield barrier devices. The Stone only amplifies her handmaidens' Talents and isn't connected in any way with the stasis chamber, which holds her body captive. It'd make Tayna a safer place to live," she said, meeting her friend's eyes. Raya got out of her chair, giving her head a nod at this plan. "And she'd still be serving her sentence as she'd been originally meant."

"I think it's the least we should do. I can see why you never told Garth the full tale. It'd be hard for any man to swallow that even as we recognize her evil, we can well understand its root. It's only that she clutches her agony so tightly to her bosom, even after all this time, that's it's a tragedy," Raya observed. "I've got to go help Chuck. See you two later," she promised, leaving quickly, still feeling as if she narrowly escaped death, herself. To consume another's soul was the worse horror she could ever imagine!

"You're getting as bad as Mitt! You shouldn't have been in on that," Ryes mildly scolded Bethy with a smile. "Maren insisted that I leave nothing out - unfiltered. It was a lot to live through, at the time," she apologized.

"But, it does explain a lot of the whys. You've learned from those women, the things you needed to survive at the time and a base knowledge of how to activate and use our own technology, later. In the end, because of all that, you managed to save us," she pointed out, smiling as she took one of the empty chairs, feeling old inside and needing to sit down. "For not being very old, you've been busy," she added, smiling in comment. Ryes finally laughed at this.

"That's the truth. It's been a very busy year so far, and it's not over, yet. We only left Matlowe Village at the start of spring!"

"So, will she hold for next spring, at least?" she asked, suddenly turning serious, seeing something was troubling Ryes.

"I think so," Ryes assured her, the smile melting.

"Then, what's the matter?" she pressed, concerned now.

"I think my Talents are fading. It has to be this pregnancy. I was thinking of asking Seena, Marla, or Rein if they knew of any family tales of what happens when a woman, who has a strong Talent, gets pregnant? Will they return, or if they do, will they be weaker? I don't know and frankly we need every little advantage we can lay our claws upon, to build this dream into a reality. I have copies of maps of Tayna taken from the ones drawn upon the walls of Berrals, but with our shuttles, we can go up and do a real survey of this world; to see what's left of it. We need to see where new settlements have begun, or older ones have disappeared. There's still so much to do," she told her, sighing with her burdens weighing her heart; her inner pain showing in her emerald green eyes.

"Ryes, you're looking too far ahead," Bethy chided her, smiling. "Let's worry about Winterhaven, before we start dragging all of Tayna into the plan. We'll go ask the others and see what they say. I'm sure with Talents as strong as yours, they'll be back as soon as your cubs are born. Otherwise, what would be the genetic advantage of passing on such traits?" she questioned. "Surely not to ONLY benefit the men!" Ryes smiled, knowing what she was getting at with this line of reason.

"Ahhhh! It's too early in the morning for any such discussions, anyway. Have you even had your breakfast, yet?" she suddenly asked.

"No. I was going to see if you wanted to come eat with me," she replied, smiling.

"Unfortunately, I could use something light again. I'll never get used to having this almost, never-ending craving for food. These little, wiggly parasites better be worth all this," she commented, turning off her screen and standing up. Bethany laughed.

"It's a good thing Darman married us. I missed my cycle and I'm usually so regular," she admitted to her friend, blushing. "I haven't even dared to tell Jim, yet."

"Let's ask Maren to check," she urged, surprised. Darman blessed the unions of four of the human couples, plus Maren and Dotti's, shortly after he did the blessings for Winterhaven, itself. He was the closest they had to a cleric. The humans put a lot of weight into such ceremonies, akin to making true-mate vows.

"That's what I was thinking," she agreed. "But, away from the clinic area. I don't want Jim to learn it from wild rumors, first."

"I'll invite you both into my office - later," Ryes suggested as they stepped out into the corridor. She didn't quite trust her Healing Talent to detect a newly begun child.

"Thanks," Bethy breathed, relieved. She had hoped... But, it was just too soon for them to be having any children!

As Mitt flew, taking a west by northwest tack, she warily watched the huge, rapidly-moving bank of black clouds sweeping eagerly toward her small chopper, with some trepidation. She had no doubt this was the storm the computer predicted. It looked far worse from in the air, than she imagined it looked from the ground. Rough winds started buffeting her small craft.

"Talk to me, Mitt!" Axel's voice demanded, coming in over her headset. He was several miles south of her and saw a massive storm front headed towards her. He KNEW she'd never flown in any storm, much less one so powerful!

"The storm's moving in fast. I'm going to try to get out of its path, in beside it if I can. I'm still not getting a clear fix from Garth's transmitter," she informed him, fearful he'd spend more time worrying about her, than watching his own situation. "Could the batteries be running too low?" she asked, her heart twisting in agony as she thought of her brother trapped in a cold, stinking, dark hole. Gann may be living with them now, but Garth had always been the one to look out for her. Gann was tied up, bending his knee to Karr! Her father was always a solid presence, but the last few years she'd grown away from asking him for advice. She couldn't lose Garth!

"The storm could be interfering," he replied. "I want you to call Garth. Tell him it's a scrub and to turn off the transmitter, to conserve what little power's left. Once this storm system's past in a few days, we'll try again," Axel suggested, knowing they were being heard back at their main base, too.

"It's too soon to give up," she protested, tears threatening to blind her eyes.

"We don't know if he has access to any light to recharge the transmitter. Do you want to waste his only chance of us finding him?" he volleyed in return, knowing where her heart lay, now after working beside her for months.

"Mitt?" Maren spoke up over the radio. "I think Axel's right. Don't waste their only chance. The storms should clear in the next couple of days and give us a chance to try again," he urged. He already put in a call for Ryes to join him in the control room. Tennan looked upset. He wasn't sure if it was because this interrupted their conversation, or if she was worried about Garth and Sabin's safety. Considering she'd never worried about the two men before, he guessed which might be the matter.

"Mitt to Garth, come in," Mitt finally transmitted, hoping he could still hear her.

"We're here, Mitt. What's going on?" Garth asked, hopeful.

"The storm's too much. I can barely hold onto the stick. We can't get a good fix, so go ahead and turn off the transmitter. We'll try again in a few days, once this storm system's out of the area," she explained, her voice betraying the stress she felt with having to tell him this bad news.

"We can't tell what the weather's like outside. So, we'll turn it on again in three days' time, about this time in the morning," Garth promised, his own throat tightening. "You better be careful and go straight back home, Mitt," he ordered.

"We'll get you out of there!" she vowed in response. Then the signal cut off and she knew he deactivated the device. She sighed. There HAD to be a way to find them!

Ryes sat down, having just heard their conversation, her face ashen. She closed her eyes, holding back her sorrow and tears. It had to be a truly fierce storm to get Mitt to back off from a search! Then she recalled her own duties to her crew.

"Mitt, Axel, get back here fast. We'll go over what maps we have of the region for the next couple of days and see if we can narrow our search," she advised.

"On the way," Axel assured her.

"Coming on in," Mitt finally added, turning for home. Now the winds were giving her craft a boost, to hurry her back. At least she had better reception of Garth's signal out here. In three days... She intended to be out here to talk to him again, no matter what happened!

"We'll find them," Maren told her, trying to find a way to reach Ryes, now that he saw the hopeless panic in her eyes. "They'll be home in time to dance around the Winterfest tree."

"I hope so," she replied, suddenly sounding so tired. "I'm going back to my room, if anyone needs me," she told him, standing up. "I left my maps there the other day." She didn't see anyone, she didn't hear anything. She was cocooned in her sorrow. All this power and Talent, yet she was helpless to find her own husband! What was the use?

"Maren, where're you going?" Tennan demanded as it looked as if he were about to follow Ryes. "We weren't finished talking," she complained. "I need to understand how my Talent works." He stopped in his tracks and sighed, feeling burdened and torn. Yes, he loved and cared for his sister, but it was very obvious Ryes needed him, too. Didn't she see it, or did she even care, he wondered? Somewhere, he realized, he'd outgrown his sister.

Trials

"That doesn't sound too promising," Sabin commented in a low voice, as Garth turned off the transmitter and put it away. They'd watched the tiny yellow light coming on, then blinking off as they sent through the carrier signals, in their efforts to get a better fix upon their position.

"What we really need is to get outside, so they can get a clear fix," Garth replied with a sigh. "I hope Mitt makes it back all right," he added, unhappy she risked herself in that flyer, in a bad storm. He could imagine the strong winds throwing it about the sky and prayed for her. At least Ryes hadn't been out in it, too. He realized he'd rather be out in the storm himself, than buried down here in Seena's "guest room." There were noises in the hallway. Sabin jumped up and went to look out the lower, floor slot.

He raised his hand to sign that there were two people outside, approaching their door. He stood and moved back, so as to stand against the wall behind the door, silently waiting.

"You in there. I want to see both of you," a voice growled out as a head appeared at the tiny, barred window, cut into the door. After a few moments of nothing happening, Sabin finally stepped out, moving next to Garth, as he still sat upon the bed. "Good. Now, if you want fresh food and water, you'll both behave and do as you're told. Otherwise, we'll use the chains and rings there on the wall, to make sure you behave and stay put," he ordered. On the far wall, away from the door, they'd noticed heavy chains hooked into stout rings embedded into the wall and floor and secured with heavy plates. They were short and looked like something from a madman's imagination. Sabin gave him a nod.

"Yes, we'll behave," Garth replied, giving him a nod of his head. He stood up, waiting; his hands empty and hanging at his sides.

"Yes, I understand," Sabin said, seeing this was what their jailer was waiting for.

"All right. Now stay exactly where you are. I'm going to open the door." Garth nodded his head, as did his friend. They weren't happy with this, but they still needed to deal with these people. Somehow, they had to win their own release!

The door opened and a man, who towered as tall as Torr and as broad in the shoulders, stood in it for a few moments, a lantern held in his hand as he surveyed the whole room slowly. He finally gave a nod of his head, then stepped in all the way, to let the other person behind him inside. She was a small woman, who looked as if she carried a heavy burden within. She was so small, thin and looked so sad that their hearts went out to her, in spite of her freedom within this place.

"May I help?" Sabin asked the tall man, indicating the way she stood with her arms laden and appeared unsure what to do now. He gave him a look, but didn't respond. Sabin was unsure, but Garth did step over, offering his arms out to take what she bore, making sure to make no sudden moves. She glanced up to him as a surprised look lit her eyes. She quickly handed over the laden tray and buckets.

"Thank you," he said, as he stepped back. She smiled and ducked her head in a shallow bow, then quickly turned and scrambled for the open door. The guard huffed out a breath, then followed her out, closing the door behind him. They heard the lock clank back into place, solid. His face was once more in the window.

"Use the empty bucket as you need. Make sure the food and water lasts you all day. You'll get no more until tomorrow," he explained.

"How long are we going to be here?" Sabin asked. "We have wives at home ready to deliver our cubs and need to be with them." The guard looked uncomfortable with this news, seeming to understand.

"As long as Senah deems you stay," he finally replied. "I can't do anything about it. As long as you behave and do as you're told, it won't be too bad a stay, at least." With this he left; checking the oil in the lamp well outside the door on his way out.

"I wonder what they did with our things and windracers?" Garth sighed out as he set down the buckets at the foot of the bed, then the tray of food. He uncovered it and noted it looked like better fare than they got when living with the Moondance Tribe.

"The bread's a little stale, but the stew doesn't taste bad," Sabin commented, inspecting what the tray held. Garth put the empty bucket in a corner behind the door, leaving the one holding water upon the bed, for now.

"Do you happen to have that deck of cards in your pack? I've got a feeling we're going to get to sharpen our card playing skills," Garth teased, grinning at last. "Let's see what we do have with us - just in case," he suggested, a little more seriously.

"Then, what we can do to get some of the locals on our side," Sabin added, in full agreement. Garth nodded his head to this, seeing it was best to have as many outs open, as possible.

After several days, Keen and Ross, the pair that were caring for them, brought out a large wooden box, a rake and broom so they could sweep up the moldy grasses and get their room clean. Keen seemed on edge for a few moments after he handed them the tools they'd need, but Garth and Sabin had a violent escape far from their minds now. They realized if they respected the restraints of the

Badge of Passage, they'd win their freedom in the rightful way. They needed to win these people over so they could get a message sent to Kyma, their great chief, as Darman advised them.

"Thank you for letting us get things cleaned up here," Garth told Ross, as Keen had stepped away for some reason of his own. She had a heavy fork in her hand, meant for serving meats; as if something to use to defend herself, in case they got out of hand. They finally finished filling the box. Sabin took both implements and handed them over with one hand, extended to appear as non-threating as possible.

"So, you're due to have cubs soon?" she asked, as she realized she'd have to hold them in her other hand and was vulnerable if they decided to try to take her. But Sabin had stepped back and both men sat down upon the hard, wooden slats of the bed.

"Our wives will have them only a few weeks apart, soon enough," Garth replied, smiling as he thought of Ryes and her merry, green eyes. "I miss Ryes so very much."

"I miss Ardis!" Sabin supplied. "We've been away from home too long!"

"Why did you leave?" she asked, wondering.

"We had to settle a peace treaty with the Moondance Tribe and after months, finally got what we needed," Garth replied, touching the edge of the Badge he still wore on his left shoulder. "Chief Dyan was hard to reason with, but Great Chief Dara took over and settled it very quickly."

"We also needed to take back a murderer from the tribe, and they put him to death for his crimes," Sabin further explained. "Their Talents verified it. And it wasn't a quick death," he added with a shudder. She grimaced at this, nodding her head.

"For a crime like that, there're no good ways to dispatch them," she replied.

"I had to kill a child murderer, myself," Sabin finally admitted while Garth nodded. Ross appeared surprised.

"How could you be sure?" she pressed. He paused, and then sighed as Garth gave his shoulder a squeeze.

"My Vision Talent opened up a surprisingly clear view of all the cubs he savaged and murdered in almost two decades. He'd wandered through the different towns, villages and farms taking cubs, using them and then leaving their broken bodies behind for their families to find, both boys and girls. It was an amazing horror and I couldn't let him live. He'd been about to use my niece, Lixi, next!" He dropped his face into his hands; the scenes running through his mind, again. "He'd stripped off her clothing and was naked from the waist down and I saw what he was going to do, as he'd done to the others before."

"It was right and wrong at the same time," Keen agreed, stepping in behind Ross, startling her for a moment.

"Talent's a two-edged sword," Sabin agreed, looking up, now appearing a little haggard.

"At least he's not around to harm any more cubs," Ross said, nodding. "I'd better get back upstairs before my cousin starts yelling," she added. She gave the men a small bow and left the room. Keen tossed the men two thick mattress pads. They weren't new, but weren't dirty, either.

"And a good man regrets killing another, even if it's to save other lives. These pads don't have any bugs and should be more comfortable," he told them, grinning. There was surprised delight upon their faces at this unexpected gift.

"Thank you," both men told him in earnest, smiling in return.

"You've both behaved and have been very accepting of your captivity," he commented.

"I bear a Badge of Passage," Garth stated. "We have to behave in the manner represented by this honor. It's your Seena who doesn't respond in the same way that's the problem. Is there any way to get word to Kyma?" he asked, being daring in this budding acquaintance. Keen shook his head and sighed.

"Even if anyone was willing to go, the winter storms outside are fierce and would quickly kill anyone caught out in them. They've been raging for days. Give it time. She may get bored and just let you go," he advised. Garth nodded his head in understanding.

"We've been sharpening our card playing skills," Sabin said with a light chuckle. "If you have the time, we can always deal you in," he invited. Keen laughed at this. He stepped out for a moment then returned with a small lantern, which he hung up on a hook near the door, inside.

"This might help, then," he said. "I have some chores to finish, but maybe later," he added with a speculative smile.

"We'll look forward to it," Garth assured him. Keen then left and closed the door, making sure the lock was secure, but hadn't shoved it into place as hard as before.

"There's some hope. He didn't seem against getting someone to go to Kyma," Sabin observed aloud after they heard Keen go up the stairs. Garth nodded his agreement.

"My prayers are deep in my heart, flying upon my hopes. Maybe the trial of this captivity will soon be over," he replied. "Let's set up our bedding for now." Sabin nodded his agreement as they turned to the wooden slats they'd been sleeping upon. Their backs would greatly love these bed pads.

"Have you seen Ryes?" Maren asked Ardis as she was talking with Torr and Shadd. The dining room was filled with laughter and music as the inhabitants of Winterhaven were celebrating their first Christmas-Winterfest together. He'd been having a fun time, until he started looking for Ryes to give her the gift he made especially for her. He couldn't find her anywhere. And some inner nagging was telling him she needed him now!

"Maybe she went to check on things in the control room?" Shadd suggested, frowning as she realized she hadn't seen her all day. "She should be in here to celebrate with the rest of us!"

"I checked the control room, her office and her quarters. She's not anywhere," he told them, his panic starting to sound in his voice. "You know how she's been the last few days. These storms have been almost constant the last four weeks."

Mitt and Axel had been unable to get anywhere near the area where they suspected the men were being held. If it wasn't fierce winter storms hitting the target area, it was fierce snow storms hitting here in Winterhaven, grounding them. Mitt had been fully frustrated and Ryes had been restless and depressed. They all missed Garth and Sabin, and every so often Ardis had to remind the others that Sabin had had other Visions which clearly shows they do get back home to be in them here, with the rest of the Winterhaveners. Her faith in his Visions was unshakable. Ryes would agree, but never quite pulled fully free of her desperation. Maren was worried.

"I'll help you look. Have you checked the shops?" Torr asked. "Maybe she's finishing up some last minute gifts? She was there yesterday, laughing at some of the colorful creations she'd been making with the machines in the shops."

"I'll check the stable. Maybe she's with Honey?" Shadd suggested, setting down her cup of eggnog. "She usually spends a little time each morning with her mare; making sure she's comfortable, brushed and as happy as can be."

"How about the Botany lab? She loves the new flowers they have blooming," Ardis put in, hoping. "She has to be somewhere! Let's all go look."

"Let's split up and find her," Maren suggested, giving them a nod; just realizing he should've asked the computer first. They each took off, as Maren headed more purposefully toward his own office, wanting some privacy.

"Computer," he addressed it directly, looking up at its pickup from within his office. "Do you know the current location of Chief Executive Officer Ryes?"

"Chief Executive Officer Ryes is currently outside this facility, approximately three point two miles from the main entrance, in a northwestern heading, beyond the Star Quest," it informed him. He looked grim as he pulled on his heavy jacket, then grabbed a blanket from a cabinet and headed for the door. Maren quickly left the office, heading for the shuttle garage.

"What're you doing out here?" Maren demanded, finally realizing the small lump ahead of him was Ryes. He'd had on all the lamps the vehicle had to help illuminate the area around it, trying to find her. She was sitting out in the middle of the ice storm, on the cold, snowy ground, facing northwest toward the storm, as if it didn't exist.

"I..." she started, then noticed him standing before her looking very frightened and angry. "Was trying to see if I could reach either of them with my Talents. My Talents are fading, Maren and I don't know what else to do," she admitted, feeling frightened. She realized she couldn't even move, as she tried to stand up.

"Come on. Let's get inside, out of this," he ordered, as he wrapped the blanket and his arms about her, hauling her back up to her feet, heading toward the rover. She was stumbling along with him, barely able to use her legs!

"I can feel them and about where they are, but I can't reach them," she complained, trying not to cry. She just started to realize there was sleet pounding them and she was shivering and couldn't stop. They were caught up in the storm, itself. He didn't reply, just loaded her into the rover and rushed back toward Winterhaven. He'd set the heaters to high, to help warm them both on this short trip back.

"You found her?" Mitt questioned, running up to them as he pulled into the garage. She helped Ryes out, grabbing her hands. "By the gods, you're ice cold!" she scolded. Maren set the garage door to close, as they headed for the main doors. He quickly caught up to them.

"I'll be all right, now," Ryes replied in a low voice, acutely embarrassed over the fuss they were making. "I didn't realize the storm..." she started but noted the anger in Maren's eyes as he threw his arm around her, again. She could feel him using his Healing Talent to repair the frost damage she caused her body. She stopped right where they were, almost to the doors leading to the inside hallway. "Look, we both saw he's not going to be here when these cubs are born. I was only hoping they'd be out hunting, or visiting over in Matlowe, or something, but now I know better!"

"They'll both be home. Sabin's had other Visions involving both he and Garth, here in Winterhaven. Don't give up!" he ordered her, pulling her along with him, back inside.

"You found her!" Bethy declared, relieved to see them, even if they were soaked through. "Let's get everyone inside and warmed up." Mitt smiled at this, but Maren looked mad, while Ryes appeared afraid and uncertain. It was something she'd never seen in her friend before, and it surprised her.

"A fresh mug of hot tea and a nice hot shower sounds about right for her," Mitt agreed, making sure the door automatically closed behind them, shutting out the raging storm. "It's COLD out there!" Bethy laughed her agreement.

"Come on, Ryes, it's a holiday. Put on a smile for everyone else, at least. I'll get your things and meet you in the showers. You should get warmed back up, first. Something hot inside and outside should do the trick," she advised smiling encouragement. Ryes finally quirked a smile in return.

"All right," she sighed, trying to break away from Maren's support, but he wouldn't let her go. "I promise to be good," she assured him as they walked down the main corridor.

"I don't believe you and I promised Garth to make sure you stayed out of trouble. He wouldn't be happy with either of us, today," he observed, mentioning Garth on purpose, so she knew he was serious.

"What were you doing outside?" Ardis demanded, frowning as she saw they were both ice-covered and soaked through.

"I was waiting for the moons to rise," she returned with a small smile. "Sure is disappointing weather we're having." Ardis didn't look amused, but Mitt huffed a laugh, giving her a nod of her head.

"The next time you want to do that, tell me sis, so I can go with you," she ordered her. Ryes noted she meant it.

"Let me get into something warmer," she told them all, as she saw Karr coming out into the hall, glaring at her.

"You'd better hurry. We're ready to open our gifts and need you. The kids are asking for you. I think they made something special, as a sort of group project," Dotti told her, stepping over to them, blocking them from Karr. She saw Maren was furious with his cousin and could well understand why. It seemed as the storms continued to rage outside, she'd slowly sunk into a hopeless depression. Nothing they did could pull her out of it for long. She gestured for Maren to get her to the showers, as she turned to fetch a large mug of hot tea for her. He saw this and gave her a nod before she left, not needing words most times between them.

"Come on, let's get you warmed up," he said, letting some of his anger go. It did no good to stay mad at her. He understood it all too well, as he recalled watching Dotti being slapped around when they were Time Walking. He hoped their Vision was wrong. He hoped Garth would be home soon... somehow.

"Ryes, everyone's waiting for you," Karr admonished, but Mitt stepped between them, smiling.

"She just needs to freshen up a bit and will be right there," she told her sister, smiling, but in a no-nonsense tone of voice. "I'll make sure," she assured her, as Maren pulled Ryes down another, nearby hallway. Bethy had disappeared down it already.

Karr stood for a moment, astounded at the attitude her younger sister had taken towards her. She wanted to slap her down, but fought that impulse as she realized Mitt was just a little taller than her now and she appeared more muscular. Not like a man, but she appeared a strong woman. She took a small step back, gave her a nod, then turned and went back to the dining hall and the rest of the celebrants. She had a mix of strong emotions running through her mind and heart as she struggled to truly understand these changes in herself and Mitt.

Ryes pulled on the white top finally, after struggling into the fancy new bra they designed for the starwomen. She had to admit to herself that she did look better in it and felt better. She'd had Mitt and Bethy standing in the changing area watching her and waiting while she showered. Their friendly banter had lightened her heart and the warm water and hot tea had thawed the rest of her. The cubs were squirming actively again, for which she was extremely thankful. She offered a prayer of thanks to the Goddess Korenda in her heart. Mitt started brushing out her long hair, while Brenda held up a bright red and green sweater for her.

"I'm giving you my gift before the others," she teased, as she saw Ryes admiring the gift she offered. She drew in a breath in surprise. "I made it just for you."

"For me? It's beautiful!" she told her fingering a sleeve, with wonder in her eyes.

"The perfect red and green to match our Christmas holiday and your hair and eyes," Bethy replied, as Mitt laughed, nodding her agreement.

"It is perfect!" she said. "Go on Ryes, try it on. I'm leaving your hair loose today." Ryes nodded and accepted the sweater, quickly pulling it on. She twirled about happily.

"Time for dancing around the tree," Bethy said, delighted that it fit her perfectly.

"It even has pockets!" Ryes said, sounding very happy. "I truly wish Garth were here to see it."

"He'll see it soon enough," Mitt assured her, noting the tiny shadow of pain behind the sparkle in her bright, green eyes. "And we'll both give him a piece of our minds about him being late for the party!" All three women laughed at this as Ryes gathered up her things.

They headed over to her room to drop them off. She then picked up a large basket she could barely carry, which held her gifts for everyone else. Soon they were walking into the dining hall, which had been converted to a crowded room for the festive celebration. A huge, fancifully decorated evergreen tree stood in the middle of the room with all the tables arranged back from it to have room for gifts and dancing. Bright garland and other festive decorations adorned the walls and hung down from the ceiling, making everything merry. As soon as they entered the room, Maren threw his arms around her and gave her a hug and a kiss on the cheek. She laughed as she returned his affections, feeling more herself once again.

"Your table's over this way," he offered, as he took her basket. He pretended to rifle through its contents, as if playfully snooping. Ryes laughed as she snatched it back from him and started towards her table.

"You!" she scolded, playfully with a grin. She set her basket down on the table in a clear spot and turned to survey the room for a moment.

"Yes, me," he return, laughing. Then every cub in the room descended upon them, wanting to greet her. They were the ones from Matlowe Village as well as from the caravan. Ryes knelt down for the younger ones, giving them hugs and kisses and laughing as they heartily returned them.

"You're late," Jons protested. "I wanted to open my gifts but grandmother said I must wait for you, first."

"We're going to eat first, Sweetling, and then pass out and open all our presents," she told her, laughing. "So, patience," she urged. "It's soon!" The promise and smile seemed to get her to subsist as she threw her arms around Ryes' neck and gave her a kiss. Ryes laughed merrily, returning it.

Finally, she got the chance to stand up and shower affection upon Sayer and Raby, whom she now accepted into her heart as her older daughters. She had her quarters expanded with extra rooms so they'd have rooms of their own to enjoy, as well as one for the coming cubs. But with the commotion at all hours of the day and night, they usually found it better if they slept in Mitt and Minn's quarters. Mitt had an extra room added as a guest bedroom, just for them.

Sayer and Raby were finally accepting of Ryes as their mom, even if she would've been fine as an older sister in their lives, too. Sayer, being younger, looked up to her more and took her direction more readily. They both found Ryes to be fair in her demands upon them to go to school and learn all there was to learn in this new, exciting and scary place. Dodi surprised them as she enrolled in classes to learn more in this new home, too. And Ryes showered each of them with simple, heart-felt love. It was something that hadn't been in either of their lives in a lot of years.

Raya and Ptan helped them both make the transition, too. With both women being from the same tribe, and Raya being familiar to them, it made things easier for the girls and Dodi. While Raya primarily loved to be second in the kitchen next to Chuck, she still loved to work with leather and hides in her spare time. She was teaching Ardis, Ptan and Raby how to make some wonderful leather goods they could use and enjoy. They'd ended up making gifts for the others using the hides, too.

The minstrels from Darman's troop were playing music, but when they took breaks to join in other fun too, there was music played by a tiny music machine Monty set up for all to enjoy. Ryes was half-listening to the song lyrics being sung on the machine. They were lively and some were puzzling to her, but she enjoyed them. She was tempted to make rounds about the room, but both Bethy and Mitt suggested she stay put and let others come to her, as it'd soon be a small crowd trying to follow her about the room. She laughed at this and finally realized they might be right, as others flocked to her table. They moved the chairs, which normally set across from hers out of the way, so to give others a clear path.

"I made this for you, from the both of us," Marla said, smiling expansively as she handed Ryes a brightly wrapped bundle. She laughed and nodded her head as she handed her a package in return, also brightly wrapped.

"And this is my gift to you and Garvin. I hope you like it," she returned.

"When are we opening them up?" Garvin asked, smiling as he realized he wanted to see it, now.

"Soon enough. After dinner," Ryes promised, seeing where Jons got her impatience.

"Thank you," Marla said as Garvin laughed and nodded. "My, you look like you're about to pop, soon," she added in comment.

"I could hope," Ryes replied, grinning and blushing. "And am hoping your son will be home in time to help with their birth."

"He'll be home soon! I feel it," Marla assured her. Ryes nodded, as it seemed the standard answer from everyone now. They left as Karr and Glyn stepped over to see her next. Glyn handed her a small packet, which surprised Ryes.

"I made something I hope you'll like," he told her. She reached into her basket and handed him a package in return.

"And I hope the both of you will like this," she offered in return. "I made it for you." There was surprise written in Karr's face at this.

"Thank you," they both told her. She smiled and nodded in return.

"And thank you, too," she said. They went over to see Mitt and Minn, next, at the next table over. This went on like this for quite some time with finally Ethan settling into the chair next to her. He smiled as the younger cubs then turned up to mob her table.

"We made you something for Winterfest," they chorused on cue from Damian Hacker, who had led them over. She laughed as she accepted the bundle Lixi and Jons handed over to her. They then sang a song together for her and everyone in the hall stopped to listen and applaud when they were done.

"What a wonderful surprise!" she replied. "And I have some Winterfest gifts for you, too," she assured them. Then was busy for a few minutes handing out a lot of small things she'd made for the cubs. They were delighted to not be forgotten and Damian released them to go back to their families.

"Thank you, Damian. That was a great presentation! I truly appreciated it!" He smiled as she handed him a special present she's made for him. He laughed and produced a small package from his pocket for her, too.

"You're very welcome and thank you," he returned. "They had a fun time making it and practicing the song."

"You all did an amazing job." He nodded as he turned away smiling, seeing others wanting to approach the table, too. She placed the gift on what had been an empty chair behind her and laughed lightly. Sayer was finally relaxed and enjoying the crowd, as they all came up to see them. Some people had small gifts for her and Raby, too. And they'd made a few small things to give others, which had surprised them.

"I've never seen so many presents," Raby commented, laughing lightly.

"It's the most I've ever gotten," Ryes admitted, blushing.

"I see you're wearing Bethany's gift," Ethan said, speaking up. Ryes turned to him, laughing and nodding.

"She insisted," she replied, grinning happily. "I love the colors and the pockets."

"It does look good on you," Brenda agreed as she now stood at the table.

"It matches your eyes," Neil added, grinning. He extended the package he had for her. She laughed and handed over one she had for them.

"Thank you," she replied. He leaned over and gave her a hug.

"And Thank you, again, for saving our lives," he told her in a low voice. Tears sprang to her eyes.

"I would've found some way to save you both, if nothing else," she replied. He let her go, giving her a nod of understanding. Brenda smiled as she hugged her for a few moments, then gave her a nod and they stepped away.

"And now, I need my kitchen helpers to step forward and lend a hand," Chuck called out to the room in general. This was greeted by cheers as far more than his usual team jumped to their feet and headed over to help out. Sayer and Raby joined the others, ready to help, too. Ryes laughed as she stood up. She still had a few gifts to pass out.

"I'll be right back," she told Ethan, who was laughing as she grabbed her basket and hurried off.

After a large and wonderful meal, there was a fun time as everyone opened their presents. Many people were surprised and there were lots of noises of laughter and delight around the gathering. The gifts that had been meant for Garth, Ryes put back into the basket still in their bright wrappings. She hoped he'd be home soon to be wonderfully surprised.

Dancing around the tree followed and while some didn't participate, Ryes found she didn't get more than a few moments' rest between dances. She danced and laughed and remembered why it was so important to be here with everyone, even if her heart wanted so much to see Garth walk into the room to surprise her for the holiday. At the end of the festivities, the whole community helped with the clean-up and they all headed off to their rooms to get some well-deserved rest.

Sayer and Raby came home with Ryes, helping her carry all her presents, as they had theirs, too. They shared a late night just talking about past Winterfests and all the things they did at today's. All three finally went to bed and for the first time in a long time, Ryes slept deeply, at peace within her soul. She belonged with Garth, and

somehow she knew they'd be together for the rest of their lives. In
her heart, she wished him a good and peaceful night.

A New Home

    "The storms have been raging for over four weeks. It's like the God Ricmon is mad at all of Tayna," Sernn told them. "I'm finally planning on leaving myself, as soon as there's a break." He sat outside the door of the room holding the two lowlands men, who were waiting upon his mother's orders. She decided to mate them both when she comes into season. It wouldn't be much longer now, he was sure. His last older sister was buried this last fall, having reached her twelfth year last spring.

    "I can feel the dying within. I heard there's a woman Talent in Kyma's hold, who can Heal. I hope to find her and that she can help me. We had a Healer here in Menna's Hold, but years ago, when my mother first came to power and discovered her cubs were dying, she had the Healer try to heal her first son, but she failed and he died. So she had her fix her body so she would come into season every two years, in hopes of a healthy cub. Then she had her put to death when she was unable to save my oldest sister, her first daughter. Still, I hope Kyma's Healer can help me." Through time, he'd come to trust them and promised to deliver a message on their behalf to Kyma, himself. And he knew Keen approved it; both his escape and the message.

    "If she can't heal you, get to Winterhaven. I know Maren's very powerful and he'll be able to heal you," Garth told the lad. He was just about to turn eleven years old this coming spring and said he knew no child of Seena's lived much beyond their twelfth birthday. He wondered why? And why she kept trying to have cubs, who only ended up dying? Was this the root of her madness?

    "A MAN with a strong Healing Talent?" he returned, smiling as he thought on it. "Usually, it's the women who carry the stronger Talents!"

    "My Talent's strong. I see Visions," Sabin offered, having seen one of this cub arriving in Winterhaven before them, and Ardis and Ryes anxious for news of their husbands. It happened yesterday morning. He told Garth about it, as both women looked so heartbroken they weren't with him.

    "What kinds of visions?" he asked. Sabin smiled into the dim lighting of their cell.

    "All kinds of things. I saw us living in Winterhaven, well before we found it. I've seen things like Garth and I piloting a huge flyer, which shoots out into the darkness of the stars to hover over Tayna herself, as our flying ships of ancient times. Since that's yet to come true, it's one that will be. I saw my cubs and wife, all out for a spring outing in a field of flowers, near Winterhaven," he told him, "and she has yet to birth our first ones."

"Flyer?" he questioned with a shake of his head. "I thought those were only stories?" Garth laughed at this, nodding his head.

"They were, but we found some in storage in Winterhaven and another machine called a computer, which taught us how to work them. They're great machines for getting far places, when you don't have the time to walk. We also have other machines we call shuttles. They travel faster than the fastest windracer, over the ground."

"Now you tell stories! If you have such wonderful machines, why weren't you using them?" he demanded, feeling like he was belittling him.

"We were afraid of the plainsmen trying to either ruin them, or take them from us. We left them at home for our wives, families and friends to use. They were out in the flyers before the storms came, looking for us," he replied, missing Ryes so very much. He thought she was trying to reach out to him earlier with her Talent, but it faded and he knew he had to be FAR from home, if she couldn't reach him with all the power she had to draw upon! He recalled her and the others touching them in their sleep when they were in Dara's camp. Suddenly, he recalled Sabin told him about her Talents fading, as the time for the cubs' birth approached. He never wanted to see her left defenseless, with him so far away! Anything could happen to her, or them! He thought of her mother's fate and shuttered.

"It's true, as you speak. They would've either tried to destroy them, or take them from you," Sernn sighed. "I would've loved to see them for myself."

"So you shall soon, and even learn to fly the machines, too," Sabin told him finally, knowing doing something like this usually led him to more trouble in the end. There was a stillness from outside the door, as Sernn stopped the small movements he was making, as they spoke. He was motionless for several long moments.

"Have you EVER been wrong, in your Visions, Sabin?" he demanded in a strange sounding voice, as hope rose within.

"Not yet, and I've had them since I was almost twelve years old," he assured him. "I saw you arriving in Winterhaven before us," he told him. "If we write you notes to carry for our wives and friends, would you please see they get them?" he suddenly asked, hoping. The cub hadn't seemed a bad person. Most of the people in this hold weren't bad people. It was only their leader, who was insane. They were all prisoners in this mad place.

"Yes, I will. I'll go to Kyma first, to tell him of your having a Badge of Passage and captured by my mother, then I'll go deliver those messages of yours. I've nothing to lose. I'll die here anyway, if I do nothing. It'll be my Winterfest Wish," he said, smiling into the dim lighting.

"Winterfest? When?" Garth questioned, his heart suddenly wringing with sorrow. Their first and he couldn't even hold her! No wonder she'd been trying to reach out to him from afar.

"It's today, Garth. I'm going to see if there's anything good left to bring you. The birds have been hanging for the last month and yesterday the cooking and baking was driving almost everyone upstairs into fits, waiting for the feast. I don't feel like celebrating, when I know next year's Winterfest will be my last," he told them.

"Maren will make sure it won't be your last," Sabin assured him, recalling that from his Vision, too. "You'll grow up to be a fine man, in your own right."

"I'll hope so," he breathed, closing his eyes. Hope could almost be as painful, as the effort to stay alive!

"As a Winterfest gift," Garth spoke up, hearing the pain in his young voice. "I give to you our windracer mare. Her name's Dancer, and she's yours. I'll write you a separate letter saying so, in case anyone questions your ownership. She bears the mark of Winterhaven upon the left side of her rump." His eyes met Sabin's and he gave him a nod in agreement. It was a very good idea. The lad deserved her.

"Thank you," he replied, then stood up. "I'm going to see what's left and check the weather outside. If it's clear enough, I'll leave before they rise in the morning. It'll be my best chance to break free of my mother and this place - for good," he explained. Sernn had a plan of action and a way to get where he needed to go, in good time. Nothing here could hold him back, now. "Best get working those letters," he suggested, wishing he knew how to read, then trotted toward the stairs upwards.

"He's going to make it," Sabin said, catching a whiff of the feast upstairs, as it wafted down towards them with his opening the door up to the next level. There were still many more levels between them and the main hall. He pondered the strange people he saw with their wives, when Sernn reaches their home. Were they humans? He hadn't told Garth about them, unsure of who they were, and not wanting him worrying more about Ryes, with her having to deal with such as they, all by herself. Her Talents would start to fade in a few weeks' time, as the birth of the cubs approached.

"We best get busy with letters to everyone," Garth suggested, standing up and going to his backpack. He was glad Ryes made everyone learn to read and write! He took out the paper, which he had from the human's leavings, and two pens. Sabin brought out his small light again, also left behind by the humans. They had the light of the small lantern, but it wasn't as bright as they wanted. Their bed had the thick mats, furs and blankets upon it now and the room had been scrubbed down and bug-free. They'd made friends with some of the people in Menna's Hold, but were still prisoners upon the whim of its mistress. They were made to stay more out of fear of what she'd do, if she ever suspected anyone of letting them out, even to merely stretch their legs. Garth handed Sabin some of the sheets of paper and a pen, as he got busy with his first letter. One he addressed to Ryes.

"Do I have to go to Matlowe?" Tossin asked, carefully schooling his voice to keep any trace of whining out of it. Rinna looked up at him and frowned thoughtfully.

"You've avoided this duty for a couple of months now," she noted aloud. Ponti nodded his head, as he stood behind him. "I need you, Ponti and Mella to all take your turn at running the shops and keeping up on our presence in Matlowe," she ordered. "I'm not giving you a choice."

"But, there's this pretty lady here who has an enchanting laugh," he started, and then darkened as he blushed. "And I'm going to freeze before we get there; it's so cold outside here," he added, knowing he sounded ineffective.

"And you'll be far warmer there," she mildly scolded while a half dozen others in the room laughed at him. "Go ahead and get going. Your lady will still be here and a few weeks there will refresh your mind and spirit, so perhaps you'll find a better way to approach her?" she advised, smiling as his shoulders slumped in surrender.

"Perhaps," he finally agreed, knowing it was pointless to resist her orders. If Rinna had to ask Darman to enforce them, he'd truly be in trouble then.

"Be packed and ready tomorrow morning," she added, considering the matter finished for now. Ponti put a hand upon Tossin's shoulder and gave it a light squeeze.

"At least we had a fine Winterfest this year," Ponti reminded him with a smile. "You'll get your chance to be with her soon. She's not going anywhere else, is she?" He shook his head in denial as they both left the conference room which Ryes gave to the caravaners to use as they needed.

"Ah, I'm going to miss that great theater room," Mella commented as she threaded her arm through Ponti's with a teasing smile. He chuckled and nodded his agreement.

"It too will still be here," he minded her, smiling. They all loved working on that grand stage! And the sound carried all the way up to the top, back seats! They had crowds of Winterhaveners watching them each evening now, which made it all the more fun.

"Mitt?" Darman called as he approached the hangar. The door was open. It was very early in the morning and he knew she was usually to be found in here, even if it was cold and stormy outside. She leaned out from behind one of the flyers, a panel was open and she was working on the machinery.

"Darman?" she questioned, wondering if she was seeing things. Behind him was Dr. Cruthers - another surprise! She quickly set down her tools and grabbed a wipe cloth, to clean her hands. "What can I do for you?"

"Could you take us up in one of these flyers? I want to see if I can get an idea where Senah's hold is located," he explained.

"The computer reports the next weather pattern won't hit the mountain regions until tomorrow morning. If you have the time?" Dr. Cruthers pressed, smiling as he spoke.

"It'd be no problem," she assured them, seeing Rowan approaching, too. "I'll have to change, first," she said, tugging on her jumpsuit. It was dirty from the regular maintenance work she was doing.

"Then please do so. But, we don't want Ryes to know we're going. She'd want to come along and with her children due soon, it wouldn't be a good idea," Dr. Cruthers suggested, seeing she caught his meaning. She smiled and nodded her head in full agreement.

"I'll be right back!" She trotted inside to her room, seeing Sayer and Raby were gone to breakfast. They were only twelve and fifteen years old, while Ardis now looked after Katas, who was fourteen. Ryes adopted them into her and Garth's family, which made them her nieces, now. She decided they could stay with her and Minn, because Ryes had people dropping by to talk with her at all hours of the day and night, and knew it'd be the only way they'd ever get any sleep. She quickly changed. As she was heading back to the hangar, she ran into Axel and Kerry, who were just coming out of the dining room with coffee mugs in hand.

"Where're you goin' girl?" Axel asked, seeing she was all cleaned up and in a flight suit.

"Got to take the elders out for a flight. They insisted it be kept low key," she informed him in a low voice, having stepped close to make sure her voice didn't carry.

"Then take one of the big ones. You're not taking any chances with any crosswinds," he ordered her, also in a low voice. "Have fun," he added, smiling.

"I didn't get to finish number three, yet," she added, "I got the problem itself, but still needed to put her back together and button her up." He smiled and gave her a thumb's up, with a nod of his head. She returned the smile, then dashed down the corridor, heading for the hanger entrance.

"What could they want?" Kerry questioned, puzzled. She wondered which elders were going?

"Who knows, but I think I might be able to guess. I saw Dr. Cruthers, Darman and Rowan discussing something this morning over breakfast. If they want it kept quiet, it'll be kept quiet. Right, wife of mine?" he warned, meeting her eyes. She wasn't known as a gossip, but there was no way he'd ever cross Dr. Cruthers!

"Don't look at me!" she protested. "I finally found where they had our personal effects stored over on the Star Quest and am planning to dig our things out today, now that the storms have quieted down a little. I've got things to do, dear sir, and no time for silly tourists," she assured him with a light laugh. He pulled her to him and gave her a warm kiss, then let her go; to do what needed to get done... while they could.

"Be careful," he cautioned. She smiled, giving him a nod of her head as she left for the rover garage, to see if the rest of her crew was ready, yet. And to distract them if they noticed the elders in the next garage over.

Axel turned for the control room. He needed to know who had watch this morning. He wanted to make sure word about the flight didn't get back to Ryes, too quickly. She was probably one of the best Exec's he'd ever worked under, but everyone was getting worried about her. She was overworking herself, to keep from thinking about her missing husband. He hoped both him and his friend would be back soon. Ardis wasn't happy, either, but she had faith in her husband's visions.

"Everything's blanketed with so much snow," Darman growled out, feeling frustrated, as he was unable to easily identify any landmarks clearly from above. Perhaps it was the details he was able to pick out clearly from flying above? The view was still amazing! They finally flew down, on the other side of the Embee peaks, to find the path which led up into the mountains, to see where the trace ran and possibly to locate Menna's Hold. The scenery was spectacular in the bright sunlight, with the ominous backdrop of dark, forbidding clouds in the far distance.

"Let me head to where the computer thought the hold might lie," Mitt suggested, taking a different tack. She set the coordinates into the craft's computer and got the best flight path projected.

"Ryes was right," Rowan commented, his inner awe plain in his voice. "This is breathtaking! I'm glad to have lived to see it."

"It truly is," Dr. Cruthers agreed, smiling as he chuckled. He kept forgetting Rowan and Darman were still very new to many things he took for granted. "Look at those," he pointed out a migrating herd of hoofed animals, heading toward the sheltered green in a high mountain valley. The racks of antlers upon their heads were majestic.

"Ah, good hunting," Rowan commented, smiling. "They're beautiful animals, though."

"Over there. That looks like smoke," Darman pointed out, just as Mitt saw it, too. She headed toward it, hoping. As they approached, they saw it was a high mountain plain and a small figure was huddled near a campfire, his windracer standing patiently, nearby. She circled, curious. Instead of running or acting panicked, he merely stood and waved to them. Even his windracer stood calm in the swirling blast of cold air caused by her rotor blades' wash.

"Land and let's see what he wants of us. He doesn't look surprised to see us," Ethan ordered, puzzled by this starman's odd behavior. Mitt set the chopper down lightly, away from the man, cutting back the engine to standby. He was now kicking out his fire and gathering his things. Amazing!

"Let me go see what he needs," she decided, unstrapping and reaching for her sidearm.

"No, child. I'm not as good a pilot as you. We'll go see what he wants," Ethan told her with a twinkle of a smile in his eyes. She paused, uncertain. While she hesitated, Darman opened his door and stepped down into the powdery snow.

"We best be quiet, or we could start an avalanche," he advised in a low voice, suddenly recalling the one main danger of living in, or near the mountains in the winter. He got a nod of understanding out of Ethan, as Rowan looked surprised, but gave him a nod of his head, too. As they walked toward the figure, they saw it was a boy who led the windracer.   A big smile was plastered across his face.

"I was told and now I believe," he said as he approached the elders. "Is there a way I could get a ride in such a great machine? I bear messages from Garth and Sabin. They're still being held captive in my mother's hold," he explained, hoping.

"Yes, I think we have room in this one for both you and your mount," Ethan agreed, speaking Dolbith and chuckling. "Do you think you could show us where your mother's hold lies?" he questioned. "My name is Dr. Cruthers, by the way. And this is the leader of the caravaners, Darman, and an elder originally from Matlowe Village, Rowan," he introduced them to the lad.

"Elders, my name is Sernn, son of Senah from Menna's Hold, and I was told that a Maren would be able to heal me. The Healer woman in Kyma's hold said she didn't have the strength to keep me from dying, but I've felt better since she tried. Sabin said he saw me learning to fly one of these machines, someday. He told me he and Garth are going to fly up into the darkness of the stars in a great flyer," he spoke, breathlessly. "So, would that mean this Maren can help?" he asked, hoping. "Either way, I'll try to show you where my old hold lies." There were smiles upon all their faces. He just proved, beyond a shadow of a doubt, that he'd truly spoken to both men.

"Come, let's get your fine mare loaded into the chopper," Rowan invited, smiling in relief. They might actually have a chance of finding their missing men now.

"She was a Winterfest gift from Garth. Even if he called her Dancer, I named her Star because of the white mark upon her head," he added, as he walked among the three men, grinning. Rowan had already noted her Winterhaven brand upon her rump and pointed it out to Ethan. It was no wonder the chopper didn't disturb her!

"If she was his gift to you, then she still is," Darman assured him. Mitt met them at the side door, seeing their smiles. "We have to load up Star, then Sernn's going to try to point out Menna's Hold for us. We have a new resident for our growing settlement." Mitt smiled in relief, giving them a nod of her head.

"Let me do that," she volunteered, extending her hand for her reins. Sernn looked at her puzzled, before giving them to her. "What?" she asked, wondering what bothered him so?

"You look a lot like Garth," he commented. She laughed; relief in her heart at hearing this.

"Yes. He's my older brother," she told him, smiling.

"Then you're Mitt," he sighed out, relieved. She merrily nodded her head at this as she recalled she still had to load the mare aboard. At least the animal was calm. Then she saw the Winterhaven brand, now understanding the comment Darman made about her being a gift. She opened the back doors, at the tail of the machine, and urged her to jump up. She so did with little trouble. She tied her securely, covered her with a blanket and made sure she wouldn't get hurt with added padding and straps, in case she started to get nervous during the flight. She secured the tail doors and went around to her own door, jumping in. She saw the elders had already gotten Sernn strapped into the copilot's seat, with the three of them sitting in the seat behind them - all smiles. She strapped in and took up her headset, once more. She began a level ascent and looked to where Sernn was pointing. It was where they'd been originally heading, before they saw his smoke. She maintained a level cruising speed for several minutes, and then slowed as she saw a greater plume of smoke up ahead.

"Does it lie over the next peak?" she asked the cub, looking to him for verification. He smiled and nodded his head, then she pointed to the mic on his headset, which practically lay upon his throat. He pulled it back up, so he could speak into it, catching on quickly.

"Yes, it does," he assured her, marveling at this great machine and all the wonders it contained.

"Okay. I'm going to take us up just enough to get a good peek at the place for our cameras, then we're heading for home. Maybe, after this next storm system breaks, we'll be able to come out and force them to let our men go?" she asked. It'd been far too long already, but it was only her, a boy and three elders. There was no way they could take on a whole hold by themselves! Even if it twisted at her heart to leave them, now.

"That's a good idea," Dr. Cruthers agreed with her plan. "We want numbers, to impress the mountain people and win the release of our missing travelers." Mitt gave him a nod and gently rose above the peak, seeing the strong house below, nestled into the side of the next one before them. She made sure the cameras were recording everything; panning from left to right, to catch everything she could. Then descended once more; turning back for home.

"You know, there're no mountains around Winterhaven," she advised young Sernn. He smiled merrily at this.

"I'm ready to try new things, once Maren heals me. I won't miss this place," he replied. Mitt laughed at this, as did the elders.

"Oh, you'll get plenty of new things to learn, now," she assured him. She homed in upon their beacon and set the engine for good speed, keeping her flight level - mindful of the windracer mare in the back. After more than two hour's flight, they set down upon their landing pad, home again. She radioed, in-flight, that they gained a new resident, and for Ryes and Ardis to meet them, as he had messages for them.

"You actually found the hold?" Ryes demanded, her eyes full of hope once more.

"Yes, but there's another snow storm heading into that area. Still, I've got some footage to show you later," Mitt affirmed, smiling. "If I had better coverage, we'd have taken them by storm, by now," she added, teasing as the three elders came up behind her with the cub and his mare.

"We have a patient for Maren," Ethan informed them, as he saw a good number of the residents had come out to greet their return, standing in the new snow. He chuckled at this, as Maren stepped forward, a puzzled frown upon his brow.

"Who?" he questioned. The cub looked up to him, smiling.

"Me. But, first, I promised these," he said as he pulled out several folded pieces of paper, extending them to the two women. Ryes and Ardis recognized their husbands' handwriting and took them, as a cascade of emotions hit them both at this sight. They sorted them out and passed out the ones which were addressed to the others.

"Let's get back inside out of this cold and read what they had to say," Ryes scolded. "Come on, Sernn. Maren can check you over as we have a nice, hot mug of tea." She put an arm around his small shoulders, her own Healing senses coming to the alert. It had to be pretty bad for her to feel it this strongly! She looked up to catch Maren's eyes, seeing he felt it, too.

"Maybe Tennan should help me with him?" he suggested. Ryes frowned at this.

"I still have the power," she assured him. "I can't utilize it, but you can draw it from me, I'm sure," she stated, refusing to put up with his sister's attitude whenever she was near. Cousin, or no, she was a pain at times. Almost as bad as Karr! He sighed, knowing what she meant. Tennan had become more territorial since she came to work in the clinic and objected to Ryes' presence. The child stood and marveled at an indoor stable area for the animals.

"How'll I know Star in here?" he asked worried, seeing the other windracers. Darman chuckled at this.

"First off, she bears the Winterhaven mark. Secondly, she trusts you and will come to you. If you feed her, brush her, ride her and spend time with her every day, she'll be yours and no other's," he advised. "Patch!" he called and a tall stallion picked up his head and came immediately to the railing nearest him. Darman chuckled as he took out a piece of sweet tuber from his pocket and fed it to him, then scratched his jawline. The windracer nudged him gently in return, affection for Darman in his bearing. Sernn understood him now and smiled.

"Yes, I'll take good care of Star," he stated, relieved. Darman helped him open the gate and get her settled inside, checking her hooves and legs, telling him that they'd come back and brush her down properly, after they had something hot to eat and drink. Most of the others had already gone back inside, but Ryes, Maren and Mitt were waiting for them, as were Rowan and Ethan. Ryes' eyes were filled with tears as she and Mitt were reading her letter. When she finished it, she folded it back up and clutched it to her breast.

"I won't be able to read this in a few days, if I keep this up," she commented to Mitt, as she pulled out a handkerchief and wiped at her eyes and nose. Mitt was doing the same.

"We know where they are now, so all we have to do is plan the best way to approach Senah," she replied. Maren was reading his letter, nodding his head as his eyes were tearing. He folded it up, putting it into his pocket. He'd show it to Dotti, later.

"Who're these other people? Garth and Sabin never mentioned them," the cub questioned, curious, but trying to be polite.

"They're the humans who originally built Winterhaven," Mitt told him with a light laugh. "We're saving them as a surprise for Garth and Sabin," she explained, as they entered Winterhaven and walked toward the dining room. His eyes were constantly roving, marveling at the many wonders around him. He smiled up at her.

"This is even better than they told me," he commented, breathlessly. "It's so nice and warm in here." They went down some stairs and turned left.

"We've made improvements," she assured him.

"Sernn, you said you took a message to Kyma?" Darman questioned, coming up beside the lad, hoping he heard him right.

"Yes. I promised Garth to deliver a message to Kyma and when I got there, I had to tell him the full tale. He wasn't happy and was calling in the chiefs from the other tribes. My mother may be in trouble because of this, but she's had it coming for a long time," he sagely informed the elder. Darman chuckled, smiling his agreement. The mountain tribes counted upon the trade agreements they held with the plainsmen and caravaners. Senah endangered all such agreements with holding one who bore a Badge of Passage against his will, and they knew it.

"Maybe, by the time the next storm clears, they'll be released and on their way home," he stated. "Yes, your mother will be in trouble if she holds them in the face of Kyma's anger." Rowan nodded his agreement, having heard of the mountain tribes through the years from him and the other caravaners.

"Let's pray so," he agreed, as they entered the dining hall. They sat and ate lunch, since it was time for it anyway, then Maren and Ryes took the child back to the clinic so they could start working on him. They wanted him to map out the inside of Menna's Hold for them, just in case, but it could wait until tomorrow. Everyone knew he needed time for healing and rest.

Maren warned him that it might take several sessions to complete, but didn't feel it lay beyond him. Sernn didn't doubt him now that he saw the wonders about him. Ryes, Maren and Tennan pooled their Talents and power, after Dr. Turner took his scans and other samples from the cub to compare with later, when he would finally be healed. Sernn felt a wonderful warmth at their touch, reveling in the way it made his entire being feel alive. After several long moments they opened their eyes, smiles upon everyone's faces.

"Not too much more, really," Maren informed him. Mitt was standing beside the door, relieved.

"Well, if you're finished for now, I'll see Sernn off to the showers, then back to Darman for his lessons on windracer care, and after that to Raya for an English lesson and dinner. We might catch the latest show, too. Then finally, get him tucked into the last bunk in our guest room. We'll have to decide who'll be adopting him, pretty soon," she reminded them.

"That's right," Ryes agreed, still trying to get used to the idea she had two daughters who needed her guidance, now. It was practically the only thing keeping her from sinking back into despair. But, there was hope. They knew where they were! "I'll take names for candidates and we'll decide this by the end of the week - with Sernn's full approval - of course." He looked puzzled.

"We want to make sure you have a new family to look after you," Maren explained, smiling. "You're still a bit young to be out on your own after all."

"I get to pick my new family?" he asked, unsure about this, but it sounded promising.

"Yes, you do," Ryes assured him. "Come on, there's still quite a lot to get accomplished today," she prompted him, smiling. With Sayer, Raby and four cubs on the way, she didn't think she could handle another one.

"I'll take him. Come on, Squirt," Mitt urged, ready to take him under her wing, for now. Ryes gave her a nod of her head.

"What did you call me?" he questioned with a smile, as they walked out the clinic door.

"It's a nickname," she explained. "Once we help you get an understanding of English, you'll know what I mean," she teased.

"It's a good thing your DNA's so clean that it's easy to see any serious changes from the norm. The preliminary on Sernn's DNA shows damage on the chromosome level. This is something inherited. It's a good thing he's young. It'll give Scott time develop remedies, in case he passes it onto his own children," Ted told them, coming back to the treatment room, his minicomp in hand with the display.

"I wonder, could you heal on that level?" Ryes asked Maren. "Could a real Talent, as powerful as your healing power, reach down to such a depth of another's being?"

"I don't know," he admitted, pondering it. Ted looked at him, speculating too.

    "My gosh, Ryes, you have so much power at your command!" Tennan spoke up, still reeling from the direct feed she provided to boost both her and Maren's Talents. It was astounding!

    "But, what use is it, if I've lost my own Talents until these little ones are born?" she returned. Then sighed. "I'll be in my office, if you need me," she told them, turning for the door. Garth felt her efforts on Winterfest Day! It warmed her heart to know he was with her, within his own. They would be together again, so very soon. She KNEW it and could hardly wait!

Long Awaited

"Garth, Sabin," they heard their names called out by Keen, as he opened their cell door. They put down their cards, having gotten into an intense game the last hour, or so. Time was relatively useless, living down here. But, they were sure it wasn't time for anything "regular" to happen, to require his presence.

"Yes?" Garth questioned, seeing a strange look upon his face.

"You're being called up to the main hall. Make sure you leave all your things - especially your beltknives - and try to look a little bewildered and downtrodden. There's something up and you're being called for questioning," he explained.

"What could it be?" Sabin asked, puzzled. "How can we be the cause of anything from down here?"

"I've no idea. I was just roused from a nap, since I had last watch, last night," Keen replied, just as puzzled.   "The whole hold is in an uproar, but no one's said why." The men stood and made sure they emptied their pockets, stowing everything in their backpacks - just in case. Then they presented themselves for his inspection. Keen gave them a nod of his head, trusting them and gestured them outside, closing the door behind them. He locked it to make sure no one disturbed their things, while they were gone. He marched them upstairs, all three playing their roles perfectly.

"Take them before Senah." Keen was ordered by one of the older guardsmen, as they emerged on the level where the main hall spread out before them. He gave him a nod, nudging them forward once more. They came before Senah's raised chair and saw she was surrounded by the Hold's elders. Keen motioned them into the circle, to wait, as he stood ready nearby. As Senah saw them, a strange gleam alit in her eyes.

"What do you know of great air machines, which fly upon strange winds?" she demanded. The elders shifted so they could clearly see their faces, too.

"We have flyers which we use at times in Winterhaven and what you say can be said to describe them," Garth answered, as calmly as possible. They must've found them at last! Were they outside, hovering, waiting upon their men's return? It took every shred of control at his command to keep his face neutral, now. She appeared even more focused upon them and evil.

"Are they dangerous?" she demanded, starting to feel panicked that these people had command of such terrible things!

"They can be," he replied. "We don't usually seek to harm others, which is why I was granted this Badge of Passage," he added, trying to get some leverage for their release, in reminding them of the status he officially held elsewhere. Her eyes fastened upon his badge again, as if seeing it for the first time. This was no game, and now she risked losing everything.

"The storms might hamper them for a few days," she breathed. "My season has come and I require your services, before I'll release you," Senah asserted. There was a murmur among the elders with her; whether approving of not, Garth couldn't tell.

"I've taken true-mate vows and you endanger your very soul by making such demands upon me," Garth assured her. "And my blood-brother is ready to offer his true-mate vows to his wife, so he cannot help you, either."

"I MUST HAVE HEALTHY CUBS!" she shouted, jumping out of her chair and stepping down and across to the two men swiftly; startling the elders. "My oldest living son stole one of your windracers and disappeared. My remaining three cubs are already displaying the same weakness, as their previous siblings. You two are my best chance and I'm not giving either of you a choice!" she declared, looking fiercely at each of them, in turn. "Take them to my room and strip them of their clothes," she ordered Keen, and then turned to deal with the Hold's elders, who were talking among themselves, sounding agitated. Keen gestured for Garth and Sabin to start walking before him with his spear. He wasn't happy with this situation, but they saw he had little choice in the matter, himself. Once they were out of the hall, heading upwards toward Senah's room and out of sight, he stopped them.

"Try your best," he begged of them. "I'm sure Sernn's gotten word to Kyma, by now. Somehow between either your machines, or the Great Chief of all the mountain tribes, you should be free of our Hold and on your way home, soon," he encouraged them, trying to win their cooperation. If Garth had spoken true-mate vows, Senah was bringing down a heavy curse upon herself with this trespass, but there was nothing any of them could do about it. She made her decision.

"We understand," Garth assured him, clasping him upon the shoulder in friendship. "This is her will and I hope she'll be the only one to suffer from it." He found he was surprised, yet not so, to hear that Keen knew of Sernn's attempt to get them help. He may have even helped the cub escape the hold, itself.

"It shouldn't be more than a few days," he said, then gestured for them to continue up the stairs. They reached her room and he opened the door. They removed all their clothing, feeling more naked than they were usually wont, in such a situation. Keen took their things, then closed and locked the door behind him.

"So, now we're deep in the viper's den," Sabin sighed. "There's no way I feel I can perform under such circumstances," he commented.

"Let's sit down," Garth suggested, gesturing toward a bench set against one wall, almost as far as they could get from the bed. His felt his stomach was tied in knots.

"What're we going to do?" he asked, looking as upset as Garth felt.

"We'll be out of here soon. Just keep remembering that and think of the look on Ardis' face, when she sees you again," he replied, clasping Sabin upon the shoulder. He smiled at this, seeing her sweet face, lively brown eyes and curling dark hair in his mind's eye. After a few minutes, the door opened and Senah came in with four guards following behind her. She saw them, then strode across to her bed, casting off her long tunic as she went.

"Come here, both of you," she ordered, removing her undergarment and sitting down upon her furs. The guards gestured with their spears, so they stood and went to the bed, standing at the foot of it, unhappy and uncomfortable. "Get into bed with me!" she demanded, seeing them hesitating.

"I can't," Garth told her, the sight of her lying upon her furs was like a dash of ice across his senses. He couldn't move to obey her command. As Sabin moved to obey her, one of the guards roughly shoved Garth from behind, down onto the bed, sneering at him as he did so. He managed to crawl up toward a more normal position, seeing he wasn't being given a choice in the matter, at all. He lay down, next to Sabin and closed his eyes.

"Relax. I don't bite," Senah scolded in a sultry voice, trying to tease these two, very-reluctant men. "Where're you from to have such fear at a time like this?" she demanded. Didn't the scent of her being in season excite them at all? She saw that it didn't. Both remained unaffected, so she started toying with them, trying to get some response. After several minutes worth of using her best efforts, she gave up with the taller one in disgust.

"You can leave!" she ordered Garth. "But, if your friend doesn't perform, I'll have you both slain for your insolence," she threatened. She rolled out of bed to get herself a goblet of mead, feeling frustrated. She'd NEVER had a man act this way around her before!

"I'll be all right," Sabin whispered to Garth, envying his escape from this madness. Didn't they have the right to refuse? He could now understand why the women of Winterhaven decided they'd chose their husbands themselves, instead of allowing challenges and having to tolerate someone they truly didn't want near them. Just because they were slaves to their urges when they're in season, didn't mean they should be forced to mate with men they hated!

"I..." Garth started, unsure of what to say of Sabin's sacrifice.

"I know," he assured him, giving him a nod of his head. "Go before she changes her mind," he urged. Garth quickly left the bed and was out the door, just as fast. He felt strange being forced to desert Sabin and even more so, as he now stood in the busy hallway without any clothing on.

"Garth!" He heard Keen's voice and saw him standing at the top of the stairs. He stepped forward, handing him back his things. Garth smiled, giving him a nod of his head and dressed quickly, seeing the other hold residents tried not to notice, as they came and went in the hallway with their duties.

"Sabin..." he started, unsure if he could even say it, now.

"I know," Keen assured him, clasping him on the shoulder. "Let's get you back downstairs," he offered, seeing his pain. He had a skin of mead stashed for special occasions; this one might rate it being brought out, he thought. It was obvious Garth needed something to dull his inner ache for his friend.

"The storms have moved back in," Mitt declared disgusted, as she threw down her minicomp onto Ryes' desktop. She sat down heavily in one of her chairs and covered her face with her hands, trying her best not to cry. "It could be days!" Ryes sighed, having seen the computer's projection, too. "I was going to ask Axel if one of the space shuttles might be able to better brave the winds?"

"We know where they are. The storms can't last forever," she stressed. This was so hard on all of them! "And we've both seen the way the space machines fly with our Inner Sight. I don't think even one of them could – even if they were operational already."

"I know," Mitt agreed, dropping her hands, looking at her. "Are you feeling all right?" she suddenly asked, concerned.

"Yeah, just a little off today is all," she related. "I think it's been all this planning and worrying about the assault. I'm going to start looking like an elder soon," she teased, smiling at last.

"How about coming to lunch with me? You look like you need the break."

"I'm not hungry today," Ryes told her. "You go on. I'm sure Shadd and Ardis would love to hear the latest, too," she urged her, turning back to her terminal. Mitt sat for a few seconds, studying her. She definitely didn't sound right, either.

"Okay, later," she agreed, getting up. She then turned for Maren's office, instead of heading for the dining room. She found him just heading out for lunch with Dotti on his arm.

"Maren, have you seen Ryes, today?" she asked. "She's not hungry and doesn't look right," she informed him. He frowned at this. It didn't sound like her, at all. She was usually found nibbling at almost all hours of the day now; like he used to do!

"It's on the way," he replied, smiling down at Dotti. She nodded her head, understanding. "Come on, Mitt. If she's all right, we'll all go to lunch together," he assured her. She smiled, feeling better about things. If anything were really wrong, he'd know right away. They went as a group back down the corridor, stopping at her open office door.

"Ryes? Want to go to lunch with us?" Dotti asked, seeing she was working at her desk. She looked over at them, then shook her head no.

"I'm not hungry," she assured them. "Oh Mitt, you forgot your minicomp," she reminded her, pointing to it on the desk. Maren stepped closer as if to retrieve it, then grabbed her hand, instead. He closed his eyes for a few seconds, then opened them in surprise. Surprise was reflected in her eyes, too.

"Guess our estimations were off. Your cubs are coming, now!" he scolded her unnecessarily, now that she'd felt what he felt through his Talent. "We'd best get you to the clinic," he advised.

"No. It's too cold a place," she decided, smiling up at him. He already knew.

"Well, let's get you somewhere!" he demanded, "or they'll be born right here in this office!" She smiled as she stood up, her heart still longing for Garth's solid presence. They had to get them back and soon!

"Calm down, Ryes," Maren ordered, finally realizing she was hampering his efforts as he was checking her cubs, seeing how they were doing. He only practiced with Myran's birth, and Marla had given birth five times before, so was an old hand at it. This was Ryes' first, and not only was this her first birth, but her heart and mind kept reaching out for Garth. She kept forgetting there was no way he could help her now! And even if her Talents were dead within her, he felt they truly weren't! It was as if they were working in the background, not deliberately blocking him, but still were.

"I'm trying, Maren," she finally stated, doing her best to relax for him, seeing he was having a difficult time with her. She was trying to hold back her tears, but not doing very well. Maren was keeping her from being swamped with labor pain, but helpless to aide with her heartache. She needed Garth! Torr peered over Maren's shoulder, concerned. It brought a smile to her lips. This was what they both saw, so long ago in Hailys.

"Is she all right?" he asked, worried, seeing her tears. Maren turned to see him; chuckling as he realized it, too.

"If I can get her to calm down, she'll be just fine," he assured him. "Go and tell the others that it won't be long now, please?" he requested. Torr smiled, giving him an affectionate cuff on the shoulder, then went back out to pass on what little he knew.

"Just exactly," she commented with a sigh, as Maren gave her a nod of his head in confirmation.

"Let me help," Bethy insisted, stepping inside the room with them. "Please?" she asked, seeing the look in Maren's eyes at her intrusion.

"Sit down here," Ryes invited her friend with a smile in her eyes, indicating a nearby chair. Torr had helped her break out of her inner torment and Bethy's presence gave her someone else to focus upon. Then another spasm of pain hit and Maren quickly extended his Talent, easing her pain without affecting her labor.

"Breathe and push, Ryes, breathe and push. The next one should be it," he promised with a smile. Bethy's presence did help after all! Bethany reached out and took her hand, mindful of her claws, which were halfway extended with the stress she was feeling.

"Sorry," Ryes saw and tried to retract them, while following Maren's directions. It took far more effort than it ever took before, in her whole life! "I really need Garth here with me. He'd be so excited and proud," she told her, seeing his face in her mind's eye. She wondered if he were thinking of her?

"He really wants to be here with you, too," Bethy assured her. "You let me read that last letter, remember," she added, seeing her puzzled frown. Ryes started to laugh at this, but she was suddenly consumed with pain, again.

"Breathe, push," Maren encouraged her, only able to muffle her pain a little, as he was concentrating upon delivering her first cub.

"What do you think I'm doing?" she returned, exasperated. She suddenly smiled as she realized she was giving birth to her and Garth's first cub.

"You have a son!" Maren told her, "but this one's not Rhin."

"He's Gareth," she told them, as he was cleaning the infant and checking him over, extending his Talent. He placed him atop of Ryes' stomach and as soon as his afterbirth was delivered, he healed the cub's umbilical connection, forming his belly button from the start. He placed the afterbirth into a waiting, steel bowl, then took Gareth and wrapped him in a small blanket, placing him in Ryes' hands. She beamed happily to finally hold her first cub.

"He's beautiful," Bethy breathed, looking at his tiny face and hands. He was so perfect and the same size as a small human baby. He looked human until you saw he lacked fingernails and had slightly larger ears.

"He sure is," she agreed, "Now only three more to go," she added, shaking her head. "One or two is definitely much saner."

"I'll tell you when it's my turn," Bethy teased. She now knew she was pregnant and from both Maren and Ted's estimations, she had been so BEFORE they boarded the Star Quest for the evacuation. It must've been that night they were out watching the moons from Hailys. Jim was proud, something she hadn't expected from him.

"Do I try to feed him now?" Ryes asked Maren. He had his eyes closed as he was checking on the remaining three.

"Wait until all four are born. That way you can be more relaxed with them," he advised, seeing she was far from that state now, but was far better than just a few minutes ago. "We'll have to move you and the cubs, get this mess cleaned up, then get you all comfortable, again. That will be the best time to start nursing." Ryes gave him a nod as she smiled, looking into the eyes of her son as he fussed at her in a low voice.

"All right," she replied, "Bethy, could you please tell the rest that Gareth is born, for me?" she requested.

"That's a good idea. It'll cut down on others coming in and constantly checking," Maren agreed. "Ryes, I need to weigh and measure your son, now. While we have a few minutes," he urged. She smiled up into his eyes, allowing her cousin to take the cub and do what he felt he must. She had found her center, once more!

"How's she doing?" Dr. Cruthers asked, as his assistant appeared out of the bedroom. The outer room was packed, with everyone who could fit inside. More chairs had been procured and so it was a very large waiting room, now. She smiled at this, nodding her head to the others in the room.

"She's had her first son, Gareth," she announced. "Maren's weighing and measuring him now. Both mother and son are doing great," she added, with a huge smile plastering her face. There arose a cheer from the rest and soon laughter and comments were exchange.

"Can we see them?" Ardis asked, wanting to be in the room with them, too.

"Let's wait until all of them are born and she's ready to introduce the newest members of her family," Ted suggested loudly to the others, to be sure he was heard. This helped take a little of the edge off the other noises in the room, as he was heard and understood.

"That would be best," Rowan assured them in full support. He wanted to be in there too, but understood keeping it a smaller number to help ease any fears Ryes might have.

"So, get back in there to help before I take your place," Mitt ordered Bethy with a big grin on her face. They all laughed at this, too.

"When they're all born, I'll be back," she replied, laughing. Bethany gave them a small quick bow and rushed back in, closing the door behind her.

"Who's all out there?" Ryes asked her as she took her seat, again.

"Everyone who could be," she merrily quipped back. "They've all been waiting for this day and want to make sure you and the cubs are all right." Ryes sighed and nodded her head, understanding.

"Thanks for keeping them at bay," she replied, chuckling for a few moments between contractions.

"What are friends for?" she returned, offering her hand as a smile lit up her eyes. Ryes nodded, trying not to look too anxiously at what Maren was doing across her bedroom with her first son.

"You'll be fine," Maren told her as he stepped back over with Gareth in his hands. He placed him on her right hand side, so she could cup him close to her, as she held onto Bethany's hand with her left one.

Before her next heavy bout of labor pains started, with Gareth returned to her, and Bethy taking her hand, Ryes was as ready as she could be for her next cub. Maren was ready, too. The following births were far easier - on all of them. She finally relaxed, letting go of her inner heartache. Rhin, the last one born, was more of a surprise. As Maren's hands touched him to deliver him, he felt his Talent's power boost tremendously.

"Rhin's a Booster!" he laughed as he held him in his hands, "and a very powerful one, too!" Ryes looked astonished while Bethy was puzzled.

"His Talent's already active and working," she explained to her friend. "He boosts, or provides added power, to other Talents. A Booster is so extremely rare, with maybe one birth in a thousand years!"

"Sort of the way you help boost Maren and Tennan, when they need it?" she asked. Ryes frowned at this, then realized she was delivering his afterbirth.

"I think it's one of your Talents, too," Maren agreed, having quickly taken care of Rhin and was now taking his measurements, before handing him over to his mother's care.

"I never thought of it that way," she admitted, then smiled as he handed him to her. She nuzzled him, nose to nose, feeling the tingle of power emanating from him, too. Her own Talents were dead within her now, but she didn't care with her cubs finally arrived.

Bethany went out to let the others know they were now all born. Ted stepped in and readily helped Maren move her and the cubs to a wide rolling cart, draping her under a light blanket, then had the other medical staffers come in to help clean up and check on the infants, now under their care. Their joy was amazing to see.

For some reason, even though she knew them all, it made Ryes nervous to have these men handle her children. Bethany quickly returned and her presence was the only thing which helped Ryes to anchor her fears and remain calm. Maren stepped over and finished healing her body, relieved she had settled down in truth. Soon they had her and Garth's bed cleaned and refreshed and made – all ready for her and the cubs. They moved her back over and then the cubs back to her arms.

"There you go. All ready for some rest, after you nurse your very large family," Maren teased, as he gave her a kiss on her forehead.

"Thank you so much, Maren, for everything," she told him, coming from her heart. She really owed him so very much! "And thank you, Bethy, for sticking beside me."

"As long as you're beside me, when my time comes," she agreed, laughing.

"That's a promise," Ryes stated with a smile. "Brenda's daughter should be due any time now," she added, concerned.

"In a few more days," Maren agreed. "I've been keeping an eye on her. You, we didn't expect for another four to five weeks, at least. Maybe we accidently tampered with the others, when we were trying to catch Rhin up?" he questioned, wondering about it.

"That's all right," she assured him with a laugh. "I'm sure they don't mind, now that they're all here - safe and sound. I know I don't mind!" she exclaimed, relieved. Ted was smiling at this, knowing of the whys behind the intense healing Maren had to do for the one cub, long before he was born. Maren told him the whole story of the challenge and what followed, so he could have a better understanding of both the way they had lived before, and why the women decided it was going to be very different here in Winterhaven.

"You make a beautiful mother," he assured her, smiling. "If you need anything, press the button on the call box and one of us will be right here," he promised, indicating the box he'd placed on the stand next to her bed. It was within easy reach. She finally smiled in return, feeling relieved they were around for support, after all.

"Thank you; all of you for what you've done to help out," she replied. "I'll remember to call if I need help." They all told her their welcomes and praised the cubs', knowing they were precious to everyone here. She smiled, nodded and laughed lightly, feeling at peace now.

"Are you ready? I'm going to let everyone in, a few at a time, to see you're okay and meet the cubs," Maren told her. "Best let them get it out of their systems now, so they're not trying to drop by constantly, when none of us is around to limit the visits."

"I'm as ready as I can be," she said, smiling. Bethany laughed.

"You really don't look it, but we understand," she assured her. "Do you want me to stay?" she asked.

"You'd better," Ryes returned, smiling. Maren went to the door and spoke to the residents of Winterhaven, briefly. "It sounds like everyone's outside, waiting," she commented in a low voice.

"Probably so. We've all been waiting for these little ones for quite some time," Bethy reminded her.

Mitt, Sayer, Raby and Sernn were the first ones in. Their delight, banter and laughter quickly put her to ease, making it easier as the next group which followed as soon as they left. After what seemed an eternity, they finally went through the entire population, with Rowan, Rinna and Darman remaining with her until her cubs were fed and they were all sound asleep.

"This I've waited to see, for a very long time," Rowan sighed out with a smile as he sat next to Ryes, watching her sleep. He reached up and damped down the lighting for her, the controls now being well-familiar devices.

"All of us have waited for this moment," Darman agreed, happy to have it over with. "And as soon as this storm system allows us, we'll go retrieve their father. Garth was so anxious to get home to her, when he'd been forced to come out to the Fall Plains Gather. I can well imagine what he's going through right now," he said, in a low voice.

"We'll get them both back," Rowan vowed. "They've been through so much with just Korman to deal with."

"That's the truth..." Rinna returned. They sat with her for a while longer, then quietly got up and left, leaving them resting peacefully. She gently kissed Ryes' head before she left, feeling so very happy.

Garth sat, meditating as Sabin taught him so long ago. It was far better than the headache he got from drinking too much of Keen's mead. It wasn't bad fare; he merely speculated that it'd been so long since he last overindulged himself that it was what he deserved. With meditation, he could ease his troubled heart and mind, in the gentle flow of his inner self. There was the sound of the door being opened, but as he let that flow past him, until he felt his shoulder being tapped. He opened his eyes to see Keen standing near him with a lantern in hand.

"Is he back, already?" he asked, puzzled by the look in his eyes.

"No. Not yet. A woman gave birth this morning and died. Senah decided that since the she-cub was fathered by a plainsman and you bore a Badge of Passage, and that your windracer was stolen by her son, she gives you the newborn. She actually said she thought the cub was cursed and you deserved her," he explained. Ross stood behind her cousin with the infant warmly wrapped in a blanket, in her arms. Her fussing and crying could be clearly heard, now.

"How will I feed her?" he questioned, surprised. "I'm not a woman!" he protested, worried for the newborn.

"We gathered fresh milk from the other, nursing mothers, but have no way to give you a nipple for her to suck," he admitted, passing over a skin filled with the milk.

"Could you please provide me with a bucket filled with ice, too? To keep the milk fresh as long as possible," he requested, standing up and taking the cub. Ross passed her over; regret in her eyes. She clearly didn't expect the infant to last too long without her mother to care for her. Garth took her and pulled aside the blanket to see her face. She had a pretty little smile, as she looked up at him and white hair adorning her head! He smiled as he realized the only name he could grant her, with such a striking feature.

"Shaysa," he named her, with a light laugh, as he looked back to his friends, here in this hold. Keen chuckled, nodding his head in agreement.

"That's what we thought, too," he stated, smiling to see Garth's acceptance for this tiny one's life.

"That windracer wasn't stolen. I granted it to Sernn as a Winterfest gift, but please don't tell Senah. It'll only make her think it was some kind of conspiracy against her, instead of merely a holiday present," he explained. "Now, I've got to figure out a way to nurse you, little daughter," he said, looking back down as the infant was starting to fuss.

"I do have this," Ross offered, extending what looked like a bounder's teat and a small length of cord.

"It might do," he agreed. He gently laid her down upon the bed as he went looking through his backpack, as she fussed. He pulled out a large plastic vial from the humans, which held some of the cooking spices Ryes packed for them. He unscrewed the lid and was going to dump it out into their waste bucket when Ross stopped him. She took it with a surprised look on her face.

"Let me have this spice. It's useful and very expensive," she requested. He shrugged with a smile as he let her have it. He rummaged and pulled out several others from his pack, extending them to her. Her eyes shone with wonder as she accepted them. As if he were giving her a precious gift. "Let me dump a couple of these out and clean them for you. I'll be right back." She hurried off.

"I never paid attention to what Ryes packed for me. I thought they were just common cooking spices," he told Keen. Keen chuckled at this, as Garth checked the small cub, to be sure she was all right. She was soon back with two of the vials empty and cleaned out.

He took one of the ones she offered with a smile. He then poured some of the milk from the waterskin into it. Taking the makeshift nipple Ross had given him before, he washed it too, then secured it with the cording to the vial. He squeezed to make sure the milk would flow, then picked up Shaysa and offered her the nipple. She quickly latched on, but almost choked as the milk flowed too fast. He then tried to let her suck upon his finger, letting the milk slowly flow down it, most of it going into her tiny mouth. This seemed to work better. He sighed in relief.

"I think we'll manage this, somehow. I used to help take care of my little sister, Mitt, when she was a tiny cub, even though I was young then. It seems I still recall some of this. I'll need some cloths for cleaning and changing her, a tunic which might fit her, and probably a few more of these nipples - just in case," he requested. Both Keen and Ross looked relieved.

"I'll go bring them right away, along with the ice," Ross volunteered, "And thank you for the cooking spices. We'll make good use of them." He chuckled and nodded his head.

"I never knew how to use them, so just left them in my pack," he admitted, chagrinned. She laughed lightly at this, giving him a nod.

"They're hard for us to come by and honestly, we would've considered them full payment for all your room rental in the hold proper, and meals for all the time you've been with us, if you were travelling guests. They're that expensive," she told him.

"Ryes gathered them in Halas. Please consider them a gift in exchange for our new daughter, here," he advised her. She nodded and laughed at this then quickly headed up the stairs. Garth smiled.

"At least Shaysa will take my mind off Sabin and worrying about my wife back home, a little," he told the guardsman.

"She'll keep you busy, for sure," he agreed. "What will your Ryes think of her?" he asked, hoping the cub would be all right.

"Her own mother died when she was a cub, so I know she'd never refuse to keep tiny Shaysa as our own," Garth assured him. He smiled down at the cub, making sure she was all right. Her bright eyes were studying his face. "Our family just increased by one."

"Good! Then, I'll leave this fresh lantern in here for you," he replied, relieved. He left, closing the door, but leaving it unlocked. It was Ross' sister, Rona, who gave Shaysa life and he knew his cousin's soul would rest easier, knowing her daughter would be loved and living far from Senah's madness.

Heading Home

Two days later, Sabin reappeared, looking exhausted. Garth was taking a nap with Shaysa beside him and awoke suddenly at sensing his presence in the room.

"Are you all right?" he questioned, sitting up, concerned for his dear friend.

"Well, I did the best I could, but still didn't make her happy. She's up there playing with the guards, who were there to make sure I stayed put and behaved. They can keep her!" he vowed, disgusted, stepping over to the bucket of water and drawing some out to wash his face. "I don't know if I'll ever get rid of her stench," he complained.

"While you've been keeping Senah entertained, I've gained a new daughter," Garth told him, pointing to the tiny, sleeping cub. "They said Senah decided to give her to me as a replacement for the stolen windracer. Her mother died birthing her and actually Senah decided she was a curse. She's the prettiest curse I've ever known," he commented with a chuckle. "I've decided to name her Shaysa." Sabin stepped over and looked down at the tiny, wrapped bundle and smiled. His face was uncertain for a moment until he got a good look at her, as she slept.

"She's so tiny," he breathed, as he gently touched one of her hands, admiring how beautiful and perfect she was. "I wonder if our own cubs will be this small? Ryes is going to be surprised," he added, looking up to see Garth's proud face. Yes, it was plain that he had his heart set upon keeping this small burden as his own.

"I wish the transmitter's batteries hadn't died, or I would've told Ryes about her by now," he said. "I don't think she'll mind, though. Her own mother died and left her orphaned." Sabin's eyes suddenly grew glassy for a few seconds, then he smiled, giving his friend a nod of his head.

"No, she won't. The first thing she'll do is put her to her own breast to nurse," he assured him, warmly clasping Garth upon the shoulder. "She's going to rename her, though," he finished, having only had a brief glimpse of Ryes and this tiny cub in his Vision.

"That's all right with me," he replied, a relieved sigh escaped his lips at this. "As long as we have her as a part of our family." There was the noise of someone coming down the stairs, which halted their conversation instantly.

"Garth? Sabin?" They heard Keen addressing them, as he stepped up to their now open door.

"Yes?" Garth asked, wondering what was up now? It wasn't time for their daily meal, yet.

"You're free to go. There's a few hours' break in the storm and Senah decided it was time for you two to leave," he explained, feeling he was shoving them out into the wicked cold to their own deaths.

"About time!" Sabin declared, while Garth smiled at hearing this good news, too.

"Is there anything left of our things?" he asked, suddenly wondering, seeing the distress in his face.

"Your packs were never touched. The elders decided when you were first brought here, that since you bore the Badge your things were to be left alone. Your two remaining windracers have been cared for and are awaiting you. Ross is preparing a food packet and we've been gathering milk from the other mothers for little Shaysa. It's not as much as I would hope," he warned them. Garth gave him a nod of his head in understanding.

"We'll make it," he vowed, "Sabin saw my wife holding Shaysa to nurse at her own breast, so we know we'll make it." He tried to assure this tall, kindly man. "I'll need to make some kind of sling to keep her warm and secure, against my chest," he added.

"I'll ask Ross. Come along, while Senah's still busy," he advised, "Before she changes her mind!"

They quickly gathered their things, making sure of them, repacking their backpacks. Garth packed the things he'd need for Shaysa at the top of his. He hung her almost-empty milk skin from his belt. They strapped on their new beltknives and were ready, as Garth gathered his new daughter up into his arms.

"Take the furs from your bed. You'll need them out there," he said in warning. They nodded and crammed them into their packs, too.

"Not enough room to do it," Sabin complained, frowning at his pack.

"No, do it this way," Keen replied, then showed them how to roll them up and put them across the top of their packs. He went and got some leather cords for them to use to tie them down and secure to their packs. Keen then led them upwards through several doors, taking a different direction. They came to the main kitchen, where they were met by several of the holders and Ross.

"Even if it wasn't the accommodations we had hoped to find, we do appreciate your doing your best to take care of us," Garth told her. She beamed at this, giving him a small bow of appreciation. "Do you have a sling, or some way for me to carry Shaysa as I ride?" he added, hoping.

"I have this for you," she offered, turning around and taking something furry from off the table next to her. She'd already foreseen the need and had fashioned one for him. It was more like a flapped pocket with straps to tie around his body. Garth smiled and nodded, passing Shaysa off to Sabin as he pulled off his jacket and outer shirt.

She helped show him how to tie it on and place her in it, to keep Shaysa warm. He then pulled back on his shirt and buttoned it up, but left it open at the top so he could see Shaysa and she could get some fresh air. It felt comfortable.

Next the elders presented both men with new, heavier coats and gloves. The coats had thick hoods, which they showed them how to tie them tight around their faces to keep the cold out. And finally, a pair of women gave them scarves and a waterskin filled with all the mothers' milk they could gather for Shaysa. They helped them wrap the scarves around their necks and across their faces to help keep the cold winds from stealing their warm.

Proper good-byes were said, with a merry escort out to their mounts. Both Pacer and Spur looked well-groomed and even a little fat from their stay here. They quickly went through their packs, gifting out the items they no longer needed, or would merely be more trouble to pack along with only the two windracers left to them. These were accepted with surprise and delight by the Menna hold residents. Ross took the small pack that contained the last of the cooking spices and empty jars and containers as if they'd handed her a bag containing gold nuggets. It made them both feel better about it all.

"Be careful," Ross advised, giving them each a kiss farewell. "Be good, little niece," she said, smiling at the tiny infant, giving her a quick kiss, as well. Garth tucked her in, snug against his chest, under his shirt and coats. He knew they'd make it home. He only hoped it'd be soon!

"If my sister, Mitt, returns in the flyer, tell her I said she'd better be good and I'll meet her at home," Garth requested, smiling, sure the message would be delivered.

"I will," she promised, returning the smile.

"I'll take you out over the pass. The rest is up to you," Keen advised; his own mount ready to ride.

"Thanks," Sabin said, grateful. The compass still worked. He had their route down and already planned out on the map, so they should be all right from there.

"Once the next storm hits, take cover - wherever you find it," he pressed. "Up here in the mountains, they're deadly!"

"We will," Garth vowed, mounting Pacer. Sabin practically jumped up onto Spur's saddle, relieved they were finally free!

They left and after an hour's hard ride crested the pass, looking down onto the snow-covered terrain below. The view was spectacular, but there was another storm threatening, at their backs.

"Be careful and ride well," Keen said as they said quick good-byes. "I'll make sure Kyma knows everything," he promised.

"Thank you, once again! Come see us in Winterhaven, sometime. We don't have any dungeons, there," Garth invited with a grin. He laughed in response, then waved as he turned his mount for home.

Then they started down the mountain, mindful of the snow and their beasts' footing. They just gained the foothills at the bottom, when the fury of the storm struck. They found a copse of evergreen trees in a small hollow, taking shelter within, quickly building a small campfire to help keep themselves warm with some old brush, fallen wood and loose forest litter. It was a pungent fire, but crackled merrily; warming their hearts while they also warmed their hands and dinner. Garth warmed some of the milk and fed Shaysa, as he and Sabin huddled under one of the blankets and the furs from their bed. Pacer and Spur were lying at their backs, providing a small windbreak. The windracers munched upon the grains the mountain folk provided for them. Garth and Sabin made a meal from what foods were still good out of their own stores along with some of the chunks of dried meat and fruits Ross packed for them.

"This looks like it's not going to let up soon," Garth commented. He didn't want any more delays. He needed to get home! He and Shaysa both needed Ryes! She was fussy and he knew she needed to be warmer.

"Let's try to get some rest," Sabin advised. "As soon as it does let up, we'll press on. I want to get to that creek on our map. I don't care how cold it is, I need a bath! I feel foul with that creature's stench still on me!" he decried. Garth smiled. He had to agree, he felt much the same about the long captivity and no bathing allowed in the hold, down in the guest room they were staying. The Moondance tribe thought they were strange with their need for frequent bathing, but let them do it.

"We'll see," he promised. "With the way this storm looks, I don't think we'll be able to tell day from night, anyway. It's just like our cell, only without walls. So, we'll sleep when we can, and travel when we can. We'll make it," he assured him, clasping his shoulder and smiling.

"I know we will," Sabin agreed. He settled back against Spur, as best he could, while Garth cleaned and changed little Shaysa's bottom. At least Garth claimed her as his own, so he didn't have to worry about changing cubs - just yet. He saw Ardis' face in his mind, then his heart wrenched as he tried to think of a way to tell her what happened, and why. Would she still want him after Senah? Would she accept his true-mate vows, now? He could only hope. His love for her was the only thing which got him through those long days in Senah's company. He hoped she could forgive him at least.

"Why it's the great Kyma, himself," Senah purred out, looking ready to pounce as he burst in her chamber door with chiefs from all the other mountain tribes attending him. She stood up from her bed, still nude and defiant about displaying it before them all.

"Where are they?" he demanded, the ice in his golden eyes finally making an impact upon her. She stepped a few paces closer to them.

"Gone. I sent them away. They were too boring," she informed him, smiling maliciously. "I mated one of them and decided he wasn't enough to fully whet my appetite. Would you like to take up where he left off?" she offered in invitation. She ran a hand down the length of her body, as if she were still young and nubile. It sickened the men, but most kept it from their faces.

"Get dressed and come downstairs," Kyma ordered, and then nodded to his own guards to keep an eye on her, until she came before him. He had witnesses to question and if she chose to take her time, it'd only give him more time alone with their testimonies.

"And that's what he said Sabin told him. He has Visionary and from before I've known Sabin to say that it's very strong," Keen related. Others had spoken before him, including the guards who had been made to force Sabin to stay with Senah. So, he wasn't sure if he'd even be heard. But when he was called, he told the whole story of all he saw and did during their time in the Hold.

"So they believe they will make it because the newborn cub will be nursed by Garth's wife?" Tonnu, Chief of Scatter Peak Hold, repeated, wonder in his eyes. "Why didn't he see them being captured in the first place?" he pressed. Keen shrugged at this.

"He never said, so I don't know," he replied. Ross gave him a nod of agreement.

"Why were they so accepting of their being locked up?" Kyma asked, wondering.

"At first, they were ready to fight, then it seemed they recalled they were bearers of the Badge of Passage and decided they needed to wait and try to seek other means of being released," Ross answered truthfully.

"A very few of us knew Sernn left to take their messages to you and their families in Winterhaven, where they came from," Keen stated. "Do you think he made it?"

"A patrol saw three people load him and a windracer into a flying machine. It took off, going straight up into the air," Kyma finally related to them all after a few moments. Ross and Keen smiled at this. "I hadn't believed what they told me, at the time," he admitted. "Then with your reports of a flyer being above the hold before the last storms, I now believe."

"I wonder if Mitt was flying it?" Ross said aloud, happy for the news. They'd all worried for the cub.

"Mitt?" he asked, wonder dancing in his eyes.

"Garth's younger sister. He said before that she loved the flyer best of all the machines they'd found in Winterhaven," Keen related.

"I want to meet this Mitt," Kyma laughed heartily. "I need such a brave wife!" The rest of the gathering laughed with him at this in agreement.

After over two hour's wait, Senah finally appeared, being brought to the circle before her own chair, where Kyma now sat. She had washed-up and dressed in her finest furs and jewelry; ready to deal with him now. He had a mug of honeyed mead in hand and had been talking with the other chiefs, laughing as if this were nothing more than a small gather to discuss tribe business. He looked at her, giving the others a nod of his head.

"What you did deserves death!" he declared. "But, since you may carry cubs from one of the Travelers, you'll be allowed to live for a while longer. Since you have no other heirs of an age to rule, I'm appointing your cousin, Ross, as chieftain until the Spring Gather. Then, either her office will be confirmed and upheld, or other candidates presented for review," he informed the assembly of the hold's population. "I'd rather have someone from Menna's Hold running Menna's Hold." This got mute nods of agreement from the holders.

"What about me?" Senah demanded, insulted that her lowly cousin was going to be given her hold, as if she had the brains to manage it alone. "The only thing she's good at is running the kitchen staff! Surely, she'd need some kind of advisor!"

"You're coming back with me as a `guest,' in my hold, just like you made the two Travelers here. If it's of any consolation, Garth said their treatment by your holders was as kind as could be, considering what it could've been. Take her away! We only have a few hours before the next storm hits," he ordered his guards, knowing they'd handle her well.

"You can't do this to me! This is my hold and my birthright!" she shouted, as she was dragged out of the main hall. "I'm the only living child of Chief Sentan! This is MY HOLD!" she screeched out, then was suddenly silenced. No one appeared to want to investigate further.

"Ross," Kyma spoke up into the sudden quiet of the room. "This hold is as much yours, as your cousin's. Take good care of it and your people. We appreciate your hospitality, but must be on our way." Ross stepped forward, bowed formally to Great Chief Kyma, and then turned to address the holders.

"I accept the responsibility placed within my claws and will do the best I can to ensure Menna's Hold thrives once more," she declared with a small smile, while shaking inside. There was a loud cheer from the rest of the holders as they accepted her pledge, and were backing her. She smiled in response, stunned. It was a lot of responsibility to take on, but with her husband and other cousins to help, she was sure she could at least start the healing process before the Great Spring Gather. Kyma stepped down from the raised seat and clasped her shoulder in pride as he chuckled. She had courage, at least.

"Your seat awaits, my lady," he told her, then gave her a bow of his head and turned for the main doors. The other chiefs made their own small comments to her, as they said their good-byes in turn. They had a ride before them. As they mounted their windracers, Kyma turned back to see the holders gathered outside, waving their farewells. He smiled, feeling good about the outcome of this ordeal. He hoped the two Travelers would make it home safely. He'd have to draft a message for Dara, to be delivered as soon as the storms broke. This spring's gather promised to be interesting, if nothing else. Senah glared daggers at everyone and her screams of outrage were quickly cut off by the winds that suddenly buffeted them, as they rode out.

        "I'll take the lead while you sit up on Pacer and feed Shaysa," Sabin ordered Garth, taking up the reins of the two stallions. The cub was fussing and needing attention. He'd helped some, the last two days, but they'd just washed up in the icy stream and he wanted the exercise to help keep him warm. The clean, dry clothing helped, at least.
        "I don't think I'll ever feel warm, again," he returned, his teeth chattering. He mounted Pacer, then took out the vial of milk and started to feed the cub. "Her milk's getting low," he warned him. "Where can we find milk for her out here?”
        "Maybe we can bring down a mother bounder and use some of her milk?" he asked, wondering if it would truly suffice?
        "You find one and I'll shoot her. We can only try. And the fresh meat would be worth it, too," he added smiling, thinking of a fresh slab of bounder meat cooking over a fire. Sabin chuckled at this, thinking much the same, himself. They still had supplies of the dried meat Ross gave them, but it was tough and the spices were not what they were used to, and it only made them thirsty when they finished.
        “Unless one's lying around for me to step on, I don't think we'll find one too soon,” he returned with a huff of a laugh. Sabin took the lead, walking the windracers through the deep snow on foot. There was light through the clouds, but they had no idea if it was morning or evening; thankfully the last storm had finally let up. So, they headed out as quickly as possible.
        There were treacherous dips and they truly had no idea where the trail lay, so used all caution as they pressed onward for home, hoping to get there soon. The mountains were well behind them, but the vast plains were still around them and there was no sign of their home beacon, yet. It looked like the storms had cleared from the mountains, but were settled down upon the plains ahead. Sabin stuck to his compass, checking the readings to make sure they were headed in the right direction. With the storms, neither of them had much sleep and knew they were reaching the limits of their endurance.
        After a few hours of walking, just as he was about to call a break, Sabin suddenly felt the "ground" shift below his feet and he fell down into a small, hidden ravine. He tumbled through the thin crust

of snow, falling eight feet before stopping at the bottom. Garth was immediately off his mount, starting to climb down to help his friend, mindful of the tiny cub sleeping in the sling against his chest.

"Are you all right?" he asked, reaching Sabin's side.

"Just feeling stupid, is all," he returned, then tried to stand up. The intense stabbing in his leg almost caused him to black out from the pain. Garth caught him with his shoulder, helping him back up, panic in his eyes.

"Not as all right as you think," he returned, seeing his ragged breathing return to something more normal, as he huffed a laugh.

"Ware the cub," Sabin warned, smiling as tears were at the corners of his eyes. "I think I'll need a little help getting back up there," he agreed.

"Let me get a rope," Garth told him, getting an idea. They still had two very-sturdy, colorful ropes from Winterhaven in their backpacks. He got one out and tied it around Sabin, then climbed back up and tied the other end to Pacer's saddle horn, urging him to back up, as he added his own strength to the effort. They got him back up to their path.

"Very clever," he complemented Garth's quick thinking. He was relieved with his solution, as he helped him mount Spur. He untied the rope, handing it back to his friend with a smile. "Remind me to bring you along on our next winter camping trip," he teased.

"I don't know. Your idea of a relaxing vacation outdoors isn't exactly what I'd call much fun," he volleyed in return; glad to see he'd regained his sense of humor the last two days, at least.

"But, you've got to admit the peace and quiet is refreshing," he replied, gesturing grandly to the open land around them. Garth chuckled at this, nodding his head.

"We'll probably be glad of this later, after a few days at home," he agreed. He examined Sabin's leg and sighed.

"It's broken," he told him. "Let me get this bound up, first. I'm not going to try to set it out here, in the wilderness. I'll let Maren truly fix it when we get home." Sabin nodded, knowing he needed care badly now.

Garth cut up the leg of his pants and then hunted about for some sticks to use. He first cleaned and bandaged his friend's leg to staunch the bleeding and provide padding, then used the sticks around the outside of his pants and tied them on to act as a brace for now. Sabin had been gritting his teeth, but now could relax his jaw; Spur had been patient through the whole thing, for which they both were thankful. Garth checked on Shaysa, since she'd been fussing during the operation, then took up the animals' leads. He used his bow stave to prod the snow before him, making sure of the path, as well as he could.

"We'll make camp soon. I want to get a better look at your leg," he told Sabin.

"I'll be all right," he complained, "We only need to get home!" he protested, not wanting the attention when it'd only delay their journey home. "I'm sure Winterhaven lies ahead of us now and those low, dark, storm clouds hide the beacon from our eyes."

"No. I'll find a good place to camp. We don't know how far we have to go, before we reach Maren," he stated, stopping to meet his blood-brother's orange-gold eyes. Sabin saw Garth was serious.

"All right. Just be careful. I don't want us both to end up injured out here in the wilderness," he gave in, feeling frustrated. The leg was going numb and that wasn't a good sign, as far as he knew.

"Ryes would hurt me if I didn't take care of both you and this little cub," he laughed, thinking of her sweet face and bright green eyes, again. He knew they had to be getting closer. It felt like it!

"Well, the computer says that the storms are only down here in the lowlands, now. The mountains are clear until tomorrow afternoon," Neil advised Ryes as she came into the control room to check up on things. "It's good to see you're already up and about, kid," he added, smiling. She smiled, grateful, feeling as if he were more like a big brother.

"I have to escape from them for a little while, or I'd go bonkers real soon," she returned with a light laugh. "How's your little girl doing? I wasn't sure if Brenda was ready for company, yet," she asked.

"Little Samantha's fine, thanks to Maren," he commented. "Drop by any time you like. I'm sure Brenda will be happy to see you."

"I will," she promised, "Right after dinner." Suddenly the computer sounded an alarm, bringing them both to the alert.

"Life threatening injury requires immediate attention," it announced, displaying the problem on the main screen. It showed a shot from one of the Star Quest's cameras. One of the women was trapped beneath a tumble of crates. Scott and Steven were trying to get them off of her.

"What's up?" Maren demanded, over the intercom. Neil shunted the display for him to see for himself. "We're on our way," he assured them, getting up and scrambling his support team.

"Jim Dawe, Quin Marcell and Damian Hacker, get out to the Star Quest's cargo hold to help in the rescue," Neil ordered, over the PA system. They saw them scrambling to action with Torr, Mason and Spann joining them. "I can't tell who's trapped," he sighed, feeling frustrated.

"Maybe I'd better get out there, too?" Ryes stated, turning to leave the control room, but Neil grabbed her wrist, halting her escape.

"No. Wait until the area's declared safe. We don't need to endanger your life as well. Those cubs need you, too," he scolded gently. Her face displayed her inner struggle for a few moments, and then she sat down upon a chair, heavily.

"And I did promise Garth that I'd be careful," she sighed. "I only feel bad about sending others out to risk their lives, while I have to hang back," she added. Dr. Cruthers came into the control room, chuckling to hear this from her.

"It's the hardest part of command to learn to deal with, my dear," he assured her, "To risk the lives of others is never easy. But if you send out people who're skilled and intelligent, it makes the burden a little lighter."

"I understand that now, only too well," she agreed, looking anxious as they all watched the main display. "This storm isn't helping things," she added, seeing their outside visibility was almost down to zero again. Thank goodness the rovers had equipment to make blind navigation easier!

"Whoever said the Fates were kind?" Neil commented, smiling as he looked over at her. The safety of the crew counted to her, very much, whether or not they were starmen. Her compassion, inner strength and warm heart were what held this motley group together, more than anything else, he realized.

They sat and watched the drama unfold. The brute strength of the men combined, managed to pull the huge crates off the woman and Maren and his team were able to stabilize her enough, to get her back to the main facility. It turned out to be Ellen Fortney, an archeologist, who was helping with retrieving what cargo they could from the derelict ship. The men shifted the cargo and locked it down, to prevent any further collapses, as they made room for the medical team to evacuate her. Then they all returned to Winterhaven.

When the medical team arrived back in the clinic, Ryes was there to help. With the strength of her pool of power to draw upon, Maren and Tennan were able to repair and restore Ellen to health, leaving her in Ted's hands, as she rested afterwards. The three of them were drained by the effort, so they went to the dining room for some tea and a short break before lunch.

"Mom!" Sayer called out, a tiny cub in her arms. "Somebody's up and needs you," she informed her as she caught them up in the hallway. Ryes was immediately by her side, seeing tiny Shaysa was indeed awake and fussing. She felt her milk letting down.

"She's the only one?" she asked, hoping.

"Yes, so far," she replied, smiling impishly, guessing why she asked. Ryes sighed in relief as she took her white-haired cub.

"Good. We're going for some tea, I'll have some sent back for you and Raby," she promised, smiling.

"Okie-dokie," she responded, "but, take your time. We can watch them for you," she assured her, then turned back for their room. "It's fun with real cubs to take care of, instead of just dolls!"

"Thanks, Sayer," Ryes called out to her laughing while meaning it. The girls had been a blessing for sure.

"It's just that they outnumber you," Tennan teased, as Ryes joined them once more. She'd relaxed somewhat now that Ryes was a mother in her own right. Ryes unbuttoned her shirt a few buttons and put the cub to her breast as they continued down the hallway, laughing lightly.

"That's too true," she agreed.

"You'll get the hang of it," Maren promised with a sigh.

"I think I'm starting to get an idea of how to manage things," she agreed, smiling as they entered the mostly empty hall. There were a handful of others there taking a short break, too.

"You go sit, I'll get something for you," Maren offered, while Tennan gave her a nod.

"Thank you," she said as she smiled and gave in with a nod of her head and headed over to her table. Maren and Tennan emerged a few minutes later, each bearing a tray. They had a small bowl of fruit with a sweet roll for each of them, along with a mug of tea.

"Oh bubblenut rolls and mint tea!" Ryes declared, happy with their choices. Maren laughed at this, nodding his head.

"I love the new tea combinations Chuck's been coming up with," he said, smiling in agreement. "And I asked if a snack could be sent to the girls," he added. Ryes grabbed her mug and added some honey from the container on the table, stirring it for a moment while enjoying the rich aroma.

"Thanks, Maren. We've got some real talent in that kitchen," she agreed, pleasure alighting her eyes. Shaysa was starting to drop off, at last. And Raby appeared with Jann in her arms. Ryes laughed, as did the others.

"Someone woke up," she told her mother. Ryes nodded, showing her Shaysa was very sleepy again.

"And someone can go back to her bed," she told her grinning. They carefully exchanged cubs with Tennan lending a hand. She seemed well practiced at it. Once Raby was on the way back, she settled back in her seat more comfortably.

"The mothers with young ones all need table top holders for them here," Tennan suggested, as ideas danced in her head.

"That sounds like the only way I'd be able to eat with everyone here, again," Ryes said, nodding her head. "It's getting hard to try to manage things from my room. All the visitors keep waking up the cubs," Ryes complained.

"Why not set up some cribs in your office so you can take care of your cubs there, while working? I have one for Tian," Tennan told her, as she saw ideas take fire in her emerald eyes at this.

"Teris has her today, correct?" Maren asked, sure he hadn't seen her today. His sister nodded her head.

"He likes to spend time with her while he practices in the garden rooms. She seems to like it better than Medical," she replied and laughed.

"I think Teris' Talent is actually a new one," Ryes added in, finally voicing when she'd felt through time. "It's not actually a regular Empath as his is more specialized just for plants and their nurturing. I have it too, but he's far more practiced at it," she smiled at the memory of their exploring a very old tree which was part of a stand of trees, further downstream along the rill that ran past them and out to the Yuri River, before her Talents had disappeared entirely. "But I haven't figured out a good name to call this new Talent," she finished, then noticed both siblings were staring at her in wonder.

"A new Talent? Truly?" Maren questioned, amazed.

"How can you be sure?" Tennan added, wondering and proud of her new husband.

"I have the memories of the Sleepers, or Handmaidens of Doran, and combed through them again and again. The abilities he's been using never existed on Kahmarr, nor her colony worlds of old. I wanted to make very sure, but nothing was ever there about them. And those women trained at prestigious academies so their Talents were honed to operate at their best potential. That is why I'm sure of it," she told them both, smiling.

"That's wonderful! I can't wait to tell him!" Tennan declared, the joy on her face said it all. "It'd be great if Tian has his Talent, too."

"If not her, then perhaps your grandchildren down the road," Maren offered as he finished off his roll. Ryes had practically wolfed hers down and was now picking up her fork to start in on her fruit, all the while Jann happily nursed. She'd learned she can do a lot of things one-handed. She nodded her head in agreement.

"And, since it's his Talent and unique, I'm going to say he deserves to name it," she stated.

"Since you both have it, why not both of you name it?" Maren countered, seeing his sister now annoyed with him. Ryes laughed, shaking her head now.

"Maybe we can work on the name together?" she replied, grinning.

"I'm going to head over and tell Teris right now!" Tennan asserted as she gulped down her tea, having finished her fruit and roll, too. She left quickly, putting her tray on the conveyer belt that led back into the kitchen. Ryes sighed and nodded her head.

"We've evolved as a people," she told Maren, "Which I feel is a good thing." He nodded and laughed.

"Truly, it's best for all of us," he agreed. "So, that means you now have thirteen Talents, not twelve as your mother possessed," he teased. She laughed at this merrily.

"Poor mom would've been driven up a tree with all four of us at once," she agreed, smiling now as she imagined it for a moment; seeing the reflection of her own life in it, too. "I think my Talents are starting to wake up again," she told Maren, "I felt my Healing aiding yours and Tennan's today."

"I thought that was you," he agreed, sipping his tea and appearing thoughtful. "So much stronger now, too. And your Booster has jumped up in strength. I noticed that as we worked." She nodded.

"I'm going to do my best to seriously work on training my Talents to their fullest capabilities. But it's a little scary to think they're coming back with far more power and far more quickly than what I was told would happen. I think I could lift the Star Quest and set her exactly where I want to now without feeling any effort."

"Wait until Garth gets back," he said, chuckling.

"He's near, Maren," she replied. "I can feel him near! I just can't pinpoint where, yet."

"Then we'll keep on the alert for them. I had hoped they'd wait for us to go rescue them, personally, from that Hold with all this bad weather," he told her, a gleam in his eyes. She gave his shoulder a squeeze as she smiled for him. "I don't want to think of them out there lost in the snow storms!"

"Since when have any of our original group been patient?" she teased. He nodded, smiling again.

"True," he agreed. "We wouldn't be here." They finished their tea in peace.

Reunited

The vicious, icy wind cut through their clothing, as the storm picked up in tempo. The cascade of falling snow was quickly turning day to night. Garth feared for their very lives in this, no matter what Sabin said about their making it home! He kept Pacer heading forward, praying no unseen obstacles would come before them, to cause his beast to fall, or break his leg. Spur's nose was almost buried in his own leg, as if the creature was seeking warmth and comfort, wherever he could find it. They crested a small hill and Garth surveyed the way ahead, seeing only a thick, white blanket of snow, through the swirling curtain.

"Keep moving!" Sabin shouted to him, seeing his hesitation. He was sure they were almost to Winterhaven. Garth gave him a sign to wait a moment as he checked on the tiny infant still bundled close to his chest, then he kneed his steed forward. She was crying and sucking on her balled fist, but there was nothing he could do for her, now. He gave her some warmed water earlier, but couldn't stop now in this storm! He continued on, hoping.

Then after another hour of agonized plodding through the storm, they unexpectedly they arrived at a massive black-metal wall. Where had this come from? What did it mean? The windracers had stopped, as it did provide a small windbreak. It appeared to have been fashioned in some manner, which hopefully meant shelter nearby, if not inside it.

"What's this?" Garth demanded of the snowy world around him.

"Who seeks passage here?" a voice demanded out of the darkness and snow. The voice came so suddenly and out of nowhere, that it startled both Garth and his steed. He reined in, calming Pacer.

"We need shelter!" he yelled back, wondering where they were?

"Who are you?" the voice demanded, as a heavily clothed figure appeared out of the wind and snow, carrying a strange weapon in his hand. It looked like a long, bulky stick, but was made of metal and wood. In his other hand he carried one of the human's lanterns. This suddenly gave him hope. Could they truly be home?

"I'm Garth formerly of Matlowe Village, now a resident of Winterhaven and my companion is Sabin," he gave in response over the wind, his voice now sounding raw even in his own ears.

"GARTH? Is that REALLY you?" a second voice questioned, as another figure appeared next to the first. "Garth's back!" he yelled into his transmitter, then rushed to Pacer's side with his arms outstretched.

"Torr?" Garth questioned, as he tried to get his legs working to dismount. He heard laughter in response and quick support to his unsteady feet. He'd been out in the cold, far too long! He was feeling too numb.

"You've been gone a long time!" Torr replied, as he put his face up next to his cousin's. "About time, too," he scolded, "Ryes is driving the rest of us crazy." This got Garth to crack a smile, as he realized he was FINALLY home… HIS HOME!

"Where is she?" he demanded, feeling the long journey crashing down upon him in this moment. "Oh, better give Sabin a hand. He's hurt his leg pretty bad." He suddenly recalled his real concern with reaching home, as quickly as possible!

"Let's get you both out of this," he told him, as they both led him and the animals around the Star Quest's bulk and after several minutes' walk down toward the main entrance to their underground base.

"Where did we get the wall?" Garth asked as Torr opened one of the large doors with a small box, to get the animals in quickly, which surprised Garth, then closed them the same way behind them and the man with the strange stick. Torr was laughing at his question.

"You'll see later, when we have better light," he answered with a grin.

Once they were inside, the warmth of the colony welcomed them home. Garth felt it was as warm in here as a spring day in the sun, and they were still in the outer holding area with the animals. He went to help Sabin down from Spur, as both animals had picked up their heads, smelling others in a small stable, across the large chamber.

"Let Torr help me," Sabin urged him, "I don't want to accidently hurt the little one you're carrying," he insisted. Torr frowned at this, wondering as he pulled off his face scarf. He was immediately beside Sabin's mount and the two of them helped him down, carefully.

"Where's Maren?" Garth asked as they supported Sabin between them. "He really needs his healing touch."

"I think Dr. Turner might be better today. Maren's been busy and I think is tapped out. He and Tennan had to heal Ellen. She was badly injured, earlier today," he told him, as the other sentry stepped over to help with their packs and getting their windracers into the paddock.

"I'll take care of this," Monty assured Torr, as he gave him a nod. He slung this rifle across his back. Torr gave him a smile.

"Thanks, Monty," he replied.

"Thank you," Sabin added, too, unsure who was helping them, but was grateful.

"Ellen, who?" Garth questioned, wondering. Torr merrily laughed again.

"You've been gone far too long," he reminded him, as he lead them toward the main door, going inside. "Ardis insisted we keep it as a surprise for your return. We now have humans living among us. They take a little getting used to, but they're not too bad. They're the ones who originally built this place." With this he opened the door onto the main corridor and Garth and Sabin both noted the number of people now living here. There were a furless people talking and interacting with more of Matlowe's population, than he recalled was living here, before. He stopped for a moment in utter surprise.

"Oh my," a slender human said, as she stopped before them, alarm in her eyes. "How long have you been out in that storm?" she asked. Her sex was easy to tell. Garth wondered how many children she had?

"For the last several days," Sabin answered for them. She activated a box in her hand and was waving it before them, a frown of concern upon her face. She suddenly stopped it right in front of Garth's chest.

"And who do we have here?" she questioned, looking him in the eye. Torr laughed.

"What was Sabin just talking about?" he asked, puzzled. Garth cast them both a chagrined smile, as he opened his coats and then his heavy shirt, to reveal the tiny she-cub nestled in a sling, against the warmth of his chest.

"We ran out of milk for her this morning, but Sabin assured me we'd make it home today. I only hoped, for she needs some now, and probably a good cleaning, too," he told them, as he gently removed her and held her in his large hands.

"Got just the thing for her," Bethany assured him, taking her from him. "Oh, she's so pretty with that white hair!" she declared as she cuddled the infant to her chest and turned for Ryes' quarters. The she-cub snuggled against her, fussing loudly as she rushed down the corridor. She saw Ted come out of the medical center.

"Ted, we have a bad leg and two cases of hypothermia, which need treatment immediately," she told him in English, pointing back the way she just came.

"Right," he replied, wondering whose cub she was carrying? "Justin, we need a wheelchair stat," he called out as he rushed over to help out. Justin was quickly on his heels, ready to help, too.

"Here," Ted offered, taking charge and helping Torr support Sabin. Justin pulled over the wheeled chair and Garth noted how efficient they were, as the second man made some adjustments to the chair and stood back up, appearing ready. Garth stepped over to Sabin and removed his backpack, moving easier now that he was cubless.

"All set," Justin offered. Ted nodded and he and Torr lowered Sabin down into it. Sabin grimaced but held himself as still as possible as they adjusted the one side to accommodate his wounded leg, keeping it raised and supported, while putting his other foot up on a small support, which was in a more normal position.

"How did you break your leg?" Ted asked as they started walking both men back to Medical.

"Not paying good enough attention," Sabin replied, feeling foolish. Garth huffed a laugh, shaking his head.

"It was a snow-covered dip that was at least eight feet deep," he told him. Sabin nodded at this. "Is Maren around? I think Sabin's leg is broken."

"I'll let him know, but he and Tennan had to heal Ellen today and are tapped out. I'll help get it reset and we'll see if either of them can finish it tomorrow," he offered him in response as they reached the Medical entrance.

"Tennan can Heal?" he asked, surprised, but as he said it, he realized it must run in their whole family.

"Yes. Ryes found her Talent some months ago," Ted assured him with a nod.

"And we need to check you over, too. We don't want you losing anything to frostbite, either," Justin added. Garth shook his head.

"I have to go find Ryes, first. I'm sure she's been waiting for me," he replied. Light dawned in their eyes at this with both men giving him a nod of agreement.

"She's been waiting," Ted assured him, smiling from ear to ear.

"I've heard driving everyone crazy," he replied, smiling in return. They both gave him broader smiles and a nod of their heads in answer.

"Welcome home," Ted said, extending his hand. Garth shook it, human-style, smiling.

"Thank you," he responded, happy to hear it. "I'll be back soon," he said. He gave Sabin's shoulder a squeeze. Sabin nodded his head, smiling through the pain. Now that he was warming up, he was feeling it more. Justin took the backpack for him.

"If you see Ardis," Sabin started. Garth laughed and nodded.

"I'll send her right to you," he promised. Then turned for the door back to the hallway and stairs he was starting to remember. Torr was nearby, ready to lead him back to the room he once called his own.

"Ryes?" Bethany queried loudly, as she turned the corner, walking quickly down the hall, approaching her door. The small one in her arms was starting to fuss loudly now and it distressed her that she couldn't do anything for her, herself.

"Come in," she heard in response.

"I have someone who needs you," she said, as Ryes met her just inside the door. There was a questioning frown in her eyes, then she saw the tiny cub she held. She put out her hands, cupped to receive her. "She's undernourished and was last fed this morning. Is this all right with you?" The cub was starting to squirm and cry even more loudly.

"Yes," Ryes assured her with a smile. She had more than enough milk to care for one more. Bethany gave the cub over to her friend with a relieved sigh. Ryes caught Garth's scent from her and looked at her strangely. "Where did she come from?" she demanded, wondering if she was imagining it?

"Two riders in out of the storm," she told her, smiling as she could guess why she asked. He had to have been Garth! Ryes pulled open her shirt and put the cub to one of her nipples. She immediately latched on and began to suckle hungrily. Soon there was a commotion out in the hallway and voices were raised in greeting. She closed her eyes, practically trembling. Yes, he had to be back at long last!

"Two men?" she asked Bethany, hoping.

"Yes," she replied smiling impishly.

"Garth," she sighed out in longing, "but, first what should we name you?" she asked the cub as she nursed. Her eyes were open as she looked up to Ryes' face.

"How about Shyla?" Bethany asked her. "It would go with Shaysa and she does have white hair, just like her," she suggested.

"Shaysa and Shyla," Ryes breathed out, "Yes. That's perfect," she agreed. She heard Maren's voice raised in surprise, and knew it for sure. But, was she really ready to face him after this long absence? "He's back Bethy, what do I say to him?" Bethany looked surprised. Ryes was always so strong, it was a new thing to see her look so uncertain.

"Say what's been in your heart for so long. From that last letter he sent, he misses you as much as you've missed him. It was only the two of them and Shyla. No one else," she reassured her. Ryes nuzzled the cub, taking in her full scent signature. No mother's scent clung to the child, only Garth and Sabin's, Garth's being the strongest. She sighed, still nervous.

"He's never going to believe the size of his family," she told her with a merry light in her eyes. "And now it's increased by one," she added with a small laugh.

"But, this one's his gift, so how can he object?" she pointed out, smiling in relief. There was a light knock on the door's casing.

"Ryes?" Maren asked, knowing she had to be up, with the commotion out in the hallways.

"Yes?" she questioned, sounding merry. She had to KNOW! He pulled back the curtain to see her and Bethany standing like they were talking, as she was nursing a cub. He suddenly stopped as he realized it wasn't Shaysa! Where had this one come from? Both women laughed, seeing the puzzled expression upon his face.

"Someone's here to see you," he told her lamely. She smiled. The first real smile he saw upon her face in several months!

"I can guess," she replied. She and Bethy stepped through the door curtain, as he held it open for them. Garth stood in the midst of his friends and looked across to see her standing in the doorway. Their eyes met and he saw the love and longing in them, as deep as that which already lay in his own heart. He stepped through the people between as he came before her and the tiny cub she held to her breast.

"You sure bring back interesting souvenirs," she teased him, smiling up into his eyes.

"I was thinking of calling her Shaysa, our moon daughter," he told her, missing her touch so much. She shook her head to this with a light laugh. Her voice and laugh went through him like a shock. He'd missed it, too!

"Our other daughter is named Shaysa, so her name will be Shyla," she informed him, as she suddenly closed her eyes and threw her other arm about him, the cub cuddled between them.

"We have a daughter?" he asked as he wrapped his arms about her, happiness bursting within his chest. She laughed at hearing this, tears in her eyes. It felt so good to have him back! A crying noise started up from inside the room. "And it sounds like she wants to eat, too," he added in comment.

"Actually, that sounds like one of our sons," she told him, pulling back to look up into his face. There was surprise written in his eyes and she had to laugh again.

"ONE?" he asked, not believing he heard her correctly.

"Yes, we have two sons and now it looks like we have three infant daughters and two teenaged daughters," she informed him. Maren, Torr and the others were laughing at the astonished look on his face.

"You matched old Talden's legendary record," Rowan told him, as he approached the growing crowd of people around them. "You now have five cubs!" Garth laughed, shaking his head. He looked around and saw Mitt and Karr working their way through the press, to reach his side. Mitt threw her arms about him too, in happiness.

"You made it back!" she declared in relief. He hugged her back, one-armed, unwilling to let Ryes go - ever again!

"Rowan?" he asked. "How did all these people get here?" He couldn't believe his eyes.

"I sent Maren and Torr back to check on things in Matlowe, before the winter snows locked us in. They just had a problem leaving them all behind," Ryes explained. Her ears caught the insistence in Gareth's voice and it tugged at her as much as her need to hold onto his father. She'd sent Raby and Sayer off to spend the night with Mitt, so they'd get some good sleep tonight. Garth saw the indecision on her face and gave her an understanding smile.

"Story telling comes later, my dear wife," he said, knowing her heart was torn. A bright smile lit her face, as she leaned up to give him a kiss, then released him to take care of things within their room. She had little ones who needed feeding, cleaning and attention, after all. Bethany followed her, closing the curtain behind them.

"They're early, aren't they?" he asked Maren, wanting to be sure.

"Yes, they are. You have no idea how much work you have cut out for you," Maren warned his friend with a chuckle, clasping a hand upon his shoulder.

"I have no idea how I'll ever repay you," Garth replied, sure in his heart that he owed Maren a great deal. He then saw a very elderly human approaching them, who moved with more grace than he knew he could manage right now. Darman followed in his wake, smiling proudly.

"Well, well," Dr. Cruthers greeted him with a cheery smile alighting his eyes and face. "So, is this young man the proud father?" he teased merrily.

"Ethan, I'd like you to meet my granddaughter's husband, Garth," Rowan introduced him. "Garth this is Dr. Ethan Cruthers, the surviving elder of the humans." Garth saw him extend his hand politely, palm up. He smiled as he crossed it with his own, noting the paper-thin texture and warmth of his skin.

"I'm pleased to meet you, elder sir. But, I want you to know that Ryes and I are not just husband and wife, but true-mates." He smiled in response at hearing this, as Karr's face was shocked horror. Maren, Mitt, Torr and Darman merely smiled with nods of agreement. Rowan laughed at this and happily threw his arms about his new family member.

"Ryes said as much, but I waited until you confirmed it," he explained, as Garth gently returned the old man's embrace, understanding what he meant.

"Glad you finally made it home," Darman told him, hugging him warmly in his turn. "We were getting a little worried about you two." He released him and looked around, suddenly noting Sabin's absence.

"Is Sabin going to be all right?" he asked Dr. Cruthers, worried about his injuries, recalling Torr said a Dr. Turner would be the one to care for him, today. Seeing the exhaustion in Maren's eyes, he could well believe why.

"Ted's looking after him right now, and I believe he'll be just fine. I would think that your first priorities would be some food and rest. We can talk about your journey later," he responded, noting his stance and exhaustion. He looked just short of a collapse.

"Yes," Rowan agreed, seeing what Ethan meant. "Let's give Garth time to rest and meet his family. He can tell us everything he saw and learned, later," he announced in a loud voice, urging the gathering of people to disperse. There were murmurs of disappointment, but they started to leave.

"Maren, aren't you getting enough sleep? You look exhausted." Garth asked in a low voice.

"There was a serious accident today, but luckily Ellen survived. And lately, Bethy, Sayer, Raby, Dotti and I take turns helping Ryes with the cubs, when she's needed elsewhere," he explained. "They're healthy, strong, more than a handful and use up every bit of extra energy you have," he chuckled. Garth clasped his arm in thanks, then turned to Torr.

"I don't know how I'm ever going to repay the both of you," he told his cousin. Torr laughed merrily.

"Just wait a l-o-n-g while before thinking of having any more cubs," he advised. "That'll be thanks, enough." Garth leaned close to his ear and asked in a low voice,

"Who's that human in there with Ryes?" Torr laughed again at hearing his question. But, he was sure she was the dark-haired woman they followed while Time Walking.

"Her name's Bethany, or Bethy and she's Dr. Cruthers' assistant. She and Ryes became good friends, almost the same moment they laid eyes upon each other," he told him, also in a low voice. "I'll tell you all about it, later. You'd better go in and get some rest, before we get into trouble for keeping you up." One of the humans rushed up with a tray in his hands.

"Ah, thank you very much, Jim," Dr. Cruthers said as he took the tray, then handed it to Garth. "Here. Now there's no reason to leave your lady's side to look for something to eat," he advised. Bewildered, but smelling a mouth-watering aroma coming from under the light metallic cover, he took the warm tray and turned for his doorway. Maren swept aside the drape, as Bethany appeared before them. She'd been about to leave, having had a quick chat with Ryes while helping her bathe and dress her new addition, while she was feeding the rest of her children.

"Oh, sorry," she told Garth with a smile dimpling her cheeks. "I was just leaving. Hope you have a good evening."

"Thank you for helping take care of my family, in my absence," he told her, hoping he wasn't offering her insult by doing so. She might've regarded it as some kind of duty.

"You're very welcome. It was no trouble, at all," she assured him, as she gave Jim a brighter smile, seeing him standing outside. Garth grinned at this, seeing there was an attachment between these two humans. She exited, allowing him access. He took his chance, then Maren let the cover fall back into place once more.

"I'm going to check on Sabin," Mitt said, looking at Maren, hinting he should be finding a reason to be elsewhere, too.

"I'm going to my room, after I check on Sabin. I'll be able to get some real rest now!" Maren declared, truly happy. They were finally home and were safe! Torr chuckled in agreement, relieved about things, himself.

"If Dotti will let you," he reminded him. "I have to go back outside. I'm still on watch," he said, as he threw his arm about Maren's shoulders and the three of them walked back around the corner, out of sight. Rowan, Ethan, Darman and Karr stood near the doorway, trying to hear what Ryes and Garth were saying as they talked in low voices within. Suddenly, Bethany realized what they were doing and turned from Jim's attention, to the rest of them.

"Come on, break it up! Let them be," she ordered in a loud voice, startling them. They turned guilty faces toward her and realized she wasn't going to let anyone bother her friend, at a time like this.

"Okay, Bethy," Ethan replied with a light chuckle. "We hear you." He, Darman and Rowan exchanged humor-filled glances, then turned for his office. Karr's face turned a deep gold as she blushed, then turned for her own quarters. She needed to talk with her brother, but this wasn't the time with this interfering human enforcing her idea of peace. Once the corridor was clear and looked to stay that way, Bethany and Jim joined hands and headed for their own room, in relief.

"Garth," Ryes breathed as she lay and nursed the hungry cubs. Little Shyla fit right in with the rest, looking to be the same age. She wasn't as intense in her nursing now, having satisfied her immediate need, just lightly sucking and getting familiar with her surrounds, siblings and new mother.

"Dr. Corothers gave me a tray of food. Would you like to share some with me?" he asked, as he approached her slowly, knowing she might be nervous about having him near with new cubs to care for, whether or not they were his. Her face beamed in happiness as her eyes filled with tears of joy, melting his fears.

"Cruthers," she corrected him. "Best set it down, so you can get out of those heavy coats, first," she advised, sure he was starting to feel too warm by now. He grinned in response, relieved she hadn't changed in all these long months. He set it on their small table out in their common room and doffed the heavy furs and Shyla's sling, hanging the coats up on the slender metal stand, which he recalled very well. Her own coat was there, ready in case of need. He sighed in relief to be in some semblance of home, at last! He returned to her and knelt down next to their bed, to meet his cubs.

"I didn't mean to be gone so long," he told her, as he stroked her cheek tenderly. She smiled as her eyes met his, knowing it came from his heart. "Senah, a mountain tribe chief, kept us prisoners in Menna's Hold for what seemed like forever. I thought I'd still be home in time for their birth," he apologized.

"They came very early. Maren thinks we accidently rushed the rest of the cubs' development when we were trying to catch Rhin up to them. I worried so much about you!" she told him, trying to hold back her tears of relief, as best she could. "What do you think of our cubs?" she finally asked, breathlessly. His eyes glistened with joy as he leaned down to nuzzle each one, tenderly. They were clean and dressed in small tunics, with clean cloths upon their tiny bottoms; each one distinct to his senses, as he reveled in his family.

"That we had too much quiet time on our way here," he teased, as he met her eyes, once more. She laughed in agreement.

"This is Shaysa, I'm sure you guessed it by now," she teased, as she introduced them to their father. "Rhin, Gareth, and Jann. There's something special about Rhin. Maren said we probably poured so much of our Talents into him to make sure he'd be all right, that he's stored it, like a little battery," she told him.

"He's a Booster?" he asked, astounded. "It's a truly rare Talent!" She gave him a nod of her head at this, smiling in pride.

"How did you come by little Shyla?" she questioned, wondering. His face took on a contemplative look as he regarded this tiny girl, who looked so like his own daughter.

"Senah had her brought to me, well before they turned us loose. They said her mother had sickened and died birthing her. She considered her the cause and a curse. The holders gave us two skins of milk to feed her. And I was relieved they let us have our windracers; otherwise, I don't think we would've made it back."

"She's not a curse, she's a blessing!" Ryes declared, recalling she survived her own mother, too. "At least she's now where she'll be loved." Garth looked into her eyes, knowing she'd say this, from her own life's trials.

"Yes, I knew she belonged with us," he agreed with a warm smile. "I love you and have missed you so much," he told her, as he leaned over and kissed her passionately.

"I love you, too," she breathed in return, as their lips parted. "And I've missed you."

"Why the second bed?" he suddenly asked, nodding toward the larger one against the wall, opposite the door. She laughed at this, smiling impishly.

"That's for us," she explained. "You don't think Sayer and Raby stay in here with me, do you? They have their own rooms here and over at Mitt's. Our cubs are too squirmy to get a good night's rest with trying to sleep with them, so I put a barrier around them and sleep over there. And, I made sure there'd always be plenty of room for you, when you returned." His eyes warmed as he thought of holding her in his arms, again. There was a light knock at their door. She recognized it.

"Yes, Maren?" she called out. He stepped into the main room, then came into their bedroom and grinned in relief, seeing them together, as if they'd never been parted. After the brief tale Sabin told him, he knew it was miracle they returned at all.

"Brought you your dinner," he said, extending the tray for Garth to take. "Just leave the trays outside and one of us will pick them up, later." Garth stood and took it with a smile.

"Thanks, but aren't you supposed to be in bed by now?" he questioned merrily, so glad to see he was well, after such a long absence. Maren yawned at this, giving him a nod of his head.

"Just heading there now," he promised and headed for the door, then paused. "Don't forget to do a health exam on Garth tonight," he minded Ryes. She nodded. He then left, letting the cloth fall back into place once outside, then as a second thought, he keyed the metal door shut, giving them some real privacy. He wasn't sure which he craved more right now, Dotti, or getting some sleep.

"Where did everyone come from?" Garth questioned, seeing Ryes get up and pull back on her shirt. She laughed at this, as she walked back out to their common room and he set her tray down next to his. She then went back and double checked the cubs to make sure they were fine, and came back out to sit next to him, leaning against him with a happy sigh. She felt centered once more, and the world was the way it should be... always!

"Matlowe's been a hotbed of unrest since we left. There's been an incursion of new people from out of the east with their own ideas of how things should be done. So, when Maren and Torr went back to fetch the rest of our things, several of the others decided they needed a better place to live, too. Including two families from out of the east. I had Raya screen them to make sure they were good people, who could fit in with the rest of us here. And even if we have far more snow here, Darman decided to winter with us, too. You and Sabin really impressed him! Oh, I officially adopted Sayer and Raby, as they're both too young to be without parents, so now we have seven children." she grinned. He laughed at this.

"Two more daughters. We men are sorely outnumbered in this family!" he declared as she grinned. "What about the humans?" he pressed, puzzled. "Did we accidently alert them with our presence in Winterhaven?"

"Our humans came from out of the sky. I figured out how to call one of their ships down and Bethy and the others were frozen inside. They were going to die because the machines were failing, and I couldn't let that happen. Maren and I saved the ones we could, and they've been a part of life here, since. After all, they're the ones who originally built it! We've been working on expanding the facility, so we now have many new hallways and work areas, which weren't here before. We're planning a new apartment building, which will go up in the spring, outside. You wouldn't believe how well everyone's been working together. Ardis swears it's because they're all more afraid of me, than each other." She laughed at this, shaking her head.

"You've been busy! It was good you saved them. All that and new cubs, too?" he asked, astounded.

"It's a good thing Sabin's back. Ardis' due to deliver hers soon," she added. Garth's eyes looked shadowed at this and she frowned, tilting her head to the side, wondering.

"In order to win our release, Senah demanded one of us mate to her. Sabin volunteered, knowing of our vows. He got little pleasure out of it. And while he was busy serving that witch, they brought me Shyla to care for. She released us shortly afterwards. I think she was disgusted with the both of us. Sabin said he had a hard time performing. His mind kept focusing upon Ardis and their cubs. I think it's the only thing which kept him going, but I know he'll tell her all about it, right off. She's not going to be happy. And he still wants to offer her his true-mate vows," he related, deeply worried for his blood-brother.

"It'll tear him apart, but I think Ardis is strong enough to get them both through it. I don't think she'll turn him down. I saw what she's been going through, too," Ryes assured him. "I'll talk with her now, if you want," she volunteered, standing up. He quickly put a hand to her arm, stopping her, pulling her back down next to him.

"No, my wife. Later. I need you, as much as I need air to breathe," he told her. Surprise was echoed in her emerald-colored eyes, then her own need arose again and she found her arms wrapped around him, as they kissed passionately. Tears sprang to her eyes, as her heart felt it was going to burst with joy. He truly was home!

"Let's eat first, then I'll really show you how much I've missed you," she teased.

"Before the cubs wake up?" he teased in return.

"Definitely!" she promised, smiling. "It's a good thing they're still little and sleep most of the time."

"In a few months, it may not be as easy," he agreed, smiling.

"Truly spoken, husband of mine!" she stated with a laugh. Her heart was light and having him home again was a living dream she'd never let go of, ever!

Home

Ted and Justin got Sabin's coats off and got him up onto the treatment table, being very careful of his leg. The screen that displayed his vitals lit up instantly, showing them the information they needed right now to help their assessment of his current health.

"This might hurt a little until we can get your leg numbed," Ted warned. Sabin nodded, having been in pain for some time now. Ted cut away the ropes binding the sticks around the leg and carefully opened up the jeans pant leg. He noted the thick roll of bandaging around the leg and smiled. Someone had gone to lengths the make sure it was immobile and protected. Justin disposed of the sticks, washed up his hands and with new gloves on was ready again to help out. As Ted was cutting away the bandaging, Ardis appeared at the doorway, saw Sabin and rushed straight over.

"Garth said you were here, when I found him in the hallway," she told him as she saw the pain in his eyes melt into wonder and then joy.

"I love you so much, my wife," he told her as both medical personnel were grinning to see their happiness. They were immediately kissing and so happy to be together.

"Get that cleaned," Ted instructed Justin, as he cleared the wounded area. "This is going to be painful. Would you like a pain killer?" he asked Sabin, noticing his distraction.

"Yes, he would," Ardis responded for him, causing all three men to laugh. "Sabin, I'd like you to meet Dr. Ted of House Turner and Justin of House Royce. They're our regular medical staff and are both good men, who take excellent care of all of us, even if they don't have Talent. They're still wonderful healers!"

"Good to meet you," Sabin said, giving them a nod. Ardis was practically clinging to his arm, as she pulled over a chair and sat down next to him, staying out the way.

"Good to meet you, too, Sabin. Ardis has missed you a lot," Ted stated, as Justin gave him a nod, having just finished the IV and started the solution with the added pain killer and antibiotic. Then he and Justin were looking at the scans they just took of his leg and talking about something in low voices.

"And the good news is that it's a clean break and will be easy to set. I'm going to let the pain killer ease things a little while I get out some rarely used supplies. We had a medical emergency today and both Maren and Tennan are fairly tapped out," Ted told him.

"I understand," Sabin responded, grinning over at Ardis. He realized she was his true pain-killer.

"How's it goin'?" Justin asked, as he put away the scanner, then got started on cleaning the wound.

"I thought all humans had left this place a long time ago," Sabin said, after kissing Ardis again.

"You'll have to talk to Ryes about that. She and Maren saved our lives," he replied, the smile was still on his face but there was a contemplative look in his eyes. "Their Talents are amazing!"

"They are," he agreed. Monty appeared in the doorway and smiled as he saw Sabin lying on the table.

"Hi! I'm Monty and I got your windracers all settled in," he said, "They were sure glad of the warmth and food," he added then stepped forward and extended his hand for Sabin, starman-style. Sabin grinned as he crossed his hand with his own, careful of the IV lead.

"Good to meet you after hearing your voice on the radio, and Thank you," he told him. "It's appreciated." Monty gave him a nod and smile.

"Gotta get back outside. See you later," he promised and left. Ted appeared with some boxes and bags in his hand which he set down. He noticed Sabin was getting sleepy and Ardis gave him a nod.

"Let's get to work," he said. Sabin waved his hand as if to give his okay to it. Ted smiled as he and Justin stepped up to get started.

After Sabin's leg was all set and he was as comfortable as he could be, Maren and Mitt stepped into the treatment room, both brandishing huge grins as they went over to greet Sabin.

"About time!" Mitt scolded, still with a big smile lighting up her eyes and face. Ardis nodded her head at this as Mitt leaned over and kissed Sabin's cheek.

"We meant to be home a long time ago and the route we were taking was supposed to get us home before the caravaners," he explained. "We just didn't count on one crazy mountain tribe leader." Maren gave him a nod. He started a quick check on Sabin, his way.

"Truly great work here, Ted and Justin," he said after a few moments. Ted smiled, giving him a nod. Justin chuckled, happy to have helped.

"Thanks, Maren," Ted replied.

"I did a tiny adjustment in the alignment, but that should hold until I can be more myself and finish it up tomorrow. There was a parasite I've never seen before," he told them, wondering. "It's gone now, but I did have this," he indicated a large drop of blood extruding from Sabin's body. Justin quickly had a clean vial out and captured it. Maren made sure none were left – even on the surface of Sabin's skin.

"Something new! Scott will love this," Justin stated, as he sealed it then got started with the label for it. Ted wiped the spot where the drop had extruded from with an alcohol wipe – to be sure. Maren nodded.

"What were you eating?" he asked, wondering.

"Intestinal?" Ted asked in English. Maren nodded and Justin added it to the vial label.

"They fed us what they ate and most of it was okay, but occasionally it was disgusting," Sabin replied, making a face.

"Whatever it is, I found it in Sernn, too, but his was a more involved infection so I didn't note it as closely as I should've, since all I did was clean it out," Maren admitted. Ted clasped him on his shoulder.

"You did great work on him," he offered in encouragement.

"Sernn made it?" Sabin asked, feeling things were falling into place.

"Mitt and the elders found him up in the mountains and brought him to us far more quickly than you both arrived," Ardis told him as Mitt nodded, grinning proudly.

"We were trying to find the place you both were being held and he showed it to us very quickly. If I'd had more than just a few elders with me, we would've taken the place by storm and demanded your release right away," she told him. "And Sernn's doing fine. Minn and I adopted him as our son."

"Sounds like I've been gone too long," Sabin sighed out, grinning. "I missed out on a lot, it seems!"

"But I wouldn't have Sernn and he wouldn't be healed, if you both hadn't asked him to help get word out of where you were," Mitt scolded. "Everything works out by Aletagga's design, it seems." He nodded at this, smiling.

"So, Sabin, let us show you how to use crutches tonight, so you and Ardis can go home and get some alone time," Maren suggested, grinning, as he suppressed a yawn.

"What're you teaching me?" he asked, which got Ted and Justin to chuckle. Maren just shook his head with a huge grin.

"I'm off to bed!" Mitt declared, giving Ardis a quick kiss, then quickly left the room, laughing lightly. Her heart was soaring with the return of her brother and Sabin. Home was now complete in her mind.

"Sabin, I don't care! You're home and right now there's only one place I want you!" Ardis told him. He wasn't sure if she even listened to what he was trying to tell her!

"Are you sure?" he hedged, uncertain. "Would such a thing be healthy with the cubs due in a few weeks' time?" he wondered aloud. Ardis went and closed the metal door to their room, came quickly back to him, pulling off her T-shirt, and ushered him into their bedroom. She tossed her shirt into the laundry basket and smiled as she looked into his eyes.

"I love you, Sabin and I heard what you said, but that's not important right now. That woman had you both at a disadvantage and you did what you had to do. I need you and our cubs are going to need us both. Do we really matter to you, or not?" she challenged him, wanting this clear, once and for all time. Sabin held out his hand before her, palm flat, inwardly quaking.

"I give to you, Ardis, all that I am, body, heart and soul, for all eternity," he stated, meeting her brown eyes in earnest, his heart hammering, as he barely balanced with the one crutch. She looked shocked, but suddenly smiled as she placed her hand, palm-to-palm with his. It was something she felt she waited for, forever!

"I give to you, Sabin, all that I am, body, heart and soul, for all eternity," she repeated. The love in her eyes was plain for him to see. Yes, this was right and what they both denied, until now. Now, he knew his Vision of them with more cubs than he thought they could ever manage was true. He took her into his arms and kissed her passionately, finally feeling relaxed and as if he was truly home. He felt their cubs moving beneath his hand and his heart bounded with joy. Her hands were already working on the lacings of his tunic.

The next morning, they all gathered in the dining room, which had been enlarged to accommodate everyone. Garth had to chuckle to himself. He couldn't believe what had sprung up from a tiny handful of adventurers, looking for a place to call their own. It seemed like it was an eternity since he left Matlowe! Now he saw the mural they were working on. It was impressive and explained much in why Ryes chose the Great Phoenix as the symbol for Winterhaven. They were truly rising up from the ashes of Hailys' destruction. He and Sabin stood upon a small dais they set up for them, telling the whole community of their journey and its conclusion, with Darman, Rinna, Dodi, Sayer, Raby and Sernn adding in comments, where they felt they were necessary.

"We've traveled afoot, now on windracers, but from now on, we're using the rovers and choppers!" Sabin assured the gathering, getting laughter and shouts of agreement. "And we now know we can use our flashlights to charge our radios! I'm NOT forgetting that one, too soon!" Garth clasped him on the shoulder with a laugh and nod of his head. "I'm looking forward to getting to know our new additions to Winterhaven, soon." Then, Sabin stepped down from the platform, leaving Garth to finish. He was walking on his own again, as Maren had finished the healing fully. Still he appreciated the work Ted and Justin did, too.

"I can't tell it any better than to say, I'm truly glad to be home again with my family and friends. I didn't think we'd been gone long enough for the whole place to be rearranged! These are exciting times! It looks like we still have a lot of work ahead, but I don't doubt we'll make it," Garth assured them, smiling as he turned off the mic, as Ryes showed him earlier. There was a cheering and clapping as he stepped down, and went over to sit back at his table, between Ryes and Mitt, both women hugged him, happily.

"Better enjoy this lull, the winter's still granting us," Dr. Cruthers advised.

"I fully intend to," Garth agreed, "I've got to get to know everyone, first! Oh, did you ever get a chance to get one of those readers from Hailys to work?" he suddenly asked Ryes, remembering.

"Eric was working on it. And he's finally found the correct frequency of light needed and has figured out how the data was encoded. I'll have to check to see where he's at on our little project," she replied with a light laugh. "From the information he's extracted, most of it was silly useless stuff like new outfits to wear, or how to tint and trim your ear fur to stand out more. It's funny, but not useful." It was supposed to be her "busy project" for the winter. Now, she was too busy to bother with it, herself. Garth was amazed that he was now in charge of the whole complex; wondering how Ryes managed it alone before? It was going to take some getting used to, with all these other people and humans, too.

"I'll excuse you this time," he teased, as he put his arm around her, hugging her close. She laughed and shook her head.

"Let's eat, then show you what we've accomplished," she suggested.

"Our beautiful family is far more valuable than anything else," he replied. "That's what I consider the accomplishment." Ryes sighed as she leaned against his side, feeling at peace with the world.

The End of Book Three

For more books, please visit my website.

www.mariedaley.com

Messenger

And a small treat... a peek at book 4 of the Adventures

of Ryes and Garth

Striding Forth

"What is that?" the watch commander demanded of the lowly man, working the scanner board. He fidgeted nervously, not liking such direct attention, especially for something as insignificant as this situation.

"Sir, it's nothing more than a very, old piece of their probing equipment, returning to their homeworld. It's moving slowly and probably just bringing them the news of our presence," Kreln replied, sitting back upon his haunches and earnestly meeting the officer's eyes, stalk-to-stalk. "In the briefing last month, it was recommended these be ignored, for they only seem to add further confusion to the entrenched enemy, as they sometimes believe that they must launch smaller, rescue missions, which are then considered easy pickings for us. This then adds to their demoralization," he explained, hoping he wouldn't be demoted for speaking to an officer in such a manner. It was his duty to remind a duty officer of the standing orders, in various situations, but sometimes the watch officers took such things as an affront to their rank.

"Very well, monitor it to see that it follows the path it's supposed to. If there are any deviations, let me know. Be sure to pass the situation down, so we can keep a watch for the rescue mission." He then returned to his own post, sitting down upon the dark, carpeted square and digging in with his claws. At least this situation promised more sport, later. He made his log entry, feeling very satisfied.

"Sir, there it is," the ensign pointed out the trace upon his screen to the watch commander, as it finally appeared, once more. The lieutenant stood at his side to confirm it, too.

"Humph. Okay, dispatch a patrol to check it out and bring it in; if it's something we should take note of," he ordered his lieutenant, then turned to handle more important matters.

"Yes Sir," Lieutenant Patton replied to his back, smiling to himself, relieved. At least it wasn't another wave of enemy fighters making a pass at their defenses. The Darkens, as they were generally called now, were getting more clever with their feints and it was rumored they might break through before much longer. What was left of the Earth fleet was a sorry sight. There was some hope in the newer prototypes being built now; that they could find a way to drive them away from the Sol system for all time. But who knew how long it would be until they'd be ready for combat?

"Ensign Feldman, have it brought in immediately," he ordered, knowing it would be done with alacrity. Funny the way this thing slipped by their outer patrols... and the Darken patrols, too. He'd have to see to it, personally.

"It really is," a crewman informed him as he stood waiting for scanner confirmations. "An old TX-127 Stinger. It may be almost a hundred years old, but it does have a primitive tesseract unit."

"Did the scans detect any lifeforms aboard it?" the lieutenant asked.

"No, Sir, it's clean. Almost factory clean," he got in response. He smiled, relieved.

"Is the data cartridge intact?" Lieutenant Patton questioned, looking down at the display, to see it for himself.

"Yes Sir. And from what I can determine from the date stamps, this was only launched three months ago. There's no coordinate information, just locational names and identifications. Looks like someone might be wary of the Darkens, too," the scan tech commented. Patton looked down at him and gave him a nod of his head; it sure looked that way to him, too.

"Consult history files about the proper procedures for data retrieval from this unit, then have it piped directly to my queue," he ordered, then turned to leave.

"Sir?" the crewman stood up, calling out to his back. Patton turned back with a look of tolerance in his eyes.

"Yes?" he asked. The tech looked calm and accepting of his attitude.

"What do we do with the Stinger, itself, Sir?"

"Stow it. We might use it to send a reply back to the colony it came from," he decided.

"Yes Sir." The crewman gave him a salute in response. He returned the salute, and then left for his office. He wanted to see what mysteries this ancient message drone held. He hoped it wasn't merely some colonists whining about their lack of supplies, or weapons. Most of the colonies got the idea real quick that if they cut off all long distance communications and interstellar travel, they were left alone by the Darkens. There was a rumor that some of the stronger, more remote colonies were planning upon striking at the Darkens from their flank, as they sat holding Sol system in siege. He smiled to himself at this, knowing there weren't ANY strong colonies left out there. Earth and her handful of inner colonies were alone, by themselves in this war. But perhaps someone will divert their attention for a short while and grant them some relief.

        "Sir, it's a report from one of those old, Amitell research stations. It says that they were recently retrieved from orbit and revived by some members of the indigenous population and are the known lone survivors of The Star Quest. I verified all given information and Dr. Cruthers' identification; everything checks out."
        "Amitell doesn't exist anymore. Are there any next of kin of the survivors to pass on the information to? Does it contain any information of interest for us?" Captain French asked.
        "Your uncle is one of those listed, a Lieutenant Paul Everett French. He was a member of the military support group for the site, Sir," Lieutenant Patton informed him. There was shock in his eyes as he sat back in his chair at this news. "But, at this time he's now younger than you, Sir, since they were in suspension tubes for about eighty years, Earth time."
        "Eighty years," he breathed. "He was my dad's youngest brother. Are there any vid shots of the survivors?" The lieutenant anticipated this and immediately handed over a chip. The Captain activated it and studied the image intently. The family resemblance was remarkable. "Copy me all the files and reports. I'll review it and kick this up to Fleet. Thank you, lieutenant, your efforts are appreciated. Dismissed," he ordered, returning the young officer's salute, before he left his office. He turned to his comp unit. He had a few calls to make back home.

        Kreln saw the exact same, ancient, probe unit returning along the exact same course. He scratched his ear, puzzled. The scans reported no sign of armament, nor anything to grant it any note, at all. Since he'd already been reprimanded on this shift for disturbing the watch officer on another trifling matter, he decided to tag it as a piece of space junk to be ignored by the patrols. It was better than have to explain why it was let to pass through their patrols, earlier. He didn't think he would survive another reprimand!